THE GREAT
DIVIDE

a concise history of the future

M.A. MARTIN

Otto

DEDICATED TO THE PRESENT

CONTENTS

ACKNOWLEDGMENTS

I give all thanks to God above, for allowing me a love of writing, even when I doubt it's what I should be doing. I am humbled by You, and give all praises.

I'd like to thank my sister, Francoise, for always telling me I was born to be a writer. Even after I told her what kind of books I wanted to write, she never thought I was insane. She's no longer here physically, but I know she walks with me every day. This one's for for, baby girl.

My mom, Carmen, for telling me stories ever since I was a kid, and sparking that love for reading in me. If not for her, I don't think I would've ever dreamed of being a storyteller. I miss you so much.

My best friend and confidant, Martina, who helped me throughout this process with everything I needed. She put up with all my ups and downs, and her advice definitely got me back on track whenever I started to slip. I appreciate you more than words can ever say.

Special thanks to artist extraordinaire, Mr. Jose Manuel Bethencourt Suarez, who never complained that I was bothering him with constant questions about the artwork he was doing for the book.

It is the year 2060. The skies grow darker with each passing day. Smoke suffocates the lungs. Mangled bodies litter the streets. Skyscrapers lie ruined across cities. The stench of death is gripping. The dying frost of a nuclear winter is only now beginning to thaw. To some, this is the end of the world —Apocalypse—Extinction. To others, it is merely a time of change, an evolution of man. But perception is an illusion, and only one thing rings true. It is Hell on Earth; the end is near.

Just imagine it, the world you've always known being torn apart right before your very eyes. Imagine everything you've ever held dear and near: family, friends, security, everything—gone. It's a frightening thing.

Cecil Greenough

Grand Magistrate: The Biography of Kiril Pordan

This wasn't war. This was carnage. Everyday people being arrested and killed? Sure, you saw this sort of thing across seas, in the Global South maybe, but this was the United States, the UK, France—the so-called civilized nations of the world. This wasn't supposed to be happening to them.

Prof. Tamara Boggier

keeper, New York Republic

You can be sure that some people were happy to see this happening to the European countries, but only for a time. It soon became a problem for everybody. You could not escape it. It was everywhere.

Tsun-chúng Hu

The Last Dynasty: The Chinese Republic's Ultimate Demise

For some religious people of the world, God was finally casting His righteous judgment upon the souls of mankind. It should have been a good thing, but no one could seem to embrace it.

It was far too hard, and far too violent. The Qur'an speaks of this, as does the Bible. To many, this was the End of Days.

Prof. Najiyah Abdullah Hassan

Crescent Moon and Pillars: The Rise of the Islamic Empire

Absolutely unheard of. Wars in cities? Famine spreading across the globe as if some great plague? It is preposterous, and all one need do is deny it. That was the foolish way of thinking back then. So I suppose you can say what happened was the product of such ignorance. Ignorance at its finest.

Prof. Jarvis Grimes

historian, *Superior and Biased: The History of the Royal European Alliance*

Ignorance which begets mutual destruction. Across the globe, man will fight to survive. Empires will become ruins. Kings turned into vagabonds. Lush lands reduced to scorching earth.

In the end, nothing will ever again be the same.

"...even Heaven had its war."

I High Magistrate George P. Hartsoe

excerpt from *Magisterium Induction Ceremony*

INTRODUCTION

Earth is a planet of over 7.7 billion people. It stands third in a solar system of eight planets, and five dwarf, yet stands alone. Many of its inhabitants are of different creeds, faiths, races, and ethnicities, but they all share one common trait—they are all human. And though they may have histories and myths as diverse from each other as the sands are from the seas, they are all the same. Herein lies the problem that has plagued them for so many millennia.

As fate would have it, the same trait that makes them human, is the same trait which begets their downfall—the want to survive. A need to endure, this driving force for survival often brings out the best in mankind: cultivation to philosophy, artistry to exploration—and his worst, in greed, tyranny, conquest, and war. A powerful, yet easily corruptible attribute, survival has raised human beings to the heights of godhood, while plunging them into the abyss of conflict and death.

This is Earth. This is where we live.

In needing to explain the age known as The Great Divide, first be enlightened as to what the world was like leading up to this time of blight. It was the early 21st century, and war seemed to be taking place almost everywhere. The end of civilization was rumored to be fast approaching. The *War On Terror: Phase II* showed no sign of slowing down. Freedom was the word on everyone's lips. Democracy was something of a crusade. The Middle East was the focus, and Islam gave the impression that is was the most dangerous ideology to have ever been born. Conflicts were taking place all over the globe, yet no one could have ever truly fathomed the darkness quickly engulfing us.

In China, reports of human rights violations were spreading like wildfire. The People's Republic of China was constantly being accused of suspiciously maneuvering its military toward bordering countries, to mass murdering its own citizens. The regime denied those reports, but the evidence could not be refuted.

In Russia, a soviet mindset had been reestablished under a new guise— Silovikism. Not quite communist, it most definitely was not Democratic. The media constantly reported on Russia committing aggressions against its neighboring satellite countries, most likely in an attempt to re-create a Soviet block under Russia's rule. But no matter the outrage, it all seemed to go unchallenged by the rest of the world.

In Africa, the shifting of governments appeared to be taking place on a daily basis. Countries like Botswana and Algeria were emerging with bright and promising futures, but Niger and Chad, and so many others, had been in a constant state of flux. But no country in the whole of Africa had been receiving more attention than that of South Sudan, where the government was enacting nothing less than a genocide. Daily reports were being leaked concerning the conflict between the government and opposition forces. A brutal civil war that had already left nearly 1.5 million dead, and over 3.5 million displaced, it demanded the world respond with utmost haste—a call that went unanswered.

The *War on Terror: Phase II* continued to be fought by both a Western Coalition and Iraqi soldiers. It was a constant struggle, but Iraq had long proven its ability to reach for the brass ring of Democracy. It was Afghanistan that remained a volatile, war-torn, battlefield. During this crisis, Iran constantly interfered by supplying arms to Shia militias, further destabilizing the region. Syria and Lebanon were not any better, but Iran's theocratic government seemed to be the most dangerous, so it was given the closest attention.

The Iranians had developed a nasty habit of flaunting their missile tests for the world to see. Its leaders' brash and provoking words never ceased in threatening nations at large. And with talks of attacking Israel, if the globally funded World Bank was moved to West Jerusalem, the Western World had reached beyond agitation with the Persian nation.

Saudi Arabia, meanwhile, remained neutral. The Saudis had long made known their decision to stay out of the *War on Terror: Phase II*. They only promised to keep stability within their own borders, and nothing more. A redundant oath to some, it was no surprise to hear the Pakistani government sprouting the same pledge. But when it came to Pakistan, all they had proven was their inability to apprehend the terrorists using their mountains as both hideouts and training hubs.

Coalition forces had long been taking it upon themselves to ignore the nation's false security, never passing on an opportunity to launch airstrikes into those very regions. Pakistan occasionally argued against such acts of aggression, but the leaders there were too busy dealing with an ever-growing crisis coming out of their neighboring country of India to overtly protest.

More so an Islamic and Hindu discord, the two countries had lived in relative peace up until the start of the *War on Terror: Phase II*. It was at that point negative Hindu sentiments toward Muslims began turning into all out attacks, while Muslim extremists retaliated with terrorist acts against India's citizens. And though both governments constantly called for peace and stability from within, they also made clear their willingness to defend their people if necessary.

With both countries being armed with nuclear weapons, the last thing the world wanted to see was a war between the two. Therefore, while pacifying Pakistan's government by constantly reminding the world of its desire to help in stopping terrorism, the United States and Europe also armed India with all sorts of state-of-the-art satellites and missile defense systems—just in case the day ever came when Pakistan crossed the line.

The duplicity was seen by some as instigation on the part of meddling Western nations. This, in turn, sparked protests around the world, and nowhere were such objections more alive than in Europe.

In Great Britain, France, Germany, and Italy, people constantly took to the streets in demand that their governments stop interfering in foreign affairs. Driven by financial struggle and an influx of foreign migrants, some were even calling on their leaders to not only step away from the Indo/Pak dispute, but to abandon the *War on Terror: Phase II* all together. These groups of demonstrators were often portrayed as nothing more than liberal fanatics who desired damaging entitlements, believing peace on Earth could be achieved by solely holding hands and singing around campfires. The activists painted their more conservative opponents as mere war mongering elitists, whose desires were nothing less than greed, ongoing bloodshed, and war.

The reports coming out of Europe presented endless footage of policemen clashing with rioters, while liberal politicians and their conservative rivals argued endlessly behind closed doors.

Constant bickering, violent acts of homegrown terrorism plaguing the streets, it was a difficult time. But across the Atlantic, things were a bit different.

In the United States, though there were protests in the streets just as frequently as there were in Europe, hostile collisions between law enforcement and activists were something of a rarity. It was the arguments taking place between the Democrats and Republicans that were far worse than anything else. The Europeans merely disagreed on issues, but in the United States, politicians had no problem portraying their opponents as nothing less than traitors to the American dream. A persistent allegation that would soon prove disastrous for everyone, the accusations began fueling people to prove their patriotism.

"Pick A Side," was the slogan, and out of this split was born the political movement known as American Revolution Two, or ART, as it was more commonly referred to. A class of Americans that neither sided with the Democrats or Republicans, the ARTists were dedicated to reclaiming their country in the name of *Liberty and Justice for All*, even if that meant risking their lives.

It was with all this in place that the world came to see its darkest hour. This was how humans brought about destruction and pain, misery and death—the harsh and changing tide of history that forever changed all our lives.

This is how we brought about The Great Divide.

M.A. Martin

2025

WAR ON TERROR: PHASE II

The Great Divide: a concise history of the future

May 9, Iraq proudly declares freedom. An estimated 2.5 million of its citizens turnout in front of Baghdad's Parliament Building in celebration. The highlight of the festivities is hearing the declaration being made by Iraqi Prime Minister, Khalil Husani, the man Iraqis merit for their Democracy. It is a day filled with fanfare and pride, and chants of '*Allahu Akbar*' can be heard ringing throughout the country.

Iraqi state media broadcasts the ceremony on all channels, while overseas stations interrupt regularly scheduled programming in honor of the historic occasion. Then after much anticipation and fanfare, Prime Minister Husani finally steps out into the public.

The leader of the Islamic country is received with praises surpassing any leader of its history. Adoration warranted by the reason so many of the country's patriots stand here, Husani affirms to his people the end of terrorism in Iraq. A grueling path engulfed in bloodshed and tears, the day they have been waiting for has finally come. After twenty-three years of war, the Iraqi people are finally a Democracy.

Ever since the U.S. was attacked on 9/11, there was this anti-Islamic sentiment alive in the world. Islam was being used in Presidential campaigns as a sort of threat to lookout for, or as some insane cult aimed at bringing about the end of the world—a sort of apocalyptic sect you can say. And not simply that, you even heard of Muslims around the world having their basic civil rights violated in the name of security. So for Muslims, Iraq declaring its freedom appeared to be a sort of hope, a belief that they would be treated with the same basic rights as everyone else—a chance to be free.

Prof. Najiyah Abdullah Hassan

Crescent Moon and Pillars: The Rise of the Islamic Empire

The world was pleased to see peace in the Middle East, even if it was only in Iraq. This was the entire reason for the War on Terror's second phase taking place, after all. So, of course, America and its military celebrated it as a victory—it's understandable. Especially when they're the ones who brought freedom to the Iraqis. It was more than just a win; it was an honor.

Cecil Greenough

Grand Magistrate: The Biography of Kiril Pordan

Husani takes it upon himself to deliver a long speech detailing the hardships taken to reach this vital moment. He gives both a meticulous history lesson concerning the country's past, and a plan on how his people are expected to move forward. His words are filled with hope, bravado, threats, and promises. Yet nothing he can say remotely sums up the way his people feel concerning their new dawn.

It was a sight seen here once before when the United States had prematurely withdrawn its troops from the country, believing the Iraqi people capable of maintaining security over their own homeland. Back then, there was a shared consensus amongst the Iraqi government and the United States that it was time for the latter to leave. Considering the reduction of violence levels low enough for American troop withdrawals to have begun taking place, it was something the American Democratic Party had been pushing for. The Iraqi government had also come to see the Western presence in their country as nothing less than an occupation.

Sentiments in the Islamic country had by then reached an apprehensive pitch, forcing then United States President, Barack Obama, to agree to the complete withdrawal of the United States military from out of Iraq. He proudly did so on December 18, 2011, leaving the Iraqi people to maintain their own.

It had been a poor choice.

No more than three years passed before Iraq once more began suffering the effects of terrorism, first by the militant group called ISIL, then at the hands of an entirely new radical group calling themselves Al-Asas. But unlike ISIL that had targeted Westerners and their Iraqi supporters, the Al-Asas movement was dedicated to the outright eradication of all those not of their fanatical dogma.

Guilty of everything from atrocious executions of innocent people to mass bombings, Al-Asas had left the United States with no choice but to return its troops in full scale to Iraq in order to halt their criminal acts. The decision was something that had lacked popularity with the American people, but needed to be done. Thus, sacrificing nearly two decades, the United States, in a joint venture with Iraq's military, battled the world's most wanted terrorist, Asim Mustafa Abdullah and his Al-Asas jihadists.

Nothing but blood and death stained their engagements. The battles were gruesome and violent, and the innocent suffered the most. But in the end, only after these casualties and bloodshed, is Iraq once more returned to a sense of normality. This time, however, Prime Minister Husani makes an oath that things will be different.

The apprehension of Abdullah and four of his lieutenants ultimately marks the administration's victory, and Husani plans on making a spectacle with which he can deter all other terrorists that might be waiting in the wings.

It is May 11, and Abdullah is hung by Iraq's Supreme Court before a cheering crowd of thousands. The execution is covered by news agencies from around the world. The United States censors it, but this only makes the capital punishment's viewing the highest rated internet search of all time —proof the Iraqi people are not alone in being satisfied by Abdullah's death.

What can be said about that time? War was everywhere, and people were getting use to seeing dead bodies on television. In some places, outside of their homes for that matter. It was a brutal age, and death was becoming a normal thing. So when you see Abdullah being hung on national television, and nobody's really complaining about it, it really shows you just where this society was headed.

Cecil Greenough

Grand Magistrate: The Biography of Kiril Pordan

With Abdullah dead, and a democratic Iraq dedicated toward a future of prosperity and growth, the United States can now focus its full attention on both a war-torn Afghanistan, and an ever threatening Iran—not to mention the growing threat of terrorism lingering in the South Pacific. But unlike its war in Iraq, the United States is not alone this time. The Americans may have been preparing to engage Iranian forces for nearly two decades, all that means nothing with Iraq's new found liberation. With that vital piece in the Middle East now in play, it can only allow for an unprecedented attack on Iran by all who deem it a threat.

Coalition forces and Iraqi troops begin crossing the Iraqi/Iranian border in droves, while the Persian Gulf is flooded with all sorts of naval convoys. The President of Iran, Farhad Seifzadeh, grows ever defiant, televising speeches throughout his country condemning the Western presence. He threatens to launch Iran's newly developed nuclear weapons into Israel if attacked. A threat his predecessors have been making for many years, with missile tests being conducted as proof of their capabilities, Coalition forces understand they must now act without hesitation, or risk a calamity unlike the world has ever witnessed. This leaves them with no other choice but to stage a full scale attack on the hostile nation, bringing the war with Iran to a head.

On July 6, military airstrikes begin taking place in Iran, destroying specific target sites believed to be housing nuclear facilities and missiles. The Iranians try retaliating with airstrikes of their own, but are greatly outnumbered by both NATO Forces and Iraqi troops, leaving them vulnerable to an all out invasion.

This was the first time that the U.S. and its Coalition had ever attacked a nation as powerful as Iran, and yet were met with almost no resistance. It was not the fight people had been saying it would be. As a matter of fact, Iraq had put up more of a fight when it was invaded. So it was no shock that, within weeks, people began hearing of utter chaos taking place all throughout the country.

Prof. Najiyah Abdullah Hassan

Crescent Moon and Pillars: The Rise of the Islamic Empire

Casualty reports begin coming out of Iran. Reports informing the rest of the world of the country's inability to match the Democratic Coalition's United Nation authorized attacks, they are utterly shocking and distressing. In time, as Iran's streets begin getting flooded with protesters demanding their government stand down in surrender to the Western forces, so are the streets throughout the world overcome by those demanding the attacks be stopped. Gripes and complaints that are for now ignored, the aid needed for the suffering people of Iran is made the focus of Western governments.

And though there are multitudes of Iranians who wholeheartedly support their leaders' decisions to resist the call of the invading army, the ones desiring freedom remain the center of attention.

The younger generation, those who have grown weary of the old ways, and want nothing more than for true freedom to flourish in Iran, they are the ones who need help, and the Democratic Coalition sees to it that they are given such. But before any aid can be received, the protestors are loathsomely branded traitors, and many are killed. An unfortunate turn of events, it never once halts Coalition Forces from continuing with their attempts at putting an end to Iran's extremist government.

Day and night, bombs rain on the cities of Tehran and Mashhad, strategically building resentment in the hearts and minds of Iranian citizens for their unyielding government. The civilian protests join the advancing invasion, dividing the Iranian military in two. NATO Forces on one side, and the engagement of its own citizens on the other, many of them University students, the split tactically cripples the once more-than-capable military force, finally allowing for an all out ground assault.

Nearby, the newly stabilized Syrian Arab Republic, and an ever-aggressive Lebanon begin voicing their discontent for the way the Iranian situation is being handled. President Zhubin Jalili of Syria, and Prime Minister Jamsheed Farahani of Lebanon accuse the unilateral military force of illegally attacking the sovereign nation. They insinuate NATO Forces deliberately kill innocent Iranian civilians with their bombs, and demand a complete withdrawal from the region. NATO denies such claims, and begins portraying both countries as supporters of a defunct regime that would use its own civilians as human shields. Arguments that go back and forth, they turn the United Nations' General Assembly into a circus of accusations and threats.

The Western Coalition charge both Syria and Lebanon with conspiring with Iran to destabilize the Middle East, while the two contend the Western presence in the Islamic world is nothing more than a rehashing of the failed Crusades of medieval times. An inflammatory accusation sprouting rumors of war being brought to the two countries, Jalili and Farahani dare such outcomes. But with the first two months of the *Persian War* seizing Iran's Tabriz, Ahvaz, Kermanshah, and Qom regions in favor of the Coalition, victory over the Persian country appears close at hand, debasing any criticism.

Whether it is fear of being next on NATO's list, or the realization of Iran's true threat to the free world, Syria and Lebanon find themselves a bit more cautious when protesting against the Western liberation of the Iranian people. At the same time, unable to deny the fact that he is quickly losing the war, Iranian President Farhad Seifzadeh reluctantly accepts to abandon his post at the urging of Iran's Supreme Leader, the Grand Ayatollah Babak Astarabadi.

The Grand Ayatollah comes to the realization he cannot allow the Western forces to enter his country as victors that have defeated Iran's mighty military, and remain powerful in the eyes of his people. Not only is he the "Great Sign of God", he is also viewed as the true power behind the government. A military loss would be a personal one. Therefore, wisely expelling Seifzadeh from out of Iran, Astarabadi chooses to extend an invitation to the Western Coalition as a sign of sincerity on his part. And though no Western leader trusts the act for a single moment, the gesture is seen as the only way to penetrate the country's heart without further bloodshed, leaving them with no other choice but to accept it.

This was a pivotal moment for both the West and Iran. Not since the Imperial Russian and British occupation had Iran been host to such a massive European presence. In one hand, you had the Iranian Revolution crumbling before a joint military venture of the U.S. and Europe, and in the other, you had a new breed of Iranians begging for true freedom—Hope—Democracy. The Supreme Leader, the Grand Ayatollah, he had to permit the long preached 'infidel' into the country before all was lost. He had no other choice. But in the same say, it would forever alter the Middle East with its passing.

Prof. Najiyah Abdullah Hassan

Crescent Moon and Pillars: The Rise of the Islamic Empire

September 14, Coalition forces march into Tehran, and are greeted as friends. Across the country and the world, people gather to watch as the United States leads the West in meeting with Ayatollah Astarabadi to declare an end to the Iranian conflict. Syria and Lebanon can say nothing when witnessing the meeting, and now find themselves pledging allegiance to the same call of Democracy they once so boastfully disavowed. But in spite of this being an historic moment, the new impression of harmony does not go without its critics.

Russia and China have long been opponents to the *War on Terror: Phase II*, and refuse to applaud its success. The two nations have been convinced for quite sometime that this *War on Terror: Phase II* is nothing more than a show of dominance by the United States and the rest of its European allies.

The Communist Chinese Republic and United Russian Republic have both repeatedly voiced adverse opinions concerning such matters, though never really interfering in the issue. In point of fact, for the better part of the 21st century, both nations had conducted themselves in a rather forthcoming manner. There was even a time when the regimes showed signs of support for the democratic challenge. Although, such affability has long since been absent by the time of Iran's supposed acceptance of Democracy.

How do you describe the Chinese mindset back then? First you have to understand there was much resentment—much resentment, and much jealousy. Not jealousy like China wanting to be the United States, but that America should not have been where it was in the world. The Chinese were prideful in their stance against the West, and they believed that they had put in place a strong enough nation to become superpower over the United States. No more accusations of ambiguity, epidemics, and human rights violations. Now China was going to be the one forging the way the world thought.

Tsun-chúng Hu

The Last Dynasty: The Chinese Republic's Ultimate Demise

What you had here were two dying empires. You'd seen it with Babylon, and you'd seen it with Egypt. You'd seen it with Greece, and you'd seen it with Rome—all of them. And among them all, China had always been there buying its time in the shadows, while Russia had already fallen once before, and only recently resurrected itself. Then the inevitable fate of all empires was brought before them, and Russia and China began trying to defy their destinies. Like I said, Russia had seen it before, and refused to taste it again. Many had been guilty of this, and the Motherland was no different. But China? Well, none had ever been as zealous as China.

Prof. Tamara Boggier

keeper, New York Republic Athenaeum

Fortunately for the Coalition, the Communist Chinese Republic currently finds itself preoccupied, leaving it no opening to engage Democracy's draping web across the Middle East. For now, the Chinese leaders believe it more important they begin pushing their forces against the Mongolian border, while continuing dialogue with the South Pacific. But when it comes to the United Russian Republic, an entirely different reason keeps this Great Mother at bay—an entirely different war all together.

The air is cool and crisp. A cloudless sky hovers above the earth. The sounds of cars, televisions, and phones have all been silenced, replaced by the crackling of gunfire, the deafening blasts of explosions, and the tortured cries of the dying. Peace is again stolen, and all that remains is pain and destruction. This is the dilemma of the Russian people, the devastation surrounding their everyday.

The Russian government remains diligent when dealing with the growing rebellion of its countrymen, but it seems impossible they will ever succeed in quelling the revolt. The rebellion is more than just a want for freedom, it is a need for freedom. And it is the movement known as SPINA leading the insurgency, making it clear that Democracy must be returned to the Russian people before the country is burned to the ground.

The very moment this farce of Silovikism was put upon the back of the Russian people, it was instantly rejected. And to make it crystal, the reaction was played out by a large majority of Russian civilians voicing their disapproval of such governmental refocus. I mean, it may have been something their former beloved leader, Vladimir Putin, dabbled in, but it was nothing like what he had tried accomplishing for his people. This Silovik regime was solely grounded in tyranny, and the amassing of untold wealth for the nation's upper echelon. It went against everything Vladimir Putin had stood for, and only proved the infectivity of Democracy's call—even within the so-called glorious United Russian Republic. For that reason, numerous outbreaks of violence began plaguing the country, but none more destructive than those committed by the rebel force calling themselves SPINA. They were remnants of the long absolved Yabloko political party, and led by a charismatic revolutionist by the name of Bogdan Kushnir. Born during an age of Democracy in Russia, Kushnir could not have fathomed living in a country where the freedoms of speech and assembly had become grounds to be either incarcerated, or worse. That was why he took up arms—him and his SPINA rebels. The very same kindred spirits sharing his vision of delivering the Russian people from their elitist oppressors, this was what began enacting the revolts that had in due time spread from Donetsk, Ukraine to Voronezh, Russia.

Prof. Jarvis Grimes

historian, *Superior and Biased: The History of the Royal European Alliance*

Clashes between Russian military forces and SPINA play throughout the world for all to see, even as the Russian government tries keeping the footage from being leaked. An obvious bloodbath on both sides of the battle, the military loses hundreds of soldiers weekly, as do the freedom fighters of SPINA. And while tanks patrol down the streets of Moscow preparing for an advancing SPINA assault, ground troops continue to ruthlessly engage the insurgency in Voronezh.

World leaders comment on the fighting, calling on the Silovik regime to furnish the rebels with their demands, or risk facing even more scenes of carnage within their country. The Russian government refuses, and continues with its assaults. These are battles which strengthen SPINA every time they are conducted, gradually fueling even greater dissensions in the hearts of the world's equally dejected citizens.

Europeans and Americans feel their governments ignore their calls to end the recent wars, and SPINA simply proves a rebellion can in fact threaten the stability of an established regime. With this made evident, the path the disheartened citizens will soon choose to follow seems almost inevitable. And with talks of Coalition Forces continuing the *War on Terror: Phase II* into the heart of the South Pacific, leading democratic governments begin preparing for a possible enacting of what is currently happening in the Silovik republic.

The discussions as to how to deal with the ever-growing threat are feverish, leading some to even suggest ending their part in the *War on Terror: Phase II*. Every word is an utterance born of concern, but no suggestion matches the desperateness of Article 412. A proposition which calls for the merging of all European banks in aiding the financial crisis fueling the mounting revolts, as well as, the drastic goal of combining the courts of laws in Europe, Article 412 is made the focal point of most European debates.

The United States faces similar threatening predicaments, but the leading bureaucrats there propose entirely different measures for dealing with the progressing problem.

The United States, much like the rest of Europe and the world, had been dealing with a financial crisis for the better part of two years. The Stock Market crash of '22 was an economic disaster the United States, like so many others, hadn't yet been able to recover from. This was the reason why they had to create the Civilian Bailout Program, a system put in place to feed the growing insolvents of the nation. Too bad it wasn't able to meet the needs of an estimated 210 million underprivileged Americans. Unemployment was at fifty-eight percent. Government programs were in shambles. And let's not forget about the riots. So yeah, a revolution did appear well in hand. But unlike their European counterparts, the American leaders saw only two alternatives concerning the troubles lingering ahead. One: they'd either have to forsake the second phase of the War on Terror to spare the escalating rebellion, or two: impose Martial Law on the citizens, and stifle the rebellion before it even got out of control. Unfortunately, that was something that could rip the nation apart. Then again, with the first proposal going against everything they'd fought so hard for, the American leaders began seeing the latter as the greater possibility.

Cecil Greenough

Grand Magistrate: The Biography of Kiril Pordan

Even with *Martial Law* in place, the United States will not avoid the similar occurrences taking place in Russia. Still, it is something both Republicans and Democrats want to prevent. For that reason, newly elected Republican President Howard Mueller goes on television to reassure the American people that not only are their economic woes coming to an end, but that the *War on Terror: Phase II* will soon render its results, and that peace will be its verdict.

He pleads with the citizens to show restraint, petitioning them to end the isolated acts of violence that have begun plaguing the more populated cities. The riots. The growing collisions with law enforcement and National Guards. The random fire-bombings taking place all around major cities. These are the things that will utterly bring about the end of the United States, things Mueller begs his fellow Americans to avoid. But just as Mueller calls for patience and calm, his political rivals constantly match his pleas with accusations concerning his administration.

The Democrats also want the wars to end, and they also want the President to focus on rebuilding government programs. But at the same time, they more so want him to fail. A constant undermining which unravels the nation with each utterance, this leaves the American people with only one place to turn. It is an ideology of freewill, a practice of absolute and unrestricted liberty, a declaration to return to the foundations on which the country was built. It is the Libertarian movement known as ART, and it fuels dissension amongst disgruntled Americans, portraying itself as the future of the United States.

ART was a party that had gained recognition around the latter part of 2022. Starting out as a group of disenfranchised Republican and Democratic officials, the ART Party had become renowned when strongly advocating against any further foreign immigration into the country; especially when the government hadn't even been unable to take care of their own. They'd gained support from anyone and everyone who had been hit the hardest by The Crash, and quickly found voice on the Senate floor. Now, that isn't to say that anyone had really taken them seriously at the time, at least not as contenders to the executive branch. But then again, all that started to change around the time of the talk of rebellion. It was during this time that ART began showing their true power—that of a second revolution.

Prof. Tamara Boggier

keeper, New York Republic Athenaeum

The ARTists have been calling for a revolution for the past two years. One that will not only see the harmonious return to a free United States, but the utter dissolving of both the Republican and Democratic parties. They are the ones who fuel the protests with their preaching of the *2nd Amendment*, passionately calling on all Americans to remove the current way of government. And while Mueller and the existing authorities have cited this petition as a form of terrorism in itself, even arresting scores of its supporters in an effort to cease its nation-wide expansion, the ARTists grow into a formidable adversary with each passing day.

They are unwilling to rest until their demands are met, and constantly make them known: the end of the *War on Terror: Phase II*, the suspension of all immigration, the end to foreign aid, and the ultimate withdrawal of all U.S. Armed Forces from foreign soil.

ART makes its point through words and violence, all the time forcing the American President to take notice of them, regardless of the consequences. In Latin America, however, no such group exists to put an end to the increasing socialism trampling over the Democracy once flourishing there.

In spite of countries such as Brazil and Mexico remaining on an economic rise, Argentina, Paraguay, Bolivia, and Ecuador have all turned toward a fascist state of mind that threatens to overrun the entire continent. A socialist tidal wave blatantly invading the structure of Democracy, Latin American leaders can do nothing as their citizens are romanced by its promises.

The Latin Liberation Front was a crushing movement spreading across both South and Central America. Its leader was a former Venezuelan gunrunner turned communist party leader by the name of Cesar Lopez—a very ruthless man. The faction had grown from a small guerrilla unit dealing mostly in kidnappings, to a fully recognized political party by 2023. They'd first made national headlines when kidnapping then Venezuelan President, Victor Hernandez—a man that had been seen throughout the United States as both a socialist and tyrant. For years, Hernandez had been instigating a fight between his country and the United States, even believing his military equaled to anything the West had to offer. He used to bark all sorts of insults at his American rivals, practically begging them to attack. And while he'd been doing that, the main display of his ruthlessness had been enacted against his own people. In time, he began burdening them beneath a dictatorship full of cruelty and human rights violations, things Cesar Lopez wanted to put an end to when he'd first began his mission. So engaging Hernandez and his military, Lopez and the LLF had enacted all sorts of terrorist acts, even up to drawing criticism from the rest of the Latin world. Nevertheless, Lopez was eventually successful in his attacks, and in the end, crushed Hernandez and his entire regime. But it wasn't long until he started displaying his true colors. A United States hating, money hungry, big shot, Lopez soon proved to be no different than his predecessor. And with a knack for attacking neighboring countries, some would even say worse. Bottom line is, Lopez was a man that would soon reach America's doorstep, and that's something the United States knew it would eventually have to deal with.

Cecil Greenough

Grand Magistrate: The Biography of Kiril Pordan

While this is taking place, the world is also paying close attention to another charismatic figure. Coming out of Africa, Abu abd Allah Muhammad is his name, and he is a man who has fully grasped his destiny.

Born in Juba, South Sudan, Muhammad, called Imam Abu, has been spreading a peaceful, but radical notion of Islamic unity. The young lawyer has watched his brothers battle and kill each other in vain for too long, and according to him, the Islam of the past ninety years or so has been nothing more than a fraud. Nothing more than a series of rites and motions, the Islam of the Prophet Muhammad is dead, and Imam Abu believes only he knows how to resurrect it. He was raised in conflict, and understands the suffering of a slave, as well as, the greed of a master.

The Mahdi, alaihi al-salaam, born Daniel Mangope, had suffered greatly beneath the ethnic cleansing that had taken place in South Sudan, and had risen above it all. Once he became of age, he converted to Islam, and worked his way up the Islamic world—first as a reformer who abolished the genocide taking place in his homeland, then as an Imam who called for Muslims to join hands across the world. Not so long after, he began summoning Islamic leaders from Egypt, Morocco, Algeria, Libya, and Chad to join him in Sudan to sign a peace agreement between all of their governments. Something he saw as forging peace, it was a call that had worried most of the European Union, including the U.S. And so it did not take long before the question of who Mahdi Abu abd Allah Muhammad, alaihi al-salaam, really was, and what his intentions truly were started sparking. And though he saw it as the usual skepticism which could only be shown by the West, the U.S. and its allies saw him as nothing less than a threat.

Prof. Najiyah Abdullah Hassan

Crescent Moon and Pillars: The Rise of the Islamic Empire

It is a question that will soon be answered. But before that mystery can be unraveled, the United States and the rest of the Western Coalition find themselves traveling the South Pacific with the ongoing *War on Terror: Phase II* as their main objective.

Led by the brave leadership of United States President Howard Mueller, British Prime Minister Edward Davies, and German Chancellor Irma Hofmann, Coalition forces prepare to mount an attack on Sumatra, Indonesia, with hopes of ending the scores of terrorists using that country as a safe haven. A move that goes against the outcries of both American and European citizens, it is one their leaders believe must be done; likewise, one that will bring about a startling new development to the world stage.

India joins the Coalition, and eagerly lends troops capable of penetrating Indonesia's terrorist organizations. But when it comes to India, their membership comes with its own set of problems. One such obstacle is that of their standing accusations regarding Pakistan's alleged support of Indonesian terrorists, the ones guilty of the attacks taking place throughout the South Pacific. They are allegations purportedly confirmed by the discovery of Pakistani born militants found amongst the acts of terror scarring the region.

Pakistani Prime Minister Maimun Ali Khan, a strong contributor to the peace process being forged throughout the Islamic world, adamantly denies the claims. Still, Prime Minister Chandra Jaiteley continues to paint her neighbor as a sponsor of statewide terrorism, threatening it with retaliation. But all countries will come to know who their true allies are in due time, especially when on November 2, the first wave of Coalition troops begin landing in Sumatra.

A massive show of naval force and soldiers all converging on the South Pacific, like an innumerable armada of steel they bring the promise of Democracy and the end of terrorism. Something that should be revered as a great day, China's Premiere, Sun Jiang, takes the attack on Indonesia personally, and makes sure his objections are duly noted.

Premiere of State Council Sun Jiang—the United States will come to hate that name. A man who will etch his name amongst the evilest men to have ever walked the face of the Earth, he will forever challenge the very idea of Democracy with one strike. And in the aftermath, death will become mere triviality to this dawning age.

The Great Divide: a concise history of the future

M.A. Martin

2026

CASUS BELLI

The Great Divide: a concise history of the future

Russia's military desperately battles SPINA at the doorsteps of Moscow's Kremlin. The conflict has seen over 15,000 deaths, and countless wounded, but SPINA has finally beaten back the elitist regime to the very heart of Russia's Republic. It is a fight to the death, more so, a final stand for the fate of the Russian people. The scene is absolute chaos. The wailing of mourners is something that cannot be made quiet. Destruction and despair collapse across the city, and innocent people die. And by mid-March, the fight for Russia is finally decided. SPINA stands victorious before the Kremlin.

Inside are Russian Prime Minister Feodore Repin and President Leonid Novikov. The two of them plea via-internet for the people of Russia to do something, but are forced to bear witness to their defeat nonetheless.

By the time Russia's Silovik regime was defeated, SPINA had by then seized control of the country's media. During that time, they had no problem with broadcasting the shear violence of the war, nor did they have any qualms broadcasting the cowardly acts of the ruling leaders for the world to see. And while the rest of his fighters continued either converting or killing the remaining country's military, it was SPINA's leader, Bogdan Kushnir, who did most of the interviews concerning his faction's next move. Of course, he never made his demands a mystery as to what he wanted in order to stop the war—not by any means. Kushnir made it clear from the beginning that in order for peace to be returned to Russia, both Repin and Novikov would have to die.

Prof. Jarvis Grimes

historian, *Superior and Biased: The History of the Royal European Alliance*

A cold Russian morning, an assemblage numbering close to 2 million gather in the center of Moscow. Crestfallen citizens who have suffered all on account of the corrupted version of the glorious future their former leader, Vladimir Putin, had once envisioned for them. They stand amongst the ruins of the once great city, eagerly watching as SPINA members storm the Kremlin to apprehend the leaders of the toppled Silovik regime.

In front of cameras and a roaring mob, Repin, Novikov, their cabinet members, and their families, are all dragged into the streets and viciously beaten to death. Brutal and traumatizing, it does not end there. Both Repin and Novikov then have their battered and bruised corpses hung from the walls of the Kremlin as a sign of SPINA's ultimate victory. And for the first time in history, no news agency censors the act, almost as if consenting to the deed.

In the United States, though precluded by warnings of containing graphic nature, the sight of the executed leaders plays for all to see. A sure sign of changing times for some, the barbaric murders are seen as nothing less than an insult to others.

Disgusted by the fact of both the West and Europe seemingly applauding such vile actions, China loudly voices its condemnation of SPINA. The Chinese see no valor in what the rebels have done, and find the murders of the Russian leaders a heinous crime demanding punishment.

You have to understand the mind frame in which Sun Jiang was operating. He saw Russia as the only functioning government allied with him in a communistic spirit, though they were not necessarily communist by any means. Second, he was watching as all other nations, the United Kingdom, France, Germany, and the United States all sat back and allowed this to happen. To him, it was clear that they refused to help Russia because of its contradicting views, and nothing else. If any other country had been in jeopardy of being hostilely taken over the way Russia was, he believed all these spectators would have jumped at the opportunity to help. But Russia was held at a different bar. So Sun Jiang felt that it was in his best interest that he defend the Silovik Republic in its time of need, and that was what he did.

Tsun-chúng Hu

The Last Dynasty: The Chinese Republic's Ultimate Demise

Chinese Premiere Sun Jiang angrily calls for an emergency meeting of the United Nations to discuss what has happened, and hopes to gain support in his campaign concerning the defense of the devastated Russian Republic. Standing there before the national assembly, Sun declares Russia a victim of terrorism, and orders the Western World do something about it.

Although, with Russia's ousted government classified as a fascist regime guilty of ignoring basic human rights, the general consensus is that they have been given exactly what they deserve. China sees this as an act of betrayal, and a sign of hypocrisy on the side of those who have sworn to battle terrorism in all its forms.

Defying those he charges with abandoning Russia during its misfortune, Sun declares his intentions of sending military aid into the war-torn nation in bringing about stability. The announcement stuns the United Nations, drawing the United States, the United Kingdom, Germany, and their coalition to denounce such undertakings. Unfortunately for them, their words are no longer credible in Sun's eyes. And on April 3, through a coerced agreement, the Communist Chinese Republic is allowed by the much weaker Mongolian government to cross through its country with a military operation numbering close to 700,000 troops.

Never before seen in modern times, the invasion of Russia is without doubt an extensive one, and proof of China's considerable might.

The United States is the most vocal critic of Sun Jiang's actions, even as the Chinese Premiere assures the rest of the world his motives are purely in line with fighting the *War on Terror: Phase II*. It is mocking propaganda in the eyes of many, but the European Union and United States do nothing to stop the invasion, or so they say.

American and European manufactured weapons begin flooding Russia in aid to SPINA. A discovery which immediately pits the Coalition against China, it amazes no one to see Sun on television every day blaming the West for its interference.

He accuses the United States of sedition, and sponsoring terrorism. He presents proof of the West arming militants, and its plans to destabilize Asia. His words precursor an evident disaster waiting to happen, and threaten the world at large. But with Coalition forces currently preoccupied with the war in the South Pacific, they seem to ignore the inflammatory allegations for the time being.

Operation: *RED STAR* has been in effect for the past nineteen months, and has seen the deaths of 473 British, 346 German, 53 French, 1209 Indian, 645 Pakistani, and 1565 American soldiers. All the same, with terrorism at an all time low in Indonesia, and the number of dead terrorists reaching well into the high 6,000's, Coalition forces see the tide of the war in their favor, and continue to spearhead their mission of Democracy.

Indonesia is their staging ground, and the united military front now begins launching attacks into Malaysia, with the Philippines as their next target. Needless to say, no one is under the false impression the war will be easily won, and the question of just how long they can actually keep fighting is discussed behind closed doors.

Regardless of the victories, the South Pacific still proves a harsh territory, and there is no telling how many innocent civilians will be lost by war's end. Likewise, Europe, as well as, the United States face near rebellion by their citizens if the war continues for much longer. A threatening dilemma for the governments of the Western World, with terrorism continuing to rear its ugly head throughout the South Pacific, the Coalition has no alternative but to continue with the fight for Democracy. It is a charge they cannot ignore, but it does not help to see two of their Coalition members going at each other's throats.

India, a major ally in the *War on Terror: Phase II*, continues voicing its allegations concerning Pakistan's suspected support for terrorists in the region. This is something Pakistan unwaveringly continues to deny, even though facts on the ground show a possible Pakistani terrorist backing in both Indonesia and Malaysia. Weapons, Pakistani born militants found daily, the proof is both overwhelming and detrimental. Despite that, the Coalition considers the Islamic country an important component in forging peace in South Asia, and try their best to absolve Pakistan of any wrong doing. A significance India disregards, the leaders there persist in their allegations, all the time refusing to accept any evidence discharging such claims.

India and Pakistan had been dealing with these sorts of allegations for years now, but never before had they been so blatantly disconcerting for the two regions. The Hindus of India hated the Muslims of Pakistan, and vice versa. But never had the governments been so adamant against each other. This was a situation that was getting out of hand, and no one could have truly fathomed the cost of what was about to follow.

Prof. Najiyah Abdullah Hassan

Crescent Moon and Pillars: The Rise of the Islamic Empire

On an early Thursday morning in April, India fires on a Pakistani freight-ship traveling through the Indian Ocean. The Indian government claims the vessel was bound for Indonesia with weapons on board, but the Pakistanis refute such charges. So in retaliation to the violent attack,

Pakistani officials authorize a full scale military assault on suspected Hindu terrorists believed to be stationed in India's eastern province of Amritsar.

India is outraged by the deliberate irruption, and accuses Pakistan of grossly retaliating against a reasonable halt of terrorist action. In response, Pakistani Prime Minister Maimun Ali Khan goes on television, and addresses the world, informing India and all others of his country's preparedness to defend itself against any attack. He promises the assault on Amritsar will be the first of many if India continues to goad a fight, daring India's leaders to test him. And as if that is all they need, India answers the call with an invasion into Pakistan's Gujranwala region, maliciously killing over three hundred people in a single day.

The deaths are unanimously seen as an act of war on India's part by all nations, but the call for a peaceful resolution is still desperately made to both sides. The United States, Great Britain, and Germany try their best to remind the two countries of what is at stake. They recall the *War on Terror: Phase II* both nations have sworn to fight, but it is a cry for restraint which falls on deaf ears. On May 4, Pakistan engages India head-on in an all out retaliation, giving birth to the Great Indo/Pak War.

Commencing in the Thar Desert, thousands of troops gather to defend their respected countries, with India displaying a might of over 500,000 soldiers to Pakistan's 145,000. A battle which threatens to weaken the *War on Terror: Phase II*, this crossing of borders, and the war it breeds, is not solely confined to the subcontinent. With the socialist conquest of Cesar Lopez and his *Latin Liberation Front* spilling their brand of fascism and violence into neighboring countries such as Colombia and Brazil, border crossing wars seem almost redundant in their performances.

Latin America had become a place of war and destruction. Its people were starving, and all sorts of small factions were pledging allegiance to the LLF movement. These militias then began attacking and killing innocent civilians, while the LLF itself battled the militaries of those same oppressed regions. The drug trade had also spun out of control, with warlords battling each other for control of its financial wealth, or lack there of. Still, it was the armed militaries of Venezuela, Bolivia, Peru, and Argentina, that furthered the LLF agenda the most. With their support, their call of Latin American dominance, and ultimate destruction of the United States, there wasn't anyway of telling who was friend or who was foe.

Cecil Greenough

Grand Magistrate: The Biography of Kiril Pordan

American leaders had known of the Latin Liberation Front threat for the past two years. Not to mention that they'd also been receiving countless requests from Brazil, Colombia, Ecuador, and Chile, for military support for even longer than that. Unfortunately, they were simply too preoccupied with the war in the Middle East to have intervened, exactly the same way they were presently preoccupied in the South Pacific. But with the ever-growing quandary in Latin America quickly becoming something that could no longer be ignored, the United States knew it would have to take serious action—and soon.

Prof. Tamara Boggier

keeper, New York Republic Athenaeum

The *Latin Liberation Front* is slowly encroaching on America's southern borders. President Howard Mueller, a Republican Congress and Senate, have no choice but to pass a controversial bill inducting private security contractors such as FLINT, Shadow Walkers Inc., Red Eagle, and Hunter-7 into the United States military. The President then authorizes the government sanctioned freelancers to enter Latin America with the support of small military regiments, and orders they quell the *Latin Liberation Front* by any means necessary. Mexico is to be the first obstacle undertaken, and the newly formed International Guards branch of the United States Armed Forces does so without mercy.

Countries aligned with the *Latin Liberation Front* begin dispatching troops of their own to meet the invasion entering Mexico. This sparks a downward spiral of violence that will see thousands killed within the span of one month, turning the whole of Latin America into an absolute killing field. Events that lead many to speculate the world is seemingly about to explode, some religious groups and zealous cults alike voice their warnings concerning the End of Days.

Christians warn of the Second Coming of Jesus Christ. Those faithful to the Holy Scriptures call on all souls to repent of their sinful ways, while they themselves fight the good fight in remaining righteous. In the same way, Muslims and Jews call for a meaningful repentance, but the majority of the world perceives the warnings as mere religious ramblings. And though a few do in fact seek a form of spirituality capable of sparing the world its impending doom, Buddhism is the one which sees the most converts, especially by those between the ages of 16-30 years old.

The young Buddhists see the religions of the Abramic faith as the primary reason behind the growing wars, and seek an alternative that would better help remedy the destruction caused by them. This eventually forges

Buddhism and its dharma into a safe haven where those seeking peace will find hope and refuge.

Before long, its numbers begin rivaling both those of Christianity and Islam, with only Hinduism maintaining its masses. Spiritual awakenings which spark all across the globe, it is during these divine revivals that China seizes control of St. Petersburg, Russia. The date is August 18, and the powerful Communist Chinese Republic's military slaughters thousands of Russians pledging allegiance to SPINA.

Violent executions and war flood news reports being broadcast from out of the country, proving even spirituality cannot halt the darkness inexorably gripping the planet. All the same, it is SPINA which broadcasts China's horrendous actions to the world, transmitting footage of Russian citizens being gunned down in the streets, while rockets destroy buildings across the city.

World leaders once more condemn the actions. They demand China abandon its unwarranted attacks on Russia and its people, and even threaten military response if their ultimatums are not met. China ignores the resolutions, and continues with its rendering of the *War on Terror: Phase II*. This leaves SPINA with no choice but to meet China's forces in a bloody clash over Russia's uncertain future, just as talks begin getting underway within the halls of the United Nation concerning the most effective way of dealing with China's deliberate spurning of the international community's demands.

The topic is presented as a detrimental attack on peace, but the world leaders soon bear witness to the most horrendous act of terrorism ever enacted, and for now, must halt any actions against their Chinese rivals.

During this entire time of war, Israel had been continuing its petition concerning the World Bank being relocated to West Jerusalem. A plan that had been encountered with a lot of anti-Semitism, the Pro-Israeli lobbyists in America had been pushing for the relocation in an attempt to show the country's resolve in the face of tyranny. Of course, the Arab and Persian nations weren't happy with the idea, but they'd recently quieted their objections as a sign of unification. This by no means meant there weren't still those elements of discontent lingering about, and this was what eventually led to the atrocious act we saw committed.

Cecil Greenough

Grand Magistrate: The Biography of Kiril Pordan

It was something no one could've ever fathomed coming true. Sure, they'd heard the threats, and had even seen the potential for such a catastrophe, but no one ever thought it could actually happen.

Prof. Tamara Boggier

keeper, New York Republic Athenaeum

Israel had been warning that this could happen for years. They had constantly reiterated their concerns regarding their country being attacked, but no one seemed to take the threat seriously. After all, Muslims expected the fulfillment of their Koran to take place there, as did Christians. So who in their right mind would have dared attacked this most holiest of cities? As a matter of fact, there had even come a time when Israel itself appeared to be the one goading a fight with the rest of the Arab and Persian world. When in reality, it was simply protecting itself from something like this occurring. I suppose it took this to happen for all the countries of the world to realize what Israel had known all along, but by then it was too late.

Prof. Jarvis Grimes

historian, *Superior and Biased: The History of the Royal European Alliance*

Saturday, August 22—the Sabbath. It is a moment that will forever be remembered. A nuclear device is detonated within the center of Jerusalem, with a radius blast powerful enough to destroy nearly the entire Holy City. It is reported an estimated 400,000 Israelis and Palestinians are killed in the initial blast, with another 3.8 million dead within two day's time from exposure to the sweeping thermal radiation aftershock. A sight that grips the entire world in fear, everyone is brought to their knees.

All over the world, media outlets display the chaos that has taken place nearest to the bombsite. Medical services: The Red Cross, CARE, the World Health Organization, and other international emergency services are deployed in vast numbers, each trying their best to aid the survivors of the iniquitous attack. Numerous quarantine zones are setup throughout the regions of Bethlehem, Jericho, and Tel-Aviv. Unfortunately, ground zero is impenetrable, leaving those who have possibly survived to perish all on their own. And for a brief moment, the world's impending doom stills the terrified frozen heartbeats of its inhabitants, but only for a short while.

World leaders quickly convene within the United Nations to discuss the paralyzing situation, as well as, to try and quell the boiling call for vengeance being echoed throughout the globe. No proof is yet found to link a specific terrorist organization to such a brutal act, but the world has already determined the most likely suspect.

In a time when Islam is considered both dangerous and capricious, the populace is all to quick to place culpability on none other than the Muslims. Because of this, anti-Islamic sentiments eventually begin flaring throughout the globe, bringing about numerous reports concerning Muslims being attacked by mobs in the streets. And though officials try their best to suppress such blatant assaults, Muslims are both beaten and killed by those believing the Islamic doctrine to be behind Jerusalem's destruction. These random attacks, in turn, fuel anger within the hearts of Muslims across the globe, establishing a mindset of retaliation in the hearts of the Islamic nations.

Muslim leaders of the world conclude they are being affronted from all sides, and see no alternative but to clear their names of being involved in the attack. Then, as if a miracle, the Iranian military, in a joint effort with an Iraqi task force, discover exiled Iranian President Farhad Seifzadeh hiding in Iran's Elburz mountainous region, and bring him in as a conspirator to the bombing.

Many people were questioning whether or not Seifzadeh had actually committed this act, or whether it was some random freelance organization hoping to disrupt the peace process of the Middle East? Either way, the leaders of Iran and Iraq made it their duty to clear Islam of such mean-spirited accusations. This is why you see Seifzadeh being brought in as a conspirator to the Jerusalem bombing, though there was literally no proof at all. It did not matter. His arrest was expected to pacify the people of the world, and the Islamic governments had no problem with pinning all culpability on this one man.

Prof. Najiyah Abdullah Hassan

Crescent Moon and Pillars: The Rise of the Islamic Empire

Iran quickly informs the world of Seifzadeh's alleged confession to being the mastermind behind Jerusalem's bombing, and declares he will be put on trial for his part in its development. In spite of this, people continue to insult the Islamic world. They call for Seifzadeh's head. They demand he immediately be put to death if the Muslims really want peace, and as a consequence, force world leaders to request of the Middle East the former Iranian leader be handed over to the international courts for further judgment as a sign of goodwill.

Iran's Ayatollah Astarabadi and Iraqi Prime Minister Husani agree to the demand, and prepare to hand Seifzadeh over. Regrettably, while awaiting transport in a highly militarized section of Tehran, Seifzadeh is apprehended by an enraged mob of Iranian citizens, and literally hacked to pieces. A gruesome killing recorded on dozens of smartphones, it is distributed around the world for all to see.

The act reminds the general public that Islam has also lost something sacred with the demise of Jerusalem. Attacks soon begin to dwindle, and Muslims can once again walk the streets. In Africa, however, though absolutely agreeing with the harsh actions taken by the Iranian people against their former leader, Imam Abu abd Allah Muhammad begins using the anti-Islamic violence seen around the globe to further advance his unified Afro Islamic agenda.

The Muslim leader makes clear the world's hatred for Islam, saying they will always lay fault on its doctrines whenever met with catastrophe. He has already gained the support of most North African countries with such talk, but that does not stop him from calling upon all Muslims within Africa to join him in pressing their governments to sign an unprecedented unification bill amalgamating all Afro-Islamic nations under one roof.

To Western powers, the strategy to unify Northern Africa under one Islamic government is seen as an effort toward displacing the Christian presence of the region. Imam Abu denies such claims, and wastes no time in charging the international consensus as being nothing more than an attempt at further oppressing the Muslim people. This triggers a growing skepticism within the heart of Islam concerning the world's true agenda for it, further strengthening the Imam.

Heated debates sparked from both sides of the argument, no one can ignore the fact of nothing less than a massacre being enacted by China's communist regime through its invasion of Russia. For while the international community has been focused on the attack on Jerusalem, the Chinese have been busy destroying what is left of the weakened SPINA rebellion.

Every day, the scenes coming out of Russia play like a symphony of death and destruction. Supporters of SPINA are either arrested, or murdered by Chinese soldiers. The city of St. Petersburg resembles an urban war-zone. Most of its aesthetic architecture is reduced to rubble. Now Moscow is the focus of the battle, trapping it in a spiral of violence and anarchy.

SPINA fighters try futilely to hold back the overwhelming Chinese forces, but with tanks, jets, and nearly 1.2 million Chinese soldiers marching through the streets of Ufa, St. Petersburg, and now Moscow, the Russian freedom fighters do not stand a chance.

SPINA leader, Bogdan Kushnir, calls on world leaders to aid him in ending the communist crush. He obliges them to determine the best way of entering the conflict before it is too late. This, in due course, sparks Chinese Premiere Sun Jiang to warn against any interference, threatening his country is more than ready to engage any intrusion.

In Sun's rationale, the world ignored Russia during its most obvious hour of need, and to try now and undermine his country's response to such crisis would only lead to a further destabilization of the region. The objection is duly noted, and rumors of going to war with China begin getting underway.

Sun Jiang knew exactly what he was doing when he took it upon himself to save Russia. He knew that the Western powers and their Coalition would not have simply stood aside and watch him takeover—not when Democracy was at stake. But to him, this was simply hypocrisy in its purist form. No one came to Russia's aid when SPINA was wrecking havoc through its streets, so why would they care now? Obviously, they did not care about terrorism, not when it served their agenda.

Tsun-chúng Hu

The Last Dynasty: The Chinese Republic's Ultimate Demise

On September 16, the massive Chinese military engages SPINA in the heart of Moscow. SPINA suffers a crushing defeat there, sealing their fate, as well as, the fate of their leader, Bogdan Kushnir.

With a sense of irony, the rebel leader finds himself making his last stand on the steps of the Kremlin, the very place where he had once been hailed as a liberator. It is here the Chinese army slaughters over 700 of his men, killing him in the process as they have promised. This sequence of events now leaves China as the only functioning government of Russia, with the unyielding Chinese Premiere, Sun Jiang, as its head.

The international community is outraged, and convenes at the United Nations to confront China and its abhorrent actions. Albeit, China is the one to take center stage when Sun Jiang delivers a speech condemning the Democratic Coalition, and their alleged hypocrisy when dealing with true threats around the world. He palpably makes the United States the primary focus of his criticisms, and then declares his intentions of indefinitely occupying Russia.

Sun calls it an effort at reconstructing the once glorious Silovik regime of the country, but the United States and its Coalition call it *casus belli*.

A case for war.

Today we witness the true character of those who claim to fight in the name of freedom. Hypocrites who would condemn sovereign nations for their justified and legal actions, simply to promote utter anarchy in the name of Democracy. It is both shameful and ghastly that these nations should dare disavow their own verdicts against terrorism solely for their own greed and self-importance. And yet, here you all are, blindly following their lead, simply to get your scraps at their table. I hear the cry of those who desire a world lacking pain, a world without hunger, a planet shared in an ideology of equality and determination. The rich desire nothing but more riches, and it is upon the backs of the poor that their insatiability finds sustenance. These reckless endorsements prove costly when you look at the world as it currently is —this world of dept, despair, and destruction. The elimination of private property is the only way toward sharing and growth, but they say the poor are needed only for the rich, and that it is the right of a few to master over the abilities of the many. They ignore the fact that every day wasted implementations of food, clothing, housing, and dignity should be distributed equally, creating a balanced system of prosperity and belonging. But they say that it is better to ration out the goods of this planet so that the goal of strangling the poor with lack of survivability should be realized. They are wrong. The world needs an honor-bound man to lead society without objection or hindrance, but they say the incompetent should be allowed to subjugate his people just long enough for another inadequate tormenter of a far different ideology to come into play. And this is why they condemn me. This is why they allow the feral nature of insurrection to dictate what plans should be allowed, what defenses one should be granted, and how far one should be permitted to develop. And this is why they stand by and watch as a mob murders recognized leaders of a lawful society. United States of America, I warn you. The Communist Chinese Republic is not a lamb, and you are no lion. The sun will always rise in the East, so do not test us in making it set permanently in the West. The Russian people need help, and we desire that you join us in aiding them, but not in the ill fashion you have demonstrated in the past. We will take lead on this mission, and you are to respect this judgment. If not, I fear your tyranny will leave us no choice but to require of you the justified contrition.

Premiere of State Council Sun Jiang

United Nations Address, October 2, 2026

The differences of opinion are stark, as well as, damaging. China has been at odds with the United States before, but this is the first time it has spoken so boastfully. Sun Jiang has put forth his challenge; now he simply waits for someone to answer. And refusing to make him wait, United States President Howard Mueller decides to be the first of the world leaders to speak on the situation.

He first condemns every word Sun has said, then reiterates the international community's original demands for China to get out of Russia. He again threatens military action if the orders are not met, and prays Sun will reconsider. A loud and commanding clarity as to the long-proven resolve of the United States, such pressure leaves China with only one option. The date is October 6, and the Communist Chinese Republic makes its statement as lurid as it can by absolving its relationship with the United Nations General Assembly.

The move is as alarming as much as it is unforeseen, and the United States of America, Great Britain, and Germany, instantly begin rallying against China, calling on their Coalition to join them in going to war against the fascist establishment. The pleas give birth to even more resentment amongst liberal politicians of both Europe and the United States, triggering an even greater resilient protest amongst rioting citizens.

France is the first of the Coalition to succumb to the demands of its people by ending its involvement in the South Pacific, and rejects taking part in any confrontation against China. The decision is respected by its European allies, but the United States condemns it as both a dangerous and cowardly neutral stance. Regardless, France's withdrawal does not change the scope of the *War on Terror: Phase II,* nor what must take place next.

The remaining Coalition is more than prepared to engage China. And when the dispute finally does commence, it will be evident no country can standby and watch as the unfolding of World War III is birthed.

The Great Divide: a concise history of the future

2028

SILENT NIGHT

The Great Divide: a concise history of the future

The #1 movie in America is *The Last Apostle*. The three hour epic details the life and ministry of the Arab prophet, Muhammad. It causes controversy around the globe, but is also seen as proof of Islam's ever-growing tolerance. It has been financed by an independent multimillionaire by the name of Frank Seager, one of the few remaining multimillionaires in the world, and promises to be worth the price of admission. It grosses 12 million dollars in three weeks.

It is a blockbuster.

The Hip-Fonika group, Nemesis, sees their latest upload, *H'dwnkT*, topping the Confirm-Graf. A fusion of heavy drums, deep grooves, and spoken word, Hip-Fonika is a musical internet platform allowing anyone to rant over the beats created by an IM (Internet Mozart). It flourishes around the globe from the fact that anyone can do it and gain notoriety, "level-ups" entitling one to a certain echelon of control, and most importantly, "Mod Status" signifying how much one modifies oneself from being a simple human being. Nemesis just so happens to be the "Signal Runner" of its craft.

In religion, Buddhism is the premier faith. Christians all over the planet retreat from society in search of a holy seclusion, while some take to the streets to condemn the world. Millions upon millions of people flock to holy sites in hopes of finding safety from the impending doom. Places such as Bodh Gaya, Varanasi, Ise, Mecca, and Vatican City are flooded, while untold numbers are kept out of Jerusalem, forcing thousands to sneak into the ravaged city, only to die from radiation, or at the hands of Bio-Hazard guards excavating its ruins.

An unmatched religious revival, those who turn to the gods pray for mercy and grace. And though hundreds of people die during these devout stampedes, the faithful still get the opportunity to stand before the sanctified settings, allowing the hopeless to find hope.

Imam Abu is an iconic figure throughout Africa and the rest of the Islamic world. Western youths view him as a symbol of revolution, and wear his bearded image on their T-shirts. Most bear his famous quote *"Everything ends, but only focus on what you can begin"*, while his more controversial statements, *"A life of lies finds truth in death,"* is embraced by those subscribing to more violent means of resistance. Indeed, Imam Abu is an idol, but he cares nothing for Western praise. The world is in upheaval, and nobody has occasion for self-glorification.

The streets of the United States, Great Britain, Germany, and many others are inundated by rioters and protestors attacking all forms of authority. The all too often violent demonstrators demand peace be found during these troubling times, and refuse to standby and watch as their world fails. Footage of hordes of people being arrested, beaten, and on a rarity, shot in the streets flash across television screens. Word of rebellion and conspiracy find life in the hearts of disgruntled citizens. Picket signs with the words: Enough Wars! The End Is Here! End The Death! Art Is The Future! bob up and down with passion, as batons, teargas, and live ammunition bring them down in keeping the law. It is definitely getting harder to live in the more developed parts of the world, and the populace of cities turn to never-ending looting, theft, and all out murder.

Absolute chaos to say the least, in Latin America, the word chaos does not do justice to the Hell it has become. In that part of the world, Democratic countries battle feverishly against the dominating might of socialism, while the United States tries supporting countries such as Brazil and Chile in their fight for freedom. Futile aid at best, the entire region will soon be overtaken by the fascist ideologies of the *Latin Liberation Front*. While across the globe, in a battle threatening world stability, Pakistan and India continue to engage each other in war. Islamabad, Lahore, and Kashmir suffer the most from ongoing bombings and deaths, but it is World War III which grips everyone's attention.

Undoubtedly a time of dread and confusion, the Coalition of the United States, Great Britain, and Germany feverishly engage the Nexus forces of

China, Occupied-Russia, and North Korea, further fueling those who believe in the words of doomsayers that the end of the world is most certainly at hand.

The battle for freedom and Democracy continues in the South Pacific. Coalition Forces defeat the terrorist groups of the Philippines, with heated battles raging on in Vietnam and Cambodia. China aggressively deploys 1.2 million of its troops to the borders of Bhutan, Nepal, and Laos in an effort to head off any invasion from its underbelly.

The Coalition begins accessing the best method for persisting with the war, and conclude Sun Jiang must fall in order for Democracy to rise. They believe the Chinese Premier sees himself a warrior taken from a mold of Genghis Khan, presenting his actions as proof. They say Sun Jiang wants to rule the world, something that absolutely cannot be allowed to happen. The very thought leaves World War III to be determined by aerial dogfights, and naval conflicts over the seas of Andaman, Philippine, Timor, and South China.

Land conflicts see the deaths of 2825 German, 13,334 British, 15,352 American, and 92,384 Asians. Clashes on the ground conveyed by news agencies from around the world, the skirmishes of the air and seas are the ones truly gaining and losing battles for both the Democratic Coalition and Nexus. Nevertheless, it is the side of the Coalition gaining ground, challenging China and all its stands for.

Chinese forces find themselves being pushed out of Bangladesh, Myanmar, and Thailand, while Guam, the Northern Mariana Islands, New Guinea, and Papua New Guinea remain free of any Chinese influence. Regardless, China backs a North Korean invasion of the South, strategically stalling a Coalition approach from the east in a maneuver which brings Japan to worry of a similar invasion.

The Land of the Rising Sun also opposes China's acts in Russia and the South Pacific, and wisely expect the Chinese to seek retribution. Therefore, Japanese Prime Minister Fushimi Heisuke opens his borders to the Democratic Coalition, joining the war as an Coalition member in late February. This does not stop Sun Jiang from contacting Fushimi in an effort to persuade him into reconsidering, tactically trying to use their common Asian ancestry as reason. But Fushimi is not swayed. On May 10, Japan joins the Democratic Coalition, and lands ground troops in South Korea in defense against its Northern attackers.

The incursion infuriates Sun Jiang, forcing him to authorize the Head General in Russia, Zhao Qi, to attack the Ukraine, Belarus, Latvia, and Estonia in an obvious effort to weaken the Coalition's European backing. Russian satellite countries are then bombarded, suffering countless dead within weeks. The onslaught even encroaches on Poland and Lithuania, finally forcing Germany to reconsider its defense of the South Pacific in order to deal with the battles taking place in its own backyard.

Soon enough, all of Europe begins reevaluating their protection of the South Pacific, convening at the Berlaymont in Brussels to discuss their next step in the global conflict.

Article 412 is once more brought to the fore, and the suggestion of merging all European banks and laws under one house seems more plausible now than ever before. Considering the fact that by July 21, the Ukraine, Latvia, and Estonia have already fallen to the Russian-Chinese communist regime, this leaves only Belarus, Lithuania, and Poland to defend against any further spread. However, nervous over what the unification could mean for the rest of the world, as well as, seeing the plan as taking one step closer toward abandoning the call of Democracy, the United States opposes such an idea.

The American leadership calls upon the European Coalition members to reassess their options, but their arguments fail in face of the inevitable Eastern European threat.

Article 412 was more than just a simple effort at preserving Europe's interests, it was a piece of legislation with which the European leaders could help solve the economic crisis facing their countries. Sadly, this point was something that had been originally believed by Nazi Germany, the very reason why the United States was so critical of its reliability. All the same, to some, it was no shock to see the Fatherland as Article 412's most prevalent advocate.

Prof. Jarvis Grimes

historian, *Superior and Biased: The History of the Royal European Alliance*

Germany is skeptical as to why the United States is so opposed to the move, and begins voicing its own distrust toward its Western ally. It is up to President Mueller to convince his European friends the move would be playing directly into China's hand, proving the communist regime correct in their propaganda regarding Democracy being a failed ideology. A reasonable objection, the world leaders meet in England to discuss the situation.

Mueller understands Chancellor Hofmann's position in needing to defend from Russia's encroachment, but also believes a loss in the South Pacific will spell certain doom for all of Democracy. The argument is taken seriously, but does not waiver Germany from systematically withdrawing its armed forces from the Asiatic regions, pulling half of its military from out of the South Pacific, with the other half to be withdrawn by the end of the year.

Undaunted by Germany's decision, the United States and Great Britain go ahead and land troops in South Korea, ruthlessly engaging the North Korean invaders in a bloody battle. The South Koreans join the fight for their freedom, and support the Allied troops as they first seize control of Pusan, and then Seoul. And though the North Koreans are relentless in their fight, the South proves freedom a more powerful weapon.

They refuse to submit to their Northern brothers, and help the Democratic Coalition to beat back communist brigade after communist brigade. The communist North soon retreats into its own territory, but the Coalition will not stop there.

The United States and Great Britain intend on following the defeated military into North Korea, and from there, launch an attack on China. A bold and dangerous assault, the Coalition is indeed able to deploy troops into both the hearts of Shenyang and Dalian, China, by early November.

Over 275,000 American and 160,000 British troops by ground, with a colossal fleet of battleships and aircraft carriers stationed in both the Yellow and East China Seas, the Democratic Coalition continually bomb the Chinese capital of Beijing, while Pyongyang, North Korea, is trampled underfoot by land and air.

The battle is waged with primal violence, with Democracy supporting news reports distorting the information concerning Coalition victories. Civilians who are not rioting are told of heroic aerial battles and crushing ground assaults gaining the Democratic Coalition more ground, including exaggerated details having to do with Chinese soldiers cowardly fleeing the battlefield in fear of the mighty West. Truth is, the United States and Great Britain lose close to 7,000 men and women of their combined armed forces within the first month of invading Shenyang. Another 5,400 are killed in Dalian within a matter of days.

This substantial loss of life does not halt the support coming from conservatives who believe in the war and its positive outcome, while those against the conflict continue to protest and riot in the streets against it. An evident fracture in Democracy, the United States' objectionable ART Party uses the split to gain the recognition it needs in presenting their candidate, Calvin Walsh, for the upcoming presidential elections. A man who, while the Democrats and Republicans contradict each other's attempts at controlling the highest office of the land, promises a future full of glory and freedom.

Regrettably for the Americans, the election of the next President of the United States will not matter. The nation is about to face a crisis it has never before believed itself vulnerable to—a crisis that will ultimately test its true loyalty to Democracy.

The date is December 25, Christmas Day. The country is gripped by violent acts of unrest and ongoing protests, but the holiday still finds people celebrating its value with family and friends. There is even a sense of normality throughout the land. Hopes of a better future is prayed for by all. Children play with whatever toys their parents have been able to get them, while adults simulate their joy at the gifts given to them by friends and loved ones.

Parents and partners wait by the phone for their nearest and dearest at war to call them. And strangers wish those same dear soldiers a Happy Holidays from all across the nation. Furthermore, as Republicans and Democrats try burying the hatchet following their grueling loss during the election season, the ART Party continues to revel in its candidate's sweeping victory.

Calvin Walsh is the United States' President-Elect, and he promises a future of peace and prosperity.

It was Christmas Day. The rioters had stopped their looting, and protestors had put down the picket signs just so they could have this day with their families. Nobody forgot about what was going on. Everybody knew there was a war, and that people were dying—that they themselves were tired, scared, and hungry. But they put all that aside just so they could have this one moment, this one day just to have peace. And then everything changed.

Cecil Greenough

Grand Magistrate: The Biography of Kiril Pordan

My mother was living in New York at the time, and she used to tell me "It was like getting punched in the chest". She could recall standing in front of her television watching the devastation, and thinking it was a movie. She always cried when she told me that story.

Prof. Tamara Boggier

keeper, New York Republic Athenaeum

It is a Christmas like all others. Crisp white snow blankets the earth. A nipping breeze caresses the cheek. The smell of winter is in the air. The songs of Noel play joyfully in homes: *Silent Night, Jingle Bells, Frosty the Snowman.* The smell of fresh baked cookies is recalled by all, and family more than makes up for any lacking with their love. Again, it is a Christmas like all others, all except for China enacting its most horrendous act of war to date.

Just as dawn breaks across the western horizon of the United States, a nuclear attack strikes the State of California. A fiery assault seen from as far as New Mexico, a portion of Los Angeles is utterly vaporized. Earthquakes measuring 7.2 on the Richter scale are recorded in Arizona, Nevada, and even Colorado. Buildings crumble, streets shatter, bridges collapse, and above all, an entire city burns like Hades. A nuclear detonation in the United States of America, within 34.8 seconds, 1.7 million people are dead.

Los Angeles to San Francisco suffer a dozen earthquakes following the attack, and with them come massive tsunamis that tear the historic *City by the Bay* apart. Nobody understands how the government did not see this coming. They immediately begin blaming their leaders for a lack of security, and the many conspiracies begin to rise. The worst attack on American soil ever recorded, it is the most brutal in all of history.

Reports concerning the blast come from as far as Utah, with the severity of the explosion losing its intensity near Texas. It grips the planet with its happening. And all over the world, the assault on America is made the focus of media frenzy.

The mighty United States has been attacked.

The American government declares a national emergency, and deploys an overhaul of emergency medical workers to California. San Diego and Sacramento are entirely transformed into quarantine zones where the injured can be brought for care, while nearby States are completely depleted of medical supplies and personnel in face of this disaster. Still, no abundance of medical care workers can meet the demands of this developing tragedy.

Everything from thermal radiation burns to injuries suffered during earthquake aftershocks are brought in for treatment, leaving the hard working doctors and nurses overwhelmed.

Meanwhile, the actual devastation suffered by *The Golden State* cannot be truly assessed due to the high levels of radiation engulfing the area. This makes the hope of contacting any possible survivors unfeasible, leaving them without any chance of survival.

The destruction was horrible. Over 2 million people were dead. Most of California was gone, and there was nothing anyone could do about it. There was this dark cloud lingering in the air—literally. And everyone in the country thought they were going to die from radiation poisoning, or that another attack was going to hit at any moment. Yet, they were calm. Maybe it was shock, or maybe it was just fear driven submission? Whatever the case, Americans had been attacked, and there hadn't been enough of a contingency plan in place to help those in need.

Prof. Tamara Boggier

keeper, New York Republic Athenaeum

Nobody saw this coming. Hell, they should've, but they didn't. Glorious landmarks were now gone. Hollywood, Rodeo Drive, The Golden Gate Bridge, even that place they used to call Disney Land—everything was gone. Almost a four hundred mile stretch of the West Coast was in absolute shambles. It boggles the mind to even imagine it. The death. The chaos. The fires. It must've been more than just terrible. It must've been Hell itself.

Cecil Greenough

Grand Magistrate: The Biography of Kiril Pordan

A sense of calm quickly sweeps over the nation. America's rebellion seems to fade in way of the stark reality of what has happened. Politics come to a standstill. What there is of commerce is frozen. The everyday lives of ordinary citizens finally succumb to the horrors around them. Their beloved United States has been attacked like never before, and their belief in her strength, her resolve, and protection is shattered. A heavy toll, a sense of hopelessness begins to rear its undesired presence in the hearts of 410 million Americans.

The citizens of the United States are devastated, and the rest of the globe mourns for each and every one of them. Even those who would wish to see the superpower brought down find it hard to believe such a thing has actually happened to the *Land of the Free*. Never before was such an attack thought truly possible. And though many had pondered it, some even come close to it, no one ever expected to see the mighty West so undeniably crippled.

The never-ending media circus blasts images of the destruction, and the brokenhearted for all to see. Throughout the country, eyes remain glued to their television screens, watching, and absorbing the darkest times they have ever known. While around the world, spectators to the mighty country's *Silent Night* watch and pray for its welfare, even as they await the emergence of a new world superpower.

The United Kingdom, France, as well as, Germany stand by the West in its moment of need, but at the same time, hasten their talks concerning Article 412. With the heinous strike against the United States making it abundantly clear the stark reality of the new order of things, that piece of legislation is made more fathomable now than ever before.

Simply the concept of a unified Europe appears the world's only chance against falling into complete anarchy. With things such as a newly realized Islamic Democracy, and the communistic views of the Far East slowly but surely taking shape, the planet is seemingly ripe for its induction. And when all is assessed, a unified Europe indeed begins to form with Great Britain and Germany leading the way.

One needs to understand that this was not, in anyway, an attempt at seizing the United States' position as world leader. On the contrary, Europe was the only region standing by America's side during this dark time. The Middle East was not. Asia was not. South America was not. No, only Europe, and it deployed medical assistance as best as it could, including whatever else its ally needed. But that did not mean it should have ignored its own welfare, and the Europeans realized this. So to them, at the time, Article 412 seemed to be that welfare.

Prof. Jarvis Grimes

historian, *Superior and Biased: The History of the Royal European Alliance*

Article 412 is well on its way, but that is merely one major change taking place in the world. In Africa, the Islamic regimes have begun drawing nearer to the ideologies of Abu abd Allah Muhammad, and ponder what they will bring about.

To the Muslims, Shia, Sunni, Ibāḍiyya, and Sufi alike, Imam Abu's plans to raise Islam beyond its design seems to be the way of the future—whether the world likes it or not. While in China, a celebration mocks all who witness it, with claims of victory and prideful rejoicing. Though it is worth mentioning Premiere Sun Jiang has twice denied being behind the strike on California, even as he continues to revel in its destruction.

As it is reported throughout the West, the Chinese believe they have done what no other nation has been able to, and that is reclaim supremacy from out of the United States' clutches. A triumph which echoes throughout the Orient, Sun Jiang vows to make China the world's only superpower. Claims cheered by all his supporters, some actually begin preaching of an age where communism is global law.

It is made evident that the stage is set for a race to claim utmost rights to the world. And just as Chinese Premiere Sun Jiang nominates himself and China for the honor of world conqueror, a defiant voice can be heard calling for strength. Amidst the fright, the pain, the hate, and the shattered remains, United States President Howard Mueller stands firm.

Speaking with a frank resound during the country's most historic Oval Office Address, Mueller implores his fellow Americans to draw together in this hour of need. He tells them times are dark. He assures them they cannot be deterred from their goals. He makes clear the world is watching to see if they have fallen, and that their enemies are cheering their impending end. No one believes they can return from this—that they can gather themselves and rise—that they can once more claim to be the *Home of the Brave.*

President Mueller tells his fellow Americans the world thinks the United States is over, but challenges them to prove the naysayers wrong.

My fellow Americans. You, the dream of liberty and justice for all. You, the benefactors of sacrifice, diligence, and patriotism. It's to you I speak tonight. You who've been afflicted, downtrodden, and assaulted all in the name of Democracy, the freewill given to all men by God, it's to you I speak tonight. We've been attacked. That which we fight every day to prevent to others has happened to us, and why? Some will say it's because of our interference. Others will say that it's because of our audacity. And others will say that it's because of our godlessness—but I disagree. You see, I know why we've been attacked. It's because of our selflessness when it comes to helping others. It's because we pride ourselves on law, order, and the right for anyone to make his or her dreams a reality. And lastly, it's because we're the children of a mighty God. He who's planted within the hearts of all Americans, the seed of goodness. That's why we've been attacked. That's why our people have been murdered. Because a coward...Cowards hate us. They're jealous of us. They desire nothing more than to be us. But behold, they chase a dream. We're the United States of America. Never before has any land functioned like us. We're not Babylon. We're not Rome. And we're not done. We're Americans. And as Americans, we must protect our land from all those who'd do us harm. I pray we're unified in this, because to be divided will only give our enemies that which they've been longing for—the fall of the United States of America. Are you going to give it to them? Not me, I refuse. And I know there are millions of you who stand with me during this dark time. It's a new show, and we play the parts of perfection, justice, might, and glory. So with that I say, God bless you all, and God bless America.

United States President Howard Mueller

Oval Office Address December 29, 2028

Mueller's mandate is to be completed by the middle of the coming year. He demands all citizens of the United States visiting, employed, or living in foreign countries be given a three month period to return home, or face possible expatriation. The military is also informed to prepare for a full overseas withdrawal, while U.S. embassies are closed throughout the world. Ultimatums never before heard of, they are understood all too well.

President Mueller refuses to answer any questions posed by even the United States' most trusted allies, leaving the rest of the world beholding the United States' fortitude limping on toward reclaiming its birthright. And while China continues to defy the truth of what it has brought upon itself, the American people are all too steadfast in handing their President the utmost power needed to do what he must in such times.

The final phase in preparing America's utmost requital, it will be an act that will both change the face of the planet, while bringing about a form of law and government never before conceived. For in the end, the United States would not have only healed itself, it will be stronger than it ever has. This is the promise of United States President Howard Mueller, and the entire world waits with bated breath.

The Great Divide: a concise history of the future

M.A. Martin

2029

THE SUN HAS FALLEN TO EARTH

The Great Divide: a concise history of the future

World War III has come to an uneasy stalemate. China slowly regains its territories, while Coalition forces either vacate the region, or simply hunker down in less strategic locations. This is not a victory for China by any means, but such an outcome cannot be seen as anything less than a defeat for the Allied Forces. And though there are rare skirmishes that continue taking place, most of the Western World finds their own survival more integral than the continued call for global Democracy.

Europe ushers in a new era with its passing of Article 412 on April 14. The United Kingdom, Germany, France, Belgium, Denmark, Italy, Portugal, Spain, and even the Republic of Ireland unanimously agree to the confederation of all European banks, more so, the laws which govern the lands being integrated into this solitary functioning body. In time, the whole of Europe is to be part of this glorious union, but that is something that will take time considering so many other countries still wait in the wings.

Countries such as Poland to Greece, the Czech Republic across to the borders of Russia, Norway, Finland, and Sweden, they all anticipate their induction into the ultimate merging. But regardless of the wait, no one can deny the mission of forging a unilaterally concurred government, though still a daunting task, is one which comes to fruition smoother than anyone could have ever expected.

The Europeans know better than to take this ease for granted, but the comfortable transition is something to be celebrated all the same. Each country works feverishly through their obvious differences in hopes of reaching an agreement on shared directives. And as expected, it is Germany which takes lead in forging a feasible structure for the hopeful unified Europe.

The Germans present their plans of grandeur to their allies. A world past Emperors and Kings could have only dreamed of, it is one where Europe as a whole will regain its standing as world leader. A structure with which it will operate as a single nation, the discussions over such an ambitious design are frenzied, as well as, awe-aspiring.

Debates take place in Brussels, Belgium, during countless Berlaymont Conferences. British Prime Minister Edward Davies heads most of these gatherings with words of determination and certainty, as does his partner in presenting the future of Europe, German Chancellor Irma Hofmann. It is her show of strength and resilience which forces her counterparts to earnestly consider their place amongst such an endeavor, in due course, sweeping Article 412 through most of Europe. But there are still those who stand against such proposals.

The never-ending protests, clashes, and riots that have been destabilizing Europe for the past seven years have found a new agenda to engage. A cause reborn in exactly the same way it was birthed in opposition to the wars, the poverty, and immigration of the past, so now does it find the unification of Europe unacceptable. And as it once spiraled toward utter chaos in objection to those tasks, so now does it begin to threaten the European leaders' plans of amalgamating their beloved countries.

Here it was. Here it finally was. This was the answer to Europe's prayers. A region with histories far more complex than any other in the world, and it was now finally becoming what it should have always been. Alexander the Great could not have done it, and neither could have Julius Caesar. No one in history had been able to unify the mighty Europe, and now Article 412 had proven all that negativity superfluous. But there was still the rebellion. There were still those who rejected this brainchild of European unification, and it was them who challenged the merger—no one else. You can even say it was made quite obvious that Europe had to conquer Europe if it was going to survive. But that was until...Well, you know.

Prof. Jarvis Grimes

historian, *Superior and Biased: The History of the Royal European Alliance*

Protests by the multitudes, they always conclude with violence and death. Thousands are killed. The bodies of victims, rioter and law enforcement, lie spread out and bloodied. It is utter anarchy, and Prime Minister Davies knows there will be no European Alliance if it continues.

Therefore, in an obvious effort to appease the rebellion, European Prime Ministers, Kings, and Presidents alike agree to the unilateral withdrawal of their militaries from out of Asia. A bold move for all involved, China considers the withdrawal a disadvantage for its enemies.

Europe is vulnerable in its unified retreat, and China sees this as a rare opportunity to strike. Thus, Chinese Premiere Sun Jiang orders General Zhao Qi of Russia's occupying Chinese military to launch a nuclear strike into the heart of Germany when the Europeans least expect it. An act rivaling that of what has taken place in the United States, China again paralyzes the planet in thought of annihilation. And once more, the people of Earth are made to watch the skies burn, as millions of people are made to die in the bounds of obliterating fire.

Germany's capital is leveled, and over 2.1 million Berliners are instantly killed. The devastation is witnessed throughout Europe, and clutches the hearts of its citizens in a vice of terror and despair. Lives are mercilessly extinguished, buildings burn, and above all, the history of Germany goes up in a fireball of ruin. It is iniquitous, but a sin British Prime Minister Edward Davies refuses to let halt any advance.

No matter the brutality of the situation, the Prime Minister can fathom no better reason than now than to display the might of a unified Europe. So while the United States has yet to respond to China's wicked attack upon it, the newly christened Royal European Alliance answers Russia's encroachment with utmost severity.

Within hours, the REA launches two nuclear warheads into both Moscow and St. Petersburg, ruthlessly obliterating the two historic cities of Mother Russia from off the face of the Earth.

St. Petersburg is the first to go beneath a mushroom cloud of raging fire, then Moscow follows by glowing brighter than the sun. 7.7 million people have their lives exterminated, and the great United Russian Republic is no more. Prime Minister Davies then goes on television, and mourns the lives lost to Russia's strike against the German people, including that of his beloved friend, Chancellor Irma Hofmann. He even tries tempering the frenzy over Russia being attacked, but leaves the world confounded as to what will happen next.

A time saturated in global newscasts reporting vehemently on Germany's demise, Russia's annihilation, Israel's efforts at salvaging a desolate Jerusalem, the Royal European Alliance's rise to power, Islam's slow but incontrovertible hour of restoration, Latin America's downward spiral into unreserved pandemonium, the United States' annulment of its recent Presidential election and struggle toward resurrecting itself, and China's ever growing show of intolerable dominance, the age of the Great Divide is here, and mankind has begun to feel its callous wrath.

Its first phase is to witness the United States' completion of its abandonment of Asia. An extraction of all US military presence from out of the Orient, the withdrawal of troops stationed around the rest of the world soon follows.

Europe, Africa, the Middle East, and Latin America are all vacated by military personnel belonging to the United States. This leaves, for the first time in nearly three hundred years, a world without American influence.

Now flooded by its own Armed Forces, the United States strategically deploys them all throughout the East Coast and Midwest. Martial Law is securely in place, and soldiers find themselves stationed in major cities. No soldier serves in his hometown, or where family may be located for the sake of avoiding conflict of interests. Instead, the redeployed soldiers of the Armed Forces are exactly that, soldiers of the United States Armed Forces. And their new orders are made clear: keep the peace, establish law and order on the streets of New York, Washington D.C., Philadelphia, and Chicago, just to name a few, and eliminate ART wherever its members are found. A military state assemblage on a massive scale, the unruly citizens of the nation are now the enemy.

A considerable homecoming which takes place within the three month expatriation set time limit, it is controversially followed up by the canceling of all inbound and outbound flights from out of the continental United States.

The Expatriation Directive that had been in effect distressed many civilians into responding with a mass migration back to the United States. This influx had momentarily hindered the process of evacuating American diplomats from out of foreign countries, leaving many to be interrogated by their hosting countries as to what the United States had been planning. And though most delegates were allowed to return home without molestation when given military escort, there were still those countries that tried banning diplomats from leaving in hopes of gaining intelligence against the United States.

A futile attempt at best, in the end, nothing stopped the nearly 32 million Americans abroad from heading home. Now the United States of America has become what it always feared—an isolationist state.

The outcome that was always foreseen, some even cursed the government for procrastinating in bringing it about. Nonetheless, the isolation of the United States is simply the product of what needs to happen next. With *Silent Night* having nearly crippled the country, the ones guilty have yet to pay the price. A demand no American need longer ask for, United States President Howard Mueller finally answers China's onslaught.

May 9, 2:34 am China Standard Time. The Eastern Hemisphere slumbers beneath a starlit sky. A military soldier stands post in front of Lüshun Naval Base. A janitor makes his rounds throughout the Commune. Prostitutes roam North Sichuan Road. A group of teens successfully break into the Shenyang Imperial Palace. A student falls asleep in his text book at Tsinghua University. And just as sirens begin to blare throughout Chinese cities, the United States launches nuclear strikes into the hearts of Chongqing, Wuhan, Tianjin, Beijing, and Hong Kong.

Those regions of the Communist Chinese regime mount into an unfeasible blaze, annihilating everything in fire and disarray. Reports as far as Europe even claim to witness the illumination of China's destruction, while sparse hearsay divulge the horrors taking place there. And while no news agency is allowed to travel out of the United States to cover the mayhem, European, Middle Eastern, South Asian, and African news organizations have no trouble reporting on the sheer nightmare engulfing the Asian continent.

"The sun has fallen to Earth!" said one eyewitness. "The sun has fallen to Earth!" That can only give us an idea of what took place, a glimpse into the horror of what people all the way in Europe claimed to see that day. It's a frightening thing. A disturbing thing, that this was the payback for what China had done to the United States. But don't get me wrong, it was justified...But my God.

Cecil Greenough

Grand Magistrate: The Biography of Kiril Pordan

You ask me, and I say it was a calculated move on the United States' part. It didn't simply attack China when it was attacked. No, it first made sure to remove all of its citizens from out of foreign countries so that it wouldn't have to worry about any of them being caught in the retaliation. Because that's exactly what this was, a well thought out retaliation. China had this coming. I dare even say that they were begging for it. Well, on May 9, I guess they got their wish.

Prof. Tamara Boggier

keeper, New York Republic Athenaeum

There were reports that when China was finally entered by medical workers, that they found children who were still on fire—alive. That they would combust without warning. They even say that people were still standing where they had been when the bombs went off. Some even looked absolutely normal, when in reality, they were not only dead, their skin may have been normal, but their insides were dust. There was nothing left. Buildings, monuments, most of the Great Wall, all of it was gone—finished.

Tsun-chúng Hu

The Last Dynasty: The Chinese Republic's Ultimate Demise

It is reported an estimated 22.9 million people are exterminated by the preliminary blasts, with an additional 40 million expected to die within a matter of days. In less than a day, the once mighty nation of China, a country that had survived thousands of years of war, is reduced to nothing more than a charred wasteland where people die in droves.

This is the last time human beings unleash such a destructive force upon the Earth. But when they do, and they will again, humanity will not survive. In the meantime, America's response is seen as an act of absolute malevolence, and is abhorred by its fellow mankind. But in no way is the United States remorseful for its actions, even removing itself from the United Nations seven days following the unspeakable retribution.

President Howard Mueller goes on television and informs his fellow Americans of what has taken place, leaving millions to speculate as to just how bad the devastation in China truly is. Mueller refuses to end his country's retribution with what has happened in China, however, quickly enacting a security measure which declares the Chinese populace of the United States enemies of the state.

The bill is called the *Loyalist Act*, and insists all Chinese Americans and nationals be detained until determined non-threatening to the well-being of the United States and its citizens.

The mandate is met with scattered protests, and cries of human rights violations. Detainees are confined in the more than one hundred significant stadiums christened Cleansing Hubs all around the country and vetted. Those found guilty of treason, sympathizing, or in legion with China, are given the harsh and firm sentencing of life imprisonment without parole, or worse. A heartbreaking assessment, it is one a portion of Americans support. And though there are still more who protest, defend, and demand social justice, the minority of American citizens simply want to feel safe.

The government shares their views, and makes sure the *Loyalist Act* guarantees them that safety. But as it is with Americans all too often, after being ignored, made to be frightened, and given a few living examples of the Chinese threat, most eventually decide to give the Cleansing Hubs a chance. By and by, the *Loyalist Act* is never hindered in its duty of arresting 4.2 million Chinese Americans and immigrants, securing the nation from any further harm.

The recent actions taken by the United States: isolationism, human rights violations, and nuclear strikes, open a doorway for North Africa's Imam Abu and his ever-growing Islamic restoration to go unchecked. Aspirations calling for a newly constructed Islamic arrangement, the turn of events breathe life into the dream of reforming Islam.

To the Islamic world, this was exactly what the Mahdi, alaihi al-salaam, had been warning them of. He had been telling them that the world was changing, and that Islam would suffer greatly if it did not also change. He wished for nothing more than Islam's survival, and made no mystery of what that would require.

Prof. Najiyah Abdullah Hassan

Crescent Moon and Pillars: The Rise of the Islamic Empire

With the obvious humanitarian infractions coming to pass in the world, Imam Abu sees no better time than now for his ultimate agenda for Islam to commence with its undertaking. Having already unified not only the people, but the militaries of Morocco, Algeria, Libya, Egypt, Niger, Mauritania, Chad, and Sudan, Imam Abu begins a sweeping march through the countries of South Sudan, Mali, Eritrea, Ethiopia, Senegal, Guinea, Burkina, and many more, in hopes of succeeding in his plans.

North Africa's Islamic reformer makes his decree loud and clear: convert or die. A slogan enforced throughout the months that follow, the northern half of the African continent comes to bear witness to unspeakable violence and cruelty with which true jihad is performed.

No infidel, indigenous African, Christian, or Jew is spared. Imam Abu either slaughters his enemies, or forces them from their homes under the threat of death. A push limited to the designated equator, the Imam orders his men to halt the onslaught at the borders of Cameroon, the Central African Republic, Democratic Republic of Congo, Uganda, and Kenya.

In less than eight months, over 6 million people are killed, while 80 million or so are displaced from their homelands. The unstoppable force of Islam rushes through North Africa like a wildfire through a forest, leaving in its wake the framework for a unified Islamic power—an Afro Islamic Union.

The United States and the Royal European Alliance have no time to object to such actions when facing crucial instability within their own borders, the latter currently preoccupied with structuring its newly drafted administration, while the United States remains busy keeping calm amongst its volatile nation. Because of this, the world remains either crippled, or without any possibility of aiding Africa. This leaves Imam Abu's Afro Islamic Union virtually unchallenged in its ever-expanding march across Northern and most of Central Africa.

After months of fighting and death, Imam Abu abd Allah Muhammad finally goes on national television to explain his intentions. He sets the border of the Afro Islamic Union, proclaiming all of Northern Africa part of the AIU, stretching its arm as far as the equator and no further. The rest of the continent is designated a no assault zone, burdening all others south of the equator with handling the wave upon wave of displaced victims flooding their lands.

African leaders throughout those countries plead with the Afro Islamic Union to cease its ousting of innocent civilians, but Imam Abu refuses to hear the cries for restraint, and continues with the final phases needed to establish a recognized Afro Islamic Union.

This is an act of violent consolidation which takes place all over the globe, with Latin America also facing an increasingly powerful *Latin Liberation Front* without any hope of international intervention.

Ever since the United States closed its borders, and denied any inbound or outbound flights, Latin America had been facing a crushing blow by the fascist LLF. It was a political move that saw the hostile takeovers of Uruguay, Paraguay, Columbia, Brazil, Ecuador, and Chile, while trapping defenseless countries such as Belize, Guatemala, and the rest of Central America between those nations and a war-torn Mexico. The International Guards had failed in their mission of preventing the LLF's cruel conquest, and now Cesar Lopez appeared unstoppable. The massacre taking place all over Latin America was a bloody one, but one nobody truly got a sense of since the international press refused to enter those regions.

Cecil Greenough

Grand Magistrate, The Biography of Kiril Pordan

The United States, Royal European Alliance, and others only get a glimpse of the violence through internet uploads being conducted by freedom fighters risking their lives to get the images out. Still, the merciless conquest of the *Latin Liberation Front* proceeds without restraint, leaving millions of people dead in its wake.

LLF leader, Cesar Lopez is undeterred by the onslaught of his fellow Latinos, and uses everything in his military arsenal to crush all those opposing him. Soon enough, he christens himself *Comadante del Mundo Latino* (Commander of the Latin World), and begins forging a new government reflecting his ultimate goal. One in which socialism will flourish without check, the LLF is determined to bring about the rise of a dominant Latin America. And just as all empires before it, this dominance is to be constructed upon the backs of the oppressed, but will not end there.

With the *Latin Liberation Front* slowly but surely creeping northward through all of Latin America, it is only a matter of time before they reach the reinforced southern borders of the United States, though Americans will confront the threat as expected. But when they do, the face of North America will be as it never has been before.

The Great Divide: a concise history of the future

M.A. Martin

2030
MAHDI

The Great Divide: a concise history of the future

On June 5, Imam Abu travels to the Middle East, holding an Islamic summit where he proposes a startling suggestion. During his revelations over the years, for as long as Islam has existed, the religion which teaches of submission to Allah has been facing a threatening divide. Sparked by the death of the Prophet, the religion has been dealing with a great rift between those who would be called Sunni, and those of the Shia faction. A blood feud born in defending their perception of the holy book, the Qur'an, countless Muslims have died because of this.

Imam Abu can conceive of only one thing capable of remedying this problem. Reaching his destination, and meeting with the leaders of Syria, Lebanon, Iraq, Iran, a newly salvaged Afghanistan, Jordan, and Saudi Arabia, the Imam risks life and limb to advocate his solution to the Islamic discord.

It is a controversial declaration he is all too aware can cause more harm than good, but one he absolutely believes must be done. A call for true unity amongst Shia and Shia, and Sunni amongst Sunni—a separation for the betterment of all involved, in Imam Abu's mind, the only way to keep Muslims from killing other Muslims is to completely relocate one faction to a designated area, while doing the same to the other. In other words, Imam Abu proposes Shias and their many factions stake claim to the whole of the Middle East: Lebanon, Jordan, Syria, Iraq, Iran, and Afghanistan, with the fate of Israel being left in their hands to decide, while Sunnis and their various denominations post land rights to Saudi Arabia, the United Arab Emirates, Yemen, Oman, and the whole of North Africa.

The response to such a suggestion is as expected. The proposal draws distress and offense from both Shias and Sunnis of the Middle East. Just the thought of separating Shias from Sunnis is seen as an insult, much less the idea of designating lands where they can live. But with Indonesia, the world's largest Muslim population, already adhering to Imam Abu's call, the declaration does not appear so overtly radical.

What the Mahdi, alaihi al-salaam, was trying to do was give both Islamic factions what they had always wanted. He was going to give them a place with which they could call their own, a land for the Shia and a land for the Sunni. That way, the two of them could work independently toward healing their wounds in becoming better Muslims. Now, some people argued against this, but many people believed, Muslims believed, that the Mahdi, alaihi al-salaam, would have eventually reunited these two denominations once they had achieved An-Nur—the light of Allah. Sadly, it would take decades before An-Nur Muslims would come to exist, leaving these Muslims of the past to deal with life the best way they knew how.

Prof. Najiyah Abdullah Hassan

Crescent Moon and Pillars: The Rise of the Islamic Empire

Imam Abu tries using what he has done in Africa as a blueprint for such a division, but understands the agenda will require much deliberation before being considered. He agrees to give his brothers time to accept his proposal, all the time praying they do not force his hand in making the decision for them. But this show of patience does not necessarily mean Imam Abu will not begin formulating a plan to takeover the lands he has already deemed part of the Afro Islamic Union. In actuality, upon returning to Sudan, Imam Abu immediately meets with his advisers, and begins commencing with the expanding feat of the Afro Islamic Union.

He knows in order to make his Islamic partition a thing of reality, he must first demonstrate such a thing can be brought on by force. So combining the militaries of Egypt, Libya, Algeria, Niger, Chad, Sudan, and Indonesia, Imam Abu mounts an unprecedented attack on Saudi Arabia in an effort to lay claim over the sovereign nation.

In a show of defiance, Saudi Arabian King, Faisal bin Salman Al Saud, refuses to stand by and allow such an attack to go uncontested, and as a result, raises an army of nearly 300,000 in response to Imam Abu's attack. Regrettably, the Saudis are no match for the Afro Islamic Union and its nearly 1.2 million soldiers.

The Saudi military meets the African war machine in Medina in a brave effort to defend their homeland. This show of bravery means nothing, however, not when the highly militarized regions of Ta'if, King Khalid Military City, and Khamis Mushayt are all overrun seemingly overnight, taken down in horrid fashion.

King Faisal desperately sends diplomats to the Middle East in hopes of receiving much needed aid, but his appeals fall on deaf ears. The Middle Eastern leaders have no desire to defend the Saudis, and silently watch as the Afro Islamic Union does in fact defeat them. And when the battle is finally over, and the smoke clears, Imam Abu has conquered the city of the Prophet, solidifying himself as the self-proclaimed Mahdi.

The Mahdi, Abu abd Allah Muhammad, alaihi al-salaam, believed he was about to usher in a great day for all Muslims. Remember, he believed they had been suffering due to their lost path, their spiritual death you can say. So now, he will breathe new spiritual life into them, and this was something he preached had been the true meaning of the day Yawm al-Qiyāmah —Day of Resurrection. And it was by doing this that he believed, and led others to recognize, that he was in fact the long awaited Guided One. The Mahdi, alaihi al-salaam.

Prof. Najiyah Abdullah Hassan

Crescent Moon and Pillars: The Rise of the Islamic Empire

In an act of total submission to Allah, Mahdi Abu enters the revered Kaaba of Mecca, and symbolically washes it with his garments. This act causes great controversy amongst Muslims throughout the Islamic world, while portraying Mahdi Abu as a savior to those who accept his claim.

Soon enough, whether out of fear, or adoration, Yemen, Oman and the United Arab Emirates yield to the Mahdi in place of suffering the royal Saudi family's fate. A triumph marked by celebration and much discussion over Islam's next step toward reformation, the newly christened Mahdi will not be satisfied until all Sunnis are brought under Afro Islamic Union rule —something he makes clear when constantly addressing the Islamic world.

The following months see much deliberation, with Middle Eastern leaders meeting constantly with the Mahdi in order to personally negotiate the terms of agreement. Above all things, it is the rights of Shias to travel into Mecca in order to perform the holy pilgrimage of Hajj that must first be guaranteed before any agreement can be reached, and Mahdi Abu has no qualms accepting such assurance. Because of this, on August 27, Islamic countries throughout the Eastern Hemisphere come to accept the proposition, and begin with the mass deportations of said peoples to their respected religious territories as per the Mahdi's ruling.

A displacement which brings about the greatest division ever within all of Islam, the expulsions will take place for years, with Sunnis of the Middle East either leaving of their own freewill, or being forced out of their native soils by military pressure.

Shias face a similar ejection from out of Afro Islamic Union territories, but their departure comes with less resistance than those of their Sunni brethren. In truth, the Shia make up less than twelve percent of the Afro Islamic Union's regions, facilitating their extraditions. But with Sunnis making up a significant sixty-three percent of the Middle East, the governments there are left no choice but to encounter harsh retaliation by those refusing to leave.

Random acts of terrorism soon being taking place throughout the Middle East because of this, claiming the lives of both military personnel and civilians. Led by a group calling themselves *Ansar al-Islam*, the resisters find themselves the target of all Middle Eastern governments.

The captures and executions of their members are broadcast all over the Middle East, but never once deter them from their agenda. Regardless of this, the removal of Sunnis from out of the Middle East becomes a joint effort by the governments there, leading to the creation of a unified regimen dubbed the Islamic People's Republic. A coalition whose sole purpose consist of eliminating the Sunni presence in the region, the Middle Eastern regimes drastically change the way they enact their affairs.

In a matter of years, the world will see the Middle East functioning at its greatest capacity, with Syria, Jordan, Lebanon, Afghanistan, Iran, Turkey, Kuwait, and Iraq marrying under one banner. A power rival that of the Afro Islamic Union, it is one unclear compared to the AIU's particular scope of peace. For while the Islamic People's Republic staggers, the Afro Islamic Union enjoys a peaceful transition from separate nation states into a cohesive people.

Pakistan soon solicits its membership to the Islamic People's Republic against the outcries of its majority Sunni population, but it is a move the country hopes will bring about an end to the Great Indo/Pak war that has been taking place for the past six years.

Worn thin, the Pakistanis have been suffering loss after loss at the hands of their far more adept Indian enemies, and can see no outcome but this in securing their nation's continued existence. This is not to say the Pakistanis have not called for a truce numerous times during the war, but India has refused to cease its bombings and occupations of Pakistani territories. However, with Pakistan now ready to join the Islamic People's Republic and its nations, India must second guess its resilience.

It is no mystery once Pakistan is considered part of the Islamic People's Republic, India will no longer be facing one country, but the whole of the Middle East. A position which puts their backs against the wall, India's leaders cautiously begin formulating a plan to bring an end to the war, but now it is Pakistan who refuses the treaty.

The Pakistanis see this an opportunity to finally end the country they feel has been the bane of their existence, and make clear their plan to destroy India. Unfortunately for them, their membership into the Islamic People's Republic comes with a convenient stipulation calling for them to spare their neighbor. This infuriates the Pakistanis, but a refusal of the prerequisite will only leave them vulnerable to India's overwhelming strength. So having no choice in the matter, Pakistan's Prime Minister agrees to a ceasefire, only demanding India vacate the Pakistani lands they have seized during the war; likewise, the country of Kashmir also relinquished.

These concessions are seen as demonstrations of Pakistan's new found power, compromises which enrage the Indian people to refuse. But with the Islamic People's Republic supporting such ultimatums, they too have no choice but to settle.

On November 10, a peace treaty is signed by both countries, bringing an uneasy end to the Great Indo/Pak war. It is an apprehensive armistice that will last the better part of five decades, eventually coming to an unfortunate end. And when it does, the blood spilled will bring about a new age upon the Earth—one neither nation will live to see fulfilled.

The Great Divide: a concise history of the future

M.A. Martin

2032

PROMETHEUS FLAME

The Great Divide: a concise history of the future

January 3, European governments begin combining their nations' offices under one roof, solidifying a stable Royal European Alliance. The United Kingdom is at its core, and over a dozen other countries anxiously await their confirmations. A paradigm of power and development, the new government will render Europe unstoppable.

The alliance champions a way of governing which sees each District: Great Britain, France, Poland, and all others of the Royal European Alliance presided over by an appointed Chief Lord. This Chief Lord governs the District with the assistance of those who preside over that District's multiple Quarters, those known as Custodians. These Custodians, in turn, are to keep law and order amongst their Quarters, while the officials who serve as Guardians to those Quarters' Sectors continue with their positions as public servants. And atop this rather functioning hierarchy stands the office of Monarch, the most powerful man in all the REA.

Former British Prime Minister Edward Davies is currently that man, and to him fall the burden of crushing the final element of a failing rebellion. Nonconformists who pledge their call to the banner of liberty calling themselves the Defiance, every day they are not stopped threatens the very existence of the Royal European Alliance's promising future. Monarch Davies refuses to let that happen.

The Defiance enacts terrorism all throughout Europe, and the leader of the REA finds himself in a formidable battle between the supremacy of law, and the dissension of chaos.

Lives are lost, structures are destroyed, and the philosophy of the Royal European Alliance, '*In Solidarity Is Strength*', shows weakness in face of the fragility of its fortitude through constant inborn conflicts. In spite of its shortcomings, the Royal European Alliance still finds itself a shining beacon of hope amongst a desolate Eastern Hemisphere. A side of the globe where two former empires suffer diseases, famines, and crimes on an unprecedented scale, the eastern half of the planet is a place full of hardships and death.

Mother Russia has become a necropolis for the demoralized and ailing. Those of the former Silovik regime now find themselves living in a country with no electricity, no running water, and shortages of food. All this is due to the nuclear strikes suffered four years earlier. In the same way, radiation levels throughout the massive continent have seen the deaths of nearly 30 million men, women, and children, all while a death gripping winter kills almost half that number in three months in itself.

Nuclear bombs detonated during World War III have undoubtedly had an effect on the planet, with a record low of -33° Fahrenheit recorded in the Sahara Desert during the summer, and a record -77° below zero in New York one winter. Nuclear winter temperatures seen as logical reasons for curbing any desire to use such weapons of mass destruction in the future, they find themselves the topic of much discussion. Still, some of Russia's surviving citizens do not hesitate robbing their neighbors, killing the innocent, or enacting feats of carnage against their fellow man.

There are even tales of rape camps, mutations, and cannibalism believed to be taking place. Rumors supported by the scarcity of food being allowed into the country, Mother Russia's fate can only be equaled by the dreadfulness taking place in China.

Cities such as Beijing, Wuhan, Tianjin, Hong Kong, and Chongqing lie in ruins, as Shanghai, Nantong, Shenyang, Baotou, and others struggle with epidemics, malnourishment, and death. The once flourishing and historical Asian country has not only been reduced to unreserved barbarism, copious fatalities have also become a conventional way of life, as have anarchy and murder. And all around the country, a people once known as the Chinese have been reduced to a fraction of what they once were.

The Chinese people were greatly suffering. International news crews, with the objection of the United States, would defy quarantine mandates, and sneak into the country simply to show the rest of the world what the Chinese people had become. I am talking about sick people. People who were losing their hair, their teeth, and their skin. It was completely horrible, and the world could not help but turn away in remorse. But then something started to happen. The people of Asia began feeling a bond with China. The same Communist Chinese Republic that had once been their enemy, now its brothers were coming to its aid. It is truly sad that something so bad had to happen in order for this unity to be found.

Tsun-chúng Hu

The Last Dynasty: The Chinese Republic's Ultimate Demise

North and South Korea are the ones to feel China's wretchedness the most. The two nations eventually come to terms with their differences, forging an alliance in hopes of aiding the wrecked country, but the Koreas are not alone. Following in their footsteps, Laos, Myanmar, Thailand, and the Philippines also begin sparing what aid they can to assist the annihilated nation. And while those countries struggle to help their distraught brethren, Japan uses its resources in airlifting food and medical supplies into the areas most needing assistance with ease.

China's pain and suffering draws the Asian countries closer together than ever before, while Southern Africa is forced to accept such things under duress.

Mahdi Abu's bias driven ousting of all who were not of the Islamic faith has created an apprehensive situation within Central and Southern Africa. With nearly 80 million plus refugees in need of medical attention and food, the African governments find themselves hectically engaged with keeping order amongst their borders.

The integration of so many amongst those already living in their countries is a burdensome one, forcing the African leaders to designate certain areas as refugee camps. Game reserves, national parks, and specified tribal areas are all sectioned off, housing close to 70,000 immigrants each throughout the entire southern African continent.

These encampments will see years and years of uprisings, criminal acts, hunger strikes, and deaths due to the intermingling of lifelong enemies and unconventional thinking. But when compared to the alternative, the camps are seen as the only hope for those thrown out of their homelands under such coercion, making the humanitarian effort one of goodwill; likewise, a chance at continued existence. A life similar to the surrounding nations of Australia, Denmark, Iceland, and Canada, in those countries christened the Freelands, the citizens there remain relatively peaceful, though feeling the effects of a financially ruined, war-torn, freezing planet.

Countries trying their best to continue with the ways accustomed to, the Freelands keep a keen eye open to the developments around them. But with most media networks utterly maneuvered by the regime's ruling over their nations, their coverage of world events can only be regarded as government propaganda at best. Ultimately, the internet becomes the most trusted source in learning daily developments throughout the planet, with new uploads informing the world's populace of the dark days taking place all around them.

By this time, the face of television had totally changed for that generation. Where there were once reality shows, game shows, and sports, there was only endless news coverage now. The worst thing was most people believed their governments were lying to them about everything, so this is why you see people turning to the internet. And with nationwide wireless connection available everywhere anybody turned, the internet starts to become this sort of rival for television. Not that it wasn't before. It's just that now, the only people watching T.V. are those who trust their governments, and accept their way of telling the news. But just to put it into perspective for you, the doubters outnumber devotees by a margin of 5 to 1.

Cecil Greenough

Grand Magistrate: The Biography of Kiril Pordan

With the internet becoming a form of rebellion in itself, it's not shocking to see insurgents using it as an outlet to get their message out. The governments couldn't do anything about it. Worldwide wireless internet connection had been in existence for years. Everybody had the internet. And though most people around the world were hungry, sick, poor even, everybody had a computer. A normal thing nowadays, it was a rather innovative reality for the people back then, and the rebellion took advantage of that as often as they could.

Prof. Tamara Boggier

keeper, New York Republic Athenaeum

There were all sorts of preposterous conspiracies bearing fruit during that time. People speculating that this was all the Illuminati's doing, that the shadow governments were somehow preparing the planet for an all out Alien invasion—all sorts of outlandish idiocies that I do not care to even repeat. But even so, these conspiracies did eventually give birth to the streaming internet reports known as Prometheus Flame. And it did not take long before that news source became the voice of the Defiance, the ART Party, Ansar al-Islam, and any other form of rebellion trying to spread their agenda.

Prof. Jarvis Grimes

historian, *Superior and Biased: The History of the Royal European Alliance*

A collection of men and women trying desperately to get information into the hands of the inquiring, the *Prometheus Flame* gains worldwide reliability due to its hard nosed journalism and risk taking exposes. Scattered rogue intranet sites serving as a voyeur's insight into the inaccessible hearts of different countries, it also allows the world to view streaming videos dealing with the hunger, conflicts, riots, and deaths plaguing the United States.

As is reported, President Howard Mueller has held office for seven years now. A natural occurrence when a president has been elected for two terms, Mueller's presidency meets controversy due to the fact of the new president elected three years earlier. The results of that presidential contest had been canceled due to the fact of a national disaster, that of California being destroyed by a nuclear weapon. An incident that had once justified Mueller's reasons behind holding office, that tragedy has been long since dealt with, and the American people now want Mueller to step down.

Mueller refuses, and states Europe's unification, the events taking place all throughout the Middle East and Africa, and Latin America's constant spiral toward absolute anarchy as motives for his concern over resigning. The United States President believes that in order to combat these obvious threats against his country, it is necessary for him to stay in power, and deal with them the best way only he knows how. He vows to hold fast to the authority he needs in order to salvage the country, no matter how long it takes. This does not sit well with many of his fellow patriots, and soon enough, talks of him needing to step down turn into cries for his expulsion.

The leaders of the United States see Europe's merger as a hopeful possibility concerning that region's ability to keep check on all those who would continue the fascist march once seen in Russia against its satellite countries. In the same way, the Middle East's internal integration poses a possibility of Islamic peace for the entire world. It was already proven the region was an ally to the United States before this Great Divide transpired, making its alteration of governments a thing of irrelevance. And when it comes to Africa and Latin America, both regions pose little or no threat to the West due to their limited technological advances.

These opposing views toward Mueller's apprehension to relinquish his seat as leader of the free world present his resistance more so a thing of ego than caution, fueling the demands for his ousting to spread across the entire nation. But Mueller continues to disagree with how he is being seen, and begins using the instability of the country as a defense to his unwillingness to surrender the Executive office. He makes clear the task facing the country, and strives to draw supporters to his side.

It was no secret that America had been facing an ever-growing dissension amongst its people, especially by those dealing hardest with the interminable isolation of the country. Riots, food shortages, protests, and constant clashes in the streets supported Mueller's logic for not wanting to give up power. And with the political group, ART, fueling the conflicts, he seemed correct in assuming that without a forceful hand, the United States was doomed to fall. It sounded good. But no matter how rational Mueller sounded, though accepted by his administration and those of the country that remained loyal to his headship, it never convinced those of the Democratic Party, or those of ART for that matter. Those two groups ignored his trepidation, and constantly demanded the Cleansing Hubs housing millions of Chinese detainees be shutdown. They also insisted that the reinstatement of inbound and outbound international air traffic be authorized before the end of the year, and that Mueller step down as president, and allow elections to be held as soon as possible. Again, Mueller condemned such demands, and that only threw more gas on the fire.

Cecil Greenough

Grand Magistrate: The Biography of Kiril Pordan

Congress prepares to impeach Mueller, hoping a guilty verdict in the Senate will give those of the Legislature temporary Executive power. Mueller opposes this plan, and uses the lapse of time between such actions to put in place an even stricter form of Martial Law. With this, the President hopes to have absolute power in performing his duties as he sees fit. Unfortunately for him, his actions are not only seen as an act of defiance, but as a pretense toward totalitarianism. But with military forces stationed all throughout the East Coast and Midwest, Mueller engages those he considers a threat to national security, and most importantly, those of ART.

Even more violent uprisings begin taking place all across the country, especially in the nation's capital of Washington D.C. It is here the more radical members of ART focus most of their rebellion, attacking government buildings without regard for innocent lives. Clashes with police officers and military personnel are ones of pure mayhem. Bloodshed, with innocent bystanders regularly being caught in the crossfire, is the norm. Protestors are arrested in masses, and most are portrayed as nothing less than terrorists. Rebels are killed in throngs, and in only a few short months, the capital is bathed in blood.

The bodies of those killed are sprawled in the streets as a reminder of the cost of going against President Mueller and his military might, but the fury is not merely one sided. For in exactly the same way the United States government battles to crush all opposing it, so does the extremist agenda of ART spare no one—military or civilian. The rest of the nation can only fret over the next horrible collision between the two rivals, but do not have to wait long.

Skirmishes are repeated over, and over again. Violent conflicts which take place at historical landmarks, traumatizing the American public the most, one such act takes place on April 9, when two dozen ART supporters take hostage over two hundred people during a siege on Union Station in Washington D.C.

An ARTist by the name of Arnold Furlong demands those he considers patriots be released from prison, or he and his cohorts will kill a hostage every hour on the hour. The threat does not faze Mueller or his political supporters, and finds the President's answer to be a brigade of soldiers in a standoff against Furlong and his men.

Furlong, a disgruntled veteran of the Indonesian war, warns the military against any siege, and vows to kill as many people as he can before being captured. And once again, his warnings and demands fall on deaf ears, bringing the altercation to a climactic end when the military storms the historic train station in full force. The nation then watches in pure disbelief as Furlong, along with his fellow radicals, blow themselves up, killing the two hundred hostages, and over forty soldiers in the wake of their violent suicide. The radicals destroy a significant portion of Union Station, and forever scar eyewitnesses.

Arnold Furlong was like many Americans who'd fought in the Third World War. They were frustrated, and prone to violence. And with their return to the States revealing a war at home, they didn't know what to do but be soldiers. Sadly, they were enacting a war on American soil, American streets, and against other Americans—those soldiers taking up the call of rebellion. Luckily for Mueller, most of them continued to obey his commands, or he would've been in even bigger trouble—not that it didn't eventually catch up with him.

Cecil Greenough

Grand Magistrate: The Biography of Kiril Pordan

The suicide bombing makes national headlines. Arnold Furlong and his band of radicals are solely blamed for what has taken place. Whereas on the internet, the Prometheus Flame lays exclusive culpability on Mueller and the United States military. Rogue intranet sites claiming the soldiers were in fact the ones guilty of detonating Furlong's bombs when hastily firing their weapons, they call on all citizens to avenge the savage attack. Either way, it changes the dynamics of the American insurgency from then on.

Because of Furlong, suicide bombings seem to occur on a weekly basis. New York, Washington D.C., Chicago, and Philadelphia lead the way in violence and all out civil war. A bleak passing for the *Land of the Free*, the future of the country is made an uncertain one like never before. Meanwhile, in Latin America, the *Latin Liberation Front* has gained considerable ground in its goal of dominance, but still finds resistance amongst those fighting for freedom.

The *Latin Liberation Front* refuses to be halted by the less armed resistance, and mounts a crushing campaign against all who stand in their way. As a result, the leader of the LLF, Cesar Lopez, stands ready to enact his most devastating attack against his own people yet.

Sending delegates north with hopes of securing a correlation between his LLF movement and the warlords that have seized control of Mexico, Lopez suggests a joining between the two factions. In response, the head warlord of Mexico's *Torreón Cartel*, a man named René Escamilla Arévalo, a.k.a. *El Oso*, The Bear, agrees to the fusion, informing Lopez that he will squeeze Guatemala, Belize, El Salvador, and Honduras, while Lopez and his LLF moves on Nicaragua, Costa Rica, and Panama.

The dangerous move seals the fates of 43.1 million Latinos under the overwhelming might of Mexico and the *Latin Liberation Front*. Although, there are those who still stand in rebellion against the two merging powers.

Rafael Salazar, a former decorated veteran from Colombia who opposes the LLF at every turn, and his ragtag group of mercenaries, believe they can topple the *Latin Liberation Front* by killing Lopez and seizing control of the group's capital of Venezuela. With that country under their control, they can then destroy the oil refineries sustaining the horrors, whereby crippling the *Latin Liberation Front*'s machines and technologies, ultimately freeing the rest of Latin America.

A possible success, the plan will take more manpower than Salazar currently has, leaving him no choice but to start a massive campaign of persuasion to begin leveling the playing field.

Salazar is aware of the difficulties ahead, but has no choice but to press on. To fail will mean all of Latin America will fall beneath the heels of oppression, while winning means freedom for all his brothers and sisters. It is a risk Salazar is willing to take, even if demanding his death. A sentiment that can be understood, halfway around the world, the Middle East faces a similar state of affairs.

Sunnis battling the Islamic People's Republic's directive expelling them from their homelands has reached a critical stage. Shias living in the Afro Islamic Union regions of Arabia, Tunisia, Morocco, and Ethiopia put up little to no resistance during their deportations, but the same cannot be said for Sunnis living in Turkey, Iraq, and Pakistan especially. In those regions, Sunnis are far too vast in number to simply be displaced without some form of belligerence. Protests and riots, the Sunnis argue against the division, while a small number take up the cry of *Ansar al-Islam*, resorting to terrorism as a way of going against the expulsion.

Everything from suicide bombings to militant conflicts comes to pass, leaving countless of innocent civilians wounded and dead. Even the isolated roads traveled by refugees being forced out of their countries are booby trapped. Landmines and roadside bombs both injuring and killing victims, they expose survivors to sweeping ambushes. Over a million people are either maimed or killed within a few years time because of this. And though the Islamic People's Republic is aware of the cost of such travels, it never once halts its ongoing eviction of Sunnis and their families.

No such uprisings take place within the borders of the Afro Islamic Union, however. On the contrary, the AIU has been enjoying a time of peace and tranquility for almost three years now, generously opening its doors to the Sunnis arriving there every day.

Upon arrival to the regions of the Afro Islamic Union, immigrants are taken to selected areas and processed, then relocated to areas capable of receiving them. Arabia, Yemen, Oman, Egypt, Libya, and Algeria are amongst the first to take in the migrants, with the rest of the Afro Islamic Union being prepared for the following waves.

Mahdi Abu is also aware of the turbulent situation taking place in the Islamic People's Republic, but the leader of the Afro Islamic Union sees the partition between Sunni and Shia as one of success and prosperity. So much so, on June 10, the Sudanese born leader comes before a crowd of thousands to proclaim the partition an accomplishment.

His appearance is televised all throughout the Afro Islamic Union and Islamic People's Republic, and is seen as a sign of hope amongst these tumultuous times. But in a daring move which threatens to jeopardize his momentous speech, the Mahdi not only declares his mission a success, he also goes as far as to rechristen his Shia brethren Mu'minūn. A Qur'anic based appellation that causes much stir amongst the Islamic People's Republic, as well as, raises some concerns, for the most part, the Shias see no wrong in making the division as clear as possible, and shockingly accept the ancient re-brand.

In the end, the Islamic People's Republic is now the residence of the Mu'minūn, while those of the Afro Islamic Union remain Muslims. And with the former being allowed to do their pilgrimage to Mecca without obstacle, peace in the Middle East has, for now at least, been managed.

M.A. Martin

2034

AR2

The Great Divide: a concise history of the future

Turmoil in the United States has reached a critical level. Most Americans demand a negotiation period commence. The lives lost during the past two years remain a thing of nightmares, and simply cannot be allowed to go on. But President Howard Mueller has already stated he will reinstate the U.S. Constitution only after the intensity of violence has gone down, and not a moment before. Although, with those of the ART Party constantly displaying a disposition toward hostility and impertinence, such an accord appears far off.

President Mueller has issued a mandate declaring all those not entirely compliant to the laws of the land are to be arrested without hesitance, or worse. This has forced ART to go underground, while fueling the imaginations of both young and old with their so-called act of revolution. And though an overwhelming portion of the country goes along with Mueller's direction either out of mere acceptance, genuine belief in his logic, or the fear of being killed, the truth remains ART draws new followers to itself with each passing day.

Seen as a reflection of resistance to many, and an example for those who truly love freedom, people yearning for a return to the ways of the past latch on to ART's passionate axiom of *"One cannot live free if told how."* A conviction in the hearts of all those who pledge allegiance to *Liberty and Justice for All*, the truism demands the patriots resist the current administration's rule by any means necessary, including their lives.

ART's slogan even trickles down to the nation's youth, giving birth to a movement even more extreme than that of its predecessor. For while the older generation of ART calls for a land reminiscent of the past, this new movement, this AR2, is driven solely by the desire for complete anarchy.

The bombings of national landmarks, the shootouts with military officers, and the tagging of the label 'AR2' on any surface left unguarded by the powers that be, all this is enacted by children embellishing the meaning of freedom. And though their actions are scorned by both their enemies and hesitant allies, AR2's constant acts of devastation up and down the East Coast never cease, gradually creating a rift amongst the anti-government faction.

AR2, now here was an interesting group during all this. They were violent. They were ruthless. They had no fear. And they liked blowing things up. That was it. There's really nothing else to say about them. And that would be a lie. This was the spiral into darkness we'd always been warned about. This was the debauchery that had sealed the fates of so many empires. And now, these children, this AR2, they go around the East Coast, heavily armed, suicide bound, and they go to war—all on the account of anarchy. They were nothing like ART. They were America's lost children, and they'd finally found their calling.

Cecil Greenough

Grand Magistrate: The Biography of Kiril Pordan

AR2 is indeed a terrible force, and it leaves nothing but absolute destruction in its rouse. Made up of the children of rebels, seditionists, and nihilists, AR2 is young—they are"Narnists", children born to a decaying world, and they are determined to be free of all laws.

They claim Hip-Fonika for themselves, and it becomes the voice of the next generation. Those who resist their call are dubbed "Feebs", and seen no differently than those abiding by fascist law. The young rebels are boys, girls, white, black, brown, insane, "Boom-Babies" or "B-B's", children of *Silent Night,* and they will not be stopped. That is not to say the spiritual movements spreading across the country have not also rooted themselves in the hearts of the youth. In point of fact, a sect calling themselves the Children of Gaea has been dispersing their own philosophy, rivaling that of AR2's message of anarchy.

Absorbing certain credos of the Abramic faith, Buddhism, New Age philosophy, and environmentalism, the Children of Gaea preach the message of spreading peace, inward reflection, the hidden elemental capabilities of human beings, and an uncompromising call to save the planet. They do this not for the betterment of man, but for the sake of the Earth and all its living things. And while most Christians view this time in history as that spoken of in the Bible's book of Revelation, the Children of Gaea flourish around the country, warning man without pause of Mother Earth turning against them.

President Mueller does not think twice about such fantasies. For him, ART remains the only fanatics he must fully defeat, or risk witnessing the end of his nation to. Therefore, the days that pass see ongoing conflicts, scores of Americans being killed, and raging infernos surging as testaments to carnage. In response to this, the military moves on urban areas with fury, killing a collection of their fellow countrymen at the urging of their Commander-in-Chief.

Their set military offensive has claimed the lives of over 1500 ART supporters, and 8000 civilians, but the conflicts keep growing increasingly dire with the passing of time. Eventually, soldiers start growing disenchanted with the way of things, and the killing of their own begins to wear them down. This begs the question of whether or not Mueller has gone too far in his commands. A doubt which surges through the minds of its cynics, the Joint Chief of Staff Chairman, a man by the name of George Hartsoe, is the one to bring the soldiers' forebodings to the President.

Chairman Hartsoe requests a compromise be reached between the administration and ART. He informs Mueller of the heartache brought on by the killing of civilians, those he and his men have sworn to protect, and fears a sense of despondency and resentment toward the leader of the free world is quickly forming amongst those same soldiers. And if not remedied, he believes it will hinder the carrying out of commands, very well leading to a military revolt.

Mueller cares nothing for Hartsoe's warnings. He refuses to reach any settlement with ART. He has already informed the American people their freedoms would be returned once the ARTists halt their attacks and turn themselves in, and callously rebuffs any notion of altering that ultimatum. So considering the Joint Chief of Staff Chairman's plea a sign of both weakness and failure, President Mueller strips George Hartsoe of his command, replacing him with someone he believes more suitable for the task.

It is a mistake the President will come to regret.

This was the exact reason why our Founding Fathers distrusted the idea of a standing military. The reason was as plain as any now. Here you had the highest ranking military officer of your country, the Chairman of the Joint Chief of Staff of the United States Armed Forces standing in opposition to you, and you strip him of his command instead of negotiating with him? It was a big mistake. The men and women of the military were loyal to Hartsoe, even though he didn't have direct command over them. To them, he wasn't just another bureaucrat, he was their brother, and Mueller was going to learn that the hard way.

Prof. Tamara Boggier

keeper, New York Republic Athenaeum

Chairman Hartsoe wastes no time in meeting with the face of ART, the man voted President seven years earlier—Calvin Walsh. During this meeting, Hartsoe reveals President Mueller's plans to destroy the ART Party, as well as, the fact that he has no intentions of reinstating the U.S. Constitution. The Chairman also accuses Mueller of being frightened, and charges the President with treason to his office.

Hartsoe completely opposes any scheme being put in place by the President, though still believing a dominant hand needs to be maintained in bringing stability to the nation. Regardless of this belief, the Chairman is willing to put aside any disagreement he may have with ART, in exchange for their support of his intended plan.

Hartsoe needs ART to suspend its terrorist acts, giving him and his military the opportunity they need in confronting Mueller. He reveals his intention of removing the President from office, and reinstating the Constitution of the United States. But it is imperative that Walsh hold back his ARTists, especially those of AR2. The last thing he needs is to have the military divided on two fronts, something Chairman Hartsoe feels would be unfortunate for all parties involved.

Walsh finds the return of the U.S. Constitution his only concern. And though the military may not be the ideal partnership, with Mueller practically trying to kill all ARTists, the Chairman's offer is good enough for ART's leader. Hartsoe is given his the trust, and those of his ART Party. AR2 is restrained by its leaders through the promise of Mueller's reign coming to an end. And by that same token, the protests and riots are also ceased to but mere infractions, granting the former Joint Chief of Staff Chairman the opportunity he needs in collaborating with those of his former outfit regarding the ousting of Howard Mueller.

Through their commanding officers and personal feelings, nearly eighty percent of the military joins the Chairman in betraying the President of the United States. Obviously, Mueller has underestimated the level of loyalty the military has for Hartsoe, and now finds himself desperate to draw their support against the man who has bled and sacrificed with them during World War III. But when it comes to the military, though Howard Mueller may be the President they have all sworn to obey, Chairman Hartsoe is the leader they are destined to follow.

In the end, Howard Mueller, and all those who remain loyal to him are proclaimed enemies of the state, and on September 4, find themselves engaging the United States military in the bleeding center of the nation's capital.

The administration still has its defenders within the Armed Forces, but they are insignificant. Their loyalty means nothing when either surrendering, or switching sides. And by November 28, Chairman Hartsoe and his men have trampled President Mueller and his administration underfoot, declaring victory at the very doorsteps of the White House, placing Mueller and his entire cabinet under arrest for the nation to see.

For the first time, the national media and Prometheus Flame concur in their reports. Bulletins informing the country of Mueller's defeat and Hartsoe's victory, after ten brutal years, Howard Mueller is no longer President of the United States.

It is a day which shows promise of the U.S. Constitution being restored, and the United States returning to its position as world leader. Most of all, it means an end to the civil war. Unfortunately, before Hartsoe can even jump-start the nation's healing process, controversy begins surrounding his seizure of power.

Things were really getting bad now. Not only had there been terrorism on American soil, now a coup d'état had taken place. Can you even imagine the frenzy, the fear the people must've had in watching their elected President being arrested, and dragged out of the White House like some common criminal? I mean, not even the unruly generation of their forefathers had done this. And now, here were the people of the 21st century acting out something they'd only seen in the Global South. You can absolutely believe that the population was scared out of its mind.

Cecil Greenough

Grand Magistrate: The Biography of Kiril Pordan

Upon deposing Mueller of authority, Chairman Hartsoe orders all Cleansing Hubs around the country be closed. All Chinese Americans are to be immediately released, while illegal immigrants are to first be vetted, and then released. Those found indeed conspiring in illicit affairs are to have their day in court, in a ruling that pleases most of the country. But in true character, the ART Party petitions that all Chinese, citizen or not, be straight away set free, and call on the Chairman to discount the Loyalist Act once and for all.

Hartsoe promises he will do his best, but at any rate, continues with the intensive probing for potential threats. His concerns over the releasing of possible radicals before screening their potential dangers promises to be fair and unbiased. A situation which remains a concern in the minds of the American people, it is compromised for the time being. On the other hand, that of the Constitution being upheld remains mandatory, and Hartsoe knows he will have to tackle it sooner than later, but refuses to make it a priority.

Congressmen and Senators released from their offices with the launching of Mueller's Martial Law edict demand Hartsoe and the military relinquish all Executive powers, and allow those elected by the people to proceed with their duties. It is an appeal Chairman Hartsoe clearly understands, but postpones due to the fact of believing he knows what is best for the current situation being faced by the nation. And taking into consideration the present state of affairs are no different than those tackled by countries of the past that have confronted insurgencies, Hartsoe maintains a strong military response is what is needed.

He promises that, unlike the attack force Mueller had made them into, the Armed Forces now stand ready to play their role as protectors of the nation. In other words, the Joint Chief of Staff Chairman refrains from allowing the politicians to return to their original status. And in the eyes of his critics, this decision contradicts his initial reason for overthrowing President Mueller. Needless to say, the ARTists believe they might have made a grave mistake.

This was the worse case scenario coming true here. The military had seized control of the Executive branch, and began conducting business the only way they knew how—militarily. That wasn't a good thing. The American people weren't soldiers. They hadn't been conditioned to operate like soldiers. And above all that, people just don't like being told what to do. And now you have the military running the show? You can be sure that things weren't going to go smoothly.

Cecil Greenough

Grand Magistrate: The Biography of Kiril Pordan

Many people believed that Hartsoe only had the nation in mind during all this, and then there were those who thought he was no better than Mueller. The bottom line was, when Chairman Hartsoe took the President of the United States out of office by force, he must've known that he couldn't have possibly implemented the demands of the common American into the equation of mending a broken nation. He would've been a fool to think so. The fact is, his coup had changed things, and there was never any chance of going back.

Prof. Tamara Boggier

keeper, New York Republic Athenaeum

The charges against Hartsoe are fueled by the media, gradually building suspicion in the hearts of those heeding their hearsay. Hartsoe denies he is going back on his word, and tries to make clear his agenda. Even so, the elected officials and the nation question such explanations, continuing their persistent demands the Joint Chief of Staff Chairman and his Armed Forces immediately handover command of the country. Hartsoe again refuses, and on December 23, orders the military begin arresting those he deems instigators of dissent amongst the nation's populace.

The arrests come as a shock to the general public, further portraying the military and their leaders as being no different than Mueller's administration. It is a comparison that rather quickly forms a fracture amongst Americans, diverging perspectives pitting an orderly society believing the military knows best against a population dedicated to returning to the way things used to be. All the while, those who believe the blood spilled by the military deserves no mercy, AR2 primarily, revert to their acts of random violence throughout the East Coast once again.

Basically, you had three types of people at this point. First you had the ones who were scared witless, fearful of the bloody clashes happening in the middle of their suburban streets, and only desiring peace. Above all, they accepted George Hartsoe and the military as their leaders, and abided by their rules. Then there were those who refused to be violent in their protests, but also refused to be forced into a military state. And lastly, you had AR2, and the people who agreed with them. They were the ones who fought and killed for what they wanted. What that was isn't entirely clear. But nonetheless, they were the ones the military needed to quell before any calm could be found. It was definitely a terrifying time. It was the time of the Great Divide.

Prof. Tamara Boggier

keeper, New York Republic Athenaeum

The nation's unity has been further shattered. A dilemma laid before United States Joint Chief of Staff Chairman George Hartsoe and his men, three factions vie for control of the land, but the Chairman knows neither standpoint can ever truly exist if two are not sacrificed. An impasse the Chairman cannot disregard, it is something he is willing to confront no differently than he has during his years of war. Thus, before the end of the year, the military seizes control of all media, immediately initiating a mass campaign of propaganda depicting the Armed Forces as the future of hope and stability—the enemy of a violent and radical faction—the law Americans must obey.

The result of such tactics waste no time in labeling those in moderate support of ART as being indistinguishable from those of AR2. Terrorists, enemies of the state, anarchists, and above all, cowards, the ART Party and its movements are once again declared traitors to the United States.

The declaration is not easy to swallow, but it must if Americans expect to live free. Freedom, the very thing at the core of this dark time, Hartsoe will not only grant it, he will do so as its master. A time of accepted tyranny. An age of desired reign. A prophesy fulfilled. The Armed Forces are about to commence with an objective they believe will bring about a glorious time for all Americans, when in fact, it will destroy the very dream that is the United States.

The media has been censored, demanding the internet flourish with its claims against the military. Each allegation is met vehemently with contrasting propaganda, but that does not halt the reports told by the Prometheus Flame from sinking into the minds of many.

A call to bring the fight to Hartsoe and his men is herald by Calvin Walsh, and others who believe the military has used them. A deception, that of Hartsoe being capable of bringing about change, was a lie they were misled into believing. And in the minds of ARTists, Chairman Hartsoe is the traitor, and it is their duty to defend their country from said traitor.

Hartsoe spreads the same dogma. Only in his words, ART is made the traitor, and the military its righteous opposition. AR2 refuses to be told how to live by anyone, military or not. Their acts of utter chaos wash over Washington D.C., with explosions, public attacks, riots, and all out terror campaigns as their proclamation. The majority of the populace cannot believe what they are seeing, and cower at the fall of their nation.

Elders weep for their land. People bicker amongst each other. And the youth either reaches for a higher consciousness, or sets the world ablaze.

It matters greatly to Hartsoe that violence levels skyrocket throughout major cities, the very reason he must prepare the military to initiate its ultimate plans for the future. He intends on challenging ART's schemes with plans of his own, putting an end to their crimes. And with a word, he sets his military on course.

Brutal clashes soon desert television screens, and play live for all to witness from outside their windows. Neighborhoods become hideouts, and nobody trusts his fellow citizen. F-16 fighters soar day and night, shadowing major cities, ominously maneuvering in battle formations. Everywhere one turns, the military stands ready to enforce its decree. It is too much, and the more moderate ART members try reaching a compromise with those of the military willing to listen. Regrettably, they are talks of little hope amongst a nation suffering internally.

'One cannot live free if told how' is the battle cry insurgents go to their graves believing. The military is now forced to present an allusion as to what it has planned in response. One that will put the declaration of the rebels to the test, it will empower those who believe in its value.

'Mercy and Reward for the Loyal' may start amongst the elite of the military, but it is soon dispensed amongst the rest of the populace. And whether out of actual loyalty, desperateness, or fear, millions upon millions, cities upon cities, States upon States, begin viewing Hartsoe as the legitimate leader of the country. Something that is intensely fed to Americans, the declaration slowly but surely begins forging a new land.

Everyone knows something is coming, but none dare speak it. They will merely accept it when it arrives, praying they will even live to see it transpire. The ART Party needs to silence its youths, but that seems impossible. The wiser rebels need to make sense of their choices in halting the military, but their children's chaos never allow that. The masses do not care how it is done; they want AR2 stopped—the country is suffering.

Chairman Hartsoe and the military are about to initiate their plan of salvation, and it will see the death of a Democratic Republic, and the birth of an Autocratic Magisterium. Everything is about to change, and the United States will have no choice but change along with it.

M.A. Martin

2036

MAGISTERIUM

The Great Divide: a concise history of the future

M.A. Martin

Times had changed, and America was about to become something it hadn't ever before imagined.

Cecil Greenough

Grand Magistrate: The Biography of Kiril Pordan

Desperate times call for desperate measures. Never before were those words truer, even if there were some people that refused to go along with those measures.

Prof. Tamara Boggier

keeper, New York Republic Athenaeum

Rubble blankets the streets of New York, New York. A bone breaking chill paralyzes Pittsburgh, Pennsylvania. Chicago, Illinois, is in shambles. Dense smoke engulfs Washington D.C. Communication is limited with the South. The Midwest is satiated with religion and dismay. Electricity is a luxury. Death and despair are all around. This is the United States of America, and these are the tribulations weeping at the feet of Acting President George Hartsoe, begging him to salvage them.

The reservoirs of crude oil that have been all but depleted, and the fact that food is getting far too scarce, these are the things destroying the country. There are still some buses driving around picking up passengers needing to travel, but most of them round up desperate people to be enslaved by gang leaders. Those who still hold to the dying ideology of

93

Democracy, those not hiding in panic, those who have not simply given up on life, they are the ones trying desperately to help others reclaim their pride, just as criminals without reins ensnare those weaker than themselves as master and lord.

Little food, hardly any running water, power outages, hopelessness, Acting President Hartsoe is all too aware of his duties, and tries obsessively, along with his military, to create a truly functioning way for the future—a peoples' second chance.

Hartsoe knows he needs to establish an infrastructure with which to create jobs, generate an economy, and bestow freedom to those who deserve it, whereas, crushing those who oppose. The task to create such designs burden all involved, especially when trying to defend the nation from the extremisms of AR2. A responsibility the military Generals and Admirals of the United States Armed Forces swear to undertake, the new diagram for the country must be set by a devotion which gives birth to the future of America.

Let me put this in perspective for you. This wasn't The Crash of '22 where people had been out of work, but were still eating. Back then, people would've said that life was hard, but at least they'd been given government assistance. At least they'd been given free food. At least they'd been warm, and with a roof over their heads. Now? Now, people were living on the streets. There was death and destruction all around them, and they were living in rubble. The temperatures were dropping every day, and they were cold. God only knows what they were eating to survive. The people who were lucky enough to still have a house of their own still got sick, and couldn't go to the hospital. This was far worse than the Great Depression and The Crash put together. Not to mention AR2 doing what they did best, and that's killing innocent people. George Hartsoe had to get these things under control, and he did... no matter the cost.

Cecil Greenough

Grand Magistrate: The Biography of Kiril Pordan

The *Affirmation of Rectification* is an Executive Order detailing the oath the Armed Forces have taken to serve their supporters, as well as, what is expected of those exact same nationals. A decree reflecting the hopes and desires of the military, the order is introduced during a terrifying time in American history.

The rebellion is at an all time high. There are more than enough casualties on both sides of the discord. The war against the rebels can only be described as a massacre, while the sacrifices of the military are constantly called brave and heroic.

All day long, the media reports on dedicated soldiers risking their own safeties against terrorists who would dare to try and cloak their acts of barbarism with the banner of freedom. Men and women of the Armed Forces maimed by roadside bombs, those kidnapped and tortured, the ones killed in the line of duty, they are all broadcast on screens for the populace to see. Images that further fuel the military's accusations against ART and their affiliates, it gradually builds resentment in the hearts of everyday Americans for the resistance's so-called fight for freedom. Then again, those who find the internet a more credible source for updates are provided pictures concerning the exploitative immoralities committed by the military, and its hostile takeover of the nation.

Prometheus Flame and its comparable rogue servers spare no one the gruesome sights of heavily armed soldiers raiding buildings, killing children, and infringing on civil liberties. They do not censor uploads alleging the governments around the world partaking in a conspiracy to enslave mankind, the only reports informing the United States of what is happening in other countries, and vice versa. And portraying the resistances, Europe's Grimaldi Defiance and the Middle East's *Ansar al-Islam*, as heroes to be imitated, the Prometheus Flames' AR2 supporters try relentlessly to gain public support concerning their own rebellion. Nevertheless, the military spearheads with its attempts of bringing some sort of normality back to the country, as ART is made to look like a fanatical group of turncoats.

In a joint effort, Acting President Hartsoe and the military find themselves working tirelessly to make their agenda a thing of acceptance. This calls for them to drive military jeeps down booby trapped streets, while daring to fly Black Hawk helicopters over war embattled urban areas, delivering food and medical supplies to those most afflicted by the uprising.

Hartsoe couldn't stand the fact that Americans, people he'd sworn to protect, were starving on the streets. The wounded, the sick, the young and the old were the people Hartsoe had been fighting all his life to safeguard from any and all threats. Of course, he had to help them, it was his duty—even if that meant flying into the middle of what could only be called war zones.

Cecil Greenough

Grand Magistrate: The Biography of Kiril Pordan

An humanitarian effort on a massive scale, ART's image is even further tainted by the fact of AR2 trying to disrupt these rescue attempts. The calculated launching of rockets at military aircraft, and the roadside bombings of support caravans trying to reach those in great need of aid are done without consideration for their fellow Americans. AR2 may have a belief in freedom, but their freedoms mercilessly infringe on the freedoms of those who disagree with them.

Their attacks on the relief efforts shame them in the eyes of many. Soon enough, even those supporting ART begin pleading with the rebel force to cease its attacks. A cry the rebels struggle to ignore, the AR2 faction of their movement never once halts its acts of terrorism. For while the populace sees these attempts by the military as a form of goodwill, AR2 sees the military's efforts as nothing less than an insincere exploitation.

The military endeavors to discredit the allegations against them. They work rigorously to initiate some form of reconstruction. And as the *Affirmation of Rectification* stated the military's desire to serve its advocates by freely supplying them with much needed food, medicine, and everyday provisions in return for loyalty, intelligence concerning possible radicals, and military service, the Armed Forces conclude a new article is needed to shape the forthcoming approach to a new America.

The *Magisterium Edict* is the proclamation that is to replace the U.S. Constitution. A new supreme law of the land renovating the now believed erroneous features pertaining to the latter's particular set of rules, the *Magisterium Edict* will reshape the United States into an image of glory.

It is a dubious and excessively amended version of the existing Constitution recomposed by a United States Naval Admiral named Kiril Gustav Pordan, and desires nothing less than to construct a country grounded in morals, allegiance, and supremacy. Plainly said, the *Magisterium Edict* is as considerate to the U.S. Constitution as the populace of the United States is going to get, and reads as so:

The Loyalist of this ordained Magisterium, in unification and understanding, hereby adhere to a cohesive excellence, function in impartiality, aspire for amity, align ourselves in steadfast defense, swear by an interests for all, and secure the sanctions of the United Republic to ourselves, do by commence and maintain this Edict for the United Republic of America.

Directive I

Element 1. *All legislative powers herein granted shall be vested in a Magisterium of the United Republic and shall consist of a Council.*

Element 2. *The Council shall be composed of abiding Vice Magistrates chosen by Councilmen of each Republic who have the qualifications requisite for electors of the limited ranks of the secondary headship.*

No person shall be a Councilman who shall not have attained to the age of twenty five years, not been born a Citizen of the United Republic, and not have served three years in the military, and who shall not, when elected, be an inhabitant of the Republic in which he shall be chosen.

When vacancies happen in the Vice Magisterium, the Executive authority thereof shall issue Writs of Election to fill such vacancies amongst supplementary Councilmen.

The Council shall choose the Vice Magistrates, and shall have voice in impeachment against that said position.

Element 3. *The Council of the Magisterium shall be composed of two Councilmen from each Republic, chosen by the Loyalists thereof, for six Years; and each Councilman shall have one vote reflecting Vice Magistrate contention.*

No person shall be a Vice Magistrate who shall not have attained to the age of thirty years, not been born a citizen of the United Republic, and not have served ten years in the military, and who shall not, when elected, be an inhabitant of the Republic in which he must serve.

The Vice Magistrates of the Magisterium shall be head of the Council, but shall have no Vote, unless they be equally divided.

The Council shall choose their other Officers in the absence of the Vice Magistrate, or when no Vice Magistrates exercise the secondary headship.

When a Vice Magistrate of the Magisterium is tried, the High Magistrate shall preside, and no person shall be convicted without the concurrence of two thirds of the Councilmen present, or by said ruling of the High Magistrate.

Judgment in cases of impeachment shall extend to Imprisonment and Death.

Element 4. *The times, places and manner of holding elections for Vice Magistrates and Councilmen, shall be prescribed in each Republic by the Council thereof; but the High Magistrate may at any time make or alter such regulations.*

The Council shall assemble at least six times in every year, and such meetings shall be on the first Monday of January, March, May, July, September and December, unless they shall by Magisterium Law appoint a different day.

Element 5. *Each Council shall be the Judge of the Elections, Returns and Qualifications of its own Members, and a Majority of each shall constitute a Quorum to do Business; but a smaller number may adjourn from day to day, and may be authorized to compel the* *attendance of absent members, in such manner, and under such penalties as each Council may provide.*

Each Council may determine the rules of its proceedings, punish its members for disorderly behavior, expel a member, and with the concurrence of the High Magistrate, have them executed.

Each Council shall keep a journal of its proceedings, and from time to time publish the same, excepting such parts as may in their judgment require secrecy; and the Yeas and Nays of the members of either Council on any question shall, at the desire of the High Magistrate or one fifth of those present, be entered on the journal.

No Councilman, during the session of Council, shall, without the consent of the High Magistrate or other Councilmen, adjourn for more than three days, nor to any other place than that in which the Council shall be sitting.

Element 6. *The Vice Magistrates and Councilmen shall receive no compensation for their services disparate to all Loyalists, or in any other form than the Interim Credit Encode of the United Republic.*

They shall in all cases, except treason, felony and breach of the peace, be privileged from arrest during their attendance at the session of their respective Councils, and in going to and returning from the same; and for any speech or debate in either Council, they shall not be questioned in any other place, unless specified differently by the High Magistrate.

Element 7. *All Credit Encodes shall originate in the office of Council; but the Vice Magistrates may propose or concur with Improvement as on other Credit Encodes.*

Every Credit Encode which shall have passed the Councils and the Vice Magistrates, shall, before it become a Law, be presented to the High Magistrate of the Magisterium; if he approve he shall sign it, but if not he shall return it, with his objections to that Council in which it shall have originated, who shall enter the objections at large on their journal, and proceed to reconsider it. If after such reconsideration two thirds of that Council shall agree to pass the Credit Encode, it shall be sent, together with the objections, to the Vice Magistrates, by which it shall likewise be reconsidered, and if approved by two thirds of those Vice Magistrates, it shall become a law. But in all such cases the votes of both Vice Magistrates and Councilmen shall be determined by the High Magistrate. If any Credit Encode shall not be returned by the High Magistrate within ten days (Fridays excluded) after it shall have been presented to him, the same shall be a law, in like manner as if he had signed it, unless the Councilmen by their adjournment prevent its return, in which case it shall not be a law.

Every Order, Resolution, or Vote to which the concurrence of the Vice Magistrates and Councils may be necessary (except on a question of Adjournment) shall be presented to the High Magistrate of the Magisterium; and before the same shall take effect, shall be approved by him, or being disapproved by him, shall be repassed by two thirds of the Vice Magistrates and Councils, according to the rules and limitations prescribed in the case of a bill until approved by the High Magistrate.

Element 8. *The Councils shall have power to lay duties, imposts and excises, to provide for the common aspiration for amity aligning in steadfast defense of the United Republic; but all Duties, Imposts and Excises shall be uniform throughout the United Republic; To provide for the Punishment of counterfeiting the Securities and current Credit Encode of the United Republic; To establish Post Offices and post Roads; To promote the Progress of Science and useful Arts, by securing for limited Times to Authors and Inventors the exclusive Right to their respective Writings and Discoveries; To constitute Tribunals inferior to the Magisterium Tribunal; To define and punish Piracies and Felonies committed on the high Seas, and offenses against the Law of Nations; And to make all Laws which shall be necessary and proper for carrying into Execution the foregoing Powers, and all other powers vested by this Edict in the Magisterium of the United Republic, or in any Department or Officer thereof.*

Directive II

Element 1. *The Executive power shall be vested in a High Magistrate of the Magisterium of the United Republic of America. He shall hold his Office during the term of one lifetime, and shall be elected as follows:*

The Councilmen shall meet in their respected Councils, and vote by ballot for a list of all the persons nominated by them, and of the number of votes for each; which list they shall sign and certify, and transmit sealed to the Vice Magistrates of the United Republic. The Vice Magistrates, in presence of the whole Secondary headship, open all the certificates, and the votes shall then be counted. The person having the greatest number of votes shall be the High Magistrate, if such number be a majority of the whole number of Councilmen appointed; and if there be more than one who have such majority, and have an equal number of votes, then the Vice Magistrates shall immediately choose by ballot one of them for High Magistrate; and if no person have a majority, then from the five highest on the list the said Secondary Headship shall in like manner choose the High Magistrate. But in choosing the High Magistrate, the votes shall be taken by Republic, the Councilman from each Republic having one vote; A quorum for this purpose shall consist of a Councilman or Councilmen from two thirds of the Republics, and a majority of all the Republics shall be necessary to a choice.

The Vice Magistrates may determine the time of choosing the Electors, and the day on which they shall give their Votes; which day shall be the same throughout the United Republic.

No Person except a natural born Citizen, at the time of the Adoption of this Edict, shall be eligible to the Office of High Magistrate; neither shall any person be eligible to that Office who shall not have attained to the Age of thirty five Years, and have served fifteen years in the military.

In Case of Death, Resignation, or Inability to discharge the powers and duties of the said Office, the same shall devolve on the Vice Magistrates, until a High Magistrate be elected.

The High Magistrate shall, at no stated times, receive for his services, a compensation disparate to all Loyalists, or in any other form than the Interim Credit Encode of the United Republic. Before they enter on the Execution of this Office, the High Magistrate shall take the following Oath or Affirmation:--"I do solemnly swear (or affirm) that I will faithfully execute the Office of High Magistrate of the Magisterium of the United Republic, and will to the best of my ability, preserve, protect, and defend the Magisterium Edict of the United Republic."

Element 2. *The High Magistrate shall be Director of the Army, Air Force, and Navy of the United Republic, and may require the opinion, in writing, of the principal Officer in each of the Military departments, upon any subject relating to the duties of their respective Offices, and he shall have power to grant reprieves and pardons for offenses against the United Republic, including in cases of Impeachment.*

He shall have power, by and with the elected advice of the Vice Magistrates, to make treaties, and he shall nominate, and by and with the elected advice of the Vice Magistrates, shall appoint Ambassadors, other public Ministers and Consuls, Judges of the Magisterium Tribunal, and all other Officers of the United Republic, whose Appointments are not herein otherwise provided for, and which shall be established by Magisterium Law: but the Vice Magistrates may by High Magistrate consent vest the Appointment of such inferior Officers, as they think proper, in the High Magistrate alone, in the Courts of Law, or in the Heads of Departments.

The High Magistrate shall have Power to fill up all vacancies that may happen during the Recess of the Vice Magistrates, by granting Commissions which shall expire at the end of their next session.

Element 3. *He shall from time to time give to the Vice Magistrates information of the state of the Republic, and recommend to their consideration such measures as he shall judge necessary and expedient; he may, on occasions, convene both parties, or either of them, and in case of disagreement between them, he may adjourn them to such time as he shall think proper; he shall receive Ambassadors and other public Ministers; he shall take care that the laws be faithfully executed, and shall commission all the Officers of the United Republic.*

Element 4. *The High Magistrate, Vice Magistrates, Councilmen and all civil Officers of the United Republic, shall be removed from Office on Impeachment for, and conviction of, treason or other high crimes.*

Directive III

Element 1. *The judicial Power of the United Republic shall be vested in one Magisterium Tribunal and in such inferior Courts as the Councils may from time to time ordain and establish. The Judges, both of the Tribunal and inferior Courts, shall hold their Offices during good behavior, and shall, at no stated times, receive for his services, a compensation* *disparate to all Loyalists, or in any other form than the Interim Credit Encode of the United Republic.*

Element 2. *The judicial Power shall extend to all Cases, in Law and Equity, arising under this Edict, the Laws of the United Republic, and Treaties made, or which shall be made, under their Authority;--to all cases affecting Ambassadors, other public Ministers and Consuls;--to all cases of admiralty and maritime Jurisdiction;--to Controversies to which the United Republic shall be a Party;--to Controversies between two or more Republics;--between a Republic and Loyalists of another Republic;--and between Loyalists of different Republics.*

In all Cases affecting Ambassadors, other public Ministers and Consuls, and those in which a Republic shall be Party, the Magisterium Tribunal shall have original Jurisdiction. In all the other Cases before mentioned, the Magisterium Tribunal shall have appellate Jurisdiction, both as to Law and Fact, with such Exceptions, and under such Regulations as the Councils shall make.

The Trial of all Crimes shall be by Magisterium Adjudicators; and such Trial shall be held in the Republic where the said Crimes shall have been committed; but when not committed within any Republic, the Trial shall be at such Place or Places as the Councils may by Law have directed.

Element 3. *Treason against the Magisterium shall consist only in levying War against them, or in adhering to their Enemies, giving them Aid and Comfort. No Person shall be convicted of Treason unless on the Testimony of two Witnesses to the same overt Act, or on Confession in open Court. The Councils shall have power to declare the punishment of treason, be it imprisonment or execution.*

Directive IV

Element 1. *Full Faith and Credit shall be given in each Republic to the public Acts, Records, and judicial Proceedings of every other Republic. And the Councils may by general Laws prescribe the Manner in which such Acts, Records, and Proceedings shall be proved, and the Effect thereof.*

Element 2. *The Loyalists of each Republic shall be entitled to all privileges and Immunities of Loyalists in the Magisterium. A Person charged in any Republic with Treason, Felony, or other Crime, who shall flee from Justice, and be found in another Republic, shall on Demand of the executive Authority of the Republic from which he fled, be delivered up, to be removed to the Republic having Jurisdiction of the Crime.*

Element 3. *The Magisterium shall situate Loyalists in this Magisterium a Resolute Form of Government, and shall protect each of them against Invasion; and on Application of the Legislature, or of the Executive (when the Legislature cannot be convened) against domestic Violence.*

Directive V

Element 1.

The Vice Magistrates and Councilmen before mentioned, and the Loyalists Members of the Magisterium, and all executive and judicial Officers of the United Republic, shall be bound by Oath or Affirmation, to support this Edict; but no religious Test shall ever be required as a Qualification to any Office or public Trust under the United Republic.

In witness whereof We have hereunto subscribed our Names,

Maine: George Hartsoe

Vermont: Cassidy Jones

New Hampshire: Alex Barnett, Thomas Shaw

Massachusetts: Kiril Pordan, Roger Billings

Rhode Island: Carlyle Brooks, Lance Porter

Connecticut: Nathaniel Woods, Paul Mancini

New York: Damon Jackson, Manuel Gonzalez, Leticia Emerson, Gary Albright

New Jersey: Andrew Saito, William Casey, Emilio Ramirez

Pennsylvania: Christopher Jones, Tamaqua Miller, Stefan Dupont

West Virginia: Hakim Douglas, Patrick Haslett, Dinah Goldstein

Delaware: Abdul Khan, Jesse Garcia

Maryland: Gideon Friedman

Virginia: Hunter Barnett, Aaron Balthazar, Tracy Weinstein

The District of Colombia, October 22, 2036

The *Magisterium Edict* is presented to the public on October 25, and is received with both enthusiasm and admiration. Seen as a second chance for the once mighty West, it makes those looking toward peace feel as if it is within their grasps. A new hope. A new way of life. A new country.

The United Republic of America.

Millions upon millions turn out to the country's capital to bear witness to its historic induction. They accept it as the only way toward harmony. The young, old, male, female, white, black, Asian, Hispanic—they all turnout to hear the promise of their country's future revisited and reestablished.

Acting President George Hartsoe is the one who delivers the oration of the *Magisterium Edict* before a heeding crowd of Loyalists, and every utterance of its wording brings the country closer to the dream of Autocracy.

Hartsoe is christened the first official High Magistrate of the United Republic of America. A title that will see the age of Presidents pass away, the High Magistrate is more than just a Commander-in-chief—he is the final authority of the nation. George Hartsoe is now unequivocally the most powerful man in all the land. But even with such a momentous occasion taking place, the fact that Americans are dying of starvation, or left out in the freezing cold due to the bombings of their homes, has not changed.

The United Republic of America is isolated. The American dollar has no value. Very few people can afford to eat a hot meal. And amongst the ruin and carnage plaguing the country, hope is being strangled by discord and violence. It is with this stage in place High Magistrate Hartsoe steps out in front of his fellow citizens, announcing with authority the creation of the Interim Credit Encode. A system conceived years before the ultimate necessitation of its existence, the Interim Credit Encode is an information databank, more so, a remedy to a financial crises, and the way of the future.

A central processing unit surgically implanted into the wrist of its carrier, the ICE-chip is capable of storing not only entire records of its owner, but is also competent in its functionality as a credit circulator. Effortless and painless in its surgical procedure, the embedding of the chip into ones wrists takes less than one hour, and less than twenty minutes to activate. With it, a Loyalist will be granted the sum of 63,000 credits a year, a lifelong connection to the Magisterium regularity databank, and a place amongst the United Republic.

Food, clothing, shelter, all this will be made possible by the Magisterium, and it will be the ICE-chip which will usher it all in. On the other hand, without this processor, one will be unable to eat, trade, or find safety within the nation's borders. An ambitious abandonment of the financial transferences understood throughout the world, it is an electronic currency that will spread like a sea over a sinking earth.

The Magisterium understands the length of time it will take to catalog all of its Loyalists, but does not fret. It will be a pleasure to see more than 30.7 million Americans cataloged before the end of 2037, each one being given a second chance at life.

Okay, now the Christians were having a field day. A chip implanted in the wrist, and without it you can't eat or trade? It's the Mark of the Beast, it's gotta be. And because America was still a predominantly Christian nation back then, regardless of the Buddhists that were taking over, everyone had heard of this myth, and most of them believed it was actually taking place right before their very eyes. So, those people didn't want it; they started to object. They started to grab their guns. And before you knew it, they started killing in the name of God. They refused to be given the Mark, and would kill anyone who tried forcing them into taking it. It was chaos. But hey, the thirteen districts, the Magisterium Republics, people were getting cataloged by the millions. To them, this was going to make everything okay again, and they'd been convinced to hate anyone who told them otherwise.

Cecil Greenough

Grand Magistrate: The Biography of Kiril Pordan

In time, every woman, every man, and every child is to be cataloged with the Interim Credit Encode—the way of the future. A person will receive his/her annual pay at the beginning of the year, and work it off in jobs established by the Magisterium. There will be no more money. Currency will no longer have value in paper or metals. Now it is a person that is found precious. Credit that is granted to all Loyalists, everyone is as never before.

There is no more debt. A man's potentials now earn him his way in life. A Loyalist is an investment, and the Magisterium will be reimbursed through the country's ascension. The United Republic of America has begun, and all bearing witness to its establishment Hail the Magisterium. And though a resistance to such comportment still beats in the hearts of many, there is no denying a new America has arrived.

My fellow Americans—Loyalists, and caretakers of a better tomorrow. Today we stand here together facing a crisis unseen by our nation since the days of the Civil War, an assault no different than what took place on the West Coast. An age when brother faces brother, sister faces sister, and the hopes of the young seem threatened by the actions of the old. A country that was forged by blood, sacrifice, and faith, we Americans now stand at a crossroad of uncertainty. We know what it is that we face: a time of cruel rebellion, trampled hopes, and nightmarish brutality. A time when those who are without are cast aside by those with. A time when the tears of our children and the cries of our loved ones intertwine as if an opus of surrender. It's a world we've only seen on distant shores, yet are astonished by now that it's at our very doorstep. We look to the East, and find the future bleak in its unveiling. To the West, we find our weakness constantly staring back at us in disdain. To the South, where the division of the nation has left our kin without leadership. And to the North, where our neighbors forsake us to our own demise. There's no discounting it my brothers, sisters, mothers, and fathers, we stand at the brink of our failed and miserable lives. But at this point of utter bereavement, I tell you there's hope. During this time of chaos and fear, I tell you there still stands order. Amongst this age of darkness, somewhere there's light. And it's with those opposing views of our reality do I say that we're not finished. It's to those who would stand in the way of unity do I say we will not falter. It's to the world that watches our time of desperation do I say we're stronger now than we've ever been. And it's to history that I do say our future will not be taken from us. My fellow Americans, even Heaven had its war. And just as God stood and proclaimed the Heavens His, so shall we in unification proclaim this country ours. So don't fret, and don't be disheartened. For I do solemnly swear that I will protect, reestablish, and march this nation in its course of glory. And as we were once known as fragmented States unified by a common goal, so shall we now be known as a single Republic unified in our future. We will survive. We will prosper. We will win. I promise you that. God bless you all, and may God bless The United Republic of America.

High Magistrate George P. Hartsoe
Magisterium Induction Ceremony, February 19, 2037

The Great Divide: a concise history of the future

M.A. Martin

2038
VEDETTE

The Great Divide: a concise history of the future

The sectarian violence of the nation has found an unsettling decline. ART remains persistent in its fight for freedom, while the violent acts of AR2 now take place along the outskirts of the United Republic. It is at last safe for the thirteen Republics of the Magisterium to begin functioning at a conventional capacity; likewise, calm enough for its Loyalists to begin living normal lives.

Magisterium owned Depots distribute food, provisions, and clothing through the usage of the Interim Credit Encode, while a majority of Americans continue to starve on the streets for denying it. Magisterium administered medical facilities see a constant flow of Loyalists needing medical care, while thousands of people deal with infections and diseases on their own, eventually dying without assistance. A massive reconstruction arrangement flourishes throughout the Republic, and helps to repair the devastated skylines of most East Coast cities, but there are still those which remain bearing scars of war, insurgency, and neglect brought on by the new order of things. Over 100 million Loyalists have already been cataloged with the ICE-chip, making the dream of the Magisterium something of a reality, all while millions upon millions of people living in the Midwest, the South, and Pacific Northwest have yet to be cataloged, and are left to fend for themselves.

All along the United Republic: Maine, New Hampshire, Vermont, all the way to the Virginias, structures that had once stood as a testament to Democracy now stood as a verification of the Magisterium. City halls, police departments, hospitals, governors' mansions, train stations, and all private estates and businesses that had once been owned by the rich and elite, all now belonged to the former U.S. Military. And they'd all been converted into what were now known as Magisterium Centers. Anything that had once displayed the selfishness of capitalism, all of them—gone now. And above all other conversions stood the alteration of the White House into the Magisterium Core, the most evident takeover of them all.

Cecil Greenough

Grand Magistrate: The Biography of Kiril Pordan

There was a new form of propulsion being experimentally utilized by the Magisterium. The dream of ending fossil fuel dependency was now a reality, with the electric battery being brought to light. No longer was gasoline and coal being depended on, and no longer was the electric battery an expensive pipe dream. With the Interim Credit Encode now in full play, nothing was too expensive to make anymore. And one of the first ways the Magisterium proved that was by introducing the electric battery. This was how they started rebuilding the country. Newly constructed bulldozers, cranes, aerial work platforms, excavators, and forklifts, everything had by now been redesigned to operate by electric battery. Even public transportation was now being run on electricity. And though this was most certainly not taking place in the entire country, the Republic definitely began benefiting.

Prof. Tamara Boggier

keeper, New York Republic Athenaeum

Home to the High Magistrate and his immediate assistants, the Magisterium Core is considered the nucleus of the Magisterium. The everyday operations remain conducted within the sacred halls of Centers, with the most important in vestibules of the Capitol Building, but it is the Magisterium Core which oversees the finality of all decrees.

At the moment, one such decree deals with the problem of those refusing to be cataloged, and the method with which they should be dealt with. It does not matter that such refusals may have been born from either a support for ART, or the fact of believing the ICE-chip to be that of the *Mark of the Beast.* It has now become an obstacle the Magisterium is determined to surmount.

The Loyalists of the Republic find pride in the respect returned to them by their sovereigns. Looking out of their windows, they rarely find an explosion waiting for them, or the sight of someone being shot in the streets. Now they shop at Depots for food, clothing, and all other necessities. The Magisterium even uses the knowledge of somatic cell nuclear transfer to produce the nourishment, and animals needed to provide for its Loyalists, and Loyalists are more than devoted to their leaders in return. Magisterium regulated electricity has also been restored throughout most of the Republic, a luxury which returns its Loyalists to the modern age.

Soon enough, news of such revolutionary modifications begin to reach far and wide, helping to trigger something around the entire globe. But for now, only the United Republic of America enjoys such advancements. It is a new age, and those who will not evolve with it will be left behind.

Taking into account the endless resources made available, all facets of life within the United Republic are converted to portray Magisterium rule. District Attorneys, Mayors, Governors, Senators, and Congressmen are all replaced by military officers dubbed Councilmen. From the extensive branches of the military they are chosen, the most highly decorated now receiving the title of Vice Magistrate, a position entitling them to more power they have ever possessed.

Meanwhile, other occupations such as judges, lawyers, policemen, and teachers are also interchanged with military soldiers capable of executing such positions. Entire zones are then seized and protected by armed soldiers, and serve as housing developments for those Loyalists who are in need of shelter. In time, nearly all cataloged citizens are provided with a warm place to stay, and find their status as Loyalists more than a blessing.

Schools throughout the Republic are eventually reopened, and children returned to their studies, but the curriculum within those instructs have also been made to reflect Magisterium rule. No longer are the days of tedious academia, now all schooling has been converted to reflect the sole purposes of math, reading, science, physical education, and Magisterium conduct. A new way of learning—a disciplined way of thinking—a loyal and subordinate American.

It is from these sets of youths the Magisterium will further build its army and society. But before that can take effect, a mandate has been implemented requiring all healthy bodied United Republic Loyalists, ages 16-35, male and female, report to their nearest Magisterium Centers, and enlist into the Armed Forces. A bitter pill to swallow, it is one that must be performed as a loyal citizen to the United Republic.

The selection process is a grueling physical and mental ordeal, and only then are servicemen selected. All cataloged Loyalists are to be evaluated and tested for potential, then separated into two groups. On one side stand the fit and the strong, while on the other stand the simple and weak. Those who do not make the cut are considered disadvantaged, and fill in the vacancies of sanitation, construction, technician, and most of all, Factory worker. Factories operating both day and night in shift intervals, producing everything the Magisterium needs from food to weapons, clothing to warships, their functions are the backbone of the country.

There is endless resource, and now the Magisterium has the bodies needed to take advantage of it all. Only those millions upon millions of Loyalists in the fields of medicine and science are permitted to continue with their disciplines, but only in association to the Magisterium. And with such cooperation flowing as gently as it does, peace has indeed been granted to this innovative institute.

If you were 16, 17, 25, all the way to 35, and were able bodied, you were in the military now. This was what George Hartsoe saw as saving the nation. He wanted all able bodied Americans that could fight for the Magisterium, fighting. Think about it. He'd already compensated the Loyalists with the ICE-chip. They only had to serve until they turned 35. That meant that if you were 34, you only had to serve for a year. And if you were 27, eight years, so on and so forth. I believe Hartsoe had already figured out his Magisterium couldn't have survived if only in the East Coast. No way. You'd have AR2 hunkering down in Ohio somewhere, and they'd attack you anytime they wanted to, then run and hide in Ohio again. Hartsoe was well aware that if he was going to take this new form of government across the entire nation, he had to do whatever it took. It's not like he was trying to create a new country, after all. He was trying to save America, and that was gonna have to include the other 39 States—maybe excluding Alaska and Hawaii. He needed an army for that. And with thirty percent of the Republic at his disposal, 38 million soldiers...he had it. The world was about to see a military like never before.

Cecil Greenough

Grand Magistrate, The Biography of Kiril Pordan

The Republic had enough people to do what they wanted done, even if there were those who sometimes resisted. Call it slavery. The people back then called it salvation. They worked in shifts, and steel, planes, machines, clothing, even food, all of them were brought to fruition in record time. It was even said that a building could go up in less than a week in those days. A clear exaggeration, of course, but you still get the idea. Now as for those chosen to be the soldiers of the country, most of the Loyalist had already seen people killed, so that wasn't an obstacle for them. But only very few had actually taken a life. Now that was something the Magisterium had to get them used to. So the training to become a soldier was grueling, violent, and soul ensnaring. And it made one apathetic to death, pain, or mercy. It made them coldly efficient.

Prof. Tamara Boggier

keeper, New York Republic Athenaeum

It truly does appear as if the Magisterium has begun to overcome its challenges. Then again, just as a new dawn breaks across the United Republic, lingering threats are being given new life. Two distinct cries struggling to be heard in an ever-changing world, they are the voices of ART and AR2.

The rebel forces have not surrendered their call of Democracy—their call of liberty—their call of freedom. The anarchist ways of the past may have been crushed to but rare infractions, but the spirit of *American Revolution Two*, both political and anarchistic, have not been exterminated. And amongst those who would dare to stand against the raging tide of the Magisterium, is one with the heart of revenge and determination. Her name is Agnes Walsh, and hers is a name that will renovate the rebellion.

It has been over five years since the ART Party, a once functioning and dignified political organization, has been made into nothing more than a fanatical movement blamed for the atrocious crimes of their more radical faction—AR2. Accused of everything from bombings to public executions, fanaticism to dissension, the defunct organization is being eliminated one by one. They are now nothing more than a dying breed of revolutionaries being hunted down by the might of an emerging empire.

They recall the history of their once great nation: George Washington, Abraham Lincoln, Barack Obama, names which have invoked a sense of pride and change in the United States of America, the patriots now find themselves voiceless.

It has been made abundantly clear uttering any sort of allegiance to ART is considered both treasonous and deadly. So they remain silent within the cities, edgily avoiding their turn at being cataloged. They mostly flee to the heartland, where military facilities function as isolated fragments, with religious movements keeping them relatively quiet, as do the longstanding militias of the region. Still, those holding out for change only have two options: the bleak life of an ARTist, or the inevitable death of an AR2 rebel —but then Agnes Walsh arrives.

Agnes Walsh had been raised with the ideology of ART coursing through her veins. It wasn't a simple movement for her, by no means. This was her life. She knew nothing else. Her father, Calvin Walsh, had been murdered during the civil unrest of the East Coast for it, and now she was ready to take up where he'd left off. But this time, the protests of ART and the terrorism of AR2 wouldn't be left divided. This time, Agnes was going to use them as a whole in bringing full out war to the Magisterium.

Cecil Greenough

Grand Magistrate: The Biography of Kiril Pordan

Born the second child of ART's premiere representative, Agnes is a young woman reared in the idealism of liberty. The Flag—its red, white, and blue, are not but mere colors to her, but a sign of glory, honor, and grace. And like so many others, she still believes in those colors, and burns every time she sees the Magisterium banner flanked atop the White House. A black eagle clinching eleven rings symbolizing the Republic's marriage to the Magisterium, and draped across a blood red background, it is but one thing that enduringly affronts Agnes' *Old Glory*.

The Magisterium has begun to emerge as the face of the United States, and that is an offense the young leader will not stand for. She begins by appealing to those willing to listen to her proposal. A conspiracy to restore the U.S. Constitution, Agnes' plan calls for even more sacrifice. It will see much blood, but she promises freedom will be its solace. The end of the Magisterium, and the resurgence of the United States of America, it is a gamble Agnes is willing to take. If it calls for her life, she will freely do so, and expects the same from everyone else.

A decision that will undoubtedly be put to the test, and a fight that will split the nation in half even further, Agnes Walsh will take back the *Land of the Free,* or die trying.

She calls for a meeting between the leaders of ART and AR2, men and women that have taken it upon themselves to lead a revolt the best way they see how. Outcasts that have taken the road of enslavement, peddling drugs to those in need of their escape as a means of living, assemblies that have turned toward pressing the rebellion through violent means, with blood and fire paying tribute to their vices, factions that make it their duty to transmit images of the Magisterium and their fascist ways, gatherings which wastes hours upon hours arguing over the best route to take, and lastly, the fanatics who simply enjoy watching the world burn, it is these splintered companies Agnes wishes to draw to her cause, offering them purpose.

Her call to arms is in the methodology of the Founding Fathers, and on August 25, finds over 100,000 people have turned out to hear her plea. They meet in the rundown, freezing, backstreets of Charlotte, North Carolina, and Agnes catches the attention of her audience by proposing a plan challenging each and every one of them.

It is a proposal to put aside their petty differences, their broken doctrines, their meaningless attacks. Agnes walks in the footsteps of her father, and knows ART must challenge the might of the Magisterium with an equally as dominant *modus operandi*. The dream that was once America can be reignited and returned to its place of glory, but the Magisterium must first fall, and only then will the flame of Democracy be rekindled— only then will the United States ever truly be free.

Welcome everybody. I've called you all out here tonight to plead with you as a fellow citizen and a patriot. Each and everyone of you forged in the fires of sacrifice and courage, blood and tears, I'm talking to you. Not for a piece of land, but for the beating heart of a dream. A dream that was given birth by people who refused to be told what to do— people who believed a person's freedom was their God given right, and not one to be dictated to by oppression and murder. Men and women who stood in the face of tyranny, and dared to defy it. Those who paved a way of living for each and every one of us to follow as an example. That dream gave us ideals, beliefs, and aspirations we weren't ever meant to surrender, a call for liberty we weren't ever supposed to reject. It's a dream I believe lives in the souls of every person calling themselves an American. I'm talking about Democracy. That dream which has been the foundation of our great country for the past two hundred and sixty-two years. A principle that calls for every person to live free of subjugation and fear. An assurance that calls for the world to lay the hungry and burden at its feet, so that they may one day be able to stand strong amidst its glory. I'm talking to you about Democracy, that dream our forefathers bled for in Valley Forge, Gettysburg, Normandy, Baghdad, and Shenyang. Democracy, that which made us the greatest country to have ever been born on the face of this planet. We're a people Modded by this dream, and it's our duty to protect its institution. Now when we, like our forefathers, stand before that dream's peril, it falls upon our shoulders to safeguard its existence. ARTists. Children of AR2. Americans. The time's come to defend our country. We have to look past her pitfalls, past her wreckage, and past her present state. Now is the time to stare into the eyes of a Feeb that has dared to sit upon her throne of justice, and smack him down from her seat. Together, you bureaucrats, you citizens, you rebels, and you Narnists can rise and meet this challenge head on. But apart, you will…We will all surely fall. So, you can either choose to squabble amongst yourselves, live in sewers, hide in hills, and suffer like animals, or you can fight and be that which you were meant to be—Americans. Remember, this is the Land of the Free and the Home of the Brave, and I find neither in my enemy, and neither should you. Together, and only together, we can return this land to its rightful station, and once more stand firm in its designation as One Nation Under God. Arise ARTists. Arise AR2. Arise Americans. And let us show this Magisterium a true revolt.

Agnes Walsh
Charlotte, North Carolina Gathering, August 25, 2038

The heartfelt call to arms is heard by the gathering, and unanimously supported by all in attendance. That night, Agnes draws thousands to her goal, and prepares to launch a massive campaign southward in order to bring more to her cause.

She is all but aware that if she attacks the Magisterium now, the chances of her making the slightest difference will be null. A mistake the young ARTist leader refuses to make, she instead takes her new band of fighters, and marches them into South Carolina, Georgia, Alabama, Florida, Mississippi, and Louisiana, preaching her brand of revolution to any and all who will listen to her.

It is a crusade without rest or charm, but one that speaks to the souls of those yearning for the past. And to those who heed the declarations of Agnes Walsh, the Magisterium is portrayed as an evil empire destined to fall by the hands of Democracy. A foretold destiny which fuels the revolution, Agnes' vision gives her fighters the strength and desire they need in order to see its ratification. As expected, however, this democratic rallying cry does not flourish without its challenges.

The States that are not part of the Magisterium suffer much. There is little to no electricity. Gasoline has not been shipped to the outer territories in years. Small towns once seen gracing the faces of postcards are now defended by armed militias struggling to keep some normality amongst them. And to much dismay, once learning of Agnes' declaration, military facilities now try seizing territories in the name of a Magisterium they share little to no contact with.

These military bases are peppered throughout the South, and stand as exiled subjects to an extreme governing, but they are loyal to this director nonetheless. Agnes must first go through them if she expects to build an army out of their people, and then she will deal with the citizens. That is something that is easier said than done, however.

How many people did Agnes Walsh have with her? 70,000? 100,000 at best? That was definitely not enough for her to engage the fractured military of the South with. Even though they weren't officially part of the Magisterium, they were still the military. They had guns, and they had soldiers—lots of them. Sure, they hardly had gasoline, and they damn sure didn't have any fancy electric batteries to use in their tanks. And yes, this created a sense of an even playing field for the rebellion. Still, that didn't mean that if Agnes planned on taking them on she wasn't going to need a plan, and a damn good one at that. Luckily, she did. She knew she couldn't just attack the military head-on, so she did the next best thing. She attacked them when they were least expecting it. Forgive me for using this old term, but she sucker punched them. And as my dad used to say "sucker punches were made for suckers".

Cecil Greenough

Grand Magistrate: The Biography of Kiril Pordan

Agnes' first obstacle is Fort Bragg. A military institution housing close to 11,000 soldiers, she must first defeat them if she is to spark her revolution into existence. So against her better judgment, she knows of only one weapon she possesses that is up to the task of weakening this hurdle. They are the ones who see death as a privilege, those who wish to see the world burn, those whose rage overruns their logic. They are the children of AR2, and chaos is their discipline. Something those at Fort Bragg do not expect, they strike without warning.

September 17, three hundred AR2 members are given the command to begin disrupting Fort Bragg's operations. The swarm approaches from the northwest of North Carolina, and paralyzes the municipality city of Fayetteville through bombings and all out attacks. Innocent civilians are either killed, or taken hostage by the group, while sophisticated improvised explosive devices destroy structures throughout the city's populated metro areas.

AR2 then floods Highway 24, forcing Fort Bragg to deploy defense forces in retaliation. The anarchists are prepared for this, and plant their members amongst those who will eventually be rescued by the military. Others, meanwhile, stand prepared to engage to the death, with the approach of Fort Bragg's seasoned veterans being more than obliged to give them such.

The military makes short work of the AR2 members, but loses numbers of their own units to roadside bombings and suicide brigades. The anarchists are very cunning in their attacks, and try weakening the military response before one bullet can be fired. But the military recuperates soon enough, and lays siege on the municipality.

A full-blown war to say the least, the military finds itself engaged in a heated battle for days, though this does not stop them from taking scores of injured civilians back to Fort Bragg for medical attention, while removing those who have fallen from the streets. Albeit, amidst those innocents wounded without cause or wrongdoing, sit anarchists patiently waiting for their moment to strike, and they do not have to wait long. The moment calm is returned to the city, and the military stands triumphant, a second wave of attacks befall Fayetteville.

Again, a horde of anarchists descend on the city, blowing themselves up amongst the military regiments just recently having gained control. Suicide bombers engaging without prejudice, they kill all soldiers in attendance, sullying the streets of Fayetteville with mutilated bodies of military and rebel. This horrendous act, in turn, leaves heavy artillery and armored vehicles unmanned throughout the municipality, up until Agnes and her units disembark on the ravaged city.

Seizing the firepower they need, the ARTists cross Highway 24 in an all out attack. Fort Bragg is all too prepared to defend itself, but their Achilles heel leaves them vulnerable. The AR2 members outfitted with concealed explosives have been brought to the base, and detonate all through the institution, raining chaos and disorder down upon the soldiers stationed there. All the distraction Agnes needs, on September 23, she and her units are allowed to launch an attack on a massive scale, granting them the unthinkable—control over Fort Bragg.

Army commanders and soldiers are placed under arrest, while a small number pledge their loyalties to ART's entreaty. Those detained are locked away in barracks, with their judgments to be left in the hands of those they have wronged—the people of North Carolina. And it is now that Agnes reveals her plans for the cities she makes free of Magisterium hold.

First she empties Fort Bragg of its arsenal, vehicles, and technologies, and then she offers the people of the city a place amongst the revolution. To those who accept her invitation, a life of war and death is what is rewarded, while those who remain do so as free men and women. The choice is theirs if they desire to make good on their freedom, or simply permit the dwindling military to return as lords over them. A decision that splits families and friends, freedom is unanimously chosen by all. And in the end, a considerable number opt the defense of their homeland with their lives, while others stay behind to protect their homes and territories.

North Carolina is the first of these rogue States. But within months, Agnes Walsh's battle cry is being heeded by scores of citizens all across the Midwest. Each of these rebel groups then begin enacting their own forms of resistance against the segregated military installations of the Magisterium, defiantly challenging the empire's planned encroachment.

Factions such as *The Defenders, The First Patriots, The Good Ol' Boys,* and the names of Xander Brown, Frank Lord, and Olivia Warner all contribute to the fight for liberty, turning ART into a formidable opposition—an opposition Agnes wages the Magisterium is resolute in defeating.

The rebel leader is correct in her assumption. By late Spring of 2039, word reaches the Magisterium of its so-called lost footholds. Distressing reports that dare to make threats against the Magisterium of the United Republic, the leaders there meet in endless sessions in the nation's capital to discuss their ultimatums.

They know they must act without clemency, crushing this insurrection, or face a growing threat that will soon overpower them. It is not a difficult decision to make, and High Magistrate George Hartsoe wastes no time in giving the order.

Charging Agnes Walsh and all others of her party with the high crime of treason, including those who would use their cities as safe havens for such turncoats, Hartsoe authorizes the all out usage of military force to defend the Magisterium. Naval fleets, fighter jets, and finally, soldiers bred to defend the Magisterium and the Republic, those whose desires are to crush the insurgency in all its forms, this show of military dominance plunges America into a civil war unlike ever before. And in conclusion, will leave the South set ablaze.

By June 14, the rogue States of North and South Carolina, Georgia, and Alabama, are all bombarded with missiles and rockets, shells and gunfire, reducing them to nothing but rubble. Thousands of people are killed, others maimed, but most are forced to flee burning cities in place of losing their lives.

Florida quickly becomes an overcrowded haven for refugees, but even it cannot suppress the horror unfolded on the victims. The South Eastern seaport is in flames, and a dark cloud of scorched earth and flesh lingers high above as a reminder of the consequences of challenging the Magisterium.

Agnes learns of the attacks just as she finds victory in Arkansas and Missouri, and accordingly alters her message from one of recruitment to one of endurance. She is aware of how the attacks on the South can jeopardize ART's agenda, but refuses to halt her petition of rebellion. So it is now that ART's adage of *"One can not live free if told how"* is truly put the test, and Agnes intends on proving its verity by launching a massive offensive against the United Republic of America itself.

She must first rally her troops to one location, and from there, march into the Magisterium Republics in order to put her plan in motion. She chooses Tennessee as her Central Command, and on August 3, commences with her attack on the Republic of Virginia.

She and her rebels enter with assurance of their impending success, killing scores of Loyalists as they penetrate further into the scarcely guarded tip of the Republic, but quickly learn just how ignorant they are of their enemy's new methods. Methods that have turned away from the days of the Army, Navy, Air Force, and Marines, the soldiers they encounter in Richmond are no longer the troops of days past, defenders of civilians and Democracy. No, the US Armed Forces are now the *Magisterium Dominion*.

They are the VEDETTE, warriors who have pledged their allegiance to the institution of Autocracy. A breed of soldiers who oppose Agnes' dream, they not only crush it and all its believers once deployed, they obliterate its very concept.

With Factories operating up and down the Republic, and millions upon millions working hard around the clock, weapons, body armor, vehicles, and aircraft were produced seemingly overnight. There were over 47 million VEDETTE ready to fight, and they'd all been made into killing machines. They were armored. They were heavily armed. And they all served the Magisterium without question. Now, some people would say that they'd sold their souls for 63,000 credits a year, and still some would say that they were just scared. But with the ferociousness with which they engaged Agnes and her ARTists, one has to question whether they were just doing their duty.

Cecil Greenough

Grand Magistrate: The Biography of Kiril Pordan

They looked like automatons from Hell, if you ask me. I've seen the uniforms, and they must have frightened anyone who encountered them. Especially if they were coming to kill you. The VEDETTE were like no other military in history. Their faces were hidden. They had these large red lenses that burned red in the dark—imagine thousands of those charging at you, not to mention the design of their armored uniforms contrasting against the snow. These hulking shells of all black, with an array of guns, knives, and compartments all over them. They really resembled the idea of the Magisterium being an Autocracized military state. And not only were they embodiments of this cause, they were its dominion. Agnes Walsh and her band of freedom fighters had lost their fight before it had even really begun.

Prof. Tamara Boggier

keeper, New York Republic Athenaeum

A 21st Century reporter named Armand Figueroa once said *"the blood which flowed in Richmond stained the concrete of the city so deeply, that to have looked upon its streets would have been to stare into an ocean of crimson"*.

No one is to ever truly know whether or not that is in fact the case. Richmond, Virginia, is eventually abandoned by all Loyalists, allowing the Magisterium to enact its final display of ruthlessness. An act with which the Magisterium solidifies its standing as the governing power of the United Republic, it also serves as a warning to all who dare consider challenging its authority.

The GBU-43/B Massive Ordnance Air Blast bomb (MOAB) is a weapon with the detonation radius of over four hundred and fifty feet, as well as, a shock wave capable of annihilating half a dozen city blocks. This is the bomb the Magisterium lets loose on one of its own Republics, not only making clear its stance in defending its establishment, but also its cruelty. Three hundred in all, the bombs destroy over thirty miles of the city, leaving absolutely nothing but devastation in their wake.

The attack leaves Richmond, Virginia burning for all to see. A pyre alight with raging flames, the 10th State of the former Union is thoroughly destroyed. And though Loyalists of other Republics remain silent out of fear and loyalty, the people of the Midwest learn of such a harsh response, and refuse to ignore it. They know in their hearts God would not want them to.

Agnes Walsh and her fighters are all killed, but her dream is only beginning. For in the aftermath of such destruction, a new voice has heeded her call, and his name is Jake Stockwell.

A man of small means, he is about to do the impossible. He will be the one to look into the eyes of the Magisterium, matching its stare with ferocity and passion. And when all is said and done, Stockwell would not have only taken up Agnes Walsh's station, he will ultimately bring about an army hellbent on victory.

The Magisterium will be tested, after all. And Jake Stockwell will be the one to do it.

2040
UNION OF NATIONS

The Great Divide: a concise history of the future

I pledge allegiance to my flag and the Republic for which it stands, one nation indivisible, with liberty and justice for all.

The American Pledge of Allegiance, 1892

Never before has this oath meant more when uttered. To those who recite it, it is priceless. They are the downtrodden, and the brave. The innocent, and guilty. The patriot, and the anarchist. They are small factions, and deadly battalions—former businessmen, contractors, farmers, and above all, children. They are the people of the Midwest.

The Good Ol' Boys of Indiana who subdued Camp Atterbury—they stand ready to defend the State with their lives. *The Defenders* of the *Wolverine State* —they are the ones who wrestled Detroit from out of the hands of Fort Custer, and they are prepared to do it again. Lastly, *The Patriots* of Ohio— those Americans who look across their dominion, *The Heart of it All,* and see the doorway into the Midwest. They are the first who will be tried by the Magisterium of the United Republic—tried, and found guilty.

Their enemy is fortified behind Kevlar-webbed armored uniforms, gas masks complete with a corrugated proboscis, steel reinforced PASGT helmets, harnessed GAU-19/E Gatling guns, tanks, jets, and enough fire power to level State after State. They are the Magisterium VEDETTE. A dreadful swarm of black and red, they leave nothing in their wake but death and destruction.

Rebels are massacred. Cities are brought to ruin. Americans are cataloged. Possibly history's most unstoppable military force, the citizens of the Midwest dare to do battle against these VEDETTE in Ohio, Michigan, and Indiana. And with nights that gleam red with fire, the rebels find each battle a struggle to maintain their way of life.

Buildings are set fire to, and people are murdered in the middle of streets. The snow blanketing the earth is made to turn scarlet with the blood that flows from such conflicts, not that it maters. With the future of the country remaining the prize, it is the duty of every man, woman, and child desiring a United States to risk it all.

They have no choice but to defend these territories from the Magisterium. And a preacher turned soldier has taken it upon himself to lead them. Jake Stockwell is his name, and he has seen enough death amongst his family and friends to know what must be done.

During this time, the world was caught in a freezing winter. People were cold, they were starving, and they were sick. And to top it all off, they were being asked to reject the only thing that could save them, and that was the Interim Credit Encode. What would you have done? The ICE-chip permitted you to eat. It gave you a roof over your head, clothes on your back, shoes on your feet. You'd be back to living a normal life, instead of living like an animal. Or worse, joining the rebellion, and getting yourself and your entire family killed. You can understand why ART and AR2 began to find a dismal end to their revolt. Then along comes Jake Stockwell, the reverend turned rebel, and everything starts to change.

Cecil Greenough

Grand Magistrate: The Biography of Kiril Pordan

Once a man of the cloth sermonizing the Coming of the Lord, Stockwell now stands for vengeance and freedom. Once urging his flock to remain diligent in the Gospels, he now believes only humanity can save itself. He has been waiting for over ten years for God to show, and all he has seen is the ongoing suffering of those nearest to him. Stockwell knows no end but one of utter destruction, and now urges his followers to take as many Loyalists with them as they can before dying. The former preacher lost his family to the wrath of the Magisterium, and in rage, abandons his Heavenly mission. The days of redemption are over; all that remains is retribution—retribution Jake Stockwell more than proudly plays herald to.

Crops are low. Food shortages plague city after city. Power can barely be supplied for warmth. And a major skirmish has recently engulfed the city of Chattanooga, Tennessee—the very home of Jake Stockwell, the reason he intends on bringing Hell to those he holds guilty.

The resistance has been without a leader for nearly two years. Acting blindly, and without direction or hope, the old ways of terrorism have been revisited. AR2 has done more harm to its kind than good. Fire burns in their stir, while blood stains their agenda at every turn. And though a call of restraint has been heard from amongst ARTists and everyday civilians, AR2's brand of belligerence harms the heartland more than the Magsiterium ever has.

With an ever emerging intrusion being committed, AR2 believes it their duty to halt such advances. Unfortunately, these children know nothing of strategic engagements, and without regard, use their violent methods of suicide bombings in order to make a difference. Their marker of carnage has injured countless of those they claim to be defending. Bloodbaths taking place on a massive scale, it soon becomes harder for the resistance to make clear their true enemy.

Citizens of the remaining United States wanted nothing more than for peace to be found. And though they'd been fighting a war, somewhere in their hearts, they still believed that a compromise could be established through dialogue. But AR2 refused to go along with those plans. The fighters and anarchists of that group wanted absolutely nothing to do with the Magisterium, or its way of governing, and they made that clear with their constant attacks. So when killing innocent people with their recklessness, they obviously started threatening any sort of bond they had between them and ART, or the unaligned civilians of the Midwest for that matter.

Prof. Tamara Boggier

keeper, New York Republic Athenaeum

This is the sort of thing Jake Stockwell, and so many others hope to stop. And like Olivia Warner who has lost her entire family, and charges her army day and night to fight with all they have, Xander Brown, a former Marine Sergeant who risks life and limb to protect those he has sworn to, and the late Frank Lord, who refused to become a terrorist, and died in heated battle over Columbus, Ohio, the former reverend understands the concerns of his peers, but also accepts the fact that AR2 has their part to play in the struggle for Democracy.

To Stockwell, the anarchists are as much a necessity as each and every other American, and he refuses to quell their hatred for the Magisterium. Regrettably, the resistance of AR2 has no headship, and combats conflicts it has no chances of winning. This leaves Stockwell to conclude that he will be their newfound savior, in turn, forging them into a true resistance.

He assures the anarchists they may continue with their suicide bombings. He gives them permission to run wild, and applauds their brutal tactics. He does not judge them, but simply asks they target only the Magisterium. He will not tell them not to embrace carnage, but pleads to give such terror a purpose. Stockwell makes it clear that Democracy is that purpose.

Months pass, and soon enough, he finds unfathomable compliance from those abandoned by the rebellion. But he promises to salvage them, and dares to engage the momentum of the Magisterium alongside those willing to put aside their differences. A move that, though brave and heroic, still finds the rebels being crushed on every front.

The weapons confiscated from seized military installations appear primitive compared to the advanced weaponry now handled by the Magisterium. Again and again, battles prove the rebellion in all its forms no match against the dominating power of the VEDETTE. F/A 18 Super

Hornets and EA-18 Growlers that are made ineffectual against sixth-generation F-Xs. M1A1 and M1A2 tanks falling prey to advanced PL-01 at every turn. Clearly, the Magisterium cannot be stopped if ART and AR2 do not alter their means of attack—yet another complication Jake Stockwell intends on overcoming.

The rebellion had been fighting a losing battle. They pulled out rocks, the Magisterium pulled out clubs. They drew swords, the Magisterium retaliated with guns. They launched missiles, the Magisterium dropped MOABs. There was nothing the rebellion could do to stop the Magisterium push, nothing except get the people of the Midwest to join them in the struggle. Because no matter how many soldiers the Republic would've been able to muster, they would've never outnumbered the average civilian. But then again, the question became how do you get the average civilian to fight on the side of anarchists? That was something Jake Stockwell and the other leaders of the Midwest had to figure out, and soon. More so Stockwell, really. After all, he was the one everybody was looking to for answers at this point.

Cecil Greenough

Grand Magistrate: The Biography of Kiril Pordan

A populace without military training, these farmers, these civilians, these everyday Americans of the Midwest, they are the ones who stand as prize for those who will win in the end. And to have them side with the resistance's dream means an army the Magisterium will be inadequate against, while their acceptance of such regime's route will only mean the end to the United States. These are the common people Jake Stockwell needs to win over, something that proves to be as difficult as winning back Democracy itself.

Ultimately, the rebel leader only has two options: the mandatory persuasion of all who hear him, or the end of the American dream. So, whether it takes coercion, petitioning, or death, the former reverend will have their loyalty instead of having them turning against him.

Jake Stockwell sees a future with the return of the United States, and all who disagree with him are made the enemy. It is only now that Stockwell begins to prove his worth as a true leader, with his exploits soon to become things of legend. But before such feats can commence, the rebel leader must first separate the civilian from the soldier, the killer from the innocent, and the weak from the strong. A similar selection process seen in the Republic, things there are not so disarrayed. In point of fact, the United Republic flourishes beyond scope, and now a momentous proposal is being enacted in proving such glory.

Considering the long isolation of the United Republic something of a drawback to future aspirations, High Magistrate Hartsoe begins preliminary dialogues with other nation leaders. The best means for such discussions is the information highway of the internet. A tool that has been used for everything from the exchanges of current events to the fueling of rebellion, the internet serves its purpose in opening talks between regimes.

In no time, encrypted messages begin flourishing throughout the globe regarding the next steps toward a unified planet, with Monarch Edward Davies of the Royal European Alliance being the first to answer the United Republic's call.

America was finally ready to open its borders again, and that was, understandably, welcomed by the Royal European Alliance. These past years, the world only had Prometheus Flame to access bulletins from across the world, and those reports were nothing more than biased filled dribble, if you ask me. I believe Monarch Davies had been anticipating this moment for quite sometime. After all, the Americans were his allies once, and to have their support once more could only mean one thing, the European power was no longer going to be alone in the world. Sure, during all this time, the Royal European Alliance had been in contact with the State of Israel and Islamic Peoples Republic, but that in no way equaled the shared power it would find with the United Republic. So now that the West was ready to once more open its borders, the REA was more than obliging in forging a joint union.

Prof. Jarvis Grimes

historian, *Superior and Biased: The History of the Royal European Alliance*

The regimes discuss the troubles facing their countries, and come to discover their predicaments are quite similar. As it is revealed, the Royal European Alliance has been facing a relentless struggle against a rebellion calling itself the Grimaldi Defiance. A group born out of opposition to Article 412 of the past, the Grimaldi Defiance has been persistent in its call to bring down the REA and its leaders. Violently attacking any and all who stand for the current establishment, they plague the Alliance with terror and death.

While in the Middle East, though the nation of Israel has been allowed to remain both independent and peaceful due to its surrendering of a ravaged Jerusalem to the Islamic People's Republic, a growing discord between the Mu'minūn and Muslims has seen the deaths of over 25,000 people due to a fueling argument between those two governments.

Due to the fact of violent skirmishes taking place between the two factions, Mu'minūn have been refused access into Mecca to perform the rites of Hajj. The primary article that had been agreed upon by both sides in facilitating the Islamic partition, the Muslims justify their decision by claiming it an effort in keeping peace in the area. But true to form, such refusals have been met with nothing but ongoing bloodshed, forcing the Afro Islamic Union to retaliate with warnings of all out war.

It is a reoccurring theme being witnessed throughout most of the developed nations, but one the leaders of the world trust they can resolve. Although, before any such resolutions can come to pass, the dedicated people of their countries must first see unification amongst the lands. This calls for a cohesive countries council to be reestablished. A place where the leaders of the world could convene for the betterment of the globe, such a congregation needs to function for the betterment all mankind, finally allowing for the Earth to begin with its much needed healing.

A thought desired by all involved, the United Republic of America, Royal European Alliance, the State of Israel, and Islamic People's Republic agree to the proposal of a new league of nations, and advocate it to the world.

A new coalition that will not be one of hearsay and seclusion, sanctions and elitists, agitators and lunatics, this Union of Nations will serve as a platform toward world peace and absolute strength, solidifying the new order of things. A symbol of mankind's quest to be exalted, it is to be conducted by logic and power.

Therefore, it comes to pass that after eleven years, from out of John F. Kennedy Airport in New York City, on March 7, 2040, the first flight from out of the United Republic is taken to Europe in preparation for this new council of united nations. A takeoff televised for all of the United Republic to see, the international flight is hailed as a glorious triumph.

Over thirty Councilmen and four Vice Magistrates are dispatched to the REA as representatives of the United Republic during this historic occasion. The Republic has been, at last, reconnected to the rest of the world. Even High Magistrate George Hartsoe is present for the momentous juncture, delivering a speech of affirmation to both the Loyalists and rebels.

He speaks of victory, he speaks of hope, and he speaks of power. He verifies the Magisterium as being invincible, and talks about a future in which the world will follow in its footsteps. He even proposes the Interim Credit Encode as the financial solution for all, and boastfully speaks of America's might. And with such powerful words resonating in the hearts of his Loyalists, it does in fact look as if the Magisterium has made good on its promises of success—but looks can be deceiving.

3:24 p.m., moments after the celebrated undertaking of the first international flight in over a decade, High Magistrate Hartsoe's convoy is ruthlessly attacked by suicide bombers, killing him and all those of his company with one vicious strike.

AR2 had struck again, but this time it was something that rattled the entire Magisterium. George Hartsoe had been assassinated. It had only been four years, and already the Magisterium was facing its darkest hour. George Hartsoe was more than just a leader, he was the father of Autocracy, and now he was dead. It was a dark time. But for the resistance, this was the win they needed, the thing that could truly spark them back to life.

Cecil Greenough

Grand Magistrate: The Biography of Kiril Pordan

The attack is humiliating for the Magisterium, as well as, a moment of horror for the world. After four years in power, George Hartsoe is dead.

The mighty Magisterium is without a leader. The Republic is shaken to its core. Even further proof of the regime's continued quandary, the High Magistrate's death is a sure victory for the resistance.

Loyalists and Magisterium affiliates mourn the loss of their beloved High Magistrate, but Jake Stockwell and his band of AR2, Olivia Warner and her *Defenders*, Xander Brown and *The Good Ol' Boys*, and of course, *The Patriots,* a band of brothers who have fully given command to Stockwell, all rejoice in their successful assassination.

To the rebels, this is a sign of weakness amongst the regime, one which leads them to believe that they can, in fact, defeat its Autocratic supremacy. And though it is only a small victory, the assassination of George Hartsoe is enough for Jake Stockwell to begin recruiting even more people to his cause. At last, the rebel leader can finally begin depicting the rebels as a formidable force against the said way of things, while preaching the end of Magisterium rule.

The Prometheus Flame transmits the call for a new army. A decree which will win back the Democracy long thought lost in America, the rebels with a voice call on their brothers and sisters to join Stockwell's fight. And as hoped, thousands upon thousands rally behind him in Iowa, Missouri, Kansas, Nebraska, North and South Dakota, and Minnesota.

An inundation of Democracy coveting souls the likes Agnes Walsh would have been proud of, it is one Jake Stockwell will ultimately need. For as the newly forming Resistance celebrates its momentary victory with cheers and augmentation, the Magisterium prepares for an ultimate counterattack that will put an end to such insolence.

The untimely death of High Magistrate George Hartsoe has left the established government feeling vulnerable and angry. They speak of vengeance and bloodshed, and soon ignite a newfound strength within themselves. Their beloved leader's death will not go unpunished, but they must first reestablish themselves as the ultimate power of the United Republic, that which calls for a new leader. This time, however, the new leader must be willing to do what it takes in order to crush the opposition. And unlike George Hartsoe who tried so kindly to draw new Loyalists every day, this leader must realize all those not of the Republic must be eliminated.

Only one man can satisfy this new standard. He is Kiril Gustav Pordan. And with a unanimous vote from all of the United Republic, he is made II High Magistrate of the Magisterium.

Kiril Gustav Pordan. Now there's a name that will forever live in history. What can be said about him? He was a soldier. He was callus. He believed in the uncompromising protection of the United Republic, and he'd kill anyone that tried standing in his way. In the end, let's not forget that he was also the author of the Magisterium Edict. Just because George Hartsoe had been the face and leader of the country, that didn't mean Pordan hadn't always been making power moves of his own. It's just that now that he'd been elected II High Magistrate, he was about to show what he'd really been made of. And it was with this goal in mind do we begin to see a drastic change in Magisterium engagement and law.

Cecil Greenough

Grand Magistrate: The Biography of Kiril Pordan

Kiril Pordan refuses to see the death of his dearly beloved Magisterium, and will stop at nothing to protect it. Thus, proudly taking the Oath of Edict on April 10, Pordan declares all those not cataloged, *persona non grata.* He demands their annihilation. He swears the knees of those who will not bend will be broken. And in due course, makes this the pledge he intends to see transpire.

The Resistance, those of the once famous ART Party, *The Good Ol' Boys, Liberty's Heirs,* AR2, and the like, they have never encountered a man like him. Kiril Pordan was born to be High Magistrate, and soon everyone will learn why. However, Pordan must first gain the full trust of the Republic, and that calls for drastic measures.

The II High Magistrate can hear the demands for retribution, and understands that it rests on his shoulders to answer. He was chosen for a reason. As the author of the creed everyone living within the United Republic has taken, the vow of allegiance every mouth has spoken, it is up to him to make good of its promises. That calls for the heads of those responsible for George Hartsoe's death, and Kiril Pordan is about to define himself.

Returning to the critical task of forging the Union of Nations, he first makes sure to dedicate the greatest strategists of the Magisterium to its cause. Pordan refuses to allow the Resistance to halt the advent of such an important design. He refuses to cower in fear of their barbarism. And just as the Union of Nations will come to pass, America will finally behold her standing as world leader revisited.

Pordan knows the Royal European Alliance needs her advancements and weaponry in order to crush the Grimaldi Defiance. He is aware of the support and technologies the Islamic People's Republic needs in order to step into the future. And he is also aware Japan's Asiatic Empire is all but isolated, and finds itself overwhelmed in an effort to be seen as the leader of the Orient. After all, with most Asian countries refusing the island nation's invitation to draw beneath one banner, Pordan expects the Japanese will soon come to appreciate the United Republic's offered aid to quell such undesired repudiation.

The II High Magistrate is dedicated to strengthening the Magisterium, with the splendor of the Republic as its fruit. The Loyalists of the land will be ushered into a new age of prosperity. Possibilities that were only before imagined, incomparability only before supposed, a day long sought by all, his loyal subordinates will see the rise of their intellect, the betterment of their health, and the ascendancy of their faith. Pordan will give them this, or his Magisterium will cease to exist.

The II High Magisterate swears to purge the nation of all who dare challenge the new order. Brown. Piper. Hunt. Warner. Knitter. And above all others, Jake Stockwell. These are the names that haunt Pordan's plan for his people—the names of rebellion—the names of anarchy. The names that must burn in order for his dream to come true.

On a late Wednesday afternoon, with frigid rain falling from a tumultuous heaven, Pordan sounds a blaring call all across the Magisterium, demanding the Admirals and Generals of the VEDETTE come before him. What transpires next is an address of ruthlessness and domination—a call to rise. It takes place in Washington D.C., with the National Mall in the nation's capital blanketed by 1.3 million Councilmen. And gracing the steps of the Capitol Building are the Vice Magistrates of the Magisterium, all this in respect of High Magistrate George Hartsoe's funeral, an occasion the Magisterium wants rectified.

The fallen High Magistrate has his onyx coffin carted though the streets, mournfully escorted by his three sons and two daughters. A sight that brings much sorrow upon the United Republic, it likewise sears a burning need for revenge with its transpiring. Even the mournful strings of Richard Wagner's *Siegfried's Funeral March* cannot quell the desire for retaliation. A hate Kiril Pordan fully understands, he uses the sight of the slain leader to speak into the hearts of all those hearing him.

Draped in the still banner of the Magisterium, George Hartsoe's casket comes to rest directly before Pordan's feet. But believing his people need a true sign of his leadership, the II High Magistrate decides to join his fellow Loyalists on the ground level of the Capitol Building, displaying his unity with each and every one of them.

His words are eloquent and lengthy. His verses, strict and direct. His warnings, boastful and assured. He speaks to not only the millions upon millions of VEDETTE awaiting his command, but to all those maintaining loyalty to the Republic. It is to them he makes a solemn vow, one he swears by the mighty one true God. They will have their revenge. They will have their justice. In the face of disbelievers who would seek to destroy this God ordained guidance, they will enact a holy war the likes of Scripture.

Kiril Pordan knows his birthright, and it is to lay siege on those threatening the United Republic. God has called him forth to smite the infidels fighting against the American dream, and he will do so with much wrath.

In the name of God, the Beneficent, and the Most Merciful. I come before you in humbleness and vehemence. You who are without fault, and scorn injustice. You who look toward the sky, and seek that which is good and right. You who value life, and speak only words of support and advancement. I come before you in homage and in ire. There is a dark presence off to our horizon, a wicked doctrine that spews venom into the hearts of those who know no better. It's a deadly poison that flows from within the deceitful fangs of vipers who would seek to destroy this country, and scorpions that stab with insanity and belligerence. They're a vile disease, these Good Ol' Boys, these so-called Defenders, these ARTists...these rats. They're a cancer that, if left unchecked, will contaminate each and every one of you. This is a malice which I present, a sinister breed spawned out of ignorance and chaos. They strike like demons, and flee like cowards. Those who have no care for the soul, and commit suicide in the sight of God. Those who would kill a defenseless mother and innocent child, only to dare and protest over inequality. Of what stench have they filled their nostrils that they would voluntarily cast their souls into the depths of Hell with such abominable acts? Amongst what filth have they laid that their minds could become so corrupted and twisted? I know the answer to such riddles, and it's called Democracy. A failed and useless banter with which the world has come to see a Great Divide. It's a living testimony to the outright disobedience to God, as it has born nothing but immoralities and transgressions in its crusade. And this is what this rebellion necessitates? This fraudulent offer of freedom? What good did it serve us? What glories did it ensue upon us? None, I say. For this country was not founded on Democracy, but on God—His divine will and merciful guidance. His commands and words. His greatness and protection. I tell you now that there's no man-made ordinance that parallels His decrees, and for far too long have we believed otherwise. And it's this sinful way of thinking which you behold in the Midwest, that which dares enters our sanctuary, and commits such atrocious acts as the one which has taken the life of my predecessor. Well, no more! No more, I say! No more shall we sit by, and allow this insult to God to continue. No more shall we ignore the dominion handed to us by His glorious hand. And no more shall we allow this godless beast to infiltrate our sanctum, just so it can spitefully hinder the opportunities given us by our Lord. No more! So, it's to you, the brave men and women of the VEDETTE that I say the time has come for a Purification Schema. A retribution that will usher in peace. God has made clear His judgment, and we shall obey. No mercy. No opinion. No matter. This heart is what I ask of you all when sending you into the Midwest, a walk ordained for each and every one of you by destiny itself. They will convert, or they will die. Kill them. Slaughter them. Tear them apart, for they are not Americans. Allow not one to remain if he doesn't bend, and only then shall you have your reward. I have said it, now let it begin. And may God have mercy on their souls, for we will not.

II High Magistrate Kiril Gustav Pordan
The Induction of the Purification Schema, July 4, 2040

Praise swells through the abundant crowd like a surging wave. Hearts pound in chests, while voices bellow a sound of renewed strength. Tears flow from the eyes of those watching their defense marching westward, already knowing peace will soon be seized. The Loyalists, as well as, the Magisterium place their future in the hands of their military, and will soon be rewarded for their well-placed confidence.

The ones who will lead the war are General Matthew Storm, and Admirals Patrick Hauser and Aaron Balthazar of the VEDETTE. Three men who have dedicated their lives to the rise of the Magisterium, they will callously tread on any and all that dare stand in the way of its victory. And upon their influx into Ohio, their mercilessness is made known to all.

With an authority reinforced by 320,000 VEDETTE, dozens of aerial fighters, hundreds of tanks, and a fleet of bombers, the General and his Admirals appear on the horizon, and launch their attacks.

First bombers soar through the air, with carpet bombings laying siege to Ohio's cities and populace. Like a downpour of flames, the bombs destroy Cleveland, and topple its structures beneath fire and brimstone. People are incinerated in the blaze, while buildings, cars, houses, and farmlands are reduced to nothing but ashes. The lamentations of those who suffer perform for all to hear, but it is a cry that is silenced by the VEDETTE that follow such destruction.

The armored combatants stalk survivors amongst ravaged steel and twisted metal. Their weapons kill all who are found hiding within basements and bunkers, while their steel hatchets hack away at any who try and flee.

Resisters are gutted, and their bodies severed into pieces. Children are ripped from out of their parent's arms, while women and men are savagely butchered to death. The victims try fighting back, but no form of defense can stop what has come upon them. The people of Ohio are not only gunned down like dogs, their corpses are put on display as warnings for all who would dare take up their cause.

This was the only way Kiril Pordan's plans could come into effect. The Resistance couldn't be seen as Americans. They had to be seen as traitors and insurrectionists, and that is how the VEDETTE saw them. To the Magisterium Dominion, they weren't killing fellow Americans. They were eliminating those who would stand in the way of peace, the way of Autocracy, the way of the future. So, of course, those of the Midwest began fighting back, if only to be slaughtered for their bravery.

Prof. Tamara Boggier

keeper, New York Republic Athenaeum

To the Dominion of the Magisterium, these animals of the Resistance deserve nothing less than unreserved annihilation. Their sons are meant to be slaughtered. Their daughters are meant to be ravaged. Their wives are meant to be cut open, and cursed for birthing such traitors. And their husbands are meant to be eradicated, as for history to never again recall any of their names. This is the agenda that finally finds itself at the doorsteps of Cincinnati. And by the time it is over, the proud home of *The Patriots*, the State of the once famous orator, Frank Lord, is finished.

Admirals Balthazar and Hauser, and General Storm want to see the Midwest obliterated by the end of the following year, only for it to rise as a Republic honorable enough to be called so. And by the time it is reported that 70,000 rebels of the Resistance have been terminated, Ohio, Michigan, Indiana, and Illinois would have all been reduced to nothing but ruins by a horror set in motion by II High Magistrate Kiril Pordan.

Although, this will only be the beginning of his ultimate plans for not only the United Republic, but the entire world. In the end, Pordan will either shape mankind into the image of perfection, or watch it razed to the abyss.

2043

No Mercy For The Wicked

The Great Divide: a concise history of the future

I hereby solemnly swear by my heart, soul, mind and body to be loyal to God and the Magisterium. And forever shall I hail the High Magistrate and his decrees, until death be given me, and my reward granted.

The Solemn Oath of the United Republic, 2036

These are the words that live in the hearts of all Loyalists, while confetti falls from the sky, and colorful banners drape the sides of buildings. While balloons of different shades and sizes are bound to all surfaces, and massive blimps soar overhead in formation in telecasting the passionate frenzy below. While barricades are lined up and down the streets of Time Square, and an estimated 1.7 million Loyalists crowd the metro area in readiness of II High Magistrate Kiril Pordan's much anticipated appearance.

A rarity, Pordan's presence only shares its magnificence with the very reason he is being seen in the first place—the official recognition of the Union of Nations. A form of governance with its premiere headquarters located in London, when it comes to the crowd in England, the British nearly double that of the Republic of New York.

From mere thought to inception, the league is a sign of things to come: the advancements of science, the merging of minds and cultures like never before, the beginning of a world-wide mandate. The Union of Nations will not only serve as a platform for world leaders, it is to be a sanctuary to the dream of Autocracy.

This wasn't the United Nations, where you'd once had countless countries bickering at each other and forming alliances, no way. The Union of Nations was a council of world leaders. People representing not only the absolute power of their governments, but with a word, could've started a war. The men and women chosen to head the Union of Nations didn't go home, and they most certainly didn't meet bi-monthly, not even weekly, but daily. Their sole purpose when in that position was to further their governments, their leaders, and their people— nothing else. What was made law in the Union of Nations, you'd better believe was made law for all. To trespass, well that would've only meant death.

Cecil Greenough

Grand Magistrate: The Biography of Kiril Pordan

The Loyalists of the United Republic come in numbers to see the union's hailing, as do others from all around the globe. Flights going to and from Europe safely reach their destinations without worry, though a fear of bombings and hijackings force a more strict code of air travel on citizens. Regardless, an astonishing 3 million people travel to celebrate the Union of Nations at any risk. Distant allies that come forth to praise their mighty governors, they await Kiril Pordan's words of enlightenment.

Iraq, Iran, Pakistan, Turkey, Syria, Israel, Spain, France, Italy, Switzerland, Finland, England, the whole of the Earth recognizes this epic achievement, and it is the honor of II High Magistrate Pordan to announce its initiation.

This was a rather momentous occasion. Nothing in history had ever drawn humanity's attention all at once such as the Union of Nations' induction ceremony. I dare say billions of people tuned in to witness this epic enacting. Not to mention America's glorious baby boy, His Honorable II High Magistrate Kiril Gustav Pordan. Anyone who lived beneath the law of the Union of Nations knew of him, the man who had birthed the pioneering idea of the Magisterium Edict. To many, quite a few to be frank, the Union of Nations was, and always would be Kiril Pordan's brainchild. He was truly the one leading the world. Once again, the West was mighty, and America took its place as the beam of hope for all—the aspiration for greatness. America was once more at the forefront, and everybody knew it.

Prof. Jarvis Grimes

historian, *Superior and Biased: The History of the Royal European Alliance*

There was a name for Kiril Pordan in the Islamic People's Republic. He was called Shahjehan, the Arabic word meaning 'King of the world'. At least, that was how the Mu'minūn saw him. To many, he was a brother of theirs, though an American, and had been given command of the planet directly from the hands of Allah. You can even imagine him surpassing the respect given to the Mahdi, alaihi al-salaam, who himself had been losing popularity amongst his people.

Prof. Najiyah Abdullah Hassan

Crescent Moon and Pillars: The Rise of the Islamic Empire

Before Pordan can even take center stage, however, a bomb goes off amongst those gathering in London. The bombing is immediately seen as an attempt on Monarch Edward Davies' life, interrupting the celebration of the Union of Nations' official presentation. Davies' safety remains the primary concern, and he is quickly removed from the area. And though the Great Hall of the Union of Nations is spared any damage, that does not change the fact of over three hundred people being killed, only for the

Royal European Alliance's SENTRIES to assume control over the situation.

The defense force knows only a handful of spectators are guilty of the crime, but their violent response leaves scores injured, with an additional six hundred dead. The motto of the Royal European Alliance's SENTRIES *'No mercy for the wicked'* is one the soldiers uphold without thought, and they make that viciously apparent to all present.

The SENTRIES of the Royal European Alliance were a deadly force in those days. The VEDETTE of the United Republic, at least I believe during this particular time in history, had failed in comparison to their proficiency. The SENTRIES were orderly, precise, and more expedient at what they did than the VEDETTE. So against civilians, they were unstoppable. Yes, sir. The SENTRIES were indeed the far more adept military in those days.

Prof. Jarvis Grimes

historian, *Superior and Biased: The History of the Royal European Alliance*

Brutality surpassing the VEDETTE of the United Republic, Pordan makes sure to speak proudly of the deadly response once being briefed on its happening. Nevertheless, the II High Magistrate's speech goes off without a hitch, further pushing the agenda of reconciling a fractured world. The same cannot be said for those of the Midwest, however. In fact, to the people of the *Heartland* fighting for Democracy, the world has never appeared so fractured. To those of the Resistance, the world is broken, and they fear they may never be able to put it back together again.

VEDETTE General Matthew Storm is the one to lead the National Offensive against the rebels. Simply the first part of the Magisterium's ultimate plan for North America, the National Offensive sees over 1.3 million VEDETTE poured into the heart of the country. Their mission is clear: obliterate the Resistance, offer the salvation of the ICE-chip to those who submit, and then have them pledge allegiance to the Magisterium. But if anyone refuses, that makes them no different than an insurrectionist, and that only brings about pain and suffering. In the end, as Kiril Pordan has already stated, those of the Midwest will either bend, or they will be broken.

The Magisterium intends on controlling the country, and nothing will stop it. In spite of this, the Resistance and its followers refuse to surrender their call of Democracy. Daily reports of entire VEDETTE battalions being decimated by enemy fire, and ruthless terrorist attacks constantly come across the desks of Councilmen and Vice Magistrates. A crushing blow every time reports such as these finally reach the office of Kiril Pordan, one name in particular appears on almost every occasion to fuel the II High

Magistrate's anger. That name is Jake Stockwell, and he leads a rebel force that is gradually becoming a true threat.

The Magisterium struggles to halt the rebel's growing army, and begins to think the task impossible. The reason is the rebel forces' methods of fighting. Guerrilla tactics unlike anything Calvin or Agnes Walsh had ever attempted, Jake Stockwell and his forces strike when the night is darkest, and vanish by dawn's earliest light. Vicious strikes that seem undaunted by the advancing VEDETTE, this is why the Magisterium feels justified in executing its horrors in slaughtering all those suspected of aiding the embattled fighters.

Kiril Pordan was crushing an insurgency at exactly the same time that he was constructing his brainchild. He constantly spoke of clearing and holding an area, making evident that he had no intention of leaving a neighborhood, a city, a State even, once it had been captured from out of enemy hands. But, at the same time, he was also making sure to do something with those areas he had captured. The clearing part was defeating the insurgents, killing the ones who were dangerous, imprisoning and rehabilitating those who'd been spared, and for some, the immediate assimilation into the United Republic—ICE-chip and all. Now came the holding process, and that's where Pordan shined. That's where the future began to present an age of Order and Excellence. That's where the face of America began to literally change. And still, the Resistance refused to go along with it. All the pretty and impressive buildings and roads the Magisterium was bringing about, and the Resistance destroyed them whenever presented the opportunity.

Prof. Tamara Boggier
keeper, New York Republic Athenaeum

First things first, let's get this picture of over one million VEDETTE fighting as a cohesive unit clear. There weren't a million men and women charging the battlefield, and shooting like a disorganized horde of psychos. That would've been just plain impossible. No, what you had here were tens of thousands of field commanders, thousands of brigades, and a deployment plan that saw organized tours of duty, as well as, well thought out strategic clear and hold operations. This was a fight for the fate of the United Republic here, after all. On on side you had the Magisterium, and on the other you had the Resistance. America was the prize, and to control the citizens was to control the land. One's a stringent, well-trained, Autocratic, war machine, and the other's a group of men and women—normal people, still believing they could restore Democracy. It was an unfair fight, but the rebels soon proved that discrepancy irrelevant.

Cecil Greenough

Grand Magistrate: The Biography of Kiril Pordan

The Resistance is truly a force to be reckoned with, and the Magisterium knows it. With the fractured doctrines of ART and AR2 giving way to a more unified way of thinking, Jake Stockwell is rapidly building a democratic army he can soon bring face to face with the vicars of Autocracy. Although, if this disease of rebellion can be somehow purged, the next phase in the Magisterium Purification Agenda can commence.

A diagram focused on the full conversion of the United States into the United Republic, the Incessant Credit Encode is to be the means by which the Magisterium will rise above its set design. Such an endeavor would abandon the unnatural necessity of computer chips being implanted into the human body, giving way to a genetically grafted cipher. Through this DNA based code, nano-microbes capable of forming an imperceptible membrane would lace the entire genetic makeup of the carrier, serving as an all inclusive databank.

An absolute collection of all information pertaining to this person, the Loyalist born with this genetic makeup would not only be a walking historical, financial, and medical disclosure, they would also be the future of all mankind.

No more would hackers be able to infiltrate the Magisterium as to play the part of viral infector, threatening the populace at large. It matters not that such advancements may be decades away, or that only a new breed of Loyalists would inherit its prize. This is a venture the entire Magisterium anticipates with great interest, and every Loyalist is prepared to be greater than anything he or she has ever dreamed of. In the meantime, the ICE-chip will have to serve its purpose of keeping order amongst the Republic, and that is something the Magisterium benignly accepts.

The rest of the Union of Nations also hopes to see such innovations in the coming future, but for now focus on the primary vexations at hand. Problems that must be resolved if either regime hopes to see their plans for the world accomplished, obstacles which halt every opportunity given them, the crisis of rebellion infecting all developing nations needs to be stopped.

In the Western hemisphere, Canadian officials argue against the Union of Nations, sighting their lack of weapons and technologies as being a hindrance to their being seen as equals amongst such an alliance. It is an argument that can be understood, but one the U.N. cares nothing for.

Canada was a region capable of serving as a strategic position for rebel forces. That was something that couldn't be allowed to happen. If the Resistance or Grimaldi Defiance had been allowed to seize control of this voluminous territory, they could've easily launched simultaneous attacks on both the United Republic and Royal European Alliance. The Union of Nations couldn't allow such threats to persist, and that was the reason Canada was given its ultimatum. The nation as a whole was to either merge with the Union of Nations, or face the full wrath of its combined military capability. Either way, the world was going to be as one, and the Union of Nations was going to be at its head. It was an admonition which

Canada had to submit to, and it officially announced that it would in fact enroll as a member of the Union of Nations on September 10, 2043.

Prof. Tamara Boggier

keeper, New York Republic Athenaeum

A wise stance, Canada hopes and waits to see if their membership in the end brings about peace or destruction. But with widespread rebellions occupying a significant amount of the Union of Nations' manpower, Canada's wait will last for quite sometime. For though the Canadians have agreed to join the global union, it is an agreement that is never really enforced.

In the East, Japan desires no such union. Instead, the island nation finds itself preoccupied with strengthening its own stance in the Orient, ignoring the requests being made by the Union of Nations concerning its support.

The Asian people had not ever forgotten what America had done to China. And though they know that China had been the aggressor, they still agreed that the punishment had not fit the crime. To them, the United States' response to it being attacked was a rehashing of unbalanced vengeance they had grown tired of. A military base, two cities. Two buildings, two countries. A State, the once glorious East. Asians refused to make the same mistake of trusting the West to be fair, and they declined being part of the Union of Nations no matter the cost.

Tsun-chúng Hu

The Last Dynasty: The Chinese Republic's Ultimate Demise

Japan does not think the Union of Nations a desirable venture, and labors without rest to convince the rest of its Asian counterparts of the same. Alternatively, the island nation proposes all the Orient enroll into a single Asiatic Empire of their own. A call to be as one, Japan wishes to reignite the fire of the dragon that is the East. But the Union of Nations opposes such rejection, and tries both day and night to correct what it believes to be Japan's faulted logic.

This does not halt the United Republic, Royal European Alliance, the State of Israel, and Islamic People's Republic from joining forces in constructing the Union of Nations by any means, leaving the piracy problem of the seas, and the militancy of the Afro Islamic Union as problems that can be effortlessly dealt with.

For far too long, the Islamic People's Republic and Afro Islamic Union have been at each other's throats. Clashes that have left numerous civilians injured or dead, the Union of Nations believes the problem sprung forth from out of betrayal and misunderstandings can be effortlessly remedied through the Afro Islamic Union's unconditional pledge to join the coalition.

The Islamic People's Republic has already pledged its oath to the new concord, leaving the Afro Islamic Union on the other side of the fence. But if it too were to join the Union of Nations, then the Afro Islamic Union would be seen as an ally against a common foe, while a rejection can only be seen as another form of insurrection. An obvious threat, the Afro Islamic Union is hesitant in accepting the proposal, leaving the Islamic People's Republic free to whisper its suspicions concerning the Muslim regime.

Mu'minūn had not been allowed to partake in Hajj for over seven years, and it was angering them more and more. Not to mention that the Muslims had suggested in the past that they do Hajj to Jerusalem instead, a place only recently healing from its devastating nuclear attack. To the Mu'minūn, the Muslims did not respect them, and they did not appear the slightest considerate of joining the Union of Nations. This could only mean one thing. If the Mu'minūn were to ever enter the holy city of Mecca again, the Muslims had to be either conquered or destroyed. This required that the Mu'minūn begin making the Union of Nations wary of the AIU's actions.

Prof. Najiyah Abdullah Hassan

Crescent Moon and Pillars: The Rise of the Islamic Empire

Rumors resurrecting the fear of Islamic extremism, the Islamic People's Republic has no problem with alleging the Afro Islamic Union's re-embracing of the long abandoned *Sharia Law*. Such talks, in turn, quickly begin drawing the skeptical eye of the Union of Nations, but it is something that must be dealt with at a later time. For now, the rebellions of the lands remain the center of attention, and it is this discussion which takes center stage at the Union of Nations' heated sessions.

Unanimously agreeing that something must be done pertaining to the insurrectionist dilemmas of the Resistance, Grimaldi Defiance, and the like, the Union of Nations demands that a solution be found, and at any cost. This is the very purpose of its design, as well as, its ultimate test. Every nation pledging itself to its cause believes this. And as expected, the Union of Nations becomes determined to not only prove its capability at handling such troubles, it will also come to be seen as something no one nation can resist.

The Great Divide: a concise history of the future

M.A. Martin

2044
NEW WORLD ORDER

The Great Divide: a concise history of the future

The date is January 17. The Union of Nations is honored by the presence of the United Republic's II High Magistrate, Kiril Pordan. A gathering of the world's leaders and their governments together in London, England, Pordan hopes to gain their support when it comes to his ultimate plan for the future.

The Resistance is gaining ground every day, and needs to be stopped. All governments have agreed to battle such insurgencies, but none have truly been able to quash the rebels threatening their rule. A reoccurring theme throughout the globe, Pordan refuses to see it go on.

To the II High Magistrate of the United Republic, the rebels desire nothing but anarchy. And to allow such ideals to prevail will only mean certain doom for the planet. Therefore, it is the duty of each and every world leader to confront this threat with the utmost determination, regardless the atrocities it will bring about. This is something Pordan has rationalized long and hard over, as should have every other world leader. And though Pordan is aware innocent people will be hurt during this cleansing period, it is something he has come to terms with.

The world will strive as one toward surviving, or it will burn in the flames of rebellion.

Kiril Pordan was a visionary. And though you and I might not necessarily agree with his vision, it's one that needs to be respected for what it truly was. Here was a government in place that said it would feed you, clothe you, put a roof up over your head, and all it wanted in return was your loyalty—your trust in the possibility that it might know, just a little better than you do, what will work for the country. Sounds good. But then again, at the same time, you had a group of Americans who constantly reminded you of Old Glory—the Red, White, and Blue. They reminded you of the Revolution, pleading with you not to forget. Basically, the freedoms of the past—Democracy. Kiril Pordan couldn't have his people being torn between these two ideas, and decided it needed to be stopped no matter the cost. He had to protect his Loyalists from such illogical, godless, and corrupted behavior, and that called for the annihilation of any idea that opposed his goals.

Cecil Greenough

Grand Magistrate: The Biography of Kiril Pordan

Operation: *Purification Schema* has already been initiated all throughout the United Republic, successfully destabilizing the rebel groups taking refuge in some Midwestern States. The rest of their cohorts are tracked down on the daily, and eliminated on all fronts. Still, the *Purification Schema* has yet to quell the violence being seen throughout North America.

To Pordan, the reason is the rebel leader known as Jake Stockwell, and his ragtag military force. A radical faction spreading a conflicting view concerning the future of North America, Kiril Pordan blames Stockwell's dissension for the horrors of the land. Something the II High Magistrate swears to remedy, the rebel leader's capture or death is expected by the end of the year. It is an oath Pordan makes before all present, daring them to swear the same.

Such fearless words stir the Union of Nations summit, breathing hope into its frail lungs. But that still does not make clear the definitive steps needed in dealing with such uprisings, a conundrum Pordan hopes to rein in.

To the II High Magistrate, the united nations coalition must be committed to an effective offensive, or suffer the wrath of their leniency. The threats of the world are real, and it is up to them to stop such terrors. Thus, to the Royal European Alliance, Pordan touches on the violence being committed by the Grimaldi Defiance.

Estimated to be over 13 million in number, the rebel group consists mostly of former statesmen, elitists, military personnel, rioters, and members of the deposed Royal family. They are guilty of everything from bombings to all out war, and have no regrets in attacking SENTRIES and Alliance members alike. Their tactics are both barbaric and vile, with the bodies of their victims all too often being hung on display for all to see.

The Grimaldi Defiance was different from the Resistance of the United Republic in a multitude of ways: their fighting tactics, their sophisticated weaponry, their agenda, not to mention that the Grimaldi fighters were mostly former military personnel. The American rebellion fought without true direction, and more than often used suicide bombings to get their points across. Sure, Jake Stockwell was building an army during this time, but he still had not created a uniformed military, unlike the Grimaldi Defiance that planned and executed without flaw. They didn't commit suicide bombings, they stood and fought head-on. They were born to fight, and they loved to kill, but they always did so as a unit. I dare say that in many ways, Edward Davies had it harder than Kiril Pordan ever did.

Prof. Jarvis Grimes

historian, *Superior and Biased: The History of the Royal European Alliance*

Using Prometheus Flame, the Grimaldi Defiance makes daily demands for the established order to step down. They want Edward Davies to remove himself from office, allow a parliament to return to its lawmaking, and in addition, stand in alliance with the Royal British Family, the brave King William V and his sons who fight alongside the rebels, and command they be returned to their status as British Royalty. But the Royal European Alliance does not bargain with terrorists, leaving the Grimaldi Defiance no choice but to seize its attention.

Their brand of diplomacy comes hand in hand with death, chaos, and the loss of innocent lives. And though the Royal European Alliance and its SENTRIES struggle with all they have in order to put a stop to the rebels, in retaliation, the Grimaldi Defiance meets them at every turn with even more savagery. Pordan sees this as a losing battle, and has no qualms stating such.

Already the REA has conceded the ravaged territories of Russia and Germany to this rebellion, with other regions such as Poland, the Czech Republic, Estonia and Lithuania hanging in the balance. Norway, Finland, and Sweden are no different, no matter if they swear allegiance to the Royal European Alliance and its leaders.

Methodologically ruled by a small organization calling itself the Saami Coalition Force, the nations of the Scandinavian Peninsula latch on to the Union of Nations with assurances of support, but refuse to aid it in ending the Grimaldi Defiance's acts of terrorism. They argue the rebels are contending for governorship of Europe, and that it is the place of the Royal European Alliance to defeat them if desiring the same role. The battle is honorable in the Saami's conclusion, and they refuse to interfere unless one contender surrenders. They side with the victors, regardless which side.

To the High Magistrate, if something is not done soon, he fears the Royal European Alliance will crumble, creating a vacuum through which the Grimaldi Defiance will seize control. The last thing Monarch Edward Davies hopes to see, he inquires of Kiril Pordan's solution concerning such dangers. However, before any resolution can be given, Pordan speaks on the issues facing the Islamic world.

As it already is, the Islamic People's Republic stands fully ready and capable of taking war to the Afro Islamic Union. A threat that is likely to jeopardize the stability of the entire region, including Israel, the only issue sparking such conflict appears to be the denial of Hajj to the Mu'minūn. A lucid but volatile topic, it must be dealt with as swiftly as possible nonetheless.

It would be like someone telling a Christian that he could no longer baptize people. Or a Jew, that now that Jerusalem was being reconstructed, and that people were slowly being let back in, that he or she could not enter. It was an insult, and the Mu'minūn were absolutely serious when warning they would bring war. Mahdi Abu, alaihi al-salaam, understood this, but he still believed that the Islamic partition was the best solution. And if that called for the Mu'minūn to be barred from Hajj, then that was what he was going to make his priority.

Prof. Najiyah Abdullah Hassan

Crescent Moon and Pillars: The Rise of the Islamic Empire

The Mu'minūn of the Islamic People's Republic refuse to be excluded from the religious pilgrimage any longer, and demand the barriers built all along the Jordanian, Iraqi and Kuwaiti borders be demolished immediately. An act that could very well still the call for war, the Muslims of the Afro Islamic Union refuse to adhere to such clamor.

As they have stated before, they believe the Mu'minūn better off enacting their pilgrimage in Jerusalem, and reject any compromise on the matter. But Jerusalem, though faring along in its recovery, has yet to even establish a fully independent infrastructure.

The nuclear damage seen there eighteen years ago still leaves a visible scar, and proves to be a region full of pitfalls and setbacks. And though it is a blessing to see the State of Israel, the Islamic People's Republic, and Europe working together in a joint effort in helping to bring the wounded city along in full recovery, all this means nothing to the Mu'minūn.

So much do they reject the thought of Jerusalem being the epicenter of their faith, the Mu'minūn have gladly returned the entire city to their once greatest enemy. A decree which has been agreed upon by all leaders of the Islamic People's Republic, it has granted full authority over the Holy Land to the State of Israel.

The agreement is called *Fatwa Bayt al-Maqdis* by those who issue it, the Ruling of the Holy House, and its binding judgment is that Jerusalem and all its surrounding regions now belong without objection to the State of Israel. From the borders of Lebanon to Egypt, Jordan and Syria, the whole of Jerusalem shall forever belong to the Chosen Ones.

Almost overnight, Israelis and Jews from all over the world flood the Holy City in seizing their long-lost birthright, while the Mu'minūn continue to recant their seriousness concerning their return to Mecca. This makes the Muslim suggestion nothing less than a outright insult, an outrage the Mu'minūn refuse to let stand.

Kiril Pordan fears the world will soon witness an outbreak of violence in that region, concluding only one way to defuse the critical circumstance. It is a solution he does not yet reveal, not until speaking on the current crises facing the rest of the planet. So turning his attention to the piracy dilemma challenging the constancies of island countries, he informs the Union of Nations of what he has come to learn.

The Pacific, the Caribbean, Indian Ocean, Tasman Sea, and all other chilled bodies of water covering the Earth, a threat equally as perilous as any rebellion also flourishes with its imperilment of the planet. The culprit is the piracy on the high frozen seas. Marauders who kill, steal, rape, and attack any and all who dare cross them, the Pirates care nothing for regional squabbles or political agendas. The icy seas are their home, and they are law.

The Pirates are steadfast in their belief of owning the freezing waters, daring to attack even Naval Fleets docked at bay or patrolling the coasts of countries. Ruthless cutthroat Pirates armed with heavy firepower, speedboats, cutters, and all types of bombs, they fear nothing, and challenge any and all who venture on the seas.

These seafaring terrorists eventually gain access and control over fortified Cruisers, Frigates, and Destroyers, jeopardizing the safety of the entire world. They traffic people across seas, and sell slaves to cruel and sadistic criminals. They smuggle anything and everything they are paid for, and care nothing for those who may get hurt. They dock in Hawaii, Jamaica, Cuba, Haiti, Mauritius, New Zealand, committing horrendous acts of violence against their designated targets. They are slaves to copious addictions; logic is something they rarely heed. And though a bone gnawing chill surrounds them, with death itself lingering in the bitter glaciation of the seas, it is here these maritime pirates rule.

The Pirates of the global waters answered to no one. There weren't any outside forces to swoop down on them, and restrict their movements and livelihoods with sanctions and threats, so they did as they pleased. They were quite violent, and they'd suffered much all these years. In hindsight, it wasn't their fault the world imploded, so why should they have to listen to anyone? Especially with everybody around them working so hard to help themselves become stronger than the next. They were warriors, and they weren't scared of anyone. So, they refused to be told what to do, and took it upon themselves to wreck havoc on the open seas anyway they saw fit. But to Pordan…Well, that was something that couldn't be permitted.

Cecil Greenough

Grand Magistrate: The Biography of Kiril Pordan

The sponsors for such reckless seamen are the self-appointed Presidents, Prime Ministers, Dictators, and Kings of the isolated islands. They are the ones who reap the rewards, offering ports in exchange for ill-gotten gains. Men and women either appointed to their positions, or seated there through the might of their arms, it is them who deal with the Pirates. Although, there are those who refuse to do business with such savages.

A rare and honest people awaiting the return of normality, some island leaders risk their lives to resist, and go to their graves without regret. But the odds of finding such an honest governor ruling an island is slim to none, so Kiril Pordan wishes to crush all those who have dared to run amok. His plan will unreservedly handle such dilemmas, but his information concerning the deadliest threat of them all must first be presented.

A structure of government rivaling the new function of things—an old way which must be extinguished in order for the new to stand true—a reminder of the failures of the past, the Freelands are a reality that cannot be allowed to persist. The greatest threat against the Union of Nations, the Freelands must be made to see the light, or be destroyed for the better good.

Alaska, Greenland, Iceland, the whole of South America, Central America, Southern Africa, India, the South Pacific, Australia, New Zealand, Korea, and finally Japan, all of them, countries remaining abiding to the ways of the past, their very existence is a living defiance to the Union of Nations, and a threat Kiril Pordan refuses to watch go unchecked.

These Freelands do not function as perfect democracies, but they do stand as absolute contradictions to the dream of Autocracy. Regions that remained neutral during the Third World War, under the radar during the Great Divide, or separate from the merging of the Union of Nations, these countries refuse to recognize the changing tides taking place around them, and try desperately to maintain hold on a dying delusion.

This way of thinking stands in contradiction of Kiril Pordan's aspirations to see the world united. And to the II High Magistrate, they are as much a threat as the resistance, the Pirates, and the false rulers of the islands.

Pordan needed the world on his side. What he was trying to do required that all nations fall into place. To have countries out there promoting different ideologies, rebel groups challenging his authority, those were things that couldn't be allowed to continue. And when he looked at these other nations, especially Japan, all he saw were instigators to his problems. So, he had to make them his enemies, them and everything they stood for.

Prof. Tamara Boggier

keeper, New York Republic Athenaeum

The world is as fractured as it has ever been, and that separation threatens Autocracy's call. For that reason, Pordan finally reveals his initiative to all present. A unified planet. A single functioning government. A cohesive unit. A perfect establishment. Before his peers, Kiril Pordan stands with absolute confidence, and proposes the creation of a one world government.

A method of direction that would call for all identities to be stripped, for all nationalities to be done away with, and for all authorities to be integrated under one crown, the II High Magistrate assures this is the only way to survive. An arrangement of a High Magistrate from each regime, Vice Magistrates from all over the globe working toward one common goal, and a society that does not see race, creed, faith, or nationality, it will be a Utopia. An Autocracy of limitless power, above it all is to be one man. He is to be the Grand Magistrate, and only God is to dictate his actions.

Such a plan is enough to think Kiril Gustav Pordan mad, and yet the Royal European Alliance, the State of Israel, and Islamic People's Republic firmly stand by his side. A world in which Autocracy will be given to all, it will be a New World Order.

Unfortunately for the Union of Nations, that dream is a long ways off.

The rebellion stands at their door. People are suffering around the planet. And death is becoming the assured way of life. With these impending scenarios in full display, Kiril Pordan now reveals his plans for the rebels, knowing of only one way to finish them off once and for all.

A sweeping march that must be taken across the lands, only together can such a task be accomplished. Simply put, Pordan calls for the REA's SENTRIES, the Tzahal of the State of Israel, and the Mujahids of the IPR to join forces with his VEDETTE, and together they will crush the insurgencies of the United Republic, Royal European Alliance, and Islamic People's Republic.

Together they will usher in the age of Autocracy. Together they will be inexorable. Together they can win.

Essentially, what Kiril Pordan was offering his peers was a chance at actually creating a New World Order. Every one of them had heard of it. There'd even been claims that it existed from since the medieval times. Either way, Kiril Pordan was offering a real, tangible, functioning New World Order. A government with absolute say so and an unstoppable military—power that still can't be fathomed even today. This authority would control the entire world. It wouldn't belong to the Americans. It wouldn't belong to the Europeans. It wouldn't belong to the Muslims, Mu'minūn, Israelis, Asians. No, it would belong to mankind, and all would be under its laws. The same laws for everyone, everywhere, throughout the world, equality and justice for all in the same manner—Autocracy.

Cecil Greenough

Grand Magistrate: The Biography of Kiril Pordan

A radical suggestion to say the least, Pordan finds his words applauded in the vestibules of the Great Hall. He is then given the words of Monarch Edward Davies, Prime Minister Jacob Manishewitz, and Ayatollah Parvaiz Makhmalbaf that he will have their support, only to return the favor when it comes to their volatile regions.

Agreed on all sides, the concurrence entails all four nations contribute troops to the cause. And on May 15, the newly created UNDO (Union of

Nations Defense Ordinance) branch of the Union of Nations is launched on its mission. 8.5 million soldiers in all, UNDO will live up to its designation. And in its wake will be devastation the likes never before imagined, at least by no one except II High Magistrate Kiril Pordan.

Therefore, on September 11, the first wave of UNDO forces from the Royal European Alliance, the State of Israel, and Islamic People's Republic set foot on American soil. Numbering over 600,000 from each regime, they arrive both by air and sea, with the ones by sea encountering hostilities en route.

Pirates caught off guard by the flood of European, Israeli, and Mu'minūn naval ships and aircraft, the marauders meet the incursion with all they have. Bombs, bullets, death, the frozen seas are turned red with blood while burning in an inconceivable rage. A similar hate that is obvious to the foreigners when finally arriving on United Republic soil, a majority of their reception is one of shared protests and slander by Americans who do not want them there.

Those who are of the United Republic are displeased by the UNDO influx, and maintain Americans should try Americans. Arguments that go no further than the occasional rally, the objectors make sure not to cross the line with their complaints. Still, this does not change the fact that the UNDO forces have arrived, and that the Magisterium can now put to rest its nation's resistance.

Some Americans weren't pleased to see the UNDO forces. This was America, after all. Why did they need foreigners to help them with homegrown problems? That was the thought process of the Loyalists who didn't like seeing aliens from other countries coming to fight their battles. And to no one's surprise, the discontent was also being seen amongst the VEDETTE and their Generals. American fighters, though a new breed unlike any before them, they still had a sense of patriotism. They still loved America, and that was why they were fighting for it. These foreigners on the other hand, they didn't have any stake in the country, if only that of killing what most Americans felt were their betters. Rebel or not, the insurgents were still Americans. And though II High Magistrate Pordan thought otherwise, there was a difference when you heard someone begging for their lives in English, only to watch them get killed by someone you yourself didn't even understand. The VEDETTE didn't like the UNDO setup, but did their duties anyway—for now, at least.

Prof. Tamara Boggier

keeper, New York Republic Athenaeum

Word reaches the rebellion concerning the UNDO forces' invasion, news no one wants to hear, least of all Jake Stockwell. And though his forces of Democracy have been making strides against the VEDETTE, they are victories that mean nothing when those of the Midwest continue to be slaughtered.

Reports of people being killed in the middle of the streets, or arrested in groups are enough to cripple the rebel leader, but the intelligence of those being cataloged in droves distress him the most. Simply the thought of those he defends bowing to the tyrannical rule of the Magisterium is enough to make him surrender his call for war, but it is a desire he ignores.

Stockwell understands that servitude can be more enticing then death, but that is exactly what he calls his fighters to do—Die.

The incursion of UNDO forces is something he must tackle before everything he fights for is lost. Thus, mounting a massive offensive against VEDETTE stationed all throughout Kansas, Jake Stockwell makes sure to validate his forces as more than capable of meeting the UNDO threat. An act that not only kills thousands of VEDETTE, it captures the attention of rebel leaders throughout the country.

Various rebellions pledge their allegiance to Stockwell's call for justice, freedom, and Democracy. They name him their General, and hoist the *Star Spangled Banner* alongside his image. He is now made the symbol of hope and rebellion. And to many, Stockwell means Resistance, and rebel leaders throughout the country have no problem heeding his decrees.

He is a man of little words, but he is beyond anything that can be said about him. Stockwell is a legend, a myth, a hero, and a savior. And standing firmly against the Magisterium, he shows why.

There were rebellions taking place all over America. South Dakota, North Dakota, Colorado, Alabama, Kentucky, even within the Republics—though the ones in the Republics were isolated and rare. The truth is, the rebellion was still alive, and each form of it had its own leader. Men and women who dared to fight an encroaching war machine, these people led thousands, and in some cases, millions in demand of Democracy. But none matched the power of Jake Stockwell's military. He was different. He wasn't a man fighting for freedom, he was freedom fighting for man. Everybody wanted to be Jake Stockwell, and they did anything he wanted. Well, almost everybody.

Cecil Greenough

Grand Magistrate: The Biography of Kiril Pordan

One such reluctant leader is named Arthur Havelock, and he is more than eager to join Jake Stockwell in the war, but as a partner and not as a minion. With forces numbering well over 16 million, Havelock has already solidified himself the leader of the Southwest. Powerfully armed, and ready to fight for liberty, the people of Oklahoma, New Mexico, Colorado, Arizona, and most of all Texas defy the Magisterium to bring their foreign legions to their door.

The Southwest wasn't always this way. It wasn't until the protests of Arthur Havelock had the Southwest rebellion gained its intensity. Before him, the Southwest had been much like the South before Agnes Walsh—regions divided, and a people without hope. Remnants of a people that bore witness to America's greatest nightmare, the residents of the Southwest had been paralyzed with fear and contrite with anger. However, their emotions were stifled and their futures determined, because at the core of their desolation was a fractured military installation of the U.S. Armed Forces. But unlike the similar fate that had befallen the South, these military soldiers had by no means pledged allegiance to the Magisterium. As a matter of fact, contrasting the servicemen of the South, the Southwestern military had seized power for themselves. Back then they were being led by a General named Carlton Peeves, a man whose ego demanded that all submit to his will. And when it came to his will, totalitarianism was what he had in mind. He produced a form of government in which his soldiers were in control, while he'd elected himself President of this fabricated administration. He called it the Western Alliance, and it was to be seen as the new way for America. The Constitution, the Pledge of Allegiance, the American Flag, all of them were removed, and a new charter was then set in stone for the land. An oath to uphold Peeves' dictatorship, it was the symbol of this tyranny that implored the Southwest's populace to stand up for their rights and fight.

Prof. Tamara Boggier

keeper, New York Republic Athenaeum

An imposter of the Lone Star flag of Texas, the Lone Star flag of the Western Alliance had raped the red of bravery, the white of strength, and the blue of loyalty, replacing it with a black of dismal despair. A travesty to which no one could have sat quiet to, so was born the Southwestern struggle known as *Night of the Longhorns*. A fight in which the control over Texas, Oklahoma, and New Mexico would be decided, it was from this conflict that Arthur Havelock was forged.

A unifier with words as sultry as a blazing sun, it had not taken long for him to become the face of the revolt. Likewise, until he had defeated the military, only to find the pledge of said forces at his service. In time, the Lone Star flag of Texas was returned to its proper place, and the Southwest given its freedom. Independence they then swore to never again surrender, the fighters of the Southwest had proven their worth. They will gladly do so again, and Havelock is the one who will lead them.

This is the type of army support Jake Stockwell knows he will need, calling on him to send delegates to petition Havelock for a rendezvous. He believes together they can indeed crush the Magisterium, but that is a decision he leaves in Havelock's hands. For now, his attack on Kansas has drawn the immediate response of the Magisterium, and Stockwell needs to engage their assault with everything he has.

A battle that blackens the sky, the fight in Kansas scorches the earth with its bombs and fires. It is a conflict that claims souls, and brings structures crashing to the ground. Bridges are burned, children are stolen, women are trampled, and men are killed, both VEDETTE and rebel numbers are depleted. Yet, after four long and grueling months, Jake Stockwell stands victorious over the entire State of Kansas.

Another defeat that comes across II High Magistrate Kiril Pordan's desk, it instructs him the time has come to launch the UNDO forces into the heart of his country. And once initiated, it will change the engagement over North America forever.

2046
SEDITION REPRESSION ACT

The Great Divide: a concise history of the future

April 9, and the preliminary UNDO forces have positioned themselves all through Michigan, Indiana, Wisconsin, and Illinois. 3 million strong, their tactics are atrocious. Rebels desperately fight to withstand their rush, but the foreign fighters are too strong. They are not Americans, and have no problem with killing those most of the population believes they have always secretly despised.

Their bombers soar overhead, and their sable rounds cut down everything in their path. In residential areas, the screams of victims drown the thunderous crackling of automatic fire, while children cry over the bodies of their parents. Resistance fighters take refuge in buildings and malls, only to draw the brutal assault upon the innocent hiding amongst them. In the cities, the fires that rage are as bright as the sun, and the smoke a black murk. Half of the Midwest is conquered in less than three months, and the Magisterium banner now waves high above what remains.

Under such a wave, the rebel forces have either fled, or met their end in the presence of the UNDO. A British General by the name of Pamela Barnett has been chosen to head the brutal assault, but even she is shocked by the lack of mercy enacted against the Americans.

Barnett is appalled when she finally enters Michigan, but such repulsions are quickly vanquished. II High Magistrate Pordan has given the UNDO forces their orders, and that means she must do as she is told. Her presence reinforces the necessity of what is taking place. A master orator, the General has already displayed a clear and indestructible loyalty toward Autocracy, and fulfills her duties of drawing such allegiance from the rest of the Republic. That is, until she is deemed capable of entrusted leadership the way Matthew Storm is.

The General is not at all pleased with her position as public pacifier, but her words do serve their purpose in downplaying the brutality enacted in the Midwest. Even so, the thought of America having to be won by Americans hounds her every assault, proving her task a rather difficult one.

The situation in America was harsh and dividing. On one side of the fence, you had Kiril Pordan believing that by bringing these foreign legions into the country he could quell the insurgents of the land. And on the other side, you had Americans who absolutely disagreed with this course of action. Vice Magistrates, Councilmen, even VEDETTE who hated the fact that European, Israeli, and Mu'minūn soldiers were trampling their land—brutally killing fellow Americans. They constantly complained about the foreigners. Sure, it was okay when they were doing it, because it was Americans fighting Americans. But now that these foreigners were here, there almost seemed to be an American pride stirring across the country. It was almost to the point where the VEDETTE had to play second fiddle to the UNDO Forces, simply because Kiril Pordan was afraid that his Loyalists wouldn't kill other Americans alongside foreigners. America for Americans, never before had this saying meant more than now.

Cecil Greenough

Grand Magistrate: The Biography of Kiril Pordan

This is the exact same sentiment lingering in the heart of General Matthew Storm, leader of the National Offensive. He makes it clear whenever communicating with Pordan—the belief that America should be won by Americans. But then again, the II High Magistrate has already weighed such grievances prior to his decision, absolutely holding fast to his belief of this being a necessary course in which they cannot fail.

II High Magistrate Pordan reiterates this to Storm, and commands him to aid the UNDO forces when they arrive at Central Command in Nebraska. A course of action that would call for the foreigners to cross through Iowa and Minnesota, two States where a little over 12.5 million restless Americans barely accept the *Magisterium Edict*, Storm can already foresee the resistance to such a foreign force asserting its power. A protest that will surely lead to untold deaths, it will undoubtedly be a fragile situation in which the mass onslaught of Loyalists only recently learning their place in the Magisterium will be butchered for their patriotism.

The inevitable horror demands Storm travel to meet Barnett and her UNDO forces instead, in hopes of sparing the massacre that will assuredly take place. Intervening, however, days after the horrors already suffered, a healing period is ordered to commence.

Every State that had been conquered by the UNDO was now going to be reconstructed. Buildings that had been burned to the ground, bridges that had been demolished, they were all going to be rebuilt. But before just one was renovated, Magisterium authority had to first be firmly established. This called for military installations to be built before anything else, if 'military installations' were what you would've called them. These weren't just simple military compounds. These intricate arrangements could have easily been called metropolises. They could sustain up to 3 million people, and had no need for outside assistance. To be frank, these military arcologies were more so blueprints for how the rest of the United Republic was to look than simple military installations. Skyscrapers, Depots, Factories, highways that resembled something out of the science fiction movies of the past, these arcological military installations were the wave of the future, and soon the entire country would look as they did —or at least, that was what Kiril Pordan was hoping would happen.

Prof. Tamara Boggier

keeper, New York Republic Athenaeum

Constructing these massive militarized municipalities in all occupied cities, as well as, rural areas, the UNDO seize possession of countless territories in the name of the Magisterium. An inevitable end for some, it is an absolute affront for others.

Whether they once disagreed with the death of their Democracy, or went along in place of being killed, the inundation of the UNDO forces is something nobody can consent to. All the same, refusing to be held hostage by such futile gripes, the II High Magistrate orders the reconstruction plan concerning the repairing of the States move forward, while making sure to deploy convoys upon convoys of much needed food, water, medicine, and clothing for those newly cataloged. Mercy Pordan hopes will help in quelling the resentment against him, he also hopes it helps to deal with the disapproval taking place in the heart of the Republics.

From Maine to North Carolina, the newly established Republics of Michigan to Alabama, and all in between, Loyalists and Councilmen argue against the II High Magistrate's current course of action. They force him to give them his undivided attention. They order him to remove the aliens from the country. They threaten to hold sessions day and night if he does not halt the atrocities of the Midwest. They voice their discontent on televised interviews, and scream at the top of their lungs for him to listen— all of which is a waste of time. Such unbefitting displays fail in budging the II High Magistrate in changing his mandate. Instead, Kiril Pordan decides to remind his Loyalists just why he is their High Magistrate.

The response comes without bloodshed or violence, but it is one which deals harshly with the objections nevertheless. For in place of attacking his Loyalists, Pordan instead freezes all ICE-chip operations, placing a sanction on all who have sworn allegiance.

No food, no clothes, no daily necessities, and no comforts to allow such blatant disrespect, Pordan puts in place an unforgiving injunction, and simply waits for his loyal citizens to come to their senses.

As planned, the sanctions do exactly what they are expected to. Before one bullet need be fired, the Republic silences its inconsequential droning, and allows their High Magistrate to continue with more important affairs. And as for those who do not cease their outrage, they are made to vanish through creative methods.

Kiril Pordan didn't have time to deal with the insurgency and his Loyalists voicing their disagreements with how he was running the country. This was a construction period for the nation, and things weren't going smoothly. Pordan had to crush the rebels, reestablish the land, and repair all the damage that had been done in the process, and didn't need the Loyalists causing problems on top of all that. So that's why he froze all ICE-chip functions. That's why he went on television, and chastised the Loyalists and his Councilmen. And that's why he arrested hundreds of protesters for all to see the consequences of dissension. He needed people to stand unified, not complaining every time something didn't go the way they wanted it to. This wasn't a Democracy, after all.

Cecil Greenough

Grand Magistrate: The Biography of Kiril Pordan

All this is legal according to the *Magisterium Edict*, and Pordan reminds his Loyalists of that every day. Correspondingly, in an effort to keep them preoccupied, the II High Magistrate adds to the propaganda concerning Servitude and Loyalty: uncut footage of VEDETTE gaining victories over the rebellion, UNDO forces helping to resurrect the Midwest, powerful misinformation portraying the peaceful life of Autocracy—the Loyalists of the Republic find it hard to argue any longer. A wise decision that not only keeps them from being killed, their silence also allows the Loyalists the normality of their lives. And with his Republic, for the time being, subdued, Pordan can return his attention toward more important things.

Meeting with his most trusted advisers, Pordan desires to further the might of the Magisterium far beyond the simple cataloging of those he most probably will never encounter. Far beyond the fragile hold he has on the Midwest, far beyond the omitted control never quite fulfilled in the Southwest, and far beyond the charred earth and foul stench of the West, Kiril Pordan intends to transform North America into a reflection of its achievements—a construction project on a massive scale.

The rise of towers reaching into the heavens, orderly streets paved for advance vehicles, an educational strive that creates masters of destiny, and elite militaries unlike any other, the attainment of the United Republic of America will see the future of man incarnated with the world adhering to such glories with equal determination. A one world brainchild, the United Republic of America is to be the inspiration for such accomplishments. But before the II High Magistrate can embark on his elaborate mission, he has problems that first need solving.

Receiving word of a meeting between Jake Stockwell and Arthur Havelock, rumors more so than intelligence, the convening of the two rebel leaders is an event Kiril Pordan's Vice Magistrates urge him to take seriously. The ideologies of ART and AR2 may have been all but suppressed, that still does not imply the Magisterium is not having enough trouble with containing the rebellion of the Midwest, much less, having to worry about the Southwestern regions.

One rebellion at a time, that is the advice Pordan is so humbly given. It is wise counsel, and for the time being, the II High Magistrate heeds the caution. He instead focuses all his attention on the Midwestern States just recently gained. Territories where much blood has been spilled, with cities that still glow from infernos, Pordan begins formulating plans for said States.

He works tirelessly both day and night to devise the best way for restoring honor to their fallen cities, while figuring out an inexpensive way to approach the Stockwell rebellion. Dedicated, Pordan allows no one within the Magisterium to remain indolent, and drives his Vice Magistrates to their maximum. And by July 22, the ultimate strategy is brought to his desk. A scheme that will heal the Midwest, on top of dealing accordingly with the rebels, the *Sedition Repression Bill* is a solution to all which concerns II High Magistrate Kiril Pordan, and he wastes no time approving its mandate.

The Midwest will indeed rise from its ashes, and it will do so on the backs of the rebellion. When all is said and done, the Resistance will no longer have the luxury of death. From now on, whoever survives an encounter with the Magisterium and its forces will have their lives spared, only to spend the rest of it performing hard labor.

Structures will rise. Streets will be repaired. Schools will be reopened. Hospitals will tend to the ill. And the Magisterium will stretch further than it ever has before, all this made possible by the back breaking work of rebel prisoners. The perfect plan, it, in due course, begins bearing the fruits of its propagation.

The Sedition Repression Bill was a way to not only penalize the rebels that had been caught, but to also hasten the reconstruction process. Those put under its bondage called it 'The Wall'. What better way to repair thousands of miles of devastation than to have millions of prisoners working for you instead of against you? It was a brilliant plan. And with over 5 million prisoners per State working hard and to the bone, cities were going to be repaired in record time. Iowa itself took less than seven months to repair, and within a year, it would be already reconstructed as to be christened a Republic. Quite soon, in an unfathomable amount of time really, the Magisterium grew from but a measly thirteen to an outstanding twenty-three Republics. Not to mention that over 190 million citizens had already been cataloged by this time.

Prof. Tamara Boggier

keeper, New York Republic Athenaeum

Penal complexes, detention centers, and all sorts of reformatories are emptied, and their inmates sent to work until rehabilitated into the Magisterium, or worse. It is a cruel, yet necessary punishment that sees the daily arrival of prisoners. And by September 15, over 33.7 million transgressors are sentenced to reconstruct the Midwest. A rather symbiotic relationship, the UNDO forces tear cities down simply for the transgressors to rebuild them in the image of the Magisterium. But despite such achievements, those rebels who retain their freedom continue with their assaults, violently attacking the Magisterium whenever and wherever they can.

In Wisconsin, VEDETTE Gen. Matthew Storm finally reaches his destination. He meets with UNDO Gen. Pamela Barnett in order to discuss the most productive way of dealing with Jake Stockwell, and finds a soldier willing to set ablaze the entire Midwest in search of her target. Storm, however, is not so eager in his desire to find the rebel leader, and tries to formulate a plan requiring less death.

The VEDETTE believes his National Offensive capable of containing the Midwestern States, while the UNDO play barricade across the boundary of the Republic. Barnett will hear of no such thing, charging Storm to play blockade instead, while she and her soldiers lead the offensive. An infantile argument that in no way furthers Pordan's agenda, this bickering forces the II High Magistrate to send word to both leaders.

Considering one more enthusiastic toward the mission than the other, Pordan orders Matthew Storm relinquish his authority over the National Offensive, and in substitution, Pamela Barnett takeover as Central Command. An infuriating demotion, Storm has no choice but to surrender his position to the endorsed leader of the UNDO. At that point, it is almost immediate that he begins feeling the effects of his relegation.

Barnett orders Storm to takeover the post of prison guard, while she and her company continue with their push westward. Obviously, she intends on entering Iowa, only to go through Minnesota with her foreign legion. To Barnett, it is a march toward solidifying the Magisterium rule in North America, while Storm views it as a bloodbath waiting to happen; likewise, a catastrophe that will set the Magisterium back years.

He, therefore, decides he must personally speak to the II High Magistrate if he intends on halting Barnett's expected genocide, and departs from his station in order to do so. In the meantime, the UNDO begin their march, taking only days before encountering rebel forces. As expected, blood begins to flow throughout Iowa, with the deaths of over 3,000 rebel members being reported in the first week.

It is yet another genocidal UNDO strike that brings chaos raining down on the Midwest, calling upon Jake Stockwell and his military forces to meet the threat head on.

Sources inform the Magisterium of a rebel offensive coming from out of Kansas, with military installation after military installation being destroyed and pillaged. And though Barnett is determined to quell such uprisings, she finds her UNDO encounter more resistance with each passing day.

The rebels are more than capable of giving her a fight, and that is something which threatens her advancements with possible failure.

Jake Stockwell hadn't let up one bit. Not with the Sedition Repression Bill in place. Not with the cataloging of nearly 200 million Americans. Not with the steel hyper-structures transforming the country into the image of the Magisterium. And not with millions of foreigners invading his land. In actuality, instead of ceasing his attacks, Stockwell intensified his assaults, and met the UNDO forces head-on. He'd heard of Pamela Barnett and her soldiers, and planned on testing them with everything he had. And when the two leaders did finally meet, only one would walk away.

Cecil Greenough
Grand Magistrate: The Biography of Kiril Pordan

Pordan logically ponders on such defeats, and finds himself troubled by their meanings. If such losses are allowed to continue, the Magisterium will undeniably fall. Enough a likelihood to crush the II High Magistrate's uncompromising spirit, it presses him to call for an emergency meeting with other nation leaders. The meeting takes place in Italy, and it is here Pordan makes clear the dark future facing all regimes.

The II High Magistrate speaks of the past, a time when rogue nations challenged peaceful governments on all fronts. He reminds them of the Persian war against Greece, the destruction of Rome by the hands of Barbarian hordes, the Nazis and their horrendous push through Europe, Al-Qaeda and their terrorist ways—tactics responsible for the horrors being seen even now. Kiril Pordan makes his case clear, and blames the division of countries for such terrors.

To him, a fractured world leaves room for nothing but rebellion and destruction, and he refuses to stand by and simply permit these dreads to persist. Hence, he again presents his design for ending said transgressions.

Once more using the dreadful situations taking place around the world, Pordan insists on the unification of all governments under the *Magisterium Edict*. A revolutionary proposition to say the least, the confederation would mean absolute Magisterium power throughout the entire world. A solitary government under which mankind would find its long awaited peace, it requires all nations consent to its existence. Pordan understands this, and makes it his primary task to make sure his counterparts understand it as well. But before any of this can come to pass, the Union of Nations must be as one in its agreement.

Therefore, with the situation in the Middle East deteriorating at such a rapid speed, Pordan suggest using that setting as a test model for global unification. The date is December 10, and the Union of Nations backs an Islamic People's Republic invasion against the northern borders of the Afro Islamic Union, sparking to life the *Islamic War of Ages*. Its goal: crush one so all may be saved. For if it can indeed be perfected, nothing will be able to halt the rise of the New World Order.

M.A. Martin

2047

THE GLOBAL MAGISTERIUM

The Great Divide: a concise history of the future

Snow blankets the outskirts of the Texas-Oklahoma border. A bright blue sky hangs above. Where there once stood a lush green landscape and thick trees, now there is only flurry dressed branches and a white expanse. This is the setting chosen by those who dare to resist the future. Far away from all populated cities, and escorted by a brigade of soldiers ready for battle, they stand guarded only by the Red River of the South. One is the leader of a Resistance daring to challenge an emerging empire, and the other is the President of a people believing themselves invincible.

Contrary to popular belief, this is the first time the two leaders of these parties are meeting. Gen. Jake Stockwell, a man in desperate need of military personnel, and President Arthur Havelock, the confident leader earnestly believing himself capable of defeating the Magisterium alone, their meeting finds Stockwell making clear the obstacles facing both their parties: the daily defeats being endured by Resistance fighters, the untold deaths suffered by those desiring Democracy, the enslavement forced upon their fellow Americans—those being cataloged as they speak, Stockwell believes the rebellions are fighting a losing battle.

The Magisterium is too organized to be overcome. Above all, Stockwell believes the country will in fact become the United Republic, and that all they know will be destroyed. A heartfelt speech affirmed by a plea for unification, Stockwell wants Havelock to join forces with him, and meet the Magisterium in all out war. A civil war to end all, it is a day he believes will be etched into the annals of history.

The petition stirs Arthur Havelock, once more proving to him that Stockwell is a fine leader, but it is not enough to convince him. Because before he can agree to any merger, he must first tackle his biggest concern with Stockwell's rebellion—AR2. A topic causing great vexation throughout the Southwest, especially to those standing firmest in their Christian faith, the problem is the reckless killing of innocents and the hell-bound act of suicide seen enacted by the adults and children of this faction.

Havelock and his army want nothing to do with these anarchists, and refuse to help Stockwell unless he distances himself from their brand of terrorism.

Arthur Havelock was a Christian. He believed in Jesus Christ as his Lord and Savior, and all his actions were dictated by the Good Book. He couldn't possibly yoke himself with a group such as AR2. Not only were they bandits and killers, Havelock had by now already discovered that they were aligning themselves with a man who'd claimed to be a Prophet up in Idaho. Those were two ungodly things the Western Alliance President and his Christian crusaders of the Southwest were willing to lose the war over, as silly as that may sound to me and you. And though he understood that a union between him and Stockwell could possibly mean the end of the Magisterium, he also believed that if anybody was going to help them win, it wasn't going to be Jake Stockwell. Only God could do that.

Prof. Tamara Boggier

keeper, New York Republic Athenaeum

It is a disquieting apprehension Stockwell can understand. He himself was once a believer, a preacher of the faith even, but those days are in the past. In the General's mind, the violent acts committed by AR2 are things the Resistance needs. The Magisterium needs to know that it is not invincible. They need to know that the American people are not helpless. And above all, they need to be put down by any means necessary. But for argument's sake, Stockwell offers Havelock proof concerning AR2 no longer operating as a separate entity of destruction, but as men and women of the Resistance.

He makes known the valiant efforts of all those once belonging to the radical group, and praises those who still carry the banner of AR2 as a reminder of all that has been sacrificed. They only target the Magisterium now. And though it is true those of the younger generation have been heeding the doctrines of a fanatical new spiritual movement, Stockwell believes that has no relevance pertaining to their desire for Democracy.

Arthur Havelock disagrees. The President of the Western Alliance sees Stockwell's reformed AR2 members as nothing more than terrorists hiding behind Democracy. He knows for a fact a number of them still the commit suicide bombings that kill innocent civilians. And though he agrees the Magisterium must be held accountable for its treacherous ascension, he refuses to sully his people with the abominable acts of such sinners as AR2.

Havelock wants nothing more than for the Resistance and the Western Alliance to join forces, and prays it will happen before the Magisterium conquers the entire country, but it is still something he is willing to risk. Righteousness which decrees the Resistance distance itself from all things AR2, Stockwell refuses, leaving Havelock no choice but to hand him over to his fate.

However, as a sign of goodwill, the President contributes 30,000 soldiers to the rebel cause, though it is not merely enough to halt the Midwestern push of the Magisterium. Disappointed, Stockwell returns to the front lines, eventually charging into Missouri in order to launch an attack on Iowa. The General can only set in stone the Resistance's agenda for the country, a course of action he hopes will entice Arthur Havelock sooner than later.

The Resistance encounters the advancing UNDO in the city of Springfield, and bravely engage them in deadly confrontation. It is pure carnage, but one Jake Stockwell knows must be done if Havelock is to realize the truth. This is a rebellion for freedom and liberty, and it cannot be lost, no matter what God says.

Halfway across the globe, in comparison, is another rebellion also risking everything it has in the name of God. A war fueled by the outcries of over 700 million dissenters, an empire threatened by a rising dominion, a people betrayed by brothers, and a doctrine that is again seen as one of extremism and destruction, it is the Afro Islamic Union, and its Muslim citizens are preparing for war.

The date is March 4, and the elderly leader of the Afro Islamic Union, Mahdi Abu abd Allah Muhammad, speaks to the world leaders of the Union of Nations. He transmits his words via the internet, and condemns the league for allowing the Islamic People's Republic to attack his people. An assault that has seen the deaths of nearly 25,000 innocent lives, and the displacement of over 12.2 million refugees, the elderly Mahdi makes known the injustice taking place, and swears the vengeance of Allah on each and every soldier trampling his land. Rhetoric the Union of Nations cares nothing to hear, it is something which eats away at the Mahdi's heart with each utterance.

It does not matter that he remains safe in his capital of Khartoum, Sudan. The suffering of his Afro Islamic Union citizens demands he feel their pain, and that is why he sends over 400,000 North African Afro Islamic Union soldiers to defend Medina and Mecca. But by comparison, it is a response that means almost nothing in view of the 2.6 million UNDO preparing to descend on his regime. Still, the Mahdi believes that if he can defeat the Mujahids of the Islamic People's Republic ahead of the crushing wave being prepared, it may deter the Union of Nations from unleashing their UNDO—a gamble at best.

The Mujahids of the Islamic People's Republic believe in Allah just as he does, they also believe in the Prophet as His last Apostle. And like the Muslims, the Mu'minūn soldiers believe in the holy words of the sacred Qur'an. But in stark contrast, they believe the Muslims of the Afro Islamic Union 'infidels' who affront God with their unrepentant sins. Crimes against the servants of Allah that deserve no mercy, the pent-up rage held captive within the Mu'minūn is expressed through a mighty military presence of nearly 650,000 soldiers.

No longer are the days of dust covered uniforms, sand packed vests, restricting robes, and hindering turbans—those warriors of the Middle East are no more. The Union of Nations backs their efforts now, and a more efficient Islamic warrior takes to the battlefield. Dragline Filament armored, Bio-guised, and adjoined with stabilized GAU-10 Gatlings, they are the unstoppable soldiers constructed from out of the men and women of the Islamic People's Republic. They are the Mujahids, an arrayed horde of sand and stone tinted battalions ready to slay all in their path.

Confronted with this, the Mahdi can do nothing as he continues to watch the conquering of the Arabian Peninsula, with the continent of Africa poised to follow. Therefore, his words to the Union of Nations are humble, but stern, respectful, but cautioning, mindful, but above all, bold. He makes clear the Afro Islamic Union will not idly standby and suffer such injustices without some sort of response. They too are a people of Allah, and no power on Earth will ever be able to crush them. He does not wish war, but is more than ready to partake in its spectacle.

The tone of the Islamic leader is something the Union of Nations is pleased to hear. In truth, they need the Afro Islamic Union to fight back, in that way they can be seen as the fanatics for which they truly are: terrorists —extremists—the enemy. Once that is accomplished, the UNDO will enter Arabia, crush the Jihadi, and be paraded as the defenders of true liberty. And in the end, the UNDO forces will reach greatness, and the Union of Nations will flourish across the globe. Law will then be reestablished, and civility will give way to superiority—a one world superiority. Rhetoric being spouted by Kiril Pordan, it gives him hope that perhaps his plans for the Union of Nations are not that far off.

It is a hopeful scenario the II High Magistrate can only wait to see made a reality. For now, a mighty war is set to wage against the Afro Islamic Union, and the Middle East is once again about to burn.

Mahdi Abu speaks to his people across the Afro Islamic Union. Nearly three quarters of a billion in number, they stand ready for his commands. Their leader's words are of compassion, but only after having vengeance. He speaks of honor, but also of the rejoicing in infidel blood. He cries out to God, holding his rifle and sword in the sky. This is Jihad, and this is what he is calling on his people to perform.

In the name of God, the Beneficent, the Merciful. Recall all you the sacred words of Sura Al Baqarah, Ayat 189 to 196. 'They ask you concerning the new moons. Say 'they are indications of times fixed for men and the pilgrimage'. It is not righteousness that you should enter your houses from behind, but the righteous one is the one who guards himself and enters his house by his doors, taking shelter in Allah so that you may be successful. And fight in the cause of Allah against those who fight you, but do not be aggressive, for Allah loves not aggressors. And slay them wherever you find them, and drive them away whence from they drove you away, for mischief is more grievous than slaughter. But fight not with them, nor unto the Sacred Mosque, until they fight with you therein. But slay them for such is the recompense of the infidels. But if they desist, then verily, Allah is forgiving and merciful. And fight them until there is no more mischief, and religion be only for Allah. But if they desist, then there should be no hostility save against the transgressors. A sacred month in reprisal for a second month; and reprisal is lawful in all things sacred. Whoever then inflicts aggression on you, you inflict aggression of the like on him as was inflicted by him on you. And fear Allah, and know that Allah is always with the pious ones. And expand in the path of Allah, and cast not yourselves with your own hands into perdition. And do good, for verily, Allah loves the beneficent ones. Complete the pilgrimage and Umra for the sake of Allah. But if you are prevented, then send whatever offering available to you, and shave not your heads until your offering has reached the place. But whoever among you is sick and has an ailment in his head, then let him effect a compensation by fasting or alms or sacrifice. But when you are secure from the hindrance, then whoever enjoys from the Umra to Hajj, let him offer whatever is available to him. But he who is not able to find any offering should fast for three days during the pilgrimage and for seven days when he returns; this makes the ten days complete. This is for him whose people dwell not near the Sacred Mosque. And fear Allah and know you that Allah is severe in requiting evil'. Allahu Akbar! Allahu Akbar! Allahu Akbar!

Mahdi Abu abd Allah Muhammad
Call for Jihad, April 16, 2047

The cry for jihad is heeded. Millions of Muslims travel to the Arabian Peninsula in search of war. No longer will there only be 400,000 Afro Islamic Union soldiers fighting for the Islamic regime, but over 3 million. A show of force led by such leaders as Idriss Hissou, Abakar El-Brazi, Kadidja Neqrouz, Pape ibn Hassan, and Ndeye Barek, the massive war machine of the Afro Islamic Union is formed out of thousands of battalions, scores of Field Commanders, and those brave enough to join them.

They say farewell to their families and friends, taking only their weapons and faith with them, staunchly joining their defenders in jihad with voices crying out to Allah. They believe God is on their side, and that they are invincible. They are prepared to do anything in order to drive the infidel from out of their land, and that means never returning to their loved ones if need be.

Crossing through Egypt and entering Aqaba, Jordan, they engage the Islamic People's Republic awaiting their arrival. They sail across the Red Sea from Eritrea, allowing them to set up bases all throughout Yemen. Resolve matching anything the Islamic People's Republic has to offer, this is the sort of drive which befalls the Mujahids when the Muslims arrive.

The Mu'minūn and Muslims believed in the same God, but that did not stop them from engaging in this brutal act. Children were there, and even that did not stop them. Mecca had to be won, and the Mu'minūn had to be pushed out. But at the same time, the Mu'minūn wanted Hajj, even if that meant the death of every Muslim living in Arabia and Africa. And in the middle of all this, was the Mahdi, alaihi al-salaam. He was the one who could stop it all, but he did not believe that to be what Allah wanted. To him, at least at this point, the Mu'minūn were no different than the infidels, and they too deserved to die. Unfortunately, it was this frame of mind that fueled the Islamic War of Ages.

Prof. Najiyah Abdullah Hassan

Crescent Moon and Pillars: The Rise of the Islamic Empire

Within days, fire rains down on Arabia. The Holy City of Mecca plays arena to its devastation. There is no mercy amongst soldiers. Blood praises their efforts. Limbs are severed. Bodies are riddled with holes. The screams of the wounded overlay loud explosions. Slaying hisses of ammunition dim in comparison to the wailing of mourners. It is absolute carnage. And before long, the cities of Riyadh, Al Jawf, Medina, and Mecca are made to typify the meaning of war.

Neighborhoods are razed to the ground. Injured citizens sob along with the sounds of bombs going off all around them. Smoke often eclipses the sun, and rubble litters streets, but none halt the detestation taking place in the Middle East. A massacre is a massacre, and the footage that makes it out of the Afro Islamic Union proves a massacre is exactly what is taking place.

All over the internet, the documentation of Mujahids decapitating men, raping and murdering Muslim women, and turning orphaned children into killers are transmitted. It is deplorable, and yet no country calls for its cease —at least, no country currently standing as a world super power. The United Republic of America and Royal European Alliance are the ones who promote this brutal discord, and neither one cares to see it end. Unfortunately for the Union of Nations, the Afro Islamic Union is stronger than they expect.

The Prometheus Flame reports what the mainstream media will not. And the truth is, the Muslim people being slaughtered in the streets are but a fraction compared to the Islamic Peoples' Republic soldiers being massacred.

Entire platoons are lost to roadside bombs. Suicide bombers rip apart dedicated defense forces. Terrorist attacks take place back in the IPR. All this is against the Mu'minūn who believe themselves invincible. Truly, the call for jihad has enticed a relentless anger from within those of the Muslim faction, an anger the Union of Nations needs to see put down.

In less than two months, the Islamic People's Republic soldiers are isolated within the Arabian Peninsula, and are left vulnerable to defeat. Their brigades are separated. Field Commanders fail to work cohesively, leading to chaotic loses. The IPR Air Force is hindered by Mujahid prisoners being used as human shields. The Muslims threaten everything the Union of Nations is working so hard to achieve, and can very well deceive the rest of the world into thinking they can do the same.

Regardless of this, the Union of Nations refuses to call the conflict to an end, not until the Afro Islamic Union recognizes their authority. So as Mujahids try hunkering down in Mecca, using the Holy City as a last line of defense, Loyalists and Alliance members alike demand a triumphant strategy toward ending the war.

The leaders of the Union of Nations keep calm amongst their populace with assurance and propaganda, but that does not stop the criticisms being heard from out of the Pacific. Because after so many years of being dormant, a once silent voice has finally decided to speak. It is Japan, and it now heads a newly formed empire prepared to express its displeasure, a displeasure everyone will take notice of—especially those of the Union of Nations.

Japan had been working long and hard at building a functioning empire. Domoto Eisaku, the former General of the Japanese Military, along with dozens of Asian leaders decided it best if they became a Coalition, and had drawn all the Asian countries to their side with a promise that they would not fall before the Magisterium. Over 2 billion in all, they were not afraid, and they were ready to show this. So, distrusting the Union of Nations the way they did, the Asian people wasted no time instigating a war with them. Of course, they could have simply waited for the Union of Nations to act against them, but they refused to wait.

Tsun-chúng Hu

The Last Dynasty: The Chinese Republic's Ultimate Demise

Late fall, and Asia's newly fashioned bond stands ready to reveal itself to the world. No longer will it be viewed as a humanitarian effort focused on salvaging China's ruined society, or a squabbling political experiment trying desperately to unify the countries of Mongolia, Myanmar, Laos, Thailand, Vietnam, Cambodia, Malaysia, Taiwan, Philippines, and Korea. After much deliberation, affairs of state, fighting, and compromise, Asia has been amalgamated into a functioning power.

Japan currently stands as its nominated director. A unity that is wholeheartedly established throughout the Orient, the recently christened Imperial Asiatic Alliance decides to make known its disapproval of the Union of Nations.

It first addresses the situation facing the Afro Islamic Union, and declares the Islamic People's Republic invasion of the region a hostile act capable of defusing the peace once seen in the Middle East. And though recognizing the fact Muslims have denied the Mu'minūn entry into Mecca for Hajj, the Imperial Asiatic Alliance warns the Union of Nations of its involvement in such matters.

The Asian empire believes this to be a dispute between brothers, and sees no benefit in foreign powers getting involved. On the contrary, the Asians make the case Union of Nations' involvement will only bring about more suffering to the region, and that an immediate withdrawal from said regions would be the wisest move to make.

It is a recommendation the Union of Nations discounts, choosing instead to portray the Imperial Asiatic Alliance as a rogue establishment dedicated toward challenging the advancements of the world. Nothing more than an allegation, it is enough of a threat to which the Union of Nations stands ready to respond.

Declaring the Imperial Asiatic Alliance an unrecognized power, the Union of Nations begins to formulate a plan concerning the dismantling of such fraud. Plans which call for the seizures of unclaimed Asiatic territories: Bhutan, Nepal, Bangladesh, Sri Lanka, and above all, India, the Union of Nations gears itself to build an evident barrier between the Imperial Asiatic Alliance and the rest of the Eastern Hemisphere. This is, of course, seen as nothing short of a declaration of war as far as the Imperial Asiatic Alliance is concerned, and it responds by sending delegates to India in order to meet with the country's leaders.

The Imperial Asiatic Alliance representatives enter Southwest Asia with the intention of merging with the nations there, as well as, to remind them of the Islamic People's Republic threat to their sovereignty. They make clear the fact if either India, Nepal, or Sri Lanka joins the UN, not only will they be merging with a fascist way of thinking, they will also be siding with their long time enemy of Pakistan. A good enough argument toward getting India to join the Imperial Asiatic Alliance, the meeting is held in New Delhi on September 24, and sees the induction of India into the Imperial Asiatic Alliance mere days later.

The move infuriates the Union of Nations, leaving it with no other alternative but to follow through with its pledge of over 2.6 million UNDO soldiers into the heart of the Middle East. A dreadful step to be taken, it is agreed upon just as the rest of the Southwestern Asiatic nations unite with the Imperial Asiatic Alliance in the following weeks.

In Europe, the Royal European Alliance needs no such impositions of the UNDO forces upon its people, not when it gladly invites their presence across its entire regime. A little under 750,000 American VEDETTE at last being contributed by the United Republic, it is an act that, as expected, riles those of the Grimaldi Defiance, while perturbing the Royal European Alliance's loyal subordinates.

No different than the positions taking place in the United Republic, rebels and the UNDO clash in battles of complete bedlam, as citizens voice their disapproval of foreigners staging war on their land. And with the situation looking as if it will only get worse before it gets better, the Royal European Alliance leaders again meet in the Union of Nations to revisit II High Magistrate Kiril Pordan's plan of governmental unification.

They now believe the ICE-chip and *Magisterium Edict* the only aid against the dissension waning their regimes, and want to ensure a more promising future for all. So they decide to adhere to the II High Magistrate's New World Order Schema.

The Magisterium will span the entire Royal European Alliance, further fortifying its ability to remain dominant, and is hailed on November 7, throughout Europe for such a promise.

Many historians believe that the REA entered this agreement due to fear and coercion. That notion is absolutely bullocks. The leaders of the Royal European Alliance saw an opportunity for greatness, and simply seized it. It was obvious that the United Republic was growing at a rapid speed, and that the more than 2 million UNDO contributed soldiers stationed in the West were aiding that process nurture. Why would they not take advantage of such a profitable procedure? They had rebels. They had wars. And they had people capable of threatening their rule. Their Alliance members needed assurance that they were safe, and that is what the REA intended on giving them—Assurance.

Prof. Jarvis Grimes

historian, *Superior and Biased: The History of the Royal European Alliance*

The dawn of the Global Magisterium has arrived, and with it, the emergence of the New World Order. Even the governments of the State of Israel and Islamic Peoples' Republic enlist in its practice, further infuriating the rest of the free world.

No longer are the UNDO to be seen as foreigners joining strength in order to quell national uprisings. No more is the Union of Nations to be seen as an assembly for various countries with hidden agendas and corrupt motives. And no more are the people of the Union of Nations to be considered a mere coalition—friends of convenience. From this day forward, the Union of Nations is but one label devoted to the Global Magisterium, the most powerful authority in the world. An Autocracy feeding the needy, clothing the poor, and educating the lost, Autocracy is now the zeitgeist of this era. And it finally perfects its veracity with the choosing of its ultimate leader, the Grand Magistrate.

To no one's surprise, it is none other than Kiril Pordan himself given the title. And almost immediately, the newly inaugurated Grand Magistrate initiates a full scale assault on the Afro Islamic Union, while the citizens of Royal European Alliance, the State of Israel, and Islamic People's Republic are abundantly cataloged.

You don't really see an outcry over the ICE-chip like you saw in the United Republic. As a matter of fact, people in Europe were flocking in droves to be cataloged. Even the Israelis, and Mu'minūn of the Islamic People's Republic wanted to be cataloged. And though there were some isolated acts of insurrection, the cataloging of these new Loyalists went rather smoothly. Now as for Kiril Pordan being made Grand Magistrate, this didn't really catch anybody off guard. Let's not forget, the people around the world had seen Pordan as the Union of Nations' leader for years. So now that the Union of Nations had been turned into the Global Magisterium, it was only fitting that Pordan be made its first official Grand Magistrate.

Cecil Greenough

Grand Magistrate: The Biography of Kiril Pordan

A sweeping force of unmatched intensity, in the same way, it is a major threat to the world ever returning to the past. Monarch Edward Davies, Prime Minister Jacob Manishewitz and Ayatollah Parvaiz Makhmalbaf all resign their ranks, and appellate themselves High Magistrates, further setting the Global Magisterium in stone. And soon enough, the Global Magisterium is indistinguishable in the wars it wages.

No longer are regimes battling internal insubordination, such egotistical objectives serve no true purpose in an Autocracy. Instead, all resistances are now only to be seen as comprehensive opponents to the world's irrefutable authority—one enemy against one order.

In time, Grand Magistrate Kiril Pordan will do what has not been done since the time of Genesis. The man who gave birth to the very law governing the conduct of this Autocratic order will unify the world. This time he believes God has ordained it, and the time has come for an end to the Great Divide. That end is the Global Magisterium, and all those beneath its rule hail its injunction.

M.A. Martin

2049
AEGIS

The Global Magisterium deploys over 13 million newly decreed AEGIS soldiers to the frozen borders of Germany, Austria, and the Czech Republic on February 10. A devoted fusion of the Royal European Alliance's SENTRIES, the United Republic's VEDETTE, the State of Israel's Tzahal, and the Mujahids of the Islamic Peoples' Republic, AEGIS is the only military force recognized in the world created by the Global Magisterium.

They are encased in anatomized bio-protected black armament. Their faces are safeguarded behind menacing menpōs with glowing infrared eyes and sallet helmets. They are adorned with an array of weapons, but primarily trademarked by devastating XM-300 Gatling railguns. Everything is reinforced with DLF technology: tanks, aerial fighters, naval crafts—everything. And trained to be the most efficient soldier to have ever existed in the whole of history, the AEGIS come complete with no fear, no pain, and no mercy.

They live only to serve the Global Magisterium, and their mission is inimitable and adamant: wrestle back the lands that have been lost during the Grimaldi Defiance's offensive, and convert those who live in those same countries to the *Magisterium Edict*. A well-plotted course to see the installation of the Global Magisterium by late June, 2049, throughout all of Europe, such campaigns do not flourish without their inevitable set of challenges.

Poverty, cries of injustice, and the slow-moving process of ICE-chip cataloging in Eastern Europe all play their part in attempting to stall the Global Magisterium advance, while the Grimaldi Defiance battles the push on every front. It is not long before the cities of Germany's already charred and desolate skyline begin to burn, with an estimated 7,000 civilian deaths reported within days.

The Prometheus Flame and other rogue internet news sources report on the violence and destruction, steadfastly portraying the Global Magisterium as a ruthless persecutor of freedom. They make sure to transmit the frightening images of people being oppressed, arrested, and shot, while blaming none other than Grand Magistrate Kiril Pordan for such horrors.

An ardent cant further infuriating those fighting for a return to the past, it is a burden to the worldwide prosperity of the Global Magisterium.

Soon enough, the world begins to see the full influence of its establishment, as word of genocide begins to ensue around the globe. This demands the Global Magisterium put in place a retaliatory campaign rejecting such gossips and mendacities, insisting it furnish its side of the facts. Thus, through Global Magisterium eyes, the mission of the *Purification Schema* is rendered a peace keeping, humanitarian, world salvaging process by which the future of the planet will be secured.

Kiril Pordan had the difficult job of not only furthering his mission, but also doing it with the acceptance of those who served him. The AEGIS was a military force that didn't see nationalities, but only insurgents. And they cut those insurgents down without any tact or restraint. It was absolutely challenging to the newly christened Grand Magistrate to have them perform their duties, and make them look like angels of mercy at the same time. But somehow, Pordan did it. With mass propaganda and well veiled coercion, Pordan didn't only have the AEGIS systematically eliminate all threats, he did it in plain view of all international Loyalists.

Prof. Tamara Boggier

keeper, New York Republic Athenaeum

News agencies throughout the Global Magisterium parade continuous footage of those without food being mercifully fed and sustained, while those who are homeless are sheltered. The rapid reconstruction plan seen in the United Republic is repeated in Europe and the Middle East. Stable apartment buildings that house millions, homes for families to find peace and comfort, as well as, Depots and Factories for them to work and shop are all constructed in record time. Somatic Cell Nuclear Transfer, a process manipulating nature's law of reproduction now produces meat, vegetables, grains, fruits, and dairy products. In the same way, those Loyalists, internationally, that are sick, are given medicine and treated for their ailments, further proving to the Loyalists of the Global Magisterium that theirs is a godly path chosen for them by the Grand Magistrate Kiril Pordan.

A misinformation driven battle for the support of over 7.3 billion souls, the conflicting views create new rebels, as well as, Loyalists every day. An agenda benefiting those who submit to the Global Magisterium, those who resist are thoroughly punished.

The fighters of the Grimaldi Defiance have been beaten back toward the former German cities of Leipzig and Munich. There, the tanks of the AEGIS fire shell after shell, destroying rebel lines, while jets streak across the sky delivering payloads of bullets and rockets. Fire appears grayish in the gloom of smoke and soot, but such bleakness spares no eye the dead stretched out across the cities.

Blood stains the snow blanketed earth, and debris of all manner dot the land, casting eerie shadows over the crimson. The beaten comrades of the Grimaldi Defiance surrender, or die to AEGIS marching across The Fatherland.

The XM-300 does its task in chopping down body after body, regardless if its sable rounds must devour concrete and steel to do so. Its hauler is also a weapon. Using such destructive techniques in subduing their enemy, AEGIS feel nothing in enacting such barbarism. But destruction is not the only thing these Autocratic warriors bring, but security and order. For as the AEGIS march effortlessly through Germany, horribly mowing down those who resist the Global Magisterium, behind them follows an equally as dedicated rescue effort.

The *Sedition Repression Act* is precise and cruel when imitated by the European Magisterium. Grimaldi Defiance prisoners are put to 'The Wall' to suffer their fate. Rebels try fleeing north away from the backbreaking tasks of constructing new European Republics, but it happens regardless of their involuntary participation. These cities and streets are no longer to be the skyline of old Europe, but a further proliferation of the Global Magisterium. Something these rebels refuse to be part of, their attempt at escaping is ceased when the developing Magisterium of the Scandinavian Peninsula stands as a blockade to their retreat.

The former Saami Coalition Force has found favor in the court of the Global Magisterium, and revises its Nordic principles to stand against the rebels. No more do they spare warriors fighting for freedom. Now the Scandinavian Magisterium keeps at bay cowards fleeing from their deaths. A perturbing view on how a war should be fought, and who to side with, and why, Finland, Norway, and Sweden abandon Eastern Europeans to their fate.

Thus, once again, even here, where the people once preferred death over being cataloged, construction projects are accomplished without stall. The homeless are sheltered. The starving are fed. The sick are healed. People receive the ICE-chip. And above all, the *Magisterium Edict* becomes the harbinger of hope. Still, the war across Eastern Europe is far from done.

The Grimaldi Defiance dare continue their insurrection, with names such as Hall, Bartok, Hänsch, and the war fashioned King himself, William V, leading the resistance. In response, the Global Magisterium first deploys well-constructed AEGIS regiments into the infinitesimal nation of Slovenia, and block all rebel attempts at using the country as a low blow. Leipzig, meanwhile, will be used to launch a bombardment of missiles into the hearts of Poland and the Czech Republic, while calculated aerial assaults lay waste to Austria. An unmerciful onslaught killing thousands, the blitzes lay ruin to structures, as bombs scorch the earth in an effort to discipline those who are disobedient.

In light of such destruction and carnage, the Southeastern European nations, the Slovak Republic to Moldova, down through Bulgaria, and across to Albania, they all unavoidably bow to such display of dominance, and pledge loyalty to the Global Magisterium. However, that is something not being seen in Belarus, not where King William V continues to make a courageous stand against the AEGIS.

He and over 7 million men and women stand primed for battle in Hrodna and Minsk, while his allies, Sir Owen Hall, Commodore Georges Hänsch, and General Karl Bartok stand in reserve throughout the Ukraine. But when the tired, war-torn rebels encounter a war machine of endless fury, the King and his reserves are crushed. And by August 21, the news of Europe being fully subdued by the Global Magisterium is reported all over the planet, with the security of Russia being made the established order's next aim.

It is a partial accuracy giving hope to all adhering to the *Magisterium Edict*, even if rebels still continue both day and night to resist its definiteness. But rebels are not the only ones to voice such arguments, not with the Imperial Asiatic Alliance joining in on the dispute pertaining to Europe's absolute conquering.

Eastern Europe had been subdued. And now all the rebels that had been living in those countries, had all been but pushed into Russia. It did not matter that minute factions still lingered in the streets of Krakow, Kiev, or Minsk. The main threat of the Grimaldi Defiance had been beaten back, and now Russia had to be taken. But let us not forget that the last time Russia had been a chess piece of sorts, the Chinese had been its players. In other words, Asia. And so, the Imperial Asiatic Alliance somehow saw an attack on the former Silovik Republic as an attack on itself. The opportunity the Imperial Asiatic Alliance had been waiting for regarding putting on display its might was finally here, and they quickly displayed what they were capable of.

Prof. Jarvis Grimes

historian, *Superior and Biased: The History of the Royal European Alliance*

The Imperial Asiatic Alliance had been waiting to join into the global conflict for a long time. They did not like the Union of Nations, and they most definitely did not like Kiril Pordan. On many occasions they had made that obvious. One Imperial Asiatic Alliance representative was even reported as saying "As long as men bow before swine, the world will be a pigpen." The hate for Pordan obviously came from his actions during World War III, where he had personally committed acts of genocide against the Chinese, but had never been prosecuted for any of it. The Imperial Asiatic Alliance had never forgotten this, and they never could. Unfortunately, the Global Magisterium had become synonymous with Pordan, and that made anyone part of its order an enemy too.

Tsun-chúng Hu

The Last Dynasty: The Chinese Republic's Ultimate Demise

The Empire of the Orient first sends word to the Scandinavian Magisterium, and makes clear it desires an audience with the men and women of the former Saami Coalition Force.

The Imperial Asiatic Alliance sees no need to have quarrel with such an honorable institution, and bargain for the Scandinavian Magisterium to stay neutral in whatever trouble may arise between itself and the European Magisterium. In exchange for said nonaligned status, the Asians will expand the Saami Coalition Force's border into Russia, from Murmansk to Petrozavodsk—a place once seen as a part of the Saami region. And as expected, seizing the opportunity of new territory without hesitation, the Nordic see the SENSHI of Asia as warriors, and agree to a neutrality up until the moment the Imperial Asiatic Alliance tries fleeing the battlefield.

The Asians assure the Saami they will die before fleeing, and depart with an oath to prove such surety. Then meeting with the elected Emperor of the Imperial Asiatic Alliance, Domoto Eisaku, the Democratic leaders of the Orient voice their concerns over the Global Magisterium push toward Russia, and order him to do something about it.

They argue the Magisterium will use its encroachment on the former Russian Republic as a platform to launch strikes against Asia, and demand that a military response be given to such intrusions. An insisting the Emperor cannot ignore, the request forces him to order the deployment of over 22 million Imperial Asiatic Alliance soldiers to the front lines of both the ruined cities of Moscow and St. Petersburg. A mission currently portrayed solely as one of defense, an engagement with Global Magisterium AEGIS is not entirely ruled out. In fact, the Magisterium sees it as nothing less, and demands the Imperial Asiatic Alliance recall its troops.

The Imperial Asiatic Alliance discounts the directive, and in turn, states its own demands of Magisterium withdrawal from said regions. This is interpreted as an obvious show of insolence and noncompliance toward Global Magisterium authority, asserting Grand Magistrate Pordan begin drawing up plans for a surefire clash with the Asiatic Empire.

Keep in mind that the Imperial Asiatic Alliance could have only entered Russia's western cities by land or sea. And with a threat of the Islamic People's Republic intercepting its underbelly while it crossed the continent of Russia, the Imperial Asiatic Alliance had no choice but to send a major fraction of its military by the latter. A journey that spanned the

Bering, up through the Chukchi, East Siberian and finally the Barents and Kara seas, by the time the Imperial Asiatic Alliance reached its destination, the ruins of Moscow and St. Petersburg had already been under attack. The AEGIS lines were impenetrable, and the Imperial Asiatic Alliance looked as if it was going to have to go up against a wall. But then the very people they were trying to save turned out to be the ones that saved them.

Prof. Tamara Boggier

keeper, New York Republic Athenaeum

The Grand Magistrate receives full support from High Magistrates Davies, Manishewitz, and Makhmalbaf, and authorizes the dispatch of a full scale assault. 5 million AEGIS in all converging on Russia sees the initial fighting between the two powers commence on October 12, with over 5,000 deaths being reported on the first day.

The devastated city of Moscow plays host to the brutality. And by the end of the month, St. Petersburg, Leningrad, Novgorod, Smolensk and Pskov have all become involved in the ravaging fray.

Desolated skylines, scorched streets, black smoke, poisonous gases, all of it joins in on the icy dreadfulness that is Russia. A bloodbath to say the least, the battle over the fallen Mother is dubbed the *Red War*, and the blood which flows more than validates its brand.

Soldiers fall in surrender of their spirits, but a sense of pride burns within their dying frames. Pride in their bravery, a pride in their oath, a pride in their belief, Kiril Pordan uses the fires of these prides to reshape the destiny of the planet, mercilessly completing the utmost erasure of all rebellion. But rebel fighters of the Grimaldi Defiance aid the Imperial Asiatic Alliance soldiers, and disclose the hidden underbellies of their nation. A horde of war wrecked insubordinates, they not only lead the Asians through the long forgotten underground passages of Kakhovskaya, Butovskaya, Koltsevaya, Kihmsko-Lyuberetskaya'; all of them once part of Russia's intricate Metro Station, they gladly die in honor of the Imperial Asiatic Alliance's demand for Democracy.

Their sacrifices and call for justice are overwhelming. No matter man, woman, or child, the rebels of the Grimaldi Defiance all die without regret. Thousand are killed—no one to ever remember their names. One of millions, it consumes Emperor Domoto to the point of tears, just as much as it wears away at Kiril Pordan.

Domoto knows his SENSHI soldiers are well-trained, formidable, and more than capable of withstanding the Global Magisterium push, but he cannot help but feel absolute sorrow for the Russo-Hungarian, Germanic, and Polish renegades dying all around them. Sacrifices that are enough to distress any leader, Pordan may believes he is offering the people something far greater than Democracy, but still struggles to understand what it is of Democracy's failed theology the rebellion craves so much.

Nevertheless, the Imperial Asiatic Alliance poses a great threat, and the Grand Magistrate must devise a plan of destabilizing them before taking on any new mission. For now, an ongoing conflict is leveling the heartland of Pordan's' own backyard, and it is a disastrous demolition further being strengthened by Gen. Jake Stockwell of the United States Resistance.

41.583202°N 93.64907°W. December 25, Christmas Day. There is no Santa Claus. There are no presents. The only trees standing are those that have not yet been burnt to the ground, or chopped for firewood. And the only tune that plays is the song of heartbeats sounding to their impending deaths—heartbeats belonging to fighters preparing themselves to die.

The rebel military known as the United States Resistance stands at the threshold of victory. A fight that has seen more than two years of tears, blood, and death, the violently waged war over Iowa will finally be decided on this day. It takes place in the very heart of Terrace Hill, Des Moines, where 5.2 million men, women, and youths dedicated to the dream of Democracy will either have their liberty, or their deaths.

These patriots stare across a frozen expanse of ice and carnage, and behold the more than 3.2 million AEGIS once more descending upon them. A Global Magisterium mass, they approach with a convoy of tanks, fighter jets, and guns. A sea of black and red is all they give the impression of being, but the military corp. of the United States Resistance knows better. Yes indeed, they know of the atrocities committed by this groundswell of pitch and crimson, as well as, what it has in store for them.

Those who are not killed will be enslaved, or face a worse fate—they will become a Loyalist. That is something neither person serving under Stockwell's command will permit of him or herself. Their leader is the man that has called them together to fight, a man who dares challenge the Global Magisterium at every turn. The one who promises them freedom, liberty, and justice for all. His name is Jake Stockwell, and he intends on giving his soldiers the State of Iowa.

It will be no different than the battles of Jefferson City, Missouri, Grand Island, Nebraska, or Little Rock, Arkansas, all of them standing as victories that have wrestled States away from Kiril Pordan's menacing grasp. States that stand as beacons of hope for all who fight, States that are Democratic, Jake Stockwell will do exactly in Iowa what he has done when facing those past challenges. He will defeat the newly fashioned AEGIS, proving once and for all Democracy is not dead.

The victory is easier said than done, however, especially with the Global Magisterium being far more advanced. But then again, it was never any different in the past, and will not be so now.

Regrettably for Gen. Stockwell, one thing has more than dramatically changed. He no longer fights an international patchwork military force led by a reluctant leader. In reality, what comes for him this time is nothing less than a cohesive Autocratic unit directed by a callous Loyalist desiring nothing but rebel blood.

When the AEGIS came and the rebellion encountered them, if any rebel was left alive, you can say it was because there were Americans amongst those particular AEGIS. That was the only form of mercy meeting the rebels during these battles, that of their fellow Americans. The Mu'minūn, Israelis, but more so the Europeans, they killed without regard, slaughtered entire families, and burned down cities without remorse, almost as if trying to destroy America's skylines. This, of course, built small rifts amongst the AEGIS, between the Americans and the rest of their so-called coalition. Nonetheless, the former VEDETTE served Kiril Pordan, and so they fulfilled their sense of duty. Not to mention that they had Pamela Barnett to answer to. A woman who, if sensing any sort of treason, would kill even her own. With her taking over for Matthew Storm, the American AEGIS had no choice but to unleash Hell.

Prof. Tamara Boggier

keeper, New York Republic Athenaeum

AEGIS Gen. Pamela Barnett has put aside her angst for her American targets, and has labeled all rebels—traitors. And though she has tasted defeat at the hands of these turncoats more than once, this day in Iowa will be different. This day, the Global Magisterium will destroy Jake Stockwell and the United States Resistance, finally bringing calm to the Midwest.

What you had here were two people with wins and losses under their belts. Shockingly though, Barnett had proven to be less of a warrior than Matthew Storm was. Jake Stockwell had beaten her in nearly a dozen different battles, and now they were about to meet on Terrace Hill. There's snow everywhere. It's cold. Stockwell's men are hungry. They're tired. And barreling down on them in a uniformed march is the AEGIS, Kiril Pordan's crushing horde. It must've been frightening, and the men and women of the United States Resistance didn't think they could win this time. This was the fight that may very well decide the war, and the odds were in the Magisterium's favor. Then again, these were the kind of odds Jake Stockwell had been leading the Resistance into so many times before. You can even say this was the way he liked it.

Cecil Greenough

Grand Magistrate: The Biography of Kiril Pordan

Tanks pound the Resistance with constant firings of shell after shell. The rebels respond with shells of their own, followed by blitzkrieg-like rocket fire from above. Their jets cry as they soar through the sky, ruthlessly carpet-bombing entire AEGIS battalions. Jet streaks carve the sky, while explosions ignite all the heavens. But in retaliation, not only are the rebels met with superior air attacks, they can do almost nothing when watching their comrades below be ripped apart by nonstop missile fire.

Dirt rushes to the high blue, and concrete is smashed to pieces by bullets being fired from all directions. Explosions rip apart entire buildings, and the sound of frantic screaming plays score to butchery. The sun barely peers through the already foggy sky, only to be blackened out by the pitch of rising smoke. And amongst this entire despondent display, this chaotic onslaught, wars Jake Stockwell, proud General of the United States Resistance, and loathed United Republic traitor.

His destiny is clear to him this day. He will win the State of Iowa, and return it to its citizens. He will then march on Minnesota, and then into the States of Wisconsin, Illinois, Indiana, Michigan, and Ohio. The Midwest will be free, and the Republic will fall. Stockwell has seen it a thousand times in his dreams, and is determined to make it a reality.

His gun rattles in his grasp, as acid burns through his muscles. His face is scarred, but his grimace of anger twists his visage even more. His heart pummels his chest with its hammering, and he surveys the clash proceeding around him. Indeed, Stockwell is nothing like Grand Magistrate Kiril Pordan. For while the architect of Autocracy hides in the capital of his dear Republic, Jake Stockwell stands amongst the unraveling, and risks his life in order to give rise to Democracy.

The United States Resistance has proven its worth on more than one occasion, and the Global Magisterium knows of its strength. So with a mighty cry, the unwavering rebellion pushes on with its fight, and dares the Global Magisterium to stop them.

Blood, sweat, and tears, the fight claims over 2.1 million souls. And by February 3, 2050, on a cold winter's morning in Des Moines, Iowa, the AEGIS once more stand defeated. The United States Resistance has won the *Battle of Terrace Hill*, and millions of Iowans cheer their triumph.

The Star Spangled Banner waves high. Democracy has been defended. Autocracy has again been shown its fallacy. From all over the Midwest these rebels have come unifying under one banner, and now they are free. Once more having beaten the so-called unbeatable AEGIS, it will now be on to Sioux City. That is, after they have celebrated. But for Jake Stockwell, the fight is not quite a success.

Receiving intelligence concerning AEGIS Gen. Barnett's retreat toward Minnesota, he gives chase with the intent of putting an end to her once and for all. She has sent word to a division ahead of her by three days, and expects to rendezvous with them as reinforcements. A reported 25.2 million AEGIS soldiers crossing all through Wisconsin and Illinois, Jake

Stockwell cannot allow it. Such a force could very well crush every rebel throughout the Midwest, especially when they are so fractured. Not to mention it also does not help that Arthur Havelock sits in the Southwest refusing to join forces, instead playing religious politics in the face of annihilation.

In the end, the United Republic of America will come to pass, but only if Barnett is allowed to converge with her reserves. Hence, with this grim possibility in sight, Stockwell and little less than 8,000 soldiers storm across the snowy heartland, desperately pursuing the routed AEGIS General and her party.

By the time the Battle of Terrace Hill had taken place, Jake Stockwell had already been a big time celebrity. Everybody knew about him. There were even kids in the Republic imitating him with their friends. A Magisterium adviser once even wrote, "The American people love Jake Stockwell so much, that when they learn of his victories, Kiril Pordan goes to bed early so that he doesn't have to hear them cheer." And this was the man Pamela Barnett had sworn to kill—the man who was the rebellion.

Cecil Greenough

Grand Magistrate: The Biography of Kiril Pordan

Stockwell ultimately catches up to Barnett in Preston, Minnesota, and engages her with the small number of rebels he has tracked her down with. He knows Barnett and her men are beaten, and does not believe he needs reinforcements. A deceitful method of clashing then fleeing which throws the AEGIS off guard, the Resistance's blitzkrieg is something the Global Magisterium soldiers cannot match.

The rebels are willing to die in fruitless attacks, only to lure the AEGIS into brutal skirmishes. They then use their knowledge of the cities to their advantage, and corner battalions in the most cramped of spaces. Unorthodox and scheming, they are capable of locking the AEGIS in bloody battles that sometime last weeks. And though the AEGIS try to force themselves free of these trapping scenarios, their attempts only leave them open to the attacks of suicide bombers.

The AEGIS never know whether they are winning or losing, that is, until it is too late. And as they have done so many times before, the Resistance drags their battle against Gen. Barnett and her losing battalion. Then, fatiguing the AEGIS with exhausting conflict, the rebels do so just long enough for their fanatical suicide attacks to bring closure.

On an early Sunday morning, Stockwell once more stands on the verge of victory. Barnett is cornered, her troops decimated, their vehicles, and aircraft pounded and charred. The General of the United States Resistance is about to be triumphant once more. Alas, it will not come to pass this time.

Barnett has held out long enough, and by February 6, the detached military force of the United States Resistance encounters the AEGIS reserves. 25.2 million soldiers determined to kill all those not of the Global Magisterium, the rebels are butchered all throughout Rochester in less than a week, with the survivors as prisoners of war. Jake Stockwell is one such prisoner, and it is AEGIS Gen. Barnett that personally supervises his detainment.

She brings him to the Republic of Washington D.C., and delivers his beaten body before the very feet of the Grand Magistrate in person. A victory beyond victories, the leader of the United States Resistance is finished, and so is his war.

On March 2, 2050, Stockwell finds himself standing before the Adjudicators of the United Republic Magisterium, with millions of Loyalists watching his trial.

"I ain't betrayin' myself by deed or facial expression. Do as you will. I'm ready!" the famous oath spoken by Jake Stockwell the last time he was on television before his trial. Kiril Pordan didn't speak to Jake Stockwell once during the trial. Though the two of them were less than twenty feet away from each other, they said absolutely nothing to one another. They didn't even make eye contact. When Jake Stockwell was standing there in the center of the Supreme Court's Chamber being charged with over 12,000 counts of treason and terrorism, he only spoke to the Judges who questioned him. You can almost say that he used his trial not to defend himself, but to try and reason with those who claimed to be protecting America. He spoke about Democracy, and how they'd all betrayed it. Even then, as Stockwell stood there bashing Autocracy and all it stood for, Kiril Pordan never uttered a single word to him. Instead, the Grand Magistrate spoke of Autocracy's benefit, condemning everyone who rejected that thought. A powerful statement on both their parts, it really showed just how much they believed in what they were fighting for. This wasn't personal. This was war.

Cecil Greenough

Grand Magistrate: The Biography of Kiril Pordan

Stockwell is found guilty on all charges. The offer of leniency in return for the rebel leader's accepted cataloging is made per *Magisterium Edict* decree, but Stockwell mulishly refuses. This leaves the United Republic Magisterium with no other choice but to sentence him to death. A day that will challenge the Resistance to persevere, it is a day that sees the death of a true democratic patriot.

Stockwell is eventually strapped to a gurney with sodium thiopental, pancuronium bromide, and potassium chloride coursing through his veins. And though still holding on to the dream of Democracy even then, and reciting the *Pledge of Allegiance* for the last four minutes of his life, Stockwell does, before dying, cease the vow if only to condemn the Global Magisterium with his final breath. A spectacle that lasts all of five minutes, at the end of it all, Jake Stockwell, General of the United States Resistance is dead.

News of Stockwell's death reaches as far as the Imperial Asiatic Alliance, and results in a worldwide mourning to such loss. Those who oppose the Global Magisterium see this as nothing less than martyrdom, and swear to avenge the rebel leader's murder. It is a threat the Global Magisterium does not panic over, the reason Jake Stockwell's death is put on display for all to see.

The world is made to observe the rebel leader's corpse hung in shame, proving that a dissenter's future holds nothing but death and humiliation. The ever-expanding Republic is reminded of his atrocities, and is made to see him as the vile killer that he was. Propaganda put in place to discredit the deceased rebel, the world bears witness to the only outcome of going against the New World Order.

The Global Magisterium will continue to rise, and all who stand in its way will fall. Stockwell is yet another example of that, and anyone wishing to join him simply need defy the masters of the planet. A threat President Arthur Havelock wishes to put to the test, he decides to do so on March 25, in a violent attack on Baton Rogue, Louisiana.

The strike catches a battalion of AEGIS stationed there by surprise, and leaves over 10,000 of them dead. Havelock then orders their corpses be put on display, and feeds the images of slaughter and mayhem through the Prometheus Flame's rogue intranet sites. In doing this, the President of the Western Alliance hopes to make clear the Global Magisterium is not the only one capable of brutality. A fact he makes resoundingly obvious, it calls upon Grand Magistrate Pordan to finally direct his attention toward the Southwest regions.

Jake Stockwell may have been eliminated, but his rebels in the Midwest have yet to be unreservedly crushed. This ultimately leaves the Grand Magistrate with only one option. He will launch a massive strike across the country, and utterly destroy the Resistance in all its forms. 30 million AEGIS in all, the Global Magisterium will further push its Autocratic agenda throughout the United States, laying its foundation on the eradicated carcasses of the Resistance and Western Alliance.

In the end, Kiril Pordan will have his control, and the United Republic will be better off for it. But all the while, as the AEGIS prepare to march across the remaining continental United States, and rebels make themselves ready for death, a new figure begins to emerge from amongst the midst of war and rebellion.

A mystic claiming he can bring about world peace, he goes by the Native American name Kuzih, and challenges both the Global Magisterium and Resistance in a way never before seen. And when all is said and done, Kuzih would not have only given birth to a new faith capable of changing the world, he will in fact help in deciding the very fate of all mankind.

M.A. Martin

2051
TREASON

The Great Divide: a concise history of the future

Early March, and the sacred words of the eco-spiritualist Kuzih can be heard echoing throughout the globe. His thousands of disciples meditate on his every sermon, while living amongst the abandoned States of Wyoming, Montana, Washington, Utah, and Oregon. Relentlessly practicing their naturalistic convictions far away from the country's war, they listen, and they learn.

Kuzih makes his presentations from amongst the snowy peaks of Mount Borah in Idaho, and call on all those who believe in the Children of Gaea faith to join him in his new devotion—Makaism.

His words are mystical, as well as, cautionary. He speaks of Mother Earth's love for Her children; likewise, Her anger for what they have done to Her: wars, pollution, chaos, and death. He warns all this angers Her, and that She will have Her revenge if it does not stop. Kuzih goes as far as to blame the frozen winters crippling the planet on Her wrath, and pleads with all governments to cease their iniquitous displays of war. A far cry from the Autocratic call to unite under one banner, and a challenge to the plea of rebellion, Makaism draws mass numbers of followers to itself, regardless of its oppositions.

Makaism is the dogma responsible for the curbing of the children of AR2. Not only does it call for the abandonment of technology, but the condemnation of war, and the adoration of the planet. The children abandoning the suicide bombings and war, it is Kuzih who calls for the return to what Mother Earth has always offered—peace.

The youth of the world gravitate toward this philosophy, and trusts their sage knows what is best to save them. Kuzih wants nothing to do with the Global Magisterium or the Resistance. To him, both doctrines breed nothing but hate and destruction. And in order for peace to return, both establishments must be forsaken. Love, work, Gaea Makawee, these are the three tenets which Makaism preaches, forever challenging all religion, all governments, and all factions.

Kuzih, now here was an interesting character among all this bloodshed and upheaval. He didn't agree with the Global Magisterium, but he also didn't agree with the Resistance. For him, the Makaism path was the only way things would ever be right. So he began drawing people away from the war, and had them join his new naturalistic approach. It wasn't only the youth of AR2 joining him either. AEGIS were breaking rank, as well—those who didn't want to fight along side foreigners, but also didn't want to betray Autocracy by joining the rebellion. You see, with Kuzih, a person simply didn't have to fight at all. Call it convenient, the people who were tired of killing, dying, and destroying everything around them saw this as the only alternative. So they went to Kuzih. And with him, they found peace.

Cecil Greenough

Grand Magistrate: The Biography of Kiril Pordan

The so-called sage known as Kuzih was actually born Marion Seager. He was the son of a Children of Gaea guru who'd made quite the living off of donations given to him by his adoring fans during the early '20s after a failed attempt at being a movie producer. Now here was his son following in his footsteps, preaching this nonsense about connecting with the planet, and allowing Her to heal the human wounds. There are still people like that even until today. Devolutionists who hide in the mountains, and forsake anything technological. You ask me, and judging by his holographs, I'd have to say that Kuzih was a good looking man with a silky tongue—a snake charmer, nothing more. And yet, somehow, he did force the entire world to take notice of him, and that was something his father could have never done.

Prof. Tamara Boggier

keeper, New York Republic Athenaeum

Kuzih believes the time has come to terminate mankind's scientific advances, replacing them with his new doctrine of Makaism. He reluctantly uses the internet highway as a means to spread its principles, preaching with a seductive voice to all who will hear him.

It is not long before computers belonging to both the Global Magisterium and Resistance begin transmitting the mystic's words, slowly but surely changing the hearts of those fighting for their causes. But that does not mean either institution faces an immediate threat from such sermons, not when war breeds more hatred with each passing day.

The the world is still spiraling into further disarray as the conflicts wage on, and nothing seems to be able to stop it.

In the Middle East, the AEGIS have beaten back the Jihadi of the Afro Islamic Union from out of Arabia, and currently prepare for a full scale assault on both Yemen and Oman. A Global Magisterium push of over 5 million AEGIS, the campaign dubbed *Al-Iithad al-Iislamia* (Unity of Islam) is scheduled to launch on April 1st, and will see the cataloging of both Afro Islamic Union regions by mid-May. This is by order of the Grand Magistrate, who desires to see the end of the *Islamic War of Ages* by the end of the year.

His confidence is due to the AEGIS having already made short work of the Afro Islamic Union's fighters, crushing them wherever they are found. Even now, the Muslims that have been spared work tirelessly to rebuild the Holy City of Mecca as per *Sedition Repression Act* dictates. The Kaaba is the only structure to not have been damaged in the skirmish. Middle Eastern High Magistrate Makhmalbaf made sure to oversee that personally, and now he stands before the holy site in awe of its majesty.

It has been far too long since he and his Mu'minūn have stood in presence of the hallowed shrine, a denial that has finally brought forth its consequence. But such victories are tainted by the fact of Muslims not entirely surrendering their call of jihad. For though the Global Magisterium has already begun cataloging multitudes of Muslims, the Jihadi have not halted their holy war.

Such acts of anarchy take place less frequently then two years before, but the suicide bombings of men, women, and children still rock both Mecca and Medina. The Global Magisterium banner may now wave atop the former Saudi palaces, a blood red eagle clinching the entire world in its claws against an ink black set, the Muslim fighters still continue to kill hundreds with their strikes.

The jihad still perseveres, though not halting the invasion of Yemen and Oman as scheduled. And by the end of the first week, both countries are set ablaze. Thousands die, buildings are destroyed, flocks are arrested, and worse, the entire Northeastern African seaport's razed to the ground.

It was complete bedlam. People were being killed left and right. Husbands had to watch their wives being killed for defending their homes, and wives had to drag the dead bodies of their husbands from off the roads. Let us not forget the poor children who had to stand amongst the carcasses of both parents and siblings. The Jihadi of the Afro Islamic Union never stood a chance against the AEGIS, and that is something the Mahdi, alaihi al-salaam, was beginning to realize. He had by now already lost Arabia, so it was time to think about his homeland of North Africa.

Prof. Najiyah Abdullah Hassan

Crescent Moon and Pillars: The Rise of the Islamic Empire

To Mahdi Abu's north stands the European front of the Global Magisterium, and to his east, the Mu'minūn shield. Now the Mahdi must brace his people for a possible invasion from both sides, and begins recoiling them south.

He orders the evacuation of all children from out of Egypt, and the Northeastern cities of Sudan and Eritrea, relocating millions of Muslims to Tumbura, Sudan's farthest Southern region. In time, the only Muslims left to meet the Global Magisterium are those men and women who either refuse to leave their homes, or the Jihadi refusing to surrender. Needless to say, it is a scene of carnage when the Global Magisterium finally does sail across the Red Sea. A stalwart flowing of history, the name that has long described the sinuous waters never befits it more than now.

Red is in fact the color of the frozen waters on an early Sunday morning in June. And on the frosty shores of North Africa, the Afro Islamic Union is once again defeated by the unmerciful mauling of the Global Magisterium. Three quarters of a million Muslims lie dead across the icy shoreline, each one an example of the AEGIS's staunched potency—Egypt has fallen.

Kiril Pordan has indeed created the perfect war machine. A military force whose only concern is to fulfill its mission by serving its commander, these young, strong, and determined futures of the Magisterium spare no one attempting to stand in the way of Autocracy. The Grand Magistrate stands as their tormented architect, dictating the onslaught at every turn. And though his mercy is absent during these appalling times, Pordan actually does grieve his fellow man.

The Grand Magistrate would like nothing more than for the wars to end, but Autocracy does not deal in fantasy. He understands peace can only be obtained through conflict, something shown even during his time as a loyal Captain in the United States Navy.

> Chaos and insurrection must be met with the utmost stern and powerful repercussions. Stability and order don't come with a soft hand. No negotiation in history has ever profited from mere words alone. Hate only understands hate. So in order for one to annihilate conflict, he must first have conflict within himself.
>
> U.S. Naval Captain Kiril Gustav Pordan
> *In support of U.S. troop deployment in Iran*, June 13, 2025

Such thinking now marks the Earth with nothing but blood, and Kiril Pordan knows it. He prays every second of every day, but can see no other alternative. The rebellion must be crushed. All resistance to the Global Magisterium must be wiped out. Autocracy must be allowed to heal every man, woman, and child. The Creator has commanded it, and Pordan believes himself His vicar. Proof of this is shown through the dismissal of his own sorrow, only to have the AEGIS move deeper into Africa. The Afro Islamic Union will be absorbed into the Global Magisterium by year's end, or there will be nothing left of it to stand alone. Kiril Pordan swears this.

Unfortunately for him, the same cannot be said for the battle in Russia, not with the Imperial Asiatic Alliance steering the Global Magisterium in reverse of its conquest. A conflict that has been waging without pause, the *RED WAR* now finds itself with an unavoidable conclusion.

It is obvious the Global Magisterium cannot defeat the Imperial Asiatic Alliance, at least not during its current dawning. Autocracy is novice when compared to the ancient honor-bound discipline of the Orient. Japan, Korea, the Philippines, Indonesia, Myanmar, Vietnam, and India, seven nations whose histories prove their resolve, it is no shock the Global Magisterium finds its failing reach stretching no further than the borders of Poland and Romania. And with a crippled China now beginning to offer up its surviving sons and daughters in service of the Imperial Asiatic Alliance, the absolute riddance of Global Magisterium influence in Eastern Europe appears imminent.

Vice Magistrates are put to work overtime, relentlessly formulating plans on how to stop the impending loss. They know that if the Global Magisterium loses this battle, rebels all over the globe will feel even more emboldened in their insurgencies. Gloomy, as much as it is dangerous, the possibility of such an outcome cannot be fathomed. Hence, the desk of Grand Magistrate Pordan is littered with diagrams and propositions regarding possible tactics, but nothing is worth implementing.

The Grand Magistrate is aware of the Grimaldi Defiance, and how their intricate knowledge of the East strengthens the Imperial Asiatic Alliance in their attacks. He must come to the conclusion that Eastern Europe is lost, and to remain there would only mean further humiliation. The Global Magisterium must never appear weak. It must not be defeated. And so it is with this in mind that Kiril Pordan opens dialogue with the Imperial Asiatic Alliance, reluctantly suggesting terms for a cease-fire.

Emperor Domoto is hesitant of the offer, but is urged to accept the proposal by his council. He tries to voice his criticism, persistently holding daily assembly meetings in order to gain support, but a majority of the council desires an end to the *RED WAR*. In the end, Domoto finds his opposing views silenced by the arguments around him.

The Imperial Asiatic Alliance is a democratic establishment, and with that Democracy comes a fractured union. It matters not that Japan is the elected head of the Alliance; it does not speak for its allied regions all on its own. The Global Magisterium has offered to send envoys, and Emperor Domoto's council has agreed. There is nothing more to discuss.

Therefore, convening without preconditions, the elected capital of the Imperial Asiatic Alliance, Tokyo, Japan, plays host to Global Magisterium Vice Magistrates, and High Magistrate Edward Davies himself to discuss the terms of agreement.

There was no doubt in the Global Magisterium that Emperor Domoto saw himself no less important than Kiril Pordan. But it would have been asking too much if the Emperor had only agreed to speak to the Grand Magistrate. Likewise, it would have been an insult for anyone else to fill Pordan's shoes. That is, anyone except Edward Davies. You see, to many people, though Makhmalbaf and Manishewitz shared the title of High Magistrate with the European leader, Davies was actually Kiril Pordan's right hand. This was why Domoto even agreed to the meeting in the first place, not that any agreement would be reached anytime soon. But at least the meeting was a civil one.

Prof. Jarvis Grimes
historian, *Superior and Biased: The History of the Royal European Alliance*

An unofficial visit as far as the two regimes are concerned, they do not allow the meeting to be televised, much less, inform their citizens of such conference. Both the Imperial Asiatic Alliance and the Global Magisterium have a lot running on this encounter, and neither one wants to appear weak in the eyes of the world. To keep the summit hidden only secures the regime conceding the most, sparing any embarrassment. It is something the Emperor and his Asiatic council expects to see gifted to the Global Magisterium, but that is until the Union of Nations makes its suggestion for ending the war.

The Imperial Asiatic Alliance is expected to cease any further push into Eastern Europe, while recognizing the legitimacy to a planned perimeter project dividing the borders of Poland, Slovakia, Hungary, and Romania from Ukraine, Belarus, and Lithuania. In return, the Global Magisterium will recognize the Imperial Asiatic Alliance as a credible power, though separate of the Global Magisterium. There will be no further hostilities toward the Asian empire; likewise, no more interference from out of the East. An offer to which Emperor Domoto voices disagreement, it is one his imperial council settles on considering. Until then, a cease-fire is put in place until the finalization of said proposals, producing a temporary truce to the *RED WAR.*

IAA SENSHI are commanded to halt any further aggression, as the AEGIS are given the respite they much desire. In point of fact, both sides take with a grain of sand the peace accord arranged between their two governments, but welcome it all the same. It has been months since either side have put down its weapons, so the opportunity to speak to distant loved ones is more than something of contentment.

Admiral Aaron Balthazar of the United Republic Magisterium Naval Fleet is even granted his request concerning a recreational exhibition for those who serve in Eastern Europe. A much needed return to normality Balthazar believes is needed by the troops, he intends on putting on a musical troupe for them.

An ensemble of Hip-Fonika signal runners the likes of White Flag Army, Atlas Autokrosē, ON-ER 5, and the ageless world-wide sensation, NEMESIS, is planned. Included, will also be MAGI-VIDS directed by prophetic M/V director, Ram Krantim. His documentaries not only boast well-edited footage of AEGIS victories, but also the more exaggerated portrayal of a future fully embraced by the Global Magisterium.

The First Annual AEGIS Day is a hearty display indeed, but the SENSHI of the Imperial Asiatic Alliance are allowed no such levity—not when people are being slaughtered every day.

Even now, a new attack on the Afro Islamic Union is taking shape, and this one promises to seal the fate of Muslims forever. An entrapping maneuver, the Global Magisterium believes this to be the most logical approach toward overthrowing the Muslim rule. And half a world away, eyes are set on Morocco, Algeria, Tunisia, and Libya.

The meetings take place within the halls of the Magisterium Core in Washington D.C. There, Grand Magistrate Pordan meets with his closest Vice Magistrates on the matter of the Afro Islamic Union, and its utter incorporation into the Global Magisterium. It is a heated debate, especially with High Magistrate Edward Davies sending word from Asia pertaining to his plans of invading Africa.

The European High Magistrate sees this moment of peace between the Global Magisterium and the Imperial Asiatic Alliance as the perfect opportunity to focus entirely on the resistance of the Afro Islamic Union. He is open to the best proposition, but makes clear all must present an absolute managing over the Islamic coalition. Something the Grand Magistrate has apprehensions over, believing the Imperial Asiatic Alliance a more prominent problem, that does not stop him from authorizing Davies to do what he feels best.

The European AEGIS militaristic aptitude is unstoppable. And in the end, Pordan gives his blessings. This allows the most Autocratic of the entire Republic to offer their superior military intellect, plans ranging from peace, to the absolute obliteration of the Afro Islamic Union. There are even suggestions that the Global Magisterium relocate its Core to the heart of Arabia, traversing all aspects of its decree to this one axis point. But as clever as it is, that insinuation is not even deliberated upon, even though similar plans of rearrangement are considered.

It would be foolish for Edward Davies to think these meetings take only days or weeks, and the High Magistrate is anything but foolish. Davies hears rumors of how Pordan surrounds himself with his most trusted advisers, but also learns there remains one voice which he desires to hear the most. That voice belongs to United Republic Magisterium Councilmen Matthew Storm, former VEDETTE General of the National Offensive. A designation Storm has not carried for years, the former decorated General now serves the United Republic from behind a desk instead of on a battlefield.

Three years ago he arrived in the Republic of Washington D.C. with a goal to end the foreign presence in the Midwest, as well as, requesting that all foreign soldiers be removed from United Republic soil. It was a bold stance which brought about his decommissioning, finally forcing him into a role he most despises, that of politician.

Matthew Storm now spends his days confined to Council meetings, stifling his rage with the Global Magisterium. He is no bureaucrat, and has nothing in common with the old men who claim to have been part of the United States Armed Forces. He is a VEDETTE, and he can no longer take the disgrace engulfing his dear and glorious United Republic.

This farce of global unity would cease to exist if he was in charge, and law would be reestablished in America. And this is the voice which the Grand Magistrate wishes to hear? Storm seriously doubts that, but still plays his part of Loyalist pawn. Then again, that is only on the surface.

Behind the scenes, the VEDETTE works assiduously to overthrow Pordan and his failed council. For even though millions of American Councilmen and Vice Magistrates pledge undying allegiance to Kiril Pordan and his directives, there are still the thousands who secretly desire to see their leader's reign come to an end.

Look, Matthew Storm was a VEDETTE. He'd been a VEDETTE all his life. He wasn't a soldier of the former United States Armed Forces, and he most definitely wasn't one of the people forced into serving the military because there hadn't been anybody else available. No way. Matthew Storm was a VEDETTE—born, bred, and trained to serve the Magisterium. He knew George Hartsoe, lived his dream even. And now he was watching as Kiril Pordan handed it over to foreigners. He refused to accept that, as did the Councilmen who shared his views. They were all once loyal to George Hartsoe, I High Magistrate. And they continued to be so toward his dream of seeing America equal to none other. To them, Kiril Pordan's Global Magisterium scoffed in the face of that dream. Matthew Storm wasn't alone. The simmering anger of 85 million of his fellow VEDETTE reassured him of that every day.

Cecil Greenough

Grand Magistrate: The Biography of Kiril Pordan

The silent dissenters convene at night, and all along the backstreets of Baltimore burn their talks of rebellion. Matthew Storm is their leader, and he has a plan on just how to eliminate Kiril Gustav Pordan.

Already he has secured the reliability of a Councilman named Christopher Cavanaugh, one of the envoys dispatched to the Imperial

Asiatic Alliance. And if what he says is true, then Cavanaugh does not go to Asia with hopes of initiating a cease-fire, but to incite the Emperor and his council to further bloodshed.

It is Storm's highest hopes that, through this deceit, he can weaken the European branch of the Global Magisterium. In truth, if the REA is occupied with halting an emboldened Afro Islamic Union, which is sure to happen if Asia weakens the AEGIS enough, then there will be no time for their interference during an American revolt. The revolt, on the other hand, needs an even more manipulative tactic, one which includes a compromise with the Resistance and Western Alliance.

The one thing George Hartsoe would have never agreed to, Storm is adamant when saying that it is the only thing that can save the United Republic.

Matthew Storm was highly intelligent. He knew that in order to truly gain a footing against the Magisterium, he needed to employ its two greatest threats, and that was unequivocally the Resistance and Western Alliance. Jake Stockwell may have been dead, but his dream of Democracy once more being placed at the fore of the United States still lived on. It was something Matthew Storm stood entirely against, but in the end, realized he would've rather had than the rubbish of allying with the REA or Islamic People's Republic. To be quite frank, Storm decided to trust Americans over outsiders—rebel or not.

Prof. Tamara Boggier

keeper, New York Republic Athenaeum

Councilman Storm proposes a Two State Solution with which the United Republic and United States would work collectively toward a cohesive ascension of the nation. There would be a recognized Democratic government functioning under an elected President, as well as, a shared Constitution for all. Except, this Western Democracy would not be allowed a standing military, nor any Weapons of Mass Destruction. In return, the Magisterium would remove all VEDETTE from said regions, placing them throughout the designated borders while maintaining a progressive *Magisterium Edict* which would not infringe on these Western States, but aid in opted cataloging for all Americans. A format Matthew Storm and his advisers have not fully envisioned, it is one the dejected Loyalist feels is more than non-discriminatory.

A portion of the continent, a land to govern with Democracy, a far fetched idea, it is promising enough to organize a coup dedicated to its realization. But before any of this can be put to the test, Storm must first gain the trust of the Resistance and Western Alliance. Thus, dispatching envoys of his own to New Orleans, Louisiana, Matthew Storm begins dialogues with none other than Western Alliance President Arthur Havelock.

Amongst the insurrectionists of the Magisterium is Admiral Patrick Hauser, a man who stands as AEGIS Gen. Pamela Barnett's highest ranking aide. Not only is he her strategic adviser, Hauser is also the one who oversees her plans being accomplished. With him on his side, Storm can cripple the AEGIS in America, as well as, topple Kiril Pordan. This is what the Councilman brings to the table when presenting an alliance between sworn enemies.

The former VEDETTE General makes clear his proposition, informing the interim leader of the Resistance of his commitment to help in defending against the *Purification Schema* being planned for the whole of the Southwestern regions. A gamble that will see him hindering the advancements of the AEGIS through confounding the Magisterium, as well as, inner-military corruption, it is a risk to say the least, but one that must be taken. In return for the Resistance's much needed support, Storm has no qualms about granting half the country to them.

Havelock is interested, but fears this deal will be no different than the pact once made between then Chairman George Hartsoe and ARTist Party leader, Calvin Walsh. A pact that, when all was said and done, saw ART betrayed and made into terrorists.

Before he agrees to anything, Havelock needs reassurance that such treasonous outcomes will not come to pass again, and leaves the challenge of gaining his trust in Storm's hands. It is not a hard thing for the Councilman to do, not when he begins leaking vital AEGIS protocol to the Resistance and their leaders.

An Achilles heel to the Global Magisterium, the AEGIS begin tasting defeat all throughout the South, where plans of building a strategic military advance is weakened by obvious betrayal. Almost overnight, a regiment in Montgomery, another in New Orleans, a military installation in Macon, and newly constructed Battery-Hubs in Tampa are attacked before implementing their phase in the *Purification Schema*. Locations and operations that were to be used as staging grounds for covert attacks on the Western Alliance, their coordinates are made known to the enemy, proving detrimental to Autocracy's capacity.

In the weeks that follow, a terrorist attack takes place in New York, killing 32 people. Then a shuttle explodes in Philadelphia, claiming 218 lives. A hostage situation in Detroit ends with the deaths of 57 Councilmen. A suicide bombing of a Magisterium Depot in Columbus, with over 17,397 victims in its aftermath. Then another in a New York subway, kills 621 innocent Loyalists.

Treason has infected the United Republic, and spreads far beyond the battlefield, threatening the Core of the Republic. The United Republic Magisterium soon, thereafter, begins to quake beneath the rise of accusations. Treason is the theme, and the utmost necessary capture of its perpetrators is demanded by all Loyalists. A disease of conspiracy drowned by a cocktail of betrayal and fear, everybody within the Magisterium becomes a suspect.

Grand Magistrate Pordan knows the attacks on specific Southern military installations are not but mere luck, and that the recent acts of terrorism seen in the Republics are bred of nothing more than treachery, and demands they be halted. It is a parallel turgidity being heard from out of the Royal European Alliance, where High Magistrate Davies insist the Grand Magistrate get control over his homeland.

Evidently, the European High Magistrate does not have complete confidence in the Grand Magistrate's regulations, especially when word of attacks taking place inside the Republic begin to surface.

It would seem the unknown conspirators have not only revealed Pordan's plans of Southern infiltration to the Resistance, but also divulge vulnerable channels by which the rebels can attack the very heart of the Global Magisterium.

High Magistrate Davies was worried, and rightfully so. And though Manishewitz and Makhmalbaf were not that vocal, Davies refused to hold his tongue. The Grand Magistrate was dealing with constant reports of internal duplicity, not to mention loses in the field of battle. He had obviously begun to lose control over his country. And though the Global Magisterium saw no nationality or land, those who were part of it still had the duty of maintaining control over their own territories. Davies had secured the Western front of Europe, Manishewitz kept peace in Israel, and Makhmalbaf had done the same in the Middle East. They could not possibly be expected to fight their own battles and Pordan's as well. He was the Grand Magistrate, after all. If he could not halt the unraveling of his regime, then what hope was there for the Global Magisterium? And now the very Core of the Republic began suffering under terrorist actions, something that had not been seen there in years. Grand Magistrate Pordan needed to get a hold on the situation, and fast.

Prof. Jarvis Grimes

historian, *Superior and Biased: The History of the Royal European Alliance*

Kiril Pordan was under a great deal of pressure. Not only was the AEGIS losing battles all throughout the South because of leaked protocols, now the suspicion of treason was hitting within his own Magisterium Core. He found himself distrusting most of his Councilmen, and couldn't even begin to figure out which Vice Magistrate was trying to take his place. All this had been unforeseen, and now it had caught up with him. It was reported that Pordan began spending hours upon hours a day praying that God would show him a way. But in the end, he'd been left all alone. He knew he had got to get control over things, and began formulating a plan as to how he should do it. Basically, the glory days of the Global Magisterium had only just begun, and already it was falling apart.

Cecil Greenough

Grand Magistrate: The Biography of Kiril Pordan

Bombings of Magisterium Centers, assassinations of key Councilmen, Loyalist casualties, they are dilemmas Kiril Pordan needs remedied. It forces him to launch, without restrictions, the AEGIS march across the remnant United States of America. 30 million AEGIS soldiers in all, their brutal attacks commence on February 18, 2052, and find the States of Louisiana, Mississippi, Arkansas, Missouri, Iowa, and Wisconsin participants in its bloody onslaught.

United States Resistance Generals Olivia Warner and Xander Brown contact President Arthur Havelock, and finalize the transference of him taking over the mission. Something the leader of the Western Alliance had once shunned, stubbornly rejecting any alliance including the movement of AR2, the obvious choice for Resistance leader has no alternative but to accept his duty now.

The Resistance and Western Alliance are one, and standing in opposition of the Global Magisterium. The most atrocious of America's sectarian violence, the *March of the AEGIS* is moderate when compared to the invasion of North Africa.

There, nothing short of genocide is about to take place, a well-organized horror enacted throughout the entire northern regions of the continent.

February 23, and High Magistrate Edward Davies launches preemptive strikes all across the Northern African shore. European and Israeli AEGIS are unleashed on the Afro Islamic Union, just as Northern Sudan and Eritrea are fully seized by the Arabian AEGIS.

Morocco, Algeria, Tunisia, and Libya are attacked by both sea and air, with Magisterium Aircraft carriers and Battle Cruisers launching both missiles and jets. The Islamic Coalition is poised to fall by year's end, only to be followed by a massive cataloging project that will see an end put to this *Sharia* driven conflict. Although, with Imperial Asiatic Alliance Emperor Domoto Eisaku informing the Global Magisterium of his regime's rejection concerning the proposed Eastern European barrier, a silver lining begins to emerge for the AIU.

Emperor Domoto had gained intelligence concerning the lies the Global Magisterium had been feeding him. He was not at all pleased when being told that the cease-fire offered to him by Pordan was only to buy time. He had it on good authority that the Global Magisterium was going to attack him the moment they quelled the violence taking place in the United Republic and Afro Islamic Union. And if he gave them this time, the AEGIS would soon be at his doorstep. Domoto knew he had to attack, and he had to attack now.

Tsun-chúng Hu
The Last Dynasty: The Chinese Republic's Ultimate Demise

The Imperial Asiatic Alliance has been given reason to distrust the Global Magisterium effort toward ending the RED WAR, threatening the regime's slow-rising dominance. The last thing Kiril Pordan needs to hear, it is a reality nonetheless.

Asia decides to continue with its aggressive stance against Global Magisterium rule, and on May 28th, reignites the RED WAR with a full-blown attack on the AEGIS stationed in both Poland and Romania. Hostility the Grand Magistrate must react to, the Imperial Asiatic Alliance threatens to bring about the downfall of his world-wide government. And once again, Eastern Europe begins to burn in the flames of war.

The Great Divide: a concise history of the future

2054
DESTINY OF SACRIFICE

The Great Divide: a concise history of the future

Man's weak. I'm not talking about man who walks the Earth, boastfully bragging to everyone he meets fantasies he himself cries at night for not succeeding a fraction at. I'm talking about mankind. Mankind's weak. And since they try force feeding us that all of mankind came from one man…Man's weak. He's weak because he's afraid. He's weak because he's selfish. He's weak because he doesn't trust. Man's weak. A sad carbon life-form no more important than an ant toiling in respect for what the Earth has given it. What man can say this? What man can truly say in his heart that he does what he does because it's always the right thing to do? Show me a man who can say this, and I'll show you a liar— the weakest amongst men. Open your eyes people. What're you fighting for? What're you killing for? Power? Power, and greed? Well, I tell you all there's no such thing as power. A man can have power beyond compare, power that puts Kiril Pordan to shame. But if he lives to be a hundred years old, and a man who's never had anything to call his own lives to be the same, then both men, no matter how different their lives, no matter their so-called "power", both men have lived a mere 36,500 days. 36,500 days. All that we are comes down to, if given a hundred years, is 36,500 days. And yet, we kill, we steal, we lie, we cheat, we do all manners of unspeakable crimes all so that we can be more than 36,500 days. Gaea Makawee. (*Om*) Is eternal. Long before we came, She was here. And long after we're gone, She'll still be here. And yet, we try everything in our power, for 36,500 days, to rape, poison, and murder the Eternal One, Gaea Makawee. (*Om*) You dig into the Earth, penetrating Her with your filthy hands, and steal Her precious life's blood—and take it where? You don't leave the planet with it. You don't hop a spaceship, and go flying off to some distant galaxy with it. You don't go anywhere with it. And no matter how precious the stone, the metal, the element, and no matter how much it means to you, what's Gaea Makawee's (*Om*) will go back to Gaea Makawee. (*Om*) That's including us. Look at all the beautiful monuments we've seen constructed throughout the past—wonders that man swore his soul to. One day a bomb fell on his petty god, and the wonder was no more. Man's glorious work was no more. But you know what was? You know what still remained, and eventually reclaimed everything man had taken from Her to make himself a god in his mind? Gaea Makawee. (*Om*) 36,500 days. That's not merely enough to give the respect deserved by something so beautiful. Something so pure. Something so much better than us. Man's weak. Turn to that which is eternal. Thank Her for her loving kindness, and Her neglect of our sins. Embrace Her, and allow Her to embrace you back. You were born of Her, and one day you'll return to Her. Be one with Her, and allow Her to do what She does best. Allow Gaea Makawee, (*Om*) Allow Her to give you life—eternal, and inextinguishable. Abandon what the weakness in you desires, and embrace that which never dies. Embrace eternity. Embrace Gaea Makawee. (*Om*).

The Weakness of Man
Sutra 274: 3rd Volume, Mt. Borah, Kuzih

May 3, paranoia best describes the infrastructure that is the Global Magisterium. Throughout vestibules of Centers, the corridors of Great Halls, and across the globe, talk of disloyalty flourishes. Vice Magistrates accuse each other of sedition, while vying for peak ranks amongst the Magisterium Council. European Councilmen request reassignments to the West, believing North America once more the future of the planet. As do some of their colleagues voice constant distrust of the Americans, while trying to convince the populace of an inescapable fallout between the nations. Some leaders enact laws without consulting the Core with hopes of impressing their superiors with such initiatives. High Magistrate Davies has reservations concerning Grand Magistrate Pordan's continued headship, voicing his discontent during televised speeches. And all throughout the United Republic, the regime's AEGIS meet defeat at the hands of subversion, proving time and time again their operations are being disclosed to rebel fighters by spies from within.

A dark web of deceit has begun to grip the powerful international establishment, a net of corruption threatening to destroy everything the Global Magisterium has worked so hard to institute. For as he struggles to keep control over all he has gained, odds are this new world order will lose even more power if things continue going the way they currently are.

As it stands, the United Republic is engaged in all out II Civil War. The entire Midwest is submerged in conflict. The death toll for the AEGIS has been put in the high ten thousands. And rebel forces meet attacks with utmost bravery and might, choosing to lose thousands of their fighters for the cause.

There are no shortages of victims on either side of the conflict, but it is the prisoners of the *Sedition Repression Act* who suffer the most. These bystanders are the ones caught in the crossfire, murdered in cold blood. Women, men, and children shot, burned, or tortured by both sides, they are the casualties of the ever turbulent *Purification Schema*. And in the end, they are the ones made into the pawns of this conflict.

Structures are destroyed during campaigns. Bridges are blown to sawdust. Children are made orphans by air raids. Women and men are made widows through outright carnage. A crimson mist stains the icy Midwestern expanse. Murky smoke billows from amongst the wreckage of the frozen South. It does not take long before even the State of Kansas begins feeling the full effects of war by late July. Yet, the *March of the AEGIS* is spearheaded, with the country torn in half because of it.

The Resistance was doing a great job in the South beating back the AEGIS. But in the Midwest, it was a stalemate that killed hundreds of thousands of people. Olivia Warner had been killed, and Xander Brown was missing. And if you weren't an AEGIS or a Loyalist, then you were an insurgent. Civilians, prisoners, children, scores of them were being eradicated, even as American VEDETTE looked on with scorn. Of course, these American AEGIS weren't innocent of the carnage, but it was the Europeans doing most of the damage. Sure, the Israelis and Mu'minūn killed people too, but they at least tried to get rebels to surrender, most of the time having no choice but to kill in self-defense. But the Europeans loved killing the rebels, and usually didn't stop until most of their enemies were dead. Meanwhile, the reconstruction effort had come to a standstill, and Americans were starving and dying again. So you can understand how there could've been a sense desperation amongst all Americans—AEGIS or not. There had to be another option to all this bloodshed. And in time, another option did eventually present itself. And as crazy as it may have sounded, it did show promise of deciding the fate of the war. I'm talking of course about Kuzih, and his Makaism philosophy—that which would tip the scales of battle.

Cecil Greenough

Grand Magistrate: The Biography of Kiril Pordan

A call for salvation—a call for peace—a call that rings out day and night to anyone who hears it, it is a way of life deeply and inherently drawing strength from the Earth. A belief in all things natural, and detest toward all things science, it is a faith in humanity's connection to all things living, and a Earth Mother's love.

Hope amongst a bleak age, and a power reserved for those who accept its truths, its broadcaster is none other than the spiritualist known as the Mystic of Mt. Borah, the diviner of the goddess Gaea Makawee. This is Makaism, and it promises sanctuary and tranquility against a ruin age.

It is spoken of from across a snowy plateau crested by mighty mountains. A place where thousands upon thousands flood into Idaho in search of deliverance and safe haven, their summoner is a man promising freedom, harmony, and love. He is Kuzih, and he seems to be the only hope one has of surviving.

People had been flocking to Kuzih for years, a slow precipitation of dejected and frightened citizens you can say. But only now during The Aegis March did mass numbers begin joining them. I am talking about non-stop caravans sometimes with up to 25,000 people, trekking the frozen Pacific Northwest, just to reach Mt. Borah, where Kuzih would make everything all right. The civil war had obviously taken its toll, and Kuzih promised people a place away from all that. Now, rationally speaking, not everyone who fled to him believed in his fantastical Makaism preaching, but they came to him nonetheless. Washington, Oregon, Montana, all those States joined Idaho in receiving these refugees of war. I can only guess that they were hoping Kuzih could indeed take them away from the violence? And it wasn't long until Kuzih's name became tantamount with harmony and protection, changing the landscape of the Great Divide forever.

Prof. Tamara Boggier

keeper, New York Republic Athenaeum

Kuzih already shares these grounds with millions who desire to know his path, as well as, walk the road he sets for them. And with a multitude from all walks of life fleeing the hardships of the Midwest, this prophet of the Makaism dharma more than easily makes himself a savior.

Under his sutras, followers of his Earth-bound belief, Makaists as they are called, are convinced to forsake their past lives, including everything that had ever bonded them to destruction. War, greed, envy, religion, technology, all of it is to be renounced in favor of a naturalistic approach toward life, and Kuzih promises his Makaists that he will be the one to teach them this approach—this positive way to conquer ones dukkha (pain and suffering).

With this rise above their design, Kuzih teaches no God has hold on them, and neither does any man. He tells them that they are one with Gaea Makawee, and that She is calling for them to embrace Her gifts. They are children of the planet, and have been gifted dominion over their Mother's playground. However, before any of these lessons can take hold on Kuzih's Makaists, he first makes sure to break their craving spirits. And the Mystic of Mt. Borah knows of only one sure thing capable of doing so, and that is backbreaking work.

The path to enlightenment demands more than just meditation, it demands pain, it demands suffering, and it demands tears. But above all, it demands a need to forsake ones human superiority. This is why under freezing temperatures and grueling labor, Kuzih encourages his followers to toil both day and night in search of a disconnect from their wants.

He allows them little sleep, denying them any man-made comforts. Instead, they are taught to live off the land, and how to hunt for food. This is a symbiotic relationship between mother and child, teaches Kuzih.

Mother Earth has given Her children everything they will ever need, and all She expects in return is respect.

Thus, through arduous exertions, the Rocky Mountains are transformed into a glorious collection of cavate cliff dwellings, and hidden temples for those of the Makaism faith. A place abandoning all sciences and technologies, Kuzih and his Makaists are successful in creating a place of living, gathering, and learning—a place truly befitting the love of Gaea Makawee—a way of thinking and living that changes the world with its every utterance and practice.

North America's long forgotten Pacific Northwest is not the only place where Kuzih is making an impact. All throughout Europe, small pockets of Makaists preach the teachings of the Western sage. They pass around flyers, and recite the exceptional sutras composed by him, while trying to stop the RED WAR taking place in Poland and Romania. Even the Grimaldi Defiance presence lingering within the European Magisterium is asked to restrain its isolated attacks, while in that same Royal European Alliance, the Makaists take their risks in urging High Magistrate Edward Davies to make peace.

They have hope their words of harmony can bring change, and pray they will be accepted. Once this happens, the sworn enemies will eventually halt their devastation of the planet, and a time of healing can commence, bringing utmost tranquility to all. A charming dream, such beautiful fantasies are exactly that—a fantasy. High Magistrate Davies has no intention of listening to such absurdities, not when he and his regime stand just one country away from having the Imperial Asiatic Alliance at their door.

The European Magisterium can feel the effects of the losses suffered by the AEGIS in Eastern Europe, and now worry only the Polish cities of Warsaw and Krakow stand in the way of the Imperial Asiatic Alliance. So as they fight with everything they have in order to halt their defeat, the European AEGIS realize they are as good as finished. Therefore, to even consider the Makaists' proposal would be seen as a sign of surrender, something the European Global Magisterium is unwilling to do.

Kiril Pordan does not take notice of his colleagues' possible doom. The Grand Magistrate is currently preoccupied with winning his own nation's II Civil War. An oversight that allows Edward Davies to take full command of RED WAR operations, the High Magistrate needs hastily to make a definitive statement when it comes to his resolve.

The situation was quite grievous for Edward Davies. The AEGIS were fighting a losing battle in Eastern Europe, and it was only a matter of time before the Imperial Asiatic Alliance pushed its self-proclaimed godsend into the Royal European Alliance itself. The

High Magistrate had to have been quite alarmed by this. The very reason, I suppose, he decided to personally attack the Muslims of the Afro Islamic Union. And though the Islamic Peoples Republic and Israel were doing a fine job of that already, Davies needed to remind the Asians that Europe was indeed strong. So what better way than to trounce on one weaker than you? At least it would allow the Europeans to vent their frustrations. For the time being, at least.

Prof. Jarvis Grimes

historian, *Superior and Biased: The History of the Royal European Alliance*

Davies decides to enact brutal AEGIS expansions all throughout North Africa, only to reestablish European Magisterium might. He kills indiscriminately, forcing the Imperial Asiatic Alliance to take notice of their possible end. It is brutal. It is a sin. It is nothing less than genocide.

The High Magistrate desires to see the lamenting of Muslims. Their soot covered faces, and tattered clothes is something which quells his rage. He wants to hear of the bombs that fall on neighborhoods, killing families in support of *Sharia*. He will not see this obsolete society interfere with Global Magisterium rule, and declares this attack on the Afro Islamic Union a warning to the Imperial Asiatic Alliance.

An act of desperation, the North African Agenda has already set ablaze the nations of Morocco and Algeria, turning both countries into pyres of death and destruction. Testaments of the European Magisterium's dominance, now Tunisia and Libya are about to be marched on, and this is where the AEGIS are expected to commit their most brutal acts of annihilation.

There will be no reconstruction effort here. The survivors will not be gifted the ICE-chip. High Magistrate Edward Davies intends on making the Muslim people an example of his wrath. And with Egypt fully under the control of both the Islamic People's Republic and the State of Israel, the populace of Tunisia and Libya will have nowhere to escape such massacre.

Regrettably, when the future of the *RED WAR* is closely examined, this entire display of savagery is nothing more than a ruse. A maltreatment of one enemy so the other will be panic-stricken enough to abandon their mission, it is the only guard the European Magisterium has toward deterring a feasible infiltration by the Asiatic empire.

This is how things are interpreted by the citizens of the Freelands, principally when witnessing such debatable measures from behind their illusions of security and freedom. Prodigious authorities attacking weaker sovereignties with the intentions of casting fears and doubts in the hearts of those attempting to ascend as world leaders, all this is obviously done in fear of losing their power to those weaker than themselves.

As seen in Canada, where the *Magisterium Edict* has been leniently imposed, the citizens there view the rumors of the establishment's fast approaching downfall as a hopeful sign of independence to come. And though they have not necessarily suffered all that much as Global Magisterium affiliates, the organization's destabilization is enough for thousands to begin heading into the streets in protest of its involvement in Canadian affairs. The same expressions can even be heard erupting from out of Greenland, Alaska, and Australia, places where the Global Magisterium has yet to even infringe upon.

The regime's recent distress over treason and corruption have more than undermined its grip on the planet, allowing island nations such as Hawaii, Cuba, Jamaica, Iceland, Madagascar, and New Zealand to begin challenging its authority. Something Grand Magistrate Pordan should be overtly concerned with, he seems to pay little to no attention to such problematic predicaments.

The Freelands were the only places where the old ways of government could still be found. The ways of life that had once governed the most developed of societies were still evident in them. Nubia, Australia, Madagascar, Hawaii, all of the Freelands were democracies. They all rejected the Global Magisterium, and tried their best to function without it. It was a difficult path they chose to walk, but they walked it anyway. They refused to be cataloged, and that's something Kiril Pordan should've taken seriously. But he didn't. Instead of crushing those who opposed him across the globe, he instead handed the problem over to others. Vice Magistrates, High Magistrates Davies, Manishewitz, and Makhmalbaf, Pordan trusted in them to make it happen without him. And in my opinion, he put way too much faith in others. Way too much faith.

Cecil Greenough

Grand Magistrate: The Biography of Kiril Pordan

Pordan leaves the obstacle of the Freelands in the hands of his most trusted Vice Magistrates to be remedied, and alternatively focuses his full concentration on the United Republic's darkest hour. With the II Civil War taking place, it is up to Vice Magistrates, public figures such as Emilio Ramirez, Abdul Khan, Tamaqua Miller, and Paul Mancini to send delegates to those Freelands, each one taking it upon him/herself to broker unity to those nations.

They commence with those countries needing the most urgent care, as well as, most ideal: Iceland, Greenland, and Alaska, and offer them incentives for joining the Global Magisterium. Theirs will be a beneficial marriage to the Union of Nations; likewise, a providential opportunity to be reborn into greatness. But, at the same time, for those who outrightly refuse the induction treaty, Australia, New Zealand, and the Polynesian Islands, a military solution is made quite probable.

They will be dealt with as insurgents, and die as so many before them have. But with such determined views focusing solely on those regions the Global Magisterium either currently fears, or finds wanting, the Union of Nations practically turns a blind eye to the southern portion of Africa.

It is a place where suffering has long made its home. A region teeming with fear, hatred, pain, courage, and mounting reprisal, the unified nation christened the Nubian Republic faces its demise at the hands of a desperate horde, but is given no care by the rest of the world. This, in turn, births a flaw in Global Magisterium security, allowing for delegates from Nubia to brave the icy pirate infested Indian Ocean in hopes of gaining audience with the Imperial Asiatic Alliance.

On August 2, Nubian Republic emissaries reach the shores of Sri Lanka, where they meet with Imperial Asiatic Alliance representatives to discuss the matter of the Afro Islamic Union onslaught, and its effect on their people.

It is no secret the embattled Afro Islamic Union is still far more dominant than the Nubian nations, and that their ever-increasing conflict with the Global Magisterium threatens Nubia each day with a possible invasion.

The Nubian Republic's emissaries explain in detail how the Global Magisterium thrust into Muslim regions force refugees to flee pass the equator, further burdening the Nubian border states. They make clear their already existing economic strife, including the suffering effects still being felt due to the Afro Islamic Union's unjust jihad over two decades earlier. And though the two governments have lived in relative peace during all these years, Nubia refuses to play host to the ones guilty of so many African deaths and displacements.

The Nubia Republic wishes for the Imperial Asiatic Alliance to interpose in the affair, in turn, keeping the Muslims from further entering their lands. A request that would see the Imperial Asiatic Alliance going against the Afro Islamic Union in the south just as the Global Magisterium crushes it from the north, the Imperial Asiatic Alliance is reluctant to partake in such formalities.

The Orient Empire recognizes a loss for the Afro Islamic Union would mean certain revitalization for the Global Magisterium, and can only see the Nubian request as a catalyst to such adverse outcomes. So, they refuse, but not entirely. Seeing another alternative to the problem, the Imperial Asiatic Alliance decides to suggest a proposal of shared benefits with the leader of the Afro Islamic Union—Mahdi Abu.

On November 21, Emperor Domoto turns back the Nubian delegates, but dispatches by sea an envoy en route to Tambura, Sudan. They are granted access by the Nubians through Kenya then Uganda, and travel until meeting with the remnant of Mahdi Abu's defiant Jihadi of Sudan.

The Asian envoys come with an offer, a chance to save the Islamic coalition. A simple compact really: handover the Arabian territories of Arabia, Yemen and Oman, and the Imperial Asiatic Alliance will help save the remaining Afro Islamic Union from the clutches of the Global Magisterium. An agreement that would forever alter the dynamics of Islam itself, it is a difficult choice for the Mahdi to make. For not only would he be surrendering a major region in exchange for Imperial Asiatic Alliance protection, he would also be giving up the holiest place in all of Islam.

Needless to say, he rejects the deal, but not without proposing one of his own.

The Mahdi, alaihi al-salaam, called this day Almaseer-Ul-Adha—Destiny of Sacrifice. Because to him, that was exactly what he knew he had to do if he was going to save the Muslims. The Asians wanted Mecca. For what, I do not know. I do not think anyone will ever truly know. But what the Mahdi, alaihi al-salaam, did know, was that the Imperial Asiatic Alliance would have to be given something comparable to their stipulation. Mecca means the world to Islam. But to an infidel, history is more important than faith. And so, the Mahdi, alaihi al-salaam, decided to make a counteroffer he believed the Imperial Asiatic Alliance could not refuse.

Prof. Najiyah Abdullah Hassan

Crescent Moon and Pillars: The Rise of the Islamic Empire

Mahdi Abu offers to surrender Egypt, Sudan, and Eritrea in exchange for Imperial Asiatic Alliance aid from the Global Magisterium. In a move that would ensure the recapture of Arabia soon thereafter, the conferral of the Northeastern region of the Afro Islamic Union to the Imperial Asiatic Alliance would pit the Israelis and Arabs of the Islamic People's Republic against the Asians, drawing the Mujahids and Tzahal from out of Arabia in defense against the SENSHI. At which time, Mahdi Abu would deploy his Jihadi into the scarcely defended city of Mecca, and seize control of the heart of Islam.

With its Northeastern front fully secured by the Imperial Asiatic Alliance, the Afro Islamic Union would be able to converge forces entirely against the European Magisterium, meeting the European AEGIS push with retaliatory aggression.

The Mahdi makes clear one particular piece of detail before finalizing the pact, however. That is, although the Imperial Asiatic Alliance would now hold title over Egypt, Sudan, and Eritrea, and would be capable of enacting laws it feels best serves its interests, the Afro Islamic Union expects those Muslims who remain in the Northeastern regions to be treated fairly.

The last thing the Mahdi desires is a future conflict between the Afro Islamic Union and its new Asian Coalition. A fair proposal in the eyes of Emperor Domoto, the Imperial Asiatic Alliance agrees to the terms on January 7, 2055. And with that, the Imperial Asiatic Alliance begins deploying troops to Africa's Northeastern regions one week later.

The Dragon Nation Naval Fleet takes to the Arabian Sea. Orchestrated to enter and seize the nations of Egypt, Sudan, and Eritrea are over 17.2 million SENSHI soldiers in an attack that immediately demands Pakistan's reaction, though that is an obligatory task the South Asian Islamic nation cannot presently carryout. A preconceived retaliation long remedied by the Imperial Asiatic Alliance, Pakistan finds itself stalled by a simultaneous buildup of SENSHI troops along the mountainous region of Kunlun China, as well as, on the borders of its longtime enemy of India.

The move cripples the once possible northern attack by Pakistan into the Arabian Sea, fully allowing the Imperial Asiatic Alliance to commence with its assault.

An unprecedented show of force against the Arabian Magisterium, the Asians do not set foot on land until igniting the skies of Northeast Africa with an assault of rockets, ballistic missiles, and fighter jets capable of laying ruin to the enemy. Of course, the Arabian Magisterium is not without its own means of defense, and launches its own array of artillery in response. The State of Israel also joins in on the fight; albeit, not in full support. Still, the conflict comes to life with fire, destruction, and death, again setting the Islamic People's Republic Occupied Northeast African regions ablaze for all to see.

The waves of both the Red Sea and Gulf of Aden jeer at the sight of massive Flag Ships shooting fighter jets from off their decks, while Battle Cruisers shutter from expulsions of rounds capable of ripping apart the most resolute of hauls. A cacophony seemingly born of opportunity and determination, the Imperial Asiatic Alliance remains resolute in taking what is now theirs.

Soon enough, the tide of the *Islamic War of Ages* begins to take a drastic turn, when the watery carnage creates nautical passages for the Afro Islamic Union to find Arabia's weakest condition. And armed with sophisticated weaponry contributed to them by the Asian empire, naval crafts, as well as over 11.5 million SENSHI soldiers at their command, the Muslims find themselves more than capable of beating back the Mu'minūn from out of the Arabian Peninsula.

With the Arabian Magisterium now separated from its North African AEGIS, the Afro Islamic Union is given the opportunity to strike at the core of the City of the Prophet itself, and hastily ascend the Red Sea northward.

They land both Jihadi and SENSHI fighters at the doorstep of Mecca by April, and dare to put on trial the whole of the Islamic People's Republic. Something High Magistrate Edward Davies takes notice of, he holds to the belief that this does not change the fate of the Afro Islamic Union struggle against the European strike.

The Muslims can do nothing when the European Magisterium push vengefully strengthens tenfold, pitting them against a force unwavering in its agenda. Enough to crush all Muslims standing in its way, fortunately for the Afro Islamic Union, the Imperial Asiatic Alliance has a means with which to push back. It takes place in Romania, and with a troop increase of over 20 million.

Edward Davies had made a horrible mistake. He had allowed his pride to fester, and now he was about to see the errors of his ways. Leaving the RED WAR behind so that he could attack the Afro Islamic Union was a poor choice from the beginning. His desperation should have never forged his thinking, but now it was too late. The Islamic People's Republic and State of Israel could not come to his aid. They were too busy trying not to fall before the Imperial Asiatic Alliance and Afro Islamic Union. Now, not only did Davies have to battle the Muslims to his south, he also had to reengage the Imperial Asiatic Alliance in Eastern Europe. Two wars on two fronts. There was no way that Davies could win, an inevitability he was becoming all too well aware of.

Prof. Jarvis Grimes

historian, *Superior and Biased: The History of the Royal European Alliance*

An unprecedented effort, the European Magisterium has no choice but to meet the threat head-on. This requires they redeploy a third of their North African AEGIS to Germany in preparation for the Imperial Asiatic Alliance assault on its western front.

Edward Davis personally sends word to the counterparts of the Scandinavian Magisterium requesting aid on the battlefront, but finds the Scandinavian Magisterium unwilling to betray their article of conduct by interfering. All the prospects needed by Mahdi Abu, the Supreme Leader of the Afro Islamic Union immediately orders all available Jihadi in Mauritania, Mali, Niger, and Chad be deployed into Libya, Tunisia, Algeria and Morocco.

It is a retaliatory rush of over 13 million, and the European AEGIS in Africa have the tide turned on them for the first time since the beginning of their battering charge. And when all is said and done, on the frosty shores of North Africa's Sahara Desert, lie the thin and shattered ranks of the European Magisterium war machine. A stalwart effort made a suicide mission through depleted numbers, the AEGIS conquest of North Africa is over by July of that year.

The war has claimed over 1.6 million souls, while leaving the Northern crown of Africa a disaster. The Muslims have proven their fortitude. Allah has granted them mercy, but has also given them a reward. For with the European Magisterium consumed in a war against the ever powerful Imperial Asiatic Alliance, the Afro Islamic Union now begins to set it sights on those who once believed them defeated.

They see Spain as their first prey, and dare to consider the unthinkable. All the same, for all the Eastern Hemisphere's shifting display of strength, all this in no way helps the situation in North America.

In the once mighty United States, a civil war between rebels and government wages on without end, proving this to be the Global Magisterium's greatest threat. Former VEDETTE General Matthew Storm has given the Revolution the tools it needs in order to defeat the AEGIS. Top secret strategies of attack, tactical assault formations, and intelligence concerning the Global Magisterium means of maneuvering its forces, the leaked data aid rebels in weakening their overlords. It is a chain of events seen all throughout the Midwest, where those battling for Democracy win skirmish after skirmish, proving the AEGIS and all their erudite weapons no match for liberty.

The Battle at Lake Michigan: 276,500 AEGIS dead. *The Jefferson City Rescue*: 743,882 AEGIS killed. *The Red Hills War*: 32,184 loyal Global Magisterium soldiers slaughtered. The *Appalachian Clear Out Agenda*: 129,000. *Grenada II*: 800,000. *The Daytona 500K*: 500,000. *The March of Montgomery* and *The Bama Slam*: 65,000. *The Cedar Rapids Massacre*: 155,000 AEGIS and Loyalists butchered. Turns of events which baffle the United Republic Magisterium each time, there seems to be no way of stopping the Revolution's treacherously promoted destruction.

The mole which exists within the ranks of those closest to Kiril Pordan proves a weakness too great for him to impede, but all this will soon begin to change. Grand Magistrate Pordan has decided to give full authority to AEGIS Gen. Pamela Barnett, and hopes she will begin designing strategies unknown to the clandestine infiltrator. A precarious choice, Pordan can only wait and see if the new stratagem helps in gaining an upper hand on the insurgents, and remarkably finds the new tactic shows promise within weeks when AEGIS march on Arkansas without suffering one casualty.

The Little Rock Lockdown: 3.8 million rebels slaughtered.

The smartest move Kiril Pordan could've done was giving control of the AEGIS to Pamela Barnett. He had spies working against him, and they were trying their best to do him in. He couldn't possibly continue giving orders from the Magisterium Core when his commands reached the Resistance before even getting to the AEGIS. But now that Barnett had been given full authority to do as she saw fit in the war, the Resistance finally encountered what the AEGIS had been meant to be.

Cecil Greenough

Grand Magistrate: The Biography of Kiril Pordan

Cities were being burned to the ground, while Americans were being arrested and killed. Sure, the VEDETTE had done similar, but the AEGIS weren't the VEDETTE. You can say that they had come to hate Americans, although they served as three quarters of their AEGIS numbers. This was America, and Americans were being slaughtered. Even the VEDETTE, those who had sworn to serve the Grand Magistrate, didn't believe that this should've been happening to their kin. The AEGIS, on the other hand, didn't care. They killed whoever stood in the way of Autocracy. It only helped that their victims were Americans whom many believed the foreigners couldn't really tolerate in the first place.

Prof. Tamara Boggier

keeper, New York Republic Athenaeum

On September 4, AEGIS General Pamela Barnett institutes a new agenda. Tossing aside the long obsolete *March of the AEGIS*, the plan Grand Magistrate Kiril Pordan constructed can no longer function as the diagram for the war. Barnett takes it upon herself to produce an effective offense. It is an intent which demands the greatest military minds of the Republic, those who serve as Geographic Consultants, Military Strategists, AEGIS Captains, and AEGIS Field Commanders lead close to 357 AEGIS battalions, 70,000 each, across Iowa, and take back what belongs to the Global Magisterium. Appropriately christened Operation: *Storm Front,* on September 18, its tumultuous wave of AEGIS strike at the very heart of Mason City.

The already snow swathed ruined city is at first bombed by air. An aerial strike that lays waste to the Badlands of the Rock Crest-Rock Glen Historic District, as well as, the perilous stretch of Iowa Highway 122, swells of fire bulge down streets consuming everything in path, while bullets break concrete and skewer flesh. A similar bloodbath and mayhem witnessed by those of Arkansas, the AEGIS are once again successful in their hostile invasion of the Midwest.

November 7, and the State of Iowa is overwhelmed from Mason City to Council Bluffs, and sees the deaths of 327 AEGIS in contrast to the

683,529 rebel fighters and 1.8 million citizens. The spy has been made obsolete, and now the true cogency of Operation: *Storm Front* may begin.

By Mid-February, 2056, the States of Missouri, Minnesota, Kansas, Nebraska, and North and South Dakota are all under Magisterium dominance. Close to 7.4 million Revolutionaries have been exterminated in the unmerciful progression, with another 39.5 million imprisoned under the *Sedition Repression Act*. Finally, after years of stalemating, the United Republic Magisterium can again begin focusing on the unification of the country, instead of fighting to maintain the Republic.

Grand Magistrate Pordan immediately initiates an uncompromising investigation into all actions taken within the Magisterium, and commences with the arrests of hundreds of Councilmen and Vice Magistrates found performing illicit affairs. It is a blunt exploit that begins to see the divulging of suspected traitors, in turn, the executions of those Pordan has no choice but to find guilty of betrayal.

From Maine to Winchester, Virginia, Rhode Island to Ohio, those who were once seen as Loyalists to the United Republic Magisterium are seized by AEGIS, and arrested under suspicion of sedition. This opens the door for people to begin accusing their enemies, their neighbors, and even family members of partaking in clandestine affairs, leading to the incarceration and death sentences of thousands. A dark time within the United Republic, with over 21,000 Loyalists being put to death by April, Councilman Matthew Storm does not deceive himself into thinking he is invulnerable.

The rumors regarding his involvement in possible duplicity have begun to rise, and the former VEDETTE General knows Pordan is bound to uncover his dealings. He decides to flee the Republic before being taken into custody, and uses the underground routes traveled mostly by rebels.

Storm travels amongst caravans being snuck out of the Republic, and in due course, finds himself hiding out in the refugee State of Florida. From there, the former VEDETTE General sends word to Admirals Balthazar and Hauser regarding his defection, including his intentions of heading to South America.

Storm does not know what is waiting for him in the enigmatic blackout zones of the Latin continent, but feels it is a chance he needs to take. Still, he makes an oath to both Admirals Balthazar and Hauser that he will return, and that they should await his signal. He says that he will come like a whirlwind from the South, and that they should be prepared to join with him when he does.

The last thing either Admiral will hear from Storm in the coming years, it leaves them anxiously awaiting his promised return, while allowing them the time needed to prepare those VEDETTE who will always remain loyal to their former General. Until then, they, like all VEDETTE, will have no choice but to serve the decree of Operation: *Storm Front*. And that only brings about more bloodshed, even as Storm does in fact reach the shores of Cancun, Mexico via the Pirate trafficking which exists in the Gulf of Mexico. Although, when he does arrive, the VEDETTE discovers the country he once knew has drastically changed.

No longer is Latin America a fractured nation of warlords and fascists. No, both Central and South America have been made into formidable players in the grand scheme of things. And standing as its supreme ruler is none other than a man named Rafael Salazar.

He is powerful, he is brave, and he commands over a billion warriors willing to kill for his glory and the betterment of the Latin Confederation. Something Storm believes he can use to his advantage, when all is said and done, Salazar is a name that will forever change the landscape of North America, as well as, the structure of the Magisterium of the United Republic.

The Great Divide: a concise history of the future

M.A. Martin

2057

TREATY OF SAMAD

M.A. Martin

The European AEGIS have failed. The perfect war machine of the Union of Nations has been defeated. The Global Magisterium has been proven vulnerable. All over Wrocław, Bucharest, Kiev, and Minsk, people take to the streets in celebration, all while the ruins of Hamburg, Berlin, Frankfurt, St. Petersburg and Moscow are embraced by their survivors. They too commemorate this historic day. It is February 13, and Eastern Europe is free.

Germany, the Czech Republic, Hungary, Romania, Ukraine, Belarus, Lithuania, Latvia, Estonia, and Russia all stand as independent nations with the freedoms deserving any Democracy. Kiril Pordan hears of this, and knows what it means. Mankind's desire for restlessness, greed, and defiance can never be tamed. Humans will never agree to live as one. And with the scriptures of Genesis whirling in his head, the Grand Magistrate cannot help but question whether or not God's decree of confounding tongues at the Tower Babel still maintains its power over humanity.

A question that haunts his every move and every decision, it is a heavy yoke helping to drive his fear of the Global Magisterium failing.

This was the point in Kiril Pordan's life when he began questioning everything he'd ever done. Keep in mind that he was no longer the strapping Admiral who'd conceived the Magisterium Edict over twenty years ago. Now, he was this old and weary, world ruler who stayed recluse, didn't really have his hands in Magisterium governance, and who doubted that the Global Magisterium could even survive. Pordan had done a lot in his lifetime, and now it was all beginning to weigh down on him. God was no longer directing his actions. It wasn't like it used to be. He didn't have that clear sense of direction anymore, and he felt his Magisterium was the one that was going to suffer all because of it.

Cecil Greenough

Grand Magistrate: The Biography of Kiril Pordan

The defeats in Eritrea, Sudan, Algeria, and Morocco have all but destabilized the Arabian branch of the regime, leaving the possibility of yet another victory dangling in front of the rebellion. And with the Imperial Asiatic Alliance sustaining the Afro Islamic Union's defense forces, this

233

bolsters the Muslim Jihadi even more. Undoubtedly a dark time for the Global Magisterium, Pordan must do something, or it will fall. Then a call comes from out of the Rocky Mountains both boisterously, and unmistakably on June 30. It is the Makaism sage known as Kuzih putting forth a challenge, one he believes will end the world's conflicts.

A summoning for all Makaists to stop their fighting, forsaking all war, not only is the call of Mt. Borah's mystic presumptuous, it is without doubt unfathomable. Over 29 million men, women, and children that have ingested this inscrutable belief, for them to simply stop fighting would indeed change the dynamics of the wars.

The powerful spiritualist believes his Makaists' are the ones fueling the battles, and calls on them to transfer their wasted energies toward healing the Earth Mother, Gaea Makawee, instead. He does not fear the outcome, but can easily tell the ones he has branded 'Enemies of Gaea' do. Panic made evident by the way both the resistances and Union of Nations react to his declaration, the apprehensive reply from both sides only prove how effective his decree truly is.

Seemingly overnight, news outlets around the world begin reporting on the arrests being made concerning AEGIS refusing to fight. Men and women that have been molded into history's greatest warriors, the AEGIS blinded by Makaism defy their orders, and cease combat.

Entire battalions refusing to carryout orders, soldiers laying down their XM-300s, and misguided words of doom against all those denying the authority of Gaea Makawee, all this plays into the hands of Kuzih, further portraying the Global Magisterium as being no match for the Earth Mother and Her loyal Makaists. But in a desperate attempt to confirm otherwise, Vice Magistrates go on television to assure Loyalists the protests are limited, and that the cohesion of the Global Magisterium remains intact.

The last thing the Global Magisterium needs is for its citizens to begin worrying about their well-being, or thinking about enacting a rebellion of their own. No, the Global Magisterium needs its Loyalists to feel protected, and therefore begins removing the ineffective AEGIS from off the battlefields.

The move sparks tense discussions amongst those questioning the legitimacy of such a verdict. A similar argument happening amongst resistance leaders, the means with which to deal with the negations to follow orders on their side also creates a tense situation.

Severe retaliations against those rebels renouncing the fight for Democracy, it is reported by the internet that Field Leaders either detain Makaists against their will, or worse. People are actually killed under the charge of treason for not wanting to fight. It is a disgrace for all involved in the rebellion, but none more than Arthur Havelock.

The President long made leader of the Revolution understands the frustrations of his commanders, but refuses to condone the horrible acts being committed against those choosing not to fight. He reminds his allies that this is the very thing they have been fighting for themselves—the freedom to choose. In that same vein, the followers of Kuzih should be allowed to do what they believe right, even if he too thinks them pathetic.

Either way, Havelock puts in place severe repercussions of his own against those who would prevent the so-called Makaists from backpedaling to the Rocky Mountains, but not before making clear his warning.

Making sure to caution the defectors that if the Resistance does fall, their faith, their homes, and their precious Kuzih will only follow, it is an admonition the now professed Makaists grasp, but one they believe Kuzih has an answer to. And though family members, friends, and comrades try convincing the converts that Kuzih and his Makaism notion is nothing more than a fraud, the Makaists know better. For them, this is about doing what they believe right. This is about doing what they know to be good. This is about fulfilling their destiny. For it is not Kuzih that is calling them, but the Earth Mother—Gaea Makawee.

By no means do they proclaim their friends consider surrendering. Their decision is about justice, but a justice only Gaea Makawee can decide—a justice Kuzih will be the one to beget. Those who reject human superiority, and instead are of the Earth will be given insight and harmony. Thus, while Makaists all around the world flee the battle scarred theaters of war, vanishing into the most deserted areas they can find, their brethren in the United Republic migrate to Idaho. 'The Blessed Ones' they are called by brothers and sisters in other countries, those privileged enough to sit at the very feet of Kuzih.

Never before in history had someone had so much power over such a broad range of the planet, someone still living during it all, at least. Apart from Kiril Pordan himself, Kuzih was the only man who millions adhered to. So when he said the Makaists were the ones empowering the war, and that they could end all conflicts by simply ceasing to fight, millions upon millions of people did just that. They stopped fighting. Now, this put the warring factions in a strange position. Because not only did rebels lay down their arms, but so did the AEGIS. It was a phenomenon being witnessed all across the globe, with the exception of the Islamic world and Israel. Either way, it was a turn of events that left the end to this global conflict vacillated, with no one knowing exactly what to expect next.

Prof. Tamara Boggier

keeper, New York Republic Anthenaeum

A substantial migration outnumbering the previous Exodus of '54, nearly 4.6 million Loyalists, rebels, and AEGIS yield to Kuzih's call within the first week. But this does not stop Resistance fighters from engaging the Global Magisterium AEGIS in Texas and New Mexico soon after. Two battles standing to decide the fate of the Western Alliance, they decide the fate of the remaining United States.

It is a warm October day, and from Fort Smith to Beaumont, Farmington to Page, stands the Western Alliance's entire defense force Beat-up and malfunctioning M1A1 and M1A2 tanks, ransacked AC-130s, confiscated AC-27Js, fleets of retired F/A-18 Hornets, EA-18G Growlers, and F15 Eagles, and over 15 million men and women willing to sacrifice themselves for freedom, justice, and the American way, this is what stands between Democracy and utter Autocracy.

15 million versus over 29 million AEGIS opponents. Naturally, the Western Alliance does not believe it can win, but they agree to give the Global Magisterium a fight it will never forget.

Arthur Havelock commands them from his headquarters in Dallas, Texas, and refuses to water down the facts of what they are facing. There will be only two options for them: servitude or death, nothing else. The AEGIS have not come to make peace, nor have they come to negotiate. They are here for one purpose, and one purpose only. The Global Magisterium will rule. The United Republic of America will rise. And in summation, Democracy will die.

Havelock tells his people the Revolution cannot stop this from happening, but they can forever taint it with the blood of Americans. It matters not that they are considered rebels, a resistance, and insurgents, the truth will forever remain. When history looks back on this day, it will have to confess the Global Magisterium was built on the carcasses of United States patriots. Unfortunately for this President, the Global Magisterium will be the one to compose history if victorious. And when it recites these final days of the war, it will say fear, terrorism, anarchy, and godlessness were all crushed for their iniquities.

Havelock does not delude himself to think differently, the very reason why he must leave proof of the Revolution's valor. Hence, sending word to his Generals and Commanders, his soldiers and his comrades, his coalition and his friends, Havelock gives word to engage the enemy.

15 million men, women, and children no different than anyone else, against 29 million military trained gladiators. The contest begins on October 25, and in one day witnesses the entire city of Port Arthur, Texas, set ablaze. An inferno rivaling the destruction of Richmond, Virginia, by its end, 571,000 resistance fighters are either shot dead, or burned alive.

The AEGIS are ruthless, and the rebels are shown no mercy. Once more, a sea of black and crimson overlays the land. People weep, the earth is scorched, the sun is blackened, and the air reeks of death. The fire that rages cannot be described, but it eventually does force the Western Alliance's preliminary defense forces to flee for their lives, pinning them deep within the State's boundary. The final days of Democracy, President Arthur Havelock watches the horror on the internet, and knows that it will be at his door by year's end.

There is nothing he can do but continue to fight, surely ending the lives of all who abide by him. So for this, he ultimately decides to stream live what he feels to be his final speech, and clarifies once and for all the inevitable for all involved.

My fellow Americans, today we stand at the door of judgment. Today's a day when all we've ever confirmed is about to burn. Tonight, I'm watchin', waitin', beggin' for the day when I too can mod in death in the name of Democracy. There's nothin' level-up 'bout me. Many have mod to this before. God willin', many'll mod again. Countless Narnists who've stood in protest against injustice, only to be killed like Feebs—as if their desires and their beliefs didn't matter. So yeah, there's a lot Feebs that would rather be deleted by being cowards. Me, I ain't that type of guy. No, sir. I'm a God fearin' American. And as a God fearin' American, it's my duty to defend these here United States of America. Old Glory. Ya'll hear that? Glory! That's what this country stands for. Democracy. Not a bunch of Autocratic Feebs who think a Mod can be told how to modify his life. God gave us Democracy. What can ya'll say against that? Sure, they done whopped us good. They killed millions. They killed Gen. Jake. They killed 'Our Girl' Olivia. They even killed the Walshes. And now they've come to kill us. Well, congratulations AEGIS, I hope ya'll are proud? But there's still a matter of that lil' thing called Democracy. 'Cause ya'll see, I got Democracy. And today, I'm fixin' on usin' that Democracy to fight ya'll 'til there ain't nothin' left. I'm gonna put a hurtin' on ya'll so bad, that whatever ya'll choose to say 'bout me and mines, ya'll gonna remember what I did...What we did. We. Americans. God's people. So go ahead, bring what it is ya'll been staticin' that ya'll got. So long as there's some Mod who believes in Democracy, they're always gonna be a monkey on ya'll's back. Jesus is waitin' for us on the other side of Uber-Mod-status, and we can't wait to Level-up. Now, to whoever can hear me, this ain't gonna be no signal runnin'. I hear there's some Feeb up in Idaho promisin' people peace, signal-runnin' as if he's Jesus Christ. If ya'll lookin' to save ya'll's asses, go on get to him, and just wait 'til the AEGIS come get ya'll there. But if ya'll trying to mod for life, ya'll better high-tail your butts up to Alaska, and from there, get to Belarus or Moldova, or some other Eastern European country. I hear they got Democracy over there. Democracy... Damn that's Mod. Well, now as for the rest of ya'll Narnists, B-B's, signal runnin', Democratic soldiers, I hear the AEGIS staticin' some deletin' feebness, and I'm 'bout to show'em why they ain't no Level-Ups I wanna confirm. What're ya'll gonna to do?

President of the Western Alliance Arthur R. Havelock
October 27, 2057

The call to arms is answered beyond expectation. A little more than 14 million soldiers stand ready to die, and Havelock joins them on the front lines.

As the Presidents of old, he not only begets a war, he is the war. It is the end of Democracy, and nothing can change that. But as long as Arthur Havelock and his 14 million patriots are still alive, they will fight for that dream. A losing battle, they engage the AEGIS with all they have, though fully knowing death will rob them of everything. Such outcomes are of no consequence, not when the final battle for Democracy begins on October 31, with Dallas, Texas exploding by dawn.

Snow blankets the city. A ruined skyline casts an eerie darkness over all things below. Fires spring up from rubble, while smoke billows high into the overcast sky. Blood gushes from the wounds of those being killed, as the fitting symphony of screams encourage such awfulness. Those clothed in heavy jackets, boots, helmets, gloves, goggles, gas masks, and anything else they can find, carry machine guns, stolen AEGIS weapons, and pride into a fight against the inexorable.

Aircraft fighters soar through the dismal heavens, meeting the AEGIS pilots on all fronts. Havelock deploys reserves to New Mexico, and as far as Albuquerque to join the 7 million making sure to guard the northern borders of both States. Alas, this show of bravery means nothing, not in the face of annihilation. Then again, there may be hope for the Southwest after all, but it is a hope yet to agree to help those needing its aid.

A power that has remained silent, might that has chosen to be recluse, a history that has been brought to life, with the United States about to be enslaved, defected United Republic Councilman Matthew Storm looks to the prodigious continent of Latin America to save his country, and is prepared to do what he must.

Having landed on the icy shores of Merida, Mexico, former VEDETTE General Storm is joined by two of his closest confidants, Councilmen Stefan Dupont and Andrew Saito. The three have been waiting for a little close to a year to meet with the leader of this Latin American conglomeration. Having traveled from the Pirate sustained outposts of Belize and Honduras, to the Latin alliance's restricted ports of Barranquilla, Colombia, and finally Caracas, Venezuela, the American trio is finally granted audience with *El Rey*, the supreme ruler of the vast Latin Confederation—Raphael Salazar.

The recently established government is equal to that of the Imperial Asiatic Alliance, Afro Islamic Union, and Eastern European League, but far from anything Storm and his fellow Americans have ever seen.

It is unification of nations once swearing to destroy each other. The countries of Mexico, Guatemala, Belize, Honduras, Nicaragua, Costa Rica, Panama, Colombia, Venezuela, Ecuador, Peru, Brazil, Bolivia, Paraguay, Chile, and Argentina have all bound themselves to one doctrine. Spawned from out of the Chibchan, the Mayas, the Toltecs, the Aztecs, the Incas, and the Olmecs, all of which were once proud rulers of this mighty continent, it is a doctrine honoring Jose Marti, Ernesto Che Guevara, Sor Juana Ines de la Cruz, and Simon Bolivar, revolutionaries who stood and died for their beliefs.

A belief born of the indigenous Záparo, Wai-Wai, Juris, Yąnomamö, Banawá, and Aymara people, those who the land has been mother to for so long, it is a way of hope, solidarity, pride, and courage.

It is the hegemonic might of the Latin Confederation.

Storm arrives in Caracas to find an empire ruling over independent nation-states. Each nation-state with its own elected leader, laws, and beliefs adhering to the utmost sovereignty of one recognized empire, it is ruled by none other than Raphael Salazar, the man who gave Latin America its freedom. And it is upon seeing this, that Matthew Storm comes to believe there is in fact still hope for his nation.

It's been two prosperous decades since the Colombian born mercenary Raphael Salazar wrestled power from the tyrant known as Cesar Lopez, and now he was sitting as the entire continent's much-admired leader. It hadn't been an easy climb, and many had died so that it could be realized. But when it had finally come to bear fruit, the Latin Confederation was exactly what the people of those lands needed. A diagram which tolerated all known ways of life to continue without interference, the hegemonic way of governance was chosen by all to be followed. And it didn't only allow all Latin nations to appoint their own leaders, it encouraged them to do so in their own way. More than just a simple governor or senator of the past, this leader was to be chosen by the people, and sponsored by their hard work. And since they'd chosen to use their countries' natural resources of gold as their currency, the people of Latin America made these men quite powerful when defending their own rights. And though some Latin nations may have still been stronger, wealthier, and more dangerous than others, they all adhered to the final council of the law. But it wouldn't have at all flourished if not for Raphael Salazar. In the end, he was their leader, and they all served him.

Prof. Tamara Boggier

keeper, New York Republic Anthenaeum

Emperor Salazar is not only the man who dethroned Latin America's greatest threat, he is also the leader who chronicled his people back to who they once were. Executing history lessons while crushing the *Latin Liberation Front* underfoot, Salazar recalled the days when he and his people created great pyramids, calendars, myths, and roads to Heaven. Eras when they constructed marvels, reshaping the Earth and its abundance, epochs when his ancestors and the ancestors of his people made cities of gold, forever basking in the immeasurable brilliance of the sun, *El Rey* is the one who reminded his people that they are Latino, Hispanics, warriors, and kings.

Ataguchu, Ek Chuah, Quetzalcoatl, Salazar told his people the gods were angry, and that it was up to them to put right everything that had gone wrong. A time before Cesar Lopez, before Socialism, before Christianity, before Cortez, Salazar called his people to be proud, and this is the sort of pride Matthew Storm now happens upon.

The VEDETTE is astounded, and knows what he must do. Beyond the glitz and glamor, the theology, the narcissism, and unyielding Latin conceit, is a military rivaling the entire world's Armed Forces.

These are not soldiers called forth to fight, nor are they proud patriots defending their homeland. No, their homeland is theirs, and fighting is something they do with pleasure. These combatants kill for the Latin Confederation. They kill for their families. They kill for their race. They kill for Raphael Salazar. And now it is up to Matthew Storm to convince their Emperor to kill for him.

It will be difficult. It will be dangerous. But most of all, it will be costly. Thus, meeting with Emperor Raphael Salazar in a meeting only known to the Latinos, former VEDETTE General Storm is prepared to make his offer. And though he knows it will change his country forever, the former American General has no choice.

Elsewhere, another offer is also being proposed. But unlike Storm's, this offer is not for victory, but for peace. It is February 10, 2058. Cadiz, Spain, 450,000 war-bound Afro Islamic Union Jihadi disembark on the Royal European Alliance's most southern tip, and begin marching northward.

They have only one thing in mind—revenge on the infidel. A call that has been dormant for far too long, the Muslims believe now to be the perfect opportunity to enact their justice. *"Allahu Akbar"* is the chant of warriors willing to die for their allegiance, as well as, a threat to the European Magisterium.

In the eyes of High Magistrate Edward Davies, the Imperial Asiatic Alliance is to blame, since it was their meddling that allowed this trespass, their weapons that strengthened a defeated people, their talks of

Democracy that sired this ongoing war. And in the eyes of High Magistrate Edward Davies, Emperor Domoto Eisaku is public enemy number one.

The IAA Emperor is the one who neutralized the AEGIS in Eritrea, Sudan and southern Egypt, with skirmishes heating up all throughout San'ā, Yemen and At Tā'if, Arabia. Now Europe stands to face similar conflicts, with doubts of its faculties being heard throughout all its nations.

Europeans were calling on their leaders to engage this threat, while fearing the fate of Spain as their own. It was something Davies tried desperately to disavow, even though he had already received word that the cities of Malaga, Seville, and Murcia had fallen to the Muslims. Valencia was next, and then it would be onto Madrid. The High Magistrate could not imagine such things, and called upon Grand Magistrate Pordan to intervene. However, the Grand Magistrate believed in the European Magisterium and the Mu'minūn Shield to hold back the menace, even as Israel started withdrawing its own AEGIS from said regions. Pordan again decided to disregard the request to send aide. Once more, when the Global Magisterium needed him the most, Pordan was nowhere to be found.

Prof. Jarvis Grimes

historian, *Superior and Biased: The History of the Royal European Alliance*

I have seen the destructive nature of rebellion, and know of its power. It's something that devours the good, while emboldening evil. Such things mustn't be allowed to transpire. But I've also witnessed the weakness of this destructive force, and know for sure that it can be crushed. It's fragile in nature, and has already been rebuked by God. Therefore, as men of God, we mustn't falter, or fear such cowardly acts. This is why I feel no need to currently supply the European or Mu'minūn branches of the Global Magisterium with additional forces. I trust in the fortitude of both regimes, and believe they will prosper over such mundane obstacles.

Grand Magistrate Kiril G. Pordan
Response to European call for additional AEGIS, March 6, 2058

Once again, Davies feels forsaken by his Grand Magistrate, and is left to manage the European Magisterium crisis alone. It is something he is not at all pleased with, and he will make that known soon enough. For now, he must put everything he has into halting the Muslim momentum, and regretfully launches airstrikes all throughout Spain's southern coastline.

The Spanish seaboard cities are bombarded with fire from the sky, unmercifully transforming them into uncontrollable infernos. The oldest of the Iberian Peninsula is laid waste to beneath missiles and rockets, incinerating the barrios of La Viña, Santa Maria, and El Populo. Traperia and Plateria are reduced to ashes, blackening nearly all of what remains of Madinat Mursiya.

The earth cries aloud with fury and disaster, with pitch smolder veiling the sun. Cathedrals crumble on fleeing souls and advancing enemies, littering the streets with baroque, rococo, Moorish, and Gothic extravagances. Hundreds of Muslims are killed, while thousands upon thousands of Spaniards are sacrificed for the security of Europe. The last thing High Magistrate Davies wants to do, he knows he has no choice. Spain must be forfeited if the Royal European Alliance is to endure. Saint Servando Teresa de Mier has abandoned her people.

The Supreme Leader of the Afro Islamic Union, Mahdi Abu, is pleased to see this momentum shift in the war, but never ceases on his primary goal, the recapturing of Arabia from out of Mu'minūn hands. That does not mean he has not come to realize a grievous mistake on his part, finally coming to terms with what he has done.

The denying of Mu'minūn from partaking in Hajj is something that was to bring peace to Islam by keeping the Islamic sects separate. Now, however, Mahdi Abu realizes such decree has brought about nothing but war and destruction to his beloved religion, and that it must stop. So having made sure the Imperial Asiatic Alliance has claimed sure victory over Sudan, Egypt, and Eritrea, the Mahdi decides to call for an end to the *Islamic War of Ages*.

He first makes clear the combined forces of the Imperial Asiatic Alliance and Afro Islamic Union can in fact crush the Islamic People's Republic, but insist peace flourish. He wants the blood to stop flowing, the young to cease their tears, the women to once more feel blessed above all others, and for the men of Islam, those chosen to be leaders, for them to stop dying.

The Mahdi wants peace, and after all these years, admits his mistake. This is why he contacts High Magistrate Makhmalbaf in order to make an offer, hoping to bring an end to the conflict.

After so many years, the Mahdi, alaihi al-salaam, finally came to realize that the Islamic partition was not working. I am sure that it was something he could not easily admit, but it was an acknowledgment he had to make nevertheless. Too many Muslims and Mu'minūn had died because of the rift, and that was something the Mahdi, alaihi al-salaam, could no longer consent to. Allah could not have wanted this, and the Mahdi, alaihi al-salaam, had to do what he felt his God would have wanted. That had become his trademark, this absolute devotion and servitude to Allah. I suppose this was the reason most Muslims agreed with him, even though many did not think the Mu'minūn deserving of such a gift. Regardless, the

Mahdi, alaihi al-salaam, made his offer, and it did not take long before he was given his answer.

Prof. Najiyah Abdullah Hassan
Crescent Moon and Pillars: The Rise of the Islamic Empire

March 28, Middle Eastern media gather in Mecca to behold a spectacle like none other. A week long exhibition to the much anticipated peace accord between the Islamic People's Republic and Afro Islamic Union, millions of people descend on Arabia to witness the honors. Even the Israelis are present, cheering on the possible end to a conflict they themselves have tried so long to avoid. More than simple peace being made amongst brothers, this is the first time a member of the Global Magisterium extends its hand to a rogue nation, seemingly accepting that country's independent sovereignty.

A blow to the laws of Autocracy as seen by Grand Magistrate Kiril Pordan, that does not stop the once great enemies from ending the *Islamic War of Ages*.

High Magistrate Makhmalbaf even agrees to cease AEGIS operations in Arabia, returning all lands seized to the Afro Islamic Union. Something he does not ask permission for, he challenges the very authority Grand Magistrate Pordan with such act. But with the Arabian AEGIS following the decree without an ounce of opposition, they also make sure to silence any disputes amongst their minute foreign comrades.

The order of banishment is then set upon those same outsiders, demanding they take the allotted time to depart in safe route to their homelands. And though Makhmalbaf recognizes his betrayal to the Global Magisterium, he finds his faith in Islamic unity more compelling in dictating his actions. Thus, making one final speech from out of Tehran, Iran, the Arabian High Magistrate bids his Mu'minūn farewell, and promises unity to them upon his return. He, of course, makes sure to reiterate the Mahdi's call for an end to the Islamic war, finally meeting with Abu abd Allah Muhammad in no other place than Mecca, Arabia, on April 12.

The two leaders gather to sign a peace accord called *The Treaty of Samad*, and almost immediately, like a miracle only now being granted, millions of Muslims and Mu'minūn alike hold back their hands of war, embracing their neighbors as brothers and sisters. An evolution of their faith, it is a reconciliation long sought by so many.

No longer will Muslims and Mu'minūn kill each other over land. Mahdi Abu tells his people it has been too long, and that there have been enough children born knowing nothing else but this hate and destruction. Now it will be up to the elders, the ones who have stained their hands with so much blood, to teach their children the truth. They are Islam. The Prophet Muhammad is the last Apostle of Allah. The Qur'an is His revelation.

The Mahdi tells them it is up to every Muslim and Mu'minūn to be a light unto the world. He repents of the war he himself brought, and now focuses on healing Islam of its scars.

Mahdi Abu will play the part of leader not only to the Muslims, but to the Mu'minūn, as well. He and High Magistrate Makhmalbaf will marshal in an age of peace and prosperity, and the world will envy its very thought. A dream of absolute submission to Allah, Mahdi Abu is sadly assassinated in front of his home on June 4, by a Muslim fanatic named Omar Kaamil Fonde, and does not live to see this age of Islamic unity come to pass.

All those who knew him mourn the slain leader; likewise, praise him as the true Mahdi. And though some will never cease their hatred, the cause of Islamic unity will not be stalled. In time, Islam will rise again, and all will bear witness to its greatness. Although, there still remains one problem that must be dealt with before seeing such eminences transpire, and that is the problem of the Global Magisterium.

The Islamic People's Republic remains a key member of the world-wide regime's existence, and cannot simply ignore its decree. The Afro Islamic Union must be merged into its system of order, or be destroyed. It is an obligation the Mu'minūn do not take lightly, especially since they know first hand of its consequences. A power that, though being subdued in Europe, remains quite visibly influential in North America.

High Magistrate Makhmalbaf is not foolish enough to think the Global Magisterium will not seek retribution for his peace treaty with the Muslim rebels. He also knows there will be nothing left of his people to be submissive if he does not fulfill his Autocratic duty. But in his mind, this will be a true sacrifice for Allah, one deserving of *Sharia*. So putting in the rear its standing at the table of the Union of Nations, the Islamic People's Republic abandons the Global Magisterium design of Autocracy, and leaves the European Magisterium to face the Afro Islamic Union alone.

With Portugal lost, and half of Spain burning as a testimony to the Afro Islamic Union's barbarism, High Magistrate Edward Davies now knows for sure that he will be defeated.

Both Eastern Europe and the Afro Islamic Union had weakened the Royal European Alliance to the point of surrender by now. But always did the REA carry on with its fight, even with the Imperial Asiatic Alliance fueling its enemies to continue. A fight that if allowed to persist, would be the end of all High Magistrate Edward Davies had worked so hard to protect. He could not allow this. And so Davies sounded the call for a cease-fire, and requested that High Magistrate Makhmalbaf himself reach an agreement with the Muslims on behalf of the Royal European Alliance. It was a very humbling experience, and Davies

M.A. Martin

does not take it well. Muslims having power over Europe? It was, and still is, to a large extent, unreservedly insulting.

Prof. Jarvis Grimes
historian, *Superior and Biased: The History of the Royal European Alliance*

Despite their rejection of compulsory Autocracy, the Islamic People's Republic seat amongst the Global Magisterium remains intact. This gives it the right to speak on behalf of the Europeans when praying the Muslims stay their encroachment. And with a new leader appointed for the Muslims, his name being Abu abd Allah Muhammad Ibn Mahdi Abu, son of Mahdi Abu, the Royal European Alliance gets its answer without misgivings.

It comes on September 15, when Afro Islamic Union forces begin withdrawing from out of Europe, sparing the REA its darkest days.

In the end, the Imperial Asiatic Alliance has tempered the European Magisterium, fully unified with Russia, gained Egypt, Sudan, and Eritrea, and stands as the most powerful force in the Eastern Hemisphere. The Islamic People's Republic, though still a member of the Global Magisterium arena, remains significant and humble alongside its equally as stable Afro Islamic Union brethren. The State of Israel is simply relieved the IPR has not been conquered, already knowing what the Muslims would have had in store for them. And the Freelands of Australia, Alaska, Greenland, Nubia, Canada, and the like, have nothing to fear from the confounded establishment.

The Global Magisterium is crumbling.

High Magistrate Edward Davies sees this, and knows exactly who is to blame. The one who lied to him. A man with dreams of grandeur. The one who turned his back on an ideology, only to make it Europe's nightmare. This is Grand Magistrate Kiril Pordan's fault, and Davies believes he must pay.

In conclusion, Edward Davies swears the Royal European Alliance will have its revenge, and that he will be the one to make the Grand Magistrate pay for his treachery. Indeed, when all is said and done, Davies still intends on seeing the Global Magisterium flourish, but it will do so without Kiril Gustav Pordan.

The Great Divide: a concise history of the future

M.A. Martin

LATE 2059
DIA DE MUERTOS

The Great Divide: a concise history of the future

August 19, and the State of New Mexico has finally fallen to the AEGIS. Texas is not far behind in its own capitulation, but defiantly continues in its resistance nonetheless. The skies are dark. Fires burn all throughout the Longhorn State. Dead bodies lay frozen all over the Southwest. And rebels are slowly, but surely eliminated on all fronts. It looks as if the United Republic of America is nearly complete in its design, but only if the Magisterium can conclude the nation's violent II Civil War.

As it already stands, Asia, Eastern Europe, Australia, Greenland, Alaska, Nubia, the islands, and the entire continent of Latin America all exist as independent governments free of Global Magisterium control. Likewise, the Middle East, Scandinavia, and Canada, though representing the extent of the Union of Nations' dominance, disregard the call of mandated Autocracy, sparing the rest of the globe their past intents of absolute control. This as a result, leaves Europe as the only true functioning ally to the United Republic.

Davies was sitting back, and watching as the United Republic flourished in the West, while the Royal European Alliance existed in a fluid state. The Muslims, the Mu'minūn, Israelis, Eastern Europeans, the Saami, and the Imperial Asiatic Alliance were all around him, while Pordan enjoyed his victory over an insignificant challenge. It was eating away at the High Magistrate, and he wanted to do something about it. Kiril Pordan deserved to feel what he was feeling, and Davies knew exactly how to give him that gift. He had to buy his time for now, though. But he would do exactly to Pordan what Pordan had done to him. It was only fair.

Prof. Jarvis Grimes

historian, *Superior and Biased: The History of the Royal European Alliance*

Kiril Pordan could feel Davies' resentment, and understood why he was so mad. But what did Davies want him to do, forsake the battle for the United Republic? He'd barely gotten control over the Midwest when Davies started hammering him for reinforcements. The REA had just as much AEGIS fighting for them as the United Republic did. Why couldn't Davies fight off the Grimaldi Defiance in the same way Pordan was doing the Western Alliance? Davies' problem was that he'd been greedy, and attacked the Afro Islamic Union for no reason. The Islamic People's Republic and Israel had beaten them, but he just had to go and stick his nose where it didn't belong. Let the Islamic People's Republic and Israel handle the Muslims, and you focus on the Imperial Asiatic Alliance! No, he just had to go and fight two wars on two fronts, and now he was trying to lay the blame on Pordan. You ask me, I think Davies lost the war about the same time he'd lost his mind, and that's just sad. Now he planned on screwing Pordan over, and the Global Magisterium was going to be the one to pay the price.

Cecil Greenough

Grand Magistrate: The Biography of Kiril Pordan

Davies makes sure to pay close attention to the developments in the West, and waits for the perfect opportunity when he can strike. And though he continues to support the AEGIS attacks on American insurgents, he has no intentions on forgetting Grand Magistrate Kiril Pordan's betrayal. A betrayal Davies holds guilty of bringing about the weakness of the Royal European Alliance, his only desire is to see the same fate befall the whole of the United Republic. So he waits for the precise moment, and then he will strike.

In the meantime, the leader of the European Magisterium congregates with his Vice Magistrates in making sure his plan will indeed work. The European Vice Magistrates and Councilmen are all aware of what Davies has in store for the mighty nation, and gladly aid him in his conquest. To them, it is an entitlement that has been forsaken for more than two hundred and eighty-three years, with the legitimacy of its reality only now finding rebirth.

The time has come for the Imperial British Royal Navy to sail across the sea, this time in the name of the Royal European Alliance, and once more stake claim over what it has bred. But Davies must postpone such triumphs for now having learned of an even greater threat, one by the name of Matthew Storm.

It has been nearly two years since the former Magisterium Councilman arrived in Latin America, only to find hope in defeating Kiril Pordan. A quest that seemed undoubtedly lost, his prayers were answered when discovering a country powerful enough to threaten the very push of Autocracy. With the hegemonic empire of the Latin Confederation, Storm has been given his instrument of war. His convincing of an emperor and his mighty empire to serve as such was his only obstacle. And though it was not easy, Storm has finally been given control of the empire's heavily armed combatants. Warriors who feed on the coca plants of Peru and Bolivia, these soldiers will bring war and horrors unimaginable.

They feel no pain, and know only death. And for far too long has Salazar kept them chained. The Emperor warns the American VEDETTE, telling him his heavily armed warriors do not go to simply kill, but to sacrifice. He tells Storm there will be blood, and loads of it. He tells him he has seen the AEGIS and their weapons, and promises the Guerreros of his empire will trample their pitch armors beneath their feet. But most importantly, Salazar tells Storm Texas will be his. And so, this is the covenant made by Matthew Storm.

In return for the Latin Confederation's guaranteed military support, the state of Texas is to be returned to their former possessors. As expected, it is a costly price for freedom, but one Storm believes necessary. Thus, having the power of over 20 million Guerreros behind him, with another assembled 35 million coming up through Central America to join them, Matthew Storm crosses the Rio Grande, and marches into the devastated Southwestern State of Texas.

It is a ghastly sight. Charred frameworks, once glorious structures. Abandoned roads, once routes to small towns. The stench of death, at one time a rich scent of freedom and decency. Houston's skyline is obscured beneath a thick pitch of gloom and death, leading the defeated and persuaded to accept the ICE-chip in hopes of solace.

Amarillo is a wasteland being made into living proof of the Magisterium's might, with rising structures birthing an advanced arcology intended on abandoning the past. Austin burns in the wake of its endless MOAB cleansing, leaving craters and devastation as testimony to the futility of defiance. And Corpus Christi ignores its neighbors and friends after realizing what they have been denying for far too long, the rebellion is over, and there is so much one can have when visiting a Depot.

This is Texas, and its people are being assimilated into the Magisterium through anguish and slaughter, bribery and fear—insults VEDETTE General Matthew Storm has come to halt.

Crossing into the few remaining strongholds of Brownsville, McAllen, Laredo, and Eagle Pass, Storm unleashes the wrath of the Guerreros upon the AEGIS, and gives birth to an invasion. The date is November 2, *Dia de Muertos*—The Day of the Dead. And never before has this appellation been more appropriate then on this day.

One eyewitness claimed the invasion seemed to take place overnight. That millions upon millions of Guerreros poured into Texas, overwhelming the State before sunlight even revealed their innumerable raid. Can you even imagine that? Millions of armed combatants crossing the Rio Grande in one fell swoop, and all of them hellbent on taking over Texas? I'm sure it was something that terrified even the rebellion, especially before they finally realized these invaders were on their side. But you have to hand it to the AEGIS. No matter how large the Guerreros' numbers, they were still there to answer the call of Autocracy.

Prof. Tamara Boggier
keeper, New York Republic Anthenaeum

The two armed forces engage, and all at once, Hell is unleashed on Earth. The AEGIS fight with purpose, and the utmost defense of the United Republic with their lives. Armed with fleets of X-44 MANTAs, and quickly proclaiming lordship over the skies, like eagles they soar, dashing, and rising into the heavens.

They dive and spin, while their rockets destroy everything targeted. Balls of fire torch the clouds, with streams of burning flames searing the earth below. Superior in every way, the AEGIS obliterate the air force of the Latin Confederation as easily as they do their tanks and brigades.

Entire squadrons and platoons are engulfed in blazing firestorms, as are convoys of trucks and reinforcements. Sable round loaded XM-300 Gatling railguns outmatch MP7s and FN P90s by a tenfold, brutally ripping apart both Guerreros and rebels alike. Smoke, silt, fire, blood, and death, this is what the AEGIS encounter Matthew Storm with, forcing him to come to the conclusion that this war machine will not be won by conventional means. But Storm counts himself lucky, for conventional is something the Guerreros do not look fondly upon.

These narcotized combatants cannot be stopped by mere-weapons, not when they flood Texas overnight, unreservedly determined to stake claim on the Southwest. 25 million intoxicated soldiers, it takes well into a little over a week, but they do eventually unleash their fury on the AEGIS. And when the Guerreros do finally reveal their true nature, a sacrifice is what is carried out.

Dissolved with chalk, the alkaloids they receive from ingesting the coca leaves cause their blood to boil, turning them into indestructible savages. They fear nothing. They scream as if animals preparing to feast on the carcasses of prey. And not only are the Guerreros well-armed, their blatant disregard for life cannot be comprehended.

Their advance never stops, giving the AEGIS no time to rest, or regroup. The Guerreros simply flood the State as if an unstoppable wave, never taking a break, consuming the land and enemies in their thrust. No battalions, no organized formation, no rest, it is a nonstop invasion of bodies upon bodies—a flood of killers.

Unlike the terrorists of the past who menacingly committed suicide bombings, and revolutionaries who died for their beliefs, the Guerreros kill only to see blood. The crimson flow of precious life force, its reddish décor is what pleases the god, Quetzalcoatl. That feathery serpent of old, he is the one who demands such carnage. And the Guerreros, as loyal servants, more than quench his thirst. An absolute massacre, not since the time of the Aztecs have these people brought forth such atrocities.

It is a tidal wave of nonstop aggression, and only now does Matthew Storm grasp the cautioning of Raphael Salazar. This is a sacrifice, and all who stand against the Latin Confederation must be made its victim. Storm has brought this bloodbath upon the AEGIS, and now he must deal with its horrors. But he is also handed a surprise—the American AEGIS on the battlefield.

Much to his shock and awe, once learning who it is who leads the Guerreros, American AEGIS refuse to defend their positions. They surrender to the onslaught, if only to join forces under Storm's command. Thousands at first, Storm finds the fracture in the AEGIS ranks yet another thing that helps his cause.

In the end, 345,000 AEGIS lie ravaged to the elements. Most of them are European and Arab, with the only American AEGIS amongst them being those not quick enough to switch sides. A scene of sheer butchery, by November 27, the cities of El Paso and San Antonio are claimed by the Guerreros and their leaders.

Matthew Storm has indeed initiated the changing tide in the war, and soon he will put his precious Magisterium to the test. Nevertheless, he must first meet with the leader of the Resistance, President Arthur Havelock, and only then will he be able to commence with his true show of aggression—one that will forever alter the United Republic of America.

Word reaches the Magisterium Core within hours of the AEGIS defeat in Texas. A crushing blow, it is the last thing Kiril Pordan needs to hear. Already torn between the near-downfall of the European Magisterium, and both the Scandinavian and Islamic Peoples Republic's perceived treachery, Storm's charge through Texas weighs heavily on the Grand Magistrate's mind. He even comes to learn of the American AEGIS defecting, and joining the invading horde. Those who are the Dominion, they betray the Magisterium. For that reason, Pordan convenes with his advisers, hoping one can deter the threat. Regrettably, not one of his aides can contribute a sensible means of defense.

It is a lack of counsel Pordan has been facing for quite some time now. A deficiency in dependence he finds quite unsettling, the Grand Magistrate cannot help but feel the Vice Magistrates and Councilmen of his Core wish to see him fail. A possible case of paranoia, Pordan is convinced he is facing a mutiny. So in response, he sets in motion a massive intelligence sweep throughout the Republic, arresting in multitudes those he deems insurrectionists. And once again, the Magisterium has a web of deception and doubt cast over its command, and that is something that does not help in solving the problem engulfing the Southwestern territories.

Matthew Storm, his traitors, and the Latin Confederation Guerreros advance on Houston with each passing day, further threatening Magisterium hold on Texas. Something the Grand Magistrate must put a stop to, the invasion leaves Pordan with no other choice but to begin increasing AEGIS numbers in that region.

He orders AEGIS in Oklahoma and New Mexico to be redeployed to Texas in mass numbers, taking station all across the cities of Dallas, Abilene, and Lubbock. The southern areas of the Longhorn State are now alienated from the rest of the territory, making it easier for the AEGIS to focus on their enemy. It is a calculative move, but Storm is not impressed.

This is exactly what he has been waiting for. The VEDETTE General has been anticipating the decks to appear stacked against him, and for anyone who stands in defiance of the Magisterium to be threatened. He already knows what is coming next. The phalanx-like attack that has subdued so many over the years, Storm is aware it is the only thing that will unify the fighters of the Resistance and the Guerreros of the Latin Confederation.

He is correct in his assumption. For when gaining intelligence concerning the massive AEGIS force preparing to attack, President Arthur Havelock finally agrees to meet with the former Councilman instead of facing sure annihilation.

Havelock had been holding back from meeting with Matthew Storm, plainly because he didn't trust him. And he had good reason not to. One, this was too similar to the deal Calvin Walsh and George Hartsoe had together, and we all know how that turned out. Two, Matthew Storm didn't really support Democracy. He was an Autocrat. And three, he'd just invaded the United States with millions upon millions of foreigners, and they're not civilians or refugees looking for a better life. No, sir. These were violent, well-trained, sadistic killers. They weren't there to help free Texas, they were there to take it. I wouldn't have trusted Storm either. But lo and behold, with an AEGIS presence of nearly a quarter of a million descending on him and his followers, Havelock had no choice but to.

Cecil Greenough

Grand Magistrate: The Biography of Kiril Pordan

The leaders gather on December 24, Christmas Eve, in the battle ravaged city of Houston. Almost immediately, Storm makes clear his proposition. The State of Texas is to be transferred to Latin Confederation governance, in exchange for wrestling Magisterium control from out of the hands of Kiril Pordan. A steep price, Storm advocates this as the only way to save North America, and asks that Havelock have his rebels cooperate.

It is an extortionate transaction, but Havelock realizes this may in fact be the Resistance's only option, and accepts his lot. But before he can agree to such terms, Havelock has concessions he too needs contracted. Three amendments that will seal the indenture of the Resistance and Guerrero merger, these are the demands of the nation's remaining patriots. All mandates concerning the Interim Credit Encode are required to be suspended, making this latest form of governmental concord a choice to be made by independent citizens. Next, the AEGIS must be dismantled and made a defense force as once in history; likewise, this Armed Force must be a body of military defense which protects, and not hinders the due processes of loyal citizens. And lastly, the *Magisterium Edict* must be dissolved, and the United States Constitution reinstated upon immediate seizing of the Magisterium.

The commands are reverse stances which Matthew Storm feels strongly about, but the propositions unquestionably address the main concerns of the Resistance and their like. Concessions the former General must obviously engage if he plans on saving his country, the requests put before him are difficult dilemmas.

In truth, Kiril Pordan and his world-wide government remain the driving force behind Storm's hostilities, and not Autocracy's assurance of prosperity and dominance. And if he fights, Storm fights to establish Autocracy, and all its decrees. However, realizing such a regime can never flourish if at constant war with half the country, Storm comes to terms with his duty to the nation as a whole, compromising his very soul.

The former Councilman weighs his options, and concludes there can indeed be prospects for both Democracy and his venerated orderly function of governance. So Storm agrees to the terms, then supplies President Havelock with the tools he needs in order to contact his scattered and imprisoned rebel fighters. Computers, encryption codes, and top secret data banks supplied to him by loyal American VEDETTE having already abandoned their AEGIS titles during the battles of El Paso and San Antonio, Storm gives Havelock and his remaining soldiers all they need in order to summon their sleeping warriors.

Those who have been humiliated and beaten, those who believe Democracy to be dead, those who once fought for liberty and justice. The details as to how Democracy and Autocracy will live harmoniously will have to wait. For now, Storm needs Havelock to rise up his army, and can only pray they will answer the call.

The Guerreros had taken most of Texas, and they were undoubtedly going to take over the other half by the end of the year. But they still weren't enough to challenge the AEGIS being geared on the southwest. Matthew Storm needed more men. So until he was able to seize control over the VEDETTE awaiting his orders, those of the overcome rebellion would have to do. That was Arthur Havelock's job. After all, if anybody was going to get these rebels who had already been defeated to fight, it would have to be the man who had fought to the bitter end to keep them free.

Prof. Tamara Boggier

keeper, New York Republic Anthenaeum

The leader of the fractured Resistance sends out an entreaty of rebellion on December 27, telling his once loyal fighters the time has come to rekindle the fire of Democracy. He begs them to stand one last time in resisting their masters. He calls on them to be soldiers, and demands their patriotism be ignited once more.

He knows many of them have already been cataloged, but Havelock declares the ICE-chip cannot stop Democracy. In the end, the United States still has a chance of surviving, and he begs his soldiers to hold fast. Democracy is on the horizon, and they must not allow it to set with the sun. Havelock calls on every able bodied man, woman, and child to fight the good fight, and promises he will join them in their struggle. God is with them, and He will deliver their enemies into their hands. A charge that is as poetic as much as it is passionate, a call of independence for the United States of America, it reaches those who are downtrodden, broken, and weak, rallying the rebellion's ultimate spark of hope.

Simultaneously, Storm puts forth his own call in triggering his stagnant VEDETTE into action. The animosity amongst the AEGIS is evident, and most Americans want the foreigners gone. Those who still consider themselves VEDETTE, their former General calls on them to rise-up and fight the foreign invasion of the AEGIS.

This was it—all or nothing. The Guerreros could only go as far as the Texas-Oklahoma border, and no further. That was the deal. After Texas had been won, Storm, and whoever else decided to join him would be on their own. The rest of America would have to be won by Americans. That's what Matthew Storm tried nailing home when he began commanding Americans to fight. He needed them, and they needed him. This had been Storm's plan all along: find a footing, and from there, call on all who share your disgust towards the Global Magisterium, and launch an attack. Storm had to convince Americans they had a common foe, uniting them as one. And the foreigners of the AEGIS just so happen to fit the bill. European, Israeli, and Mu'minūn alike, they all had to go.

Cecil Greenough

Grand Magistrate: The Biography of Kiril Pordan

Storm is finally prepared to bring about the time of decision. And in his eyes, there are only two forms of soldiers fighting in his country: those who stand for America's honor, America's glory, America's dream—Americans. And those who dare sully the land with their foreign presence, and tacit occupation. America for Americans. Storm calls upon his VEDETTE to rise.

Brave Loyalists of the National Offensive, this is Central Command, VEDETTE General Matthew Storm. Do you read me? It's come to my attention our dream is being tampered with from within our ranks. That everything we've fought so hard for is being stolen from right beneath our noses. That a poison has infested our very core, and is slowly but surely killing us. Do you read me? I sit here a man broken of heart, and enraged in spirit. I'm discontented with the order of things, as I'm sure you all are. Autocracy, the ideology of our honorable High Magistrate of fore, George Hartsoe. Wasn't it him who begot this trial for us, only to make us fervent in our belief in Autocracy? He who dared to look across a broken nation, only to see hope and courage. Wasn't him who brought forth this Magisterium, solely for the glory of America? America, VEDETTE. America for Americans. Do you read me? This was the dream of High Magistrate George Hartsoe. The dream of Autocracy. Not this union of foreigners and barbarians sired by an egomaniac in service of his own glory. His glory, not ours. Not the nation's. And not Autocracy—His. Do you read me? But not anymore. No more shall I betray the dream of Autocracy for that of global domination. I'm a VEDETTE, the Dominion of the Magisterium. And it is my duty to defend this United Republic against all threats. But above all, my duty is to sustain America's greatness above all other nations with none being her equal. I'm a Loyalist, and I stand for order and glory. Do you read me? I refuse to share my birthright with outsiders. I'm an American, and my land stands indivisible, with liberty and justice for all. Do you read me? Now I ask you, VEDETTE, guardians of Autocracy, protectors of America, now I ask you, will you continue to eradicate your American brothers alongside those who, during our darkest hour, smiled and rejoiced at our suffering? And though they challenge us with their Democratic views, are you going to continue killing those who are Americans alongside those who've hated us for so long? I don't think so. I've served with each and every one of you. I've bled alongside each and every one of you. I'm VEDETTE General Matthew Storm. You know our code and our pledge. Do you read me? We are the Dominion of the Magisterium, and we pledge solidarity to the institution of Autocracy. Therefore, if we are to compel the supremacy of our land, the foreigners must go. There is no Global Magisterium. There is no Union of Nations. And there is, categorically, no AEGIS. This is America, and all others must depart, or taste her wrath. My fellow Americans, *"even Heaven had its war. And just as God stood and proclaimed the Heavens His, so shall we in unification proclaim this country ours,"* remember that? Do you read me? I hereby solemnly swear by my heart, soul, mind, and body to be loyal to God and the Magisterium. And forever shall I hail its decrees, until death be given me, and my reward granted. Arise VEDETTE. Arise Americans. Arise. And let us cleanse our lands of these illegal aliens. God bless the Republic, and God bless America.

VEDETTE General Matthew Nicholas Storm
Launch of the Purification War, December 31, 2059

The directive millions upon millions of AEGIS have been waiting to hear, those who still classify themselves as VEDETTE take heed of their obligation to obey the order given to them. And in a bar, an American AEGIS voices his lewd agreement with Storm's words in front of his European comrades, and starts a brawl. The 38th NECRO Brigade nearly open fire on each other, when American AEGIS refuse to carryout an execution order against a known terrorist cell of the Resistance. A Councilman in Kansas and a Vice Magistrate in Pennsylvania defend any and all acts of violence being acted out by American Loyalists against Magisterium Centers. And it is not take long before news agencies begin flashing breaking news reports of American AEGIS battling European counterparts all throughout the Republic.

Random acts that make clear a division amongst the warriors of the Global Magisterium, American AEGIS all over the country make known their true allegiance. They are the Dominion of the Magisterium— VEDETTE.

Still, much to Matthew Storm's dismay, it is only a small number of VEDETTE that immediately react to his demand. And though isolated skirmishes between Americans and foreign lieges do spark throughout the country, they are all quickly quelled by AEGIS Gen. Pamela Barnett, and her demand for order.

Matthew Storm had been gone for quite some time. The VEDETTE had been tainted by their fighting, and weren't thinking straight. They didn't know who to trust. Matthew Storm, who, though their former leader, abandoned them in their time of need? Or Pamela Barnett, who has been there in the trenches with them, though murdering their fellow Americans? It wasn't the reaction Storm had been hoping to receive, but one he'd long anticipated. He knew full and well that his decree would take time to fester in the hearts of his men and women of the VEDETTE Order, but at the same time, hoped it wouldn't take too long.

Prof. Tamara Boggier

keeper, New York Republic Anthenaeum

Regardless of such setbacks, Storm persists with his attack on the foreign members of the AEGIS either way, and comes to find more than enough support from rebels all across the land once more engaging their overseers. They fight for Democracy and its ideals, and it is enough of a disruption to allow Storm to begin conducting his *Purification War.*

The Magisterium Core learns of such violent outbreaks, and hectically riles the establishment's everyday functions. Hundreds of Vice Magistrates and Councilmen alike agree with Storm's statements, and begin voicing their disgruntled opinions over foreigners enacting bloodshed on American soil. Some even outrightly challenge the Grand Magistrate, and what he believes to be a necessary sanction, calling for all foreign soldiers to be extracted from out of the nation. An opposition Kiril Pordan refuses to bow on the subject of, those who dispute the regulations of the Global Magisterium are either arrested, or executed under the indictments of treason and dissension.

These acts of punishment prove Pordan's continued authority over the Magisterium, but only add more fuel to the fire as Loyalists commence taking to the streets in protest of Kiril Pordan's continued upholding of the Global Magisterium. Rallies that do not undermine their adherence to Magisterium Autocracy, they more than agree with the demands to end the nation's occupation by foreigners.

These turn of events began taking place literally overnight. Loyalists, those of the Republic, began taking to the streets and actually began protesting. At first there were picket signs, and then before one knew it, there were clashes. This was something that hadn't been seen in nearly twenty years, at least not in the original thirteen Republics. But even they were being disrupted by riots and demonstrations. Kiril Pordan couldn't stand for this, and again he passed his verdict for such brashness. Unfortunately, this time around, the response he received was one of absolute defiance.

Cecil Greenough
Grand Magistrate: The Biography of Kiril Pordan

Grand Magistrate Pordan once more places a round of sanctions against the Republic, but primarily the embargo on all ICE-chip functions. All Depots are closed for business, public transportation is halted, schools are dismissed, Factories are shutdown, and utilities are all cut off, plunging the Republic into a primitive state. A rehashed subjugation, Pordan demands the Loyalists halt their unbecoming barbarisms, or remain in the dark. And with the technology behind the Interim Credit Encode being the main upgrade to the nation over the years, the Grand Magistrate simply waits for his Loyalists to bend. It is an assumption that is proven faulty this time around.

The repeated usage of the ICE-chip as a form of reprimand has gone too far, and is this time met with an immediate uprising. Violent unrest breakout all through the Republics of Kansas, Nebraska, Iowa, Georgia, New York, and Washington D.C., steadfastly demanding the Interim Credit Encode be put back online. Loyalists unleash their anger in forms of looting, vandalism, and arson, never putting to rest their demands for all ICE-chips to be reactivated. They burn the Global Magisterium flag, demanding all foreigners be ejected from the country. And they even begin hailing Matthew Storm as their leader, daring to threaten of a coup against Kiril Pordan himself if he does not heed their plea. Intimidation the Grand Magistrate will not be dictated by, he instead deploys thousands of AEGIS to suppress the demonstrations. Unfortunately for him, even those who are amongst his military promote the aggressive disputes, and refuse the orders.

The uprising of Loyalists, the invasion of Texas through the Republic's underbelly, and Matthew Storm's discordant call for VEDETTE betrayal rightly disturb Kiril Pordan to the point of defeat. Without a doubt, the Grand Magistrate can feel his grip on things slipping, but refuses to succumb to its reality. Still, in face of such blatant challenge to his authority, Pordan does reinstate all ICE-chip functions in hopes of allaying the turmoil, a sure sign to all involved of his abating power. But it does not stop with that, not when High Magistrate Davies demands from half a world away that something be done about the constant reports he has been receiving relating to European AEGIS being attacked by their supposed American colleagues.

By March, 2060, there had already been hundreds of cases involving AEGIS on AEGIS crime, as well as, European AEGIS being attacked by Loyalists. The Arabs and Israelis would have suffered the same amount of backlash, but those cowards started choosing to take a step back. Texas had been laid siege to, and the Guerreros stood poised to move on a fractured military standing guard in Dallas. It was a rapid and dismal spiral of inner-turmoil, and Matthew Storm was to blame. It was his venomous declaration concerning dissolving the AEGIS that had indeed begun to contaminate the Global Magisterium, and now it even threatened the regime's once successful amalgamation of nations. Well, Edward Davies was not going to stand for this, and who could blame him? Kiril Pordan was losing control, and it was up to High Magistrate Davies to salvage what he could.

Prof. Jarvis Grimes
historian, *Superior and Biased: The History of the Royal European Alliance*

The United Republic is not the only place where Americans are reacting to Matthew Storm's declaration. In both Europe and the Middle East, American AEGIS begin protesting as well, but theirs is not a demand of deportation, but an insistence to return home.

No longer believing in the Union of Nations and its mandate of world governance, the insubordinate Americans begin disrupting Global Magisterium protocols all across the Eastern Hemisphere. Within days, news of such defiance reaches the heart of the Royal European Alliance, forcing High Magistrate Davies to make his intolerance of the situation as clear as possible.

He immediately puts in place a decree condemning all acts of sedition, and begins placing thousands of American AEGIS under arrest in Europe, with the charges of treason and discord behind each detainment. Detainment that are both harsh and grueling, the American prisoners are then condemned to Europe's own version of the *Sedition Repression Act*. Thousands of Americans forced into enslavement overseas, it is enough to outrage any American back home.

It does so in the forms of even more attacks against European AEGIS stationed in the United Republic, as well as, in protests occurring right outside the Magisterium Core—the very home of Grand Magistrate Pordan.

There, the demands are clear and nonnegotiable. Europeans have to leave the United Republic of America, or face severe reprisals. The deaths of 1156 Americans, 1342 Europeans, 286 Israeli, and 495 Mu'minūn is proof enough of what this threat entails, slowly but surely unraveling all of what Kiril Pordan has realized.

On April 19, the Islamic People's Republic and State of Israel simultaneously begin instructing their AEGIS to abandon operations in the United Republic. High Magistrates Makhmalbaf and Manishewitz contact Pordan, and inform him of their intentions concerning ending their regions' continued military support. Pordan argues against the withdrawal, warning the High Magistrates that such decisions carry heavy consequences, but Manishewitz and Makhmalbaf go behind his back and ransom the safety of their soldiers by surrendering their forces to the will of the American consensus. And in a matter of days, all across the United Republic, Mu'minūn and Israelis abandon the battlefield, offering themselves up as prisoners to the American AEGIS. It is a gamble, but one General Storm supports.

The former VEDETTE General broadcasts his demands to those aligning themselves to his cause, and orders the Israelis and Mu'minūn be allowed safe passage. A risk in any case for those seeking to flee the United

Republic, the Arabian and Israeli AEGIS nonetheless abandon their European Coalition in face of a losing battle.

The act is to be followed by the withdrawal of over 2 million Mu'minūn and Israelis in the coming months, in a decision which brings Europe's High Magistrate, Edward Davies, to carefully affront the Islamic People's Republic and State of Israel for their desertion. And though he does not admonish the Arab Magisterium too harshly, he does demand Grand Magistrate Pordan take into custody any deserter attempting to leave the battlefield, citing the defections as treason, and a direct violation of the *Magisterium Edict.*

The executions of those defecting from the AEGIS is unreservedly protected under that code of conduct's *Directives,* and should not be offset for any reason. A charge the Grand Magistrate ponders, the Mu'minūn and Israelis are without care for such plea, and commence withdrawing from the United Republic by early May.

The Islamic world had no stake in the United Republic, and saw no reason for its people to die. Obviously, the Americans did not want them there, and the Mu'minūn did not want to be there in the first place. It would have been a stupid move on their parts if the Mu'minūn had remained. The country was falling apart, and the last thing Makhmalbaf wanted to see was his people getting caught in the collapse. And I suppose the leaders of the State of Israel were thinking the same thing. High Magistrate Davies could have complained all he wanted. When the Mu'minūn decided to leave the United Republic, they did so without anyone's permission. Not that they ever needed it.

Prof. Najiyah Abdullah Hassan
Crescent Moon and Pillars: The Rise of the Islamic Empire

On addresses to the United Republic Magisterium, High Magistrate Davies repeatedly demands the Israeli and Mu'minūn exodus be stopped, and challenges Pordan to do so. Although, in Europe, Arabs and Israelis stepping off the battlefield find no such punishments. Needless to say, Davies finds his own hands tied when faced with the Arab desertion of his regime, knowing the slightest offense could lead to them calling on their Muslims brothers for support. The Israelis also benefit from Europe's apprehension, but such hesitations never spare defiant American AEGIS refusing to do their duties.

Pordan, in the end, decides to ignore Edward Davies, and instead puts in place a deportation mandate facilitating the ejection of all Israelis and Mu'minūn. Although, in an attempt to salvage his relationship with Davies, the Grand Magistrate sanctions the deaths of those in Europe that would bring dissension to the Global Magisterium. A mandate that is as bleak as it is frank, the proclamation paints Pordan, in the eyes of many Americans, as nothing more than a European pawn.

First of all, let me make myself absolutely clear when I say that this was the dumbest thing Pordan could've ever done; even I have to say that. The sanctioning of Americans to be murdered because they don't agree with the Global Magisterium? You're just giving Davies a license to kill Americans abroad. Those same brave men and women you'd sent to Europe to help them in their time of need, you've just given a man full of jealousy the right to kill them. On national television, no less. Yeah, you can say that Kiril Pordan sealed his own fate, as well as, the fate of the entire order of things with this move.

Cecil Greenough

Grand Magistrate: The Biography of Kiril Pordan

The verdict is an obvious offense to nearly all Americans, and Matthew Storm addresses what he considers to be nothing less than unforgivable treason on the rebel run Prometheus Flame.

The VEDETTE General addresses a bulk of his accusations against any American AEGIS still harboring loyalty toward the Global Magisterium, and points out the flaw in their beloved institution. Americans are being arrested and killed in Europe for their patriotism. And at home, those same Europeans dare attempt to overrun their beloved country. To Matthew Storm, Kiril Pordan is a traitor, and anybody who supports him is one as well.

Storm declares the time for American unity has come. And by late June, begins to find both the members of the Magisterium Council and leaders of the VEDETTE Order heeding his words concerning the immediate removal of Grand Magistrate Pordan from office; likewise, the sanctioned purging of all European AEGIS from out of the nation.

Such news inevitably finds High Magistrate Davies, and he conveniently proclaims he too no longer finds confidence in the supreme leader or his council. Furthermore, he asserts it has been made clear Kiril Pordan can no longer control his own nation, and finds that to be a clear weakness threatening to destabilize the Global Magisterium even further. Therefore, in the end, these two faults leave Davies with no other recourse but to take matters into his own hands.

He holds a European Magisterium recognized trial in the Great Hall of London, England. And on September 12, after months of propaganda and televised reproach, High Magistrate Davies denounces Kiril Pordan as Grand Magistrate, declaring himself the official Grand Magistrate of the Global Magisterium. A bold move, it is one Kiril Pordan resentfully retaliates against.

The Grand Magistrate proclaims Edward Davies a traitor to the Global Magisterium, and insistently orders his arrest. Sadly, Pordan's words hold as much ground in Europe as Davies' assertion of leadership does in the United Republic. This is an obvious impairment to the Global Magisterium that causes VEDETTE all across the United Republic to abandon the suppression of American insurgents, only to uniformly turn their brutal assaults against those of the European AEGIS.

At last, Storm has begotten an all out insurrection on American soil, a conflict soon aptly compared to the first American Revolution. And though an alien warmth now bathes the nation, beneath bombs and bloodshed, the coldness of death lingers across the land. Those who were once prisoners under the *Sedition Repression Act* now find themselves side by side with their wardens defending a common goal. Rebel and VEDETTE alike, battling and dying for America, it is a unification Matthew Storm seizes when all American VEDETTE crossover to his side, finally allowing him to charge into Dallas, Texas.

Violent, brutal, and bloody, in the end, it will be the push inevitably bringing 281 million Americans face to face with AEGIS Gen. Pamela Barnett and her Royal European Alliance. A clash that will ultimately decide the fate of the United Republic, it will unquestionably change the order of things. And, in due course, bring forth from its ashes, a new nation.

M.A. Martin

2061
BIG MUDDY

The Great Divide: a concise history of the future

May, Friday the 13th, Dallas, Texas. The sun blazes on high, baking the land below. The snow blanketing the earth begins to melt, revealing the horrors it once concealed. Charred earth, rubble, shards of steel, and twisted metal. A decaying stench, and the macabre bodies of combatants both recently, and long dead are exposed to the elements. The sight is enough to think the Makaist sage, Kuzih, justified in his condemnation of technology, and all things born of man's corruption. A reality for those of the Revolution, it does not halt 16.3 million Guerreros from celebrating their bloody victory over the Global Magisterium.

To the Latinos who parade up and down the streets of Main, Ross, Elm, and the West End Historic District, blaring their chants of triumph, this Friday the 13th is a good day. The AEGIS have been defeated. The Global Magisterium banner no longer waves above the State. The ground is littered in black and red. And reaching the heart of Dallas, Texas, escorted by over 3,000 of his personal guards, is the enigmatic Emperor of the Hegemonic Empire, *El Rey*—Raphael Salazar. Texas now belongs to the Hispanic people. The Kings. The Latin Confederation.

Indeed, to these foreigners, today is a good day.

American leaders Matthew Storm and Arthur Havelock are there to greet the Emperor, bringing with them more than enough soldiers of their own for the occasion. VEDETTE and rebel alike, perpetrators of a treacherous attack, they are here to perform a heartbreaking act. And although the Americans find absolutely no pride in what they are about to do, they are still prepared to hand over Texas to the Latin Confederation, if only to gear up for a glorious march into Oklahoma.

What you had here was a bittersweet victory; a victory without glory if you'd rather. Sure, the Mexicans of the Latin Confederation were overjoyed, and the AEGIS had been defeated. But for the Americans, this win means nothing. Technically, if Texas belonged to the Latinos, then that meant the Global Magisterium, technically, had its unified United Republic. Yeah, the Northwestern States were still free, but what kind of fight were they going to put up? Texas was lost, and Matthew Storm couldn't have his army crying over it. Because if he did, he could've very well have faced a jeopardizing situation. One in which his revolutionary soldiers began fighting the Guerreros over the State of Texas, inevitably losing sight of the AEGIS gearing up to make war against them. It was a fragile situation Storm had to take control of, and he did so as humbly as he could.

Cecil Greenough

Grand Magistrate: The Biography of Kiril Pordan

Fireworks, gunshots, cheers, coca plants, and alcohol, this is how the Guerreros celebrate their victorious battle. A festival to mark the day when they reclaimed the land long lost to them, the Americans who have helped them in their venture do not partake. For them, it is an embittered day. One in which they have proven their worth, just as they desecrate the very nation they have fought so hard to defend.

Matthew Storm cannot allow the sentimental connection to the State to interfere with the direction the VEDETTE and their rebel peers need to take. His covenant with Salazar must be honored, and they need to accept that. More to the point, the rest of the country still needs to be won, and only then will Storm deal with the loss of Texas. Thus, meeting with Emperor Salazar in Dallas' Old Red Courthouse building, Storm officially relinquishes the whole of the State of Texas to Salazar and his Latin Confederation.

More a symbolic gesture to be later ratified, it is not broadcast as not to bring about unnecessary objection by those in other States. Storm's loyal supporters already know of his understood, logical, saddening, and wretched deal, and do not need to have it rubbed in their faces. Instead, the compact is carried out peacefully, all the time burrowing into the guts of those it exasperates.

A heavy heart that kills Storm as much as it does every one of his revolutionaries, the rechristened VEDETTE General orders all Americans vacate the Longhorn State within a month. Provisions have already been made for them in Oklahoma, and it is there both VEDETTE Admirals Aaron Balthazar and Patrick Hauser await their restored General's much desired arrival.

The Revolution was now ready to stake claim on the rest of the nation. The deal Matthew Storm had made with the Latin Confederation has been put behind them, if simply for now. America was awaiting them. So amongst seasoned veterans of the VEDETTE Order, those who were once AEGIS themselves, rebels, Loyalists, prisoners of the Sedition Repression Act, all of them as one began marching toward Oklahoma. This was the Revolutionary Army of America. And as their numbers began growing from city to city, they only became a more dominant force rivaling the Magisterium itself. It only helped that Admirals Balthazar and Hauser had nearly 60 million VEDETTE of their own waiting to merge with them.

Prof. Tamara Boggier

keeper, New York Republic Anthenaeum

It is early summer when Storm and Havelock arrive in the city of Lawton. With them is an army of over 8.6 million VEDETTE and rebel soldiers. An ensemble of thousands of heavily armed brigades, vehicles pulverizing stone beneath their massive tires, X-44 MANTAs shrieking across the skies, the combined forces of the VEDETTE Order and Resistance arrive at the newly constructed military hyper-structure christened Bastion-31 to start a war.

A militarized metropolis of smoked steel, darkened glass, and fully powered by Nuclear Fusion Technology, the highly fortified installation is the latest in Magisterium defense and design. And it is here most American AEGIS gather, having defected from the overpopulated European presence in the Northeast. The gateway into the United Republic, the II American Revolution is set to begin.

On May 21, Storm and Havelock find over 64 million men and women of the VEDETTE standing ready to serve with them in the cause for American freedom. A marriage between Autocracy and Democracy, America will once more be for Americans. Autocracy will be unsoiled by delusion, and honor will be granted to America—and only to America. Whilst Democracy will see a powerful establishment of Americans, and only for Americans. The battles that have taken place all throughout Oklahoma prove such determinations through gruesome sights of European corpses being burned in piles, while the State itself shimmers from still raging fires; the city of Bastion-31 is the only true sign of order.

It is a sight that has been repeated all over the southwest ever since the commencement of the *Purification War*. Millions of European AEGIS that have either been killed, or have fled to Missouri and Kansas in an attempt to find safety in numbers before a unified American Army can be forged, and a retaliatory march across the United Republic begun. VEDETTE Gen. Matthew Storm and his leaders must first understand the existing rules of engagement; not to mention, the next step for the country.

The leaders of the Revolution setup Central Command in Lawton, and meet for over three days to discuss what each of them brings to the table. Fleet Admiral Aaron Balthazar, the director of all naval activities seen in recent years, and leader of the X-44 MANTA program. Admiral Patrick Hauser, second only to AEGIS Gen. Pamela Barnett during the *March of AEGIS* campaign and Admiral of the Fleet during World War III. President Havelock, leader of the Resistance and Western Alliance defense forces. And lastly, but most definitely not least, VEDETTE Gen. Storm, leader of the *National Offensive,* and unifier of both the United States and United Republic of America. It is on their shoulders that it lies to deliver the rest of the nation, and they accept such tasks without question. Storm will lead them, and victory will be theirs.

Hauser delivers top secret schematics concerning the AEGIS recent fighting tactics, while Balthazar reassures his ability to seize control over the entire American naval armada by year's end. And then there is Arthur Havelock, who leads over 47.2 million former rebels, each determined to see the downfall of the AEGIS. Men and women prepared and dedicated to fulfilling his orders, Storm finally begins using the nation's media to make known his agenda. And though the Prometheus Flame does continue with its rallying of rebels across the land, the declarations made to the Loyalists and remaining VEDETTE find even greater support from the mainstream media being seen everywhere in the country.

In every Bastion the Revolution passed through, they were hailed as heroes. Loyalists who couldn't go to war for whatever reason, stood on the streets, rooftops, following, and cheering the soldiers on. There were parades and speeches, all of them hailing the arrival of their deliverance from Global Magisterium Rule. It was a spectacle, and it had all been made possible by the media. The very thing the Magisterium had once used to gain control over its people was now being used by one of their own to destroy them. But unlike the Magisterium, Storm didn't need to force the news agencies to promote his agenda. No way. Storm was a celebrity, and the reports declared him 'Savior of America'. Storm didn't need to demand propaganda, propaganda was already endearingly his.

Cecil Greenough

Grand Magistrate: The Biography of Kiril Pordan

The nation itself is fractured, but its people cannot be more unified. In Ohio, such unification threatens to unravel all of what AEGIS Gen. Pamela Barnett has achieved. The date is June 3, and Barnett finds herself facing a crisis.

All over the country, entire battalions have either redeployed themselves to Oklahoma, or stand fighting against their once European allies in forms of all out rebellion. From Ohio to North Dakota, Kansas to South Carolina, American AEGIS betray their European associates, proudly taking up the summons of Matthew Storm regarding the ousting of all foreigners. An act of treason too swift in its enacting, the British General can only watch in horror as she and her remaining AEGIS now fight desperately for their lives.

From her headquarters located in Columbus, Ohio, Barnett learns of the devastation brought against her fellow Europeans, as her own eyes behold the necessary onslaught against Americans in her midst. She warns the Loyalists about interfering, and imposes Martial Law. A decision she has all the authority to enact, anyone found defying the order is considered a traitor, and immediately executed. This is by adherence to the Global Magisterium, a worldwide government that is undeniably seeing its final days. But unlike the massacres being committed in the South and Southwestern territories, the attacks Barnett and her men meet in the Midwest are quickly subdued by the sheer size of European AEGIS stationed there.

Only now does Barnett accept it as no coincidence that she had decided long ago to keep the European AEGIS close together, dispatching mostly American AEGIS during the final days of the cruel *March*. A decision that had once been criticized as favoritism and cowardice, it is now the only reason the AEGIS General stakes claim over strategic pockets of the Midwest.

The Southwest may be entirely free of Europeans, while New Mexico, Oklahoma, Arkansas, Tennessee, Alabama, and Georgia continue to slaughter entire AEGIS regiments, that does not change the fact Barnett still holds on to well-positioned Midwest command centers, sturdily prepared to stand against whatever the Americans can muster.

AEGIS were dying and fleeing all over the country, and it was only a matter of time before Barnett joined them. She had been fighting a massive incursion in Ohio against the Americans who had turned against her there, and had already lost three quarters of the State because of it. She was only really in control of Columbus, while holding a few fragmented military Bastions throughout Indiana, Illinois, Missouri and Kentucky. The AEGIS stationed in places like Iowa, Minnesota, Nebraska and the rest of the Midwest had all been but left without direction, and were being attacked from all sides. And yet amongst all this disarray and failure, II Grand Magistrate Edward Davies never once ordered Barnett to surrender. It did not matter that the Americans had enacted their treachery without flaw; Barnett was made to stand her ground. Alas, she was also left to watch her ruin.

Prof. Jarvis Grimes

historian, *Superior and Biased: The History of the Royal European Alliance*

With the odds obviously stacked against her, AEGIS Gen. Barnett sends word to the only man she believes can aid her in her hour of need—Grand Magistrate Kiril Pordan. Unfortunately for her, it is a request that finds no response. For as she battles to maintain her grounds, so does the Grand Magistrate fight to stay in command of his empire.

It is June 14, and the nation's capital is alive with the insisting Kiril Pordan step down. A demand being heard all throughout the entire Magisterium Core, it is one the Vice Magistrates cannot ignore. They too begin to speak on the matter, holding sessions both day and night as to what direction they should take. A threat that should urge the Grand Magistrate to flee for his life, he instead decides to leave the situation in the hands of God.

It is a decision that bears much consequence, leaving Pordan with absolutely no power over his Magisterium. Needless to say, the lack of leadership in Washington D.C. only fuels Matthew Storm and his army even further, leading the VEDETTE General to announce his ultimatums to said regime.

Today, you who've sworn allegiance to Kiril Gustav Pordan now see the retribution for such oath. The Global Magisterium is no more, as is its founder. This wasn't what the Honorable High Magistrate George Hartsoe had in mind when beginning our direction—this debauchery of global union. George Hartsoe brought forth this Magisterium in hopes of raising America above her wrecks, not so that it could share its glory with the entire world. Of what corrupt ideology did such rouse spring from, that you all accepted its fruits? By whose authority did it flourish, as to contaminate the entire country with foreigners? Who's to blame for our precious Magisterium being proven faulty? Obviously, the culprit can be but only one man. He who dared to make himself master over us all. He who dared to betray our foundations. He who must be removed from all status, as to spare the rest of you this Revolution's crushing might. So it's now that I make the demand of the people, for the people, to you...the people. If the Magisterium is to be salvaged, and its founding ideals preserved, Kiril Gustav Pordan must step down as Grand Magistrate, or you all will fall. This is the demand of the American people. America for Americans. All Europeans must go.

VEDETTE General Matthew Nicholas Storm
Proclamation for Peace, July 2, 2061

The order is loud and clear. Kiril Pordan must be evicted from leadership if the Magisterium is to survive. A stipulation that cannot be compromised, the Magisterium Council immediately begins taking the suggestion seriously. Nonetheless, it is but one thing captivating the nation, especially with the Revolution preparing for an all out offensive on the peppered AEGIS installations of the Midwestern States.

July 21, and a Revolutionary Army numbering close to 100 million stand on the warm banks of the Missouri River. The VEDETTE are still dressed in their AEGIS uniforms, but no longer hide their faces in shame. Whereas, those of the former rebellion continue to wear their rags and tattered clothes, if only to veil their faces behind the masks their VEDETTE brethren have discarded. A symbol of unity amongst those calling themselves Americans, the sight of them overruns the 12 or so million European AEGIS standing across the river. A pathetic sight to the Americans about to unleash their fury, they simply await a word from their leader to attack.

The 12 million AEGIS are all that are left before meeting the real opposition in Ohio. Nothing more than a cutoff military company left as a buffer to the advancing Revolution, they do not want to be there, but have been given no choice. AEGIS Gen. Barnett has given her orders. No AEGIS is to attempt an escape, and there is to be no retreat. The insurrection must not be allowed to enter into the Republic's Core, making this fight a deciding factor in the war.

Matthew Storm, however, sees nothing more than a pitiable and stubborn refusal to bow, and keeps his eyes on Ohio. To the leader of the Revolution, he sees a battle lost before it has even begun. Ohio remains the true test. The AEGIS are about to fall, and *The Battle of Big Muddy* is about to initiate the end of the Global Magisterium.

Matthew Storm had been anticipating this day for over two years now. The day when he and an American military stood face to face against an AEGIS horde. He'd been waiting to reclaim his rightful place as General of the United Republic VEDETTE, and now he was standing as leader of the American Revolution. It was a proud moment for every American there, but a day of destiny for the man leading them. If he was going to bring war to the Global Magisterium, Matthew Storm was going to do so with everything he had. He'd already made sure to send Fleet Admiral Balthazar off in preparation for the naval battle that was quickly growing in the Atlantic, and believed he'd be rendezvousing with him before the middle of the following year.

Cecil Greenough

Grand Magistrate, The Biography of Kiril Pordan

The scenery for The Battle of Big Muddy was both startling and awe inspiring. Just picture it. You had a military of over 100 million men and women, thousands of Field Commanders, hovering helicopters, soaring X-44 MANTAs, tanks and all other sorts of instruments of war spanning from Kansas to Kentucky, all armed and all ready to fight. And at the same time, they were facing a suicide brigade of only 12 million AEGIS who were as equally ready to fight. It was a massacre waiting to happen, one Matthew Storm knew would solidify his agenda of ending the Global Magisterium.

Prof. Tamara Boggier

keeper, New York Republic Anthenaeum

This is what Matthew Storm has begotten on this day. And standing ahead of his Revolution, the VEDETTE General finally gives word to attack.

It will be recorded that the war began at 2:18 pm, but that the first bullet was actually fired at 2:17. The reason for the discrepancy? The first VEDETTE to plunge into the Missouri, Daniel Coates, does so without command, only to be killed a minute later. Regardless, the Revolution does in fact meet the AEGIS, and war is waged in honor of the II American Revolution.

Thunderous explosions shatter a once peaceful river front, just as the flash of firings turn the day into a bemused spectacle. All along the waters burn the fury of pent-up rage. An anger to ravage all they despise, the enemies clash without restraint.

Rockets soaring through the air, destroying everything they target. Likewise, missiles racing across the heavens, obliterate not only the aircraft challenging their supremacy, but also the tanks and vehicles treading the ground below. The air is thick. Each breath draws a cloud of smoke into the lungs, filling them with silt and heat. Eyes sting, tearing when assaulted by dirt and smolder. Chocking, some collapse, allowing the dampness of the ground to offer some form of deliverance. While those who fight, battle through the pain and through the stifling, only to bear witness to the horror mocking their misery. It is pure chaos. And by the end of the first hour, 33,000 men and women lie dead across Big Muddy. They are AEGIS, and they are finished.

Within the first month, the Revolutionary Army stands victorious in the heart of Jefferson City, Missouri. Their leader, Gen. Matthew Storm is pleased, but has his eyes set on Illinois and Kentucky, and it is a victory he wants as soon as possible. So sending word to Admiral Hauser in Springfield, Storm authorizes him to march a battalion of over 40 million soldiers into Louisville. A small fraction of an ever growing military, the Revolution easily boasts close to 128 million soldiers.

Those Americans who do not fight are either in company of the mystic Kuzih, too old, too young, ailed, or dead. Nonetheless, the fact remains the AEGIS are outnumbered, and AEGIS Gen. Pamela Barnett knows it.

It does not help that Storm deploys Arthur Havelock with nearly 60 million men to the States of Nebraska, South and North Dakota, Colorado, Wyoming, Montana, Iowa, and Minnesota in an attempt to expunge them all of AEGIS. At this rate, America will belong to the Revolutionary Army by year's end. Therefore, with victory within his grasp, Storm sends communication to Barnett, and swears it will be her one and only chance to survive.

No love is lost between the two Generals. Storm, the VEDETTE who had worked his way up the ladder, honorably bearing the weight of Magisterium glory, and Barnett, the eager young prototype of a one world government who replaced him. The correspondence Storm sends to Barnett is both cautionary and daring, and her response can be no less bold.

Dear AEGIS General Barnett,
In circumstances such as this one, I would normally offer the opponent with which my quarrel is engaged an opportunity to accept the deliverance of the Interim Credit Encode. Sadly, I find that this has been my main purpose for serving my Magisterium, but that was until this AEGIS business hired my wrath upon it. You and your AEGIS may keep your Global Magisterium, for this United Republic no longer adheres to your welcome. He who stood you against us will be dealt with. And unless such fate fancies you, consider this your sole circumstance for abandoning his futile mission. After this, your repentance will have to be pronounced before God Almighty. Of this, I am staunch.

With the Deepest Intent,
VEDETTE Gen. Matthew Storm
August 23, 2061

Mr. Storm,
Let it be known that I have found your previous correspondence lacking and offensive. The day we meet, it is either you or I who is deleted. This is the only mod I ask of you.

A Resounding Pledge,
AEGIS Gen. Pamela Barnett
August 25, 2061

Lacking the usual flare for which she is known, Storm understands Barnett is ready to die. And on August 28, he gladly decides to oblige her by launching an air assault resolutely set on annihilating the Republic of Ohio.

Loyalists who learn of the attack from Revolution-run newscasts flee the city of Columbus, convinced Barnett's headquarters will be the target. They are joined by the Revolutionary soldiers that have been defending them, leaving Barnett and under 7 million AEGIS to control the capital city. A daring show of bravery on the part of the AEGIS General, it is one which fails in its encounter against the American Revolution.

The sky above Barnett burns as bright as the sun, all the while basking her in the horror of AEGIS being dismantled before her eyes. It is a glorious radiance, a dizzy dance, and it grips her heart with its terror when declaring her strength's negation. Columbus is made victim by MOAB after MOAB dropping from the sky. Each bomb destroys buildings, flattens monuments, and kills thousands. Structures are reduced to mere shambles, as the sheer force of the bombs punch craters all throughout the Republic's capital.

What was once thought to be a major confrontation is nothing more than a vicious pummeling. In the end, Gen. Storm does not waste his men on Barnett, not when she does not expect this merciless assault. And within days, the lamenting of the defeated Europeans is alive for all to hear, and all Americans are made to heed this solemn orchestra of absolute devastation.

> X-44 MANTAs streak across heavens, engaging their like without concern. A disturbance to sight, the sky itself burns. Are these not the same crafts that fight so chaotic? No, upon the greatest are signs patriotic. Red, Blue, and White streaks most bare, those who devour all with bombs bursting in air. No morning gives proof that our banner waves high, not when Barnett wails, with her tears flowing whilst she cries. America the Great is what we are called. Accept this or not, we never shall fall.
>
> *Unknown*, dated October 3, 2061
> Columbus, Ohio

October 17, the State of Ohio belongs to the Revolution. The Gateway to the Midwest has been conquered, and the AEGIS have again been defeated. AEGIS Gen. Pamela Barnett has lost, but still lives to fight. And though she would have preferred to have died in Columbus, she has finally been sent direct orders from II Grand Magistrate Edward Davies commanding her to redeploy the remaining AEGIS to a secure port in Raleigh, North Carolina.

As per her orders, Barnett is to rendezvous with the Royal European Alliance's recently deployed Naval Armada, and await word. She heeds the command, but has no idea what awaits her. A battle that may very well give the AEGIS a chance at victory, it is one that will display the Royal European Alliance's legendary ability to fight at sea.

The greatest battle for the United Republic is about to be fought on all fronts, and the prize is none other than America itself.

M.A. Martin

2062

THE UNITED REPUBLIC STATES OF AMERICA

The Great Divide: a concise history of the future

March 10, and the Atlantic Ocean is tumultuous with the performance of war. Fire, destruction, and death are its actors, and the screams of the dying are its applause. The once united fleets of the Global Magisterium blasts their railgun canons, and wreck havoc upon the surging waters.

The United Republic Navy against the Royal European Alliance Armada is a scene of murky depths consuming sinking naval carriers, while electrically charged ammo annihilate entire battleships. Blazing infernos are engulfed with disturbing black smoke reaching high into the sky, while the deafening groans of mangled steel belong to devastated vessels and frigates fighting not to be claimed by the cold blackness. All the while, a paralyzing war of the heavens ultimately decides who the victor will be, sparing no witness its celestial marvel.

The American pilots are the best in the world, and the Europeans soon realize it. The X-44 MANTA is untouchable in its technology, and in all ways, superior in its engagements. But it is the pilot of this craft which proves its greatness, and Americans who refuse to be crushed confirm to be better than all.

Fleet Admiral Aaron Balthazar commands his fleet from a massive flagship stationed off the coast of New York Harbor, leading his seamen to victory. Europe is losing its conquest faster then it can scheme new courses of action. A weakness which costs the Royal European Alliance dearly, the losses in the same way threaten to destroy the regime itself. But all this does not insinuate the AEGIS do not commit their own horrors. In actuality, though losing the fight, the Europeans make the Americans pay with air raids against the populated Eastern seaport Republics.

From Massachusetts to the nation's capital of Washington D.C., the Aerial AEGIS fleets bombard Loyalists in blitzkrieg attacks adopted from fighting the former rebels, and bring devastation to the crown of the United Republic. These are suicide missions, of course. And though entire AEGIS airborne armadas are destroyed before being allowed to return to their flagships, they never cease in bringing about chaos.

These suicide attacks eventually force the Magisterium to relocate thousands of Loyalists to underground bunkers recently constructed during a renovation program to incorporate Fission Technology into the original Republics. And as they were created to safeguard Loyalists in an event of unforeseen nuclear fallout, so do these subterranean strongholds now protect tens of thousands from merciless acts of air bombings.

Regardless, the violent air raids pale in comparison to the hammering of the Revolution's offensive against said institution's ground forces. It is April 4, and Pamela Barnett, the British General of the AEGIS, is desperately trying to keep hold on North Carolina.

In all, 12.7 million European AEGIS lie betrayed and slaughtered, not to mention their general, Pamela Barnett, has been driven from her post countless of times. She is miserably losing every battle she fights. And with Wyoming, Minnesota, Kentucky, Ohio, and everywhere in between now standing as Republics guarded by both VEDETTE and Resistance fighters in a sort of Autocratic and Democratic fusing, the full expulsion of foreigners seems fast approaching.

There still remains reports of isolated skirmishes between VEDETTE and rebels in pockets of the Republics, but Matthew Storm's command to the Revolutionary Army has been accepted as law nonetheless.

> Before any American takes to judging his brother, let those who are outsiders be ruled out. Spectators to our feud are unnecessary, and insolent. First the eviction of our enemies, and then to the remedying of our unity.
>
> VEDETTE General Matthew Nicholas Storm
> *Battle of Chattanooga*, January 15, 2062

And that is what they do. VEDETTE and rebel alike, Loyalist and Patriot, Autocrat and American, they put aside their differences, and callously try the European trespassers without leniency.

The Americans in the Royal European Alliance that have been murdered on live television will be avenged, and the AEGIS will pay the price. VEDETTE General Matthew Storm is their leader, and he desires nothing more than to exterminate every last living European. Still, there is one thing the VEDETTE General not only desires, but requires to see happen more than anything else, and that it the expulsion of Grand Magistrate Kiril Gustav Pordan.

Storm believes that, unlike himself who heavy heartedly handed over Texas in exchange for America's continuance, Pordan is a man blameworthy for Europeans near controlling their in every way better. The VEDETTE general will not allow that, and in his mind only one thing can bring end to such debacle. Kiril Gustav Pordan, the architect of the

Magisterium, the Grand Magistrate of the Global Magisterium, must evacuate his supreme leadership position immediately.

Matthew Storm must have been feeling real good about himself right about now. Not only was he commanding a Navy more than capable of defeating any in the world, he'd also forced the AEGIS out of most of the country. The Republics were being cleared of AEGIS presence day by day, and it was because of Matthew Storm's design that such things transpired. He was the leader of the whole United Republic, and I doubt anybody even dared challenging him. This was supposed to be Kiril Pordan. Instead, the true leader of the Magisterium sat defeated in the Magisterium Core. He hadn't even been trying to bring back order, not that anyone would've listened.

Prof. Tamara Boggier

keeper, New York Republic Anthenaeum

There were reports that Kiril Pordan began delving even deeper into his Islamic faith during the time the Revolution marched across the country. For some people, this was the first time they'd even known that Pordan was a Muslim. Nonetheless, he did remain with his title of Grand Magistrate, though he didn't have any power. Even when they spoke of him in the news, they still referred to him as the Grand Magistrate. But it didn't mean a thing, not while he was detained in a sort of self-exile. This was the same man Matthew Storm held responsible for treason, another torment Kiril Pordan had to face. He believed he wasn't going to be Grand Magistrate for long, and neither was he going to live to see his retirement. Kiril Pordan believed he was going to die.

Cecil Greenough

Grand Magistrate: The Biography of Kiril Pordan

Pordan desolately suffers, and knows of the talks concerning his ousting. His Councilmen, Advisers, and Vice Magistrates may have been temporarily forced underground, meeting in elaborately submerged command centers, that does not stop them from considering the Revolution's adamant demands. It is a proposal which heats the entire Magisterium. The only option for its Councilmen and their Vice Magistrates, it is one Storm has warned decides their own futures as well.

A threat they take seriously, the leaders of the United Republic have already bore witness to its horrid possibilities, and refuse to be its victims. So constantly pondering on how exactly to eject their Grand Magistrate, the Councilmen and Vice Magistrates can only watch as the Revolution violently collides with the European AEGIS daring to take control of North America.

It is June 3, and the American fighters are unforgiving and brutal in their attacks, laying waste to European AEGIS after European AEGIS. The cities of Charleston, Columbia, Charlotte, and Raleigh mainly play host to such ferociousness, as coastlines are bombarded with bombs and falling debris. From Maine to South Carolina, the devastation is terrifying, but bomb shelters are quickly activated to halt a multitude of deaths.

The Southeast Republic is as much under attack as the AEGIS are. But even amongst this fierce war over the United Republic, it is easy to see Europe being forced out of the country soon enough. This is why AEGIS begin abandoning their posts, fleeing to the nearest seaports in retreat. There, they board naval vessels too damaged to fight, and wait for the moment when self-proclaimed Grand Magistrate Edward Davies calls them home. A decree they have been anticipating ever since the betrayal by the Americans commenced, it is one they have yet to receive.

Nevertheless, the fight for America continues with acts of pure ferocity, making the decision to oust Pordan one of utmost importance. A calmer violence storming throughout the Magisterium Core, with accusations and threats running rabid, the decision is clearly the catalyst to the Magisterium's end.

July 28. The nexus of the Magisterium quakes beneath an impossible act that will essentially dissolve the *Magisterium Edict.*

The Vice Magistrates, as well as, their Councilmen, argue over what steps to take next. As it stands, Matthew Storm has already arrested control of the VEDETTE Order, and his words are without question their commands. Now he intends on marching his Revolutionary Army up through the East Coast, only to seize control over the Republic itself, with only the expulsion of Kiril Pordan capable of sparing them the planned destruction.

It is a verdict that will absolutely betray the very foundations of the Magisterium, shattering everything it holds most precious—Autocracy itself. In spite of this, ensuring their own survival, Vice Magistrates and Councilmen decide to impeach Pordan on the grounds of treason, and force him to take leave of office, even going as far as to sully his name in the media. Accusations solely blaming him for every misstep that has taken place, the debauchery of the Global Magisterium is made entirely his fault.

The Grand Magistrate submissively agrees to the ruling of his Council without protest, and is placed under house arrest until his sentence has been decided. A downfall that should easily rattle any man, Pordan maintains his composure, and comports himself as a prisoner of honor and dignity.

Kiril Pordan once wrote, "There was never any living for one who dies without accomplishment. But for the one who achieves, death merely hinders his abilities to see his own glory". It was the motto that dictated his life. You see it in his deeds, and you see it in his thoughts. So even when Pordan was facing the lowest point of his life, and being slandered by the very people he put in power, he never once lowered his head. Even at the very end, he still kept his pride, and all could see it. He was the ruler of the world, and nothing would ever change that.

Cecil Greenough

Grand Magistrate: The Biography of Kiril Pordan

The date is October 2, and members of the Magisterium begin arguing amongst each other, submitting themselves as the new leader of the failing establishment. Obviously, somebody will need to represent them when VEDETTE General Matthew Storm arrives, and that somebody must be capable of salvaging the framework of Autocracy's establishment.

Their institution cannot be allowed to be dismantled, and they know there is a place in Storm's heart where he feels the same. The General of the II American Revolution may be ready to officially recognize a Democratic counterpart to the West of the United Republic, that does not to imply the Magisterium will not find its existing stance amongst such a merger. Therefore, someone must be there to stand across from Matthew Storm and negotiate a continued Magisterium representation. And though this is the main concern amongst the Magisterium Council, while Loyalist come to both pleased and saddened terms with the ousting of Kiril Pordan in the streets, that does not change the fact the United Republic has no current leader.

A vacancy II Grand Magistrate Edward Davies is pleased to see, only now does the European leader decide to begin withdrawing his troops from out of the United Republic. He has done his damage. To see Kiril Gustav Pordan humbled and disgraced, and his precious Magisterium in shambles is more than what Davies can ask for. The hostile conquest of seizing control over its lost custody is something Europe cannot afford the price, so the confounding of the guilty rebellion will have to do. Edward Davies feels he simply has to sit back now, and watch as the mighty West falls before its lack of direction.

He first makes sure to broadcast his regime's intentions through both televised international newscasts and subversive internet bulletins, then commences with suspension of all Royal European Alliance operations in the West. A show of good faith toward the Revolution, with hopes the remaining European AEGIS will be allowed to leave the country unharmed, it is wisely led by a command for all AEGIS to surrender. It is October 19, and the Royal European Alliance concedes to the Revolution, handing themselves over as prisoners of war.

The Councilmen of the former European Magisterium send word to the leaders of the Revolution, and not only hail their decision of removing the Grand Magistrate, but also agree to the termination of the Global

Magisterium as a whole. They offer their assistance in whatever the United Republic may request of them in the future in salvaging their past comradeship, and initiate the withdrawal of all naval craft from United Republic waters. They even begin the systematic release of all Americans detained in Europe, and offer them safe passage back home. An act Davies and his Councilmen commit to without duplicity, the AEGIS submission comes with a plea for unmerited leniency.

It was something seen with the Israelis and Mu'minūn nearly two years earlier. And as it spared the lives over 2 million Arabs and Israelis back then, so now do the Europeans plea for such mercy toward their European Loyalists.

General Matthew Storm is the man forced to make the decision, and he weighs the outcomes with a heart sullied by hate. To allow the Europeans to simply leave after so much bloodshed and tyranny would bring both insult and chaos upon those victimized during Operation: *Storm Front*. But to find them guilty and punish them according to their acts would require that all VEDETTE that partook in such actions be equally penalized. A dilemma Gen. Storm requests the mindset of Arthur Havelock on, the Revolution's leader must first gain a clear view on where the former rebellion rests before making any decision.

Havelock is flown from the recently conquered state of Wyoming, and meets with Storm at Central Command in Lawton, Oklahoma. The meeting lasts but for a few hours, and in the end, both Stockwell and Havelock unanimously agree to the halting of bloodshed against the AEGIS.

They cannot guarantee a few people will not try violently stopping the Europeans from leaving, but the VEDETTE will do their best in protecting their eviction. The European AEGIS will be allowed to leave, and Americans cannot be more pleased. Unfortunately, the same cannot be said of AEGIS Gen. Pamela Barnett.

In opposition to such defeat, while her European brethren begin fleeing the United Republic through both military and commercial means, Barnett stays behind in a blatant show of defiance. Her actions are not toward Edward Davies or his command; Barnett makes that clear to her personal regiment. Her defiance is to the thought of Matthew Storm and his treacherous Revolution bringing about her end. She would rather die first before surrendering, and countless of her loyal subordinates make an oath to do the same.

The war was over. Edward Davies had called on all AEGIS to cease and desist their activities, but yet Pamela Barnett remained behind. It is unclear as to why, and I cannot help but wonder what it was she was trying to prove? But by this point in the war, she knew there was nothing she could do. Yet she stayed behind. And though I would like to speak boastfully of her need to make this final stand in the name of her country, it is one myself and most Europeans still regret she made.

Prof. Jarvis Grimes

historian, *Superior and Biased: The History of the Royal European Alliance*

On an early Thursday morning, November 23, in the ruined center of North Carolina, the AEGIS General does in fact make one final stand against the Revolution.

AEGIS Gen. Pamela Barnett leads a small platoon of 32,000 AEGIS against a Revolution battalion of 1.8 million, and is wounded during the battle. Likewise, her entire regiment, those daring to stand with her until the bitter end, they are all slaughtered during the battle. Barnett is then flown to an outpost located at Cape Fear, where she encounters VEDETTE Gen. Matthew Storm as a prisoner.

The exchange between the two leaders is unknown. All that is revealed is that Pamela Barnett eventually succumbs to her injuries, and that Storm personally sees to it that her body is relinquished to the Royal European Alliance. He even makes sure to praise her as a fine military leader when talking about her in the media, going as far as to call her death a brave sacrifice. Regardless of all this pageantry, in the end, her death is seen as the ultimate victory to those who despise her, and her demise made fun of by bitter Americans who served beneath her.

It is official, the war is over. The time has finally come for Americans to begin forging a new horizon for their land, one in which both Democracy and Autocracy can survive as one. A test that will prove to be even more difficult than their nation's darkest days, it does not stop Americans from rejoicing in their reestablished glory.

From Portland, Oregon, to Missoula, Montana—Phoenix, Arizona, to Miami, Florida— America is alive with song of triumph. The foreigners are gone, and the country cleansed. A near Xenophobic revelry burns through the country, and even puts the Latin Confederation on guard. But once again, Matthew Storm reminds his people a deal has been struck with the Latinos, and there are deadly consequences for breaking that deal. The warning is made clear, but the disdain remains. Still, America has won its war, and its loyal citizens celebrate their survival.

All across the mighty nation, '*America for Americans*' blare for all to hear. All across the mighty nation, a stir of pride stands for freedom and liberty. All across the mighty nation, the sun shines through a long winter. Big Muddy. Chattanooga. Richmond. Raleigh. Port Arthur. Fort Bragg. All across the might nation, America is great.

All across the mighty nation, tears fill the eyes of the humbled. All across the mighty nation, questions fill the eyes of the wary. All across the might nation, pride swells the *Star Spangled Banner* and *Magisterium Standard*. Olivia Warner. Jake Stockwell. George Hartsoe. Agnes Walsh. Arthur Havelock. Matthew Storm. All across the mighty nation, America is strong.

All across the mighty nation, no foreigner stands. All across the mighty nation, the Constitution and *Magisterium Edict* are professed. All across the mighty nation, God is praised. Democracy. Autocracy. America. All across the mighty nation, America is free.

Abel Kane
All Across the Mighty Nation: A Composition of Post-Great Divide Prose
Library of Madam Myna Nova, [circa. 2062-2088]

Bombs no longer fall from the skies. Alarms no longer blare in warning of attacks. The business of Loyalists being shoved into underground bunkers is no longer a need. Children are no longer separated from their parents. All is quiet now, and joyous Americans take to the streets in celebration.

Gatherings hosting a band of performers, parades, and guest speakers, the festivities go on for days. Even the leaders of the Revolution partake in the celebrations, with Arthur Havelock getting together with a mass of millions all throughout Oklahoma, Patrick Hauser traveling from Kentucky to Ohio as part of a healing process on behalf of the VEDETTE Order, Aaron Balthazar orchestrating a naval display of fanfare and fireworks all across the eastern seaboard, and Matthew Storm in Washington D.C. during the United Republic's official First Annual *19th of October* Independence Day Parade. These are days of happiness and peace for Americans. And for a moment, the country is as one.

All the fights. All the battles. All the deaths. For a moment, all is forgiven, and the nation is given pause to heal. But for all their praises and wonders, the celebrations of those who have won their war pale in comparison to those of the Northwestern territories of Idaho, Oregon, and Washington. In those territories, another commemoration is also underway, but this salute is not for freedom. The cause for such festivities is the Earth Mother, Gaea Makawee, and the mercy She has shown Her children.

Unlike the rest of the nation, the Makaists of the Makaism ideology were never abandoned to war, not when accepting the tranquility offered by Gaea Makawee. Their Goddess never inflicted upon them the bloodshed and devastation seen by the rest of the nation. The carnage and chaos was something they never felt, not in the midst of the Makaism sage, Kuzih. He is the one who promised them peace, if only they would forsake the battles and come to salvation. And just as there were many who blasphemed, criticized, and doubted such hope, so were there many who came in search of peace.

They are the ones spared the horrors and deaths—The ones who memorize the sutras of Kuzih, and submit to his teachings—The ones who continue to create natural dwellings, and a community full of harmony and respect. Above all, they are the ones loved by the Earth Mother—Gaea Makawee.

Unlike the nonbelievers who are now left frail and leaderless facades of themselves, the Makaists believe in Gaea Makawee, and they know She will always work through the wisdom of Her sage, Kuzih. It was his sutras that prophesized there would be no need to flee their homes, as the AEGIS would never reach them. Now it would seem his words have been proven correct, for all Makaists now praise the Earth Mother without care or fear.

Most of the world deems such fantastical and inane levity foolish, but there are still some in the Republic who actually wish they were a Makaist during this time. A heavy burden is beginning to bear its weight upon their shoulders, and the time to plan a new course has arrived.

Isn't it ironic? The very same people the Resistance and VEDETTE had once considered fools for not fighting, just so happen to be the only ones who never had to fight? They even got to enjoy an uninterrupted peace, praising their sage, and his ever-merciful Earth Mother. It wasn't fair, but it didn't change the facts. The Europeans were gone. The AEGIS were gone. Kiril Pordan was finished. And in some ways, so was the Magisterium. It was time to pick up the pieces, and for every American to help put back the country. As expected, the moment they realized this, was about the same exact time they started bickering again.

Prof. Tamara Boggier

keeper, New York Republic Anthenaeum

It is December 19, 2062. The Capitol Building's House of Representatives Chamber is bursting with words of anger, threats, mourning, and dismay. The topic is America, and the arguments range from hard-lined institutions to outright anarchy.

For the first time in history, Vice Magistrates and Councilmen find themselves face to face with the very people they once considered rebels, heatedly discussing the future of their country. The words of venerated statesman Daniel Webster guides the exchanges. "*Let us develop the resources of our land, call forth its powers, build up its institutions, promote all its great interests, and see whether we also, in our day and generation, may not perform something worthy to be remembered"*. A powerful decree alive in the hearts of all involved, it does not keep the Councilmen from wisely making sure to keep order through armed VEDETTE standing vigilantly nearby.

Merely a precaution, the soldiers are there just in case the former rebels prove to be indeed too savage to deal with. But it is their General, Matthew Storm, who has called forth this meeting, and by his commands are the former rebels given voice in this most sacred edifice of the Magisterium.

The most argumentative subject being discussed is that of the United States Constitution versus the United Republic's *Magisterium Edict*, and which of the two rules will govern the land. One side argues society is corrupt, and the goals of individuals are self-glorifying. If there is no one to guide those who are guideless, then the road to success and power will never be treaded. A powerful call to abandon the needs of freedom in exchange for superiority, the cry for independence is just as emotive.

A cry dealing with the foundations of the country, a dream for which the Founding Fathers bled and died for, the hope that all men would be created equal, it is Democracy, and the day has come for it to find its rightful place.

Matthew Storm had realized Democracy's strength for quite some time now, and had also promised the rebels a compromise in which both Autocracy and Democracy could flourish. And it didn't take long before his original offer was revisited, with a two state proposal proving quite a gamble. Once again, Storm believed that America should in fact be partitioned into two governing bodies—a sort of hegemonic rule in itself, almost similar to what he'd seen in the Latin Confederation. The Republic of the East Coast would be seen as the central axis of the entire country, while the Midwest and Southwest existed as Commonwealths independent in their laws, but voluntarily united with the Magisterium under the Constitution of America. Sounded good, but nobody was buying it.

Cecil Greenough

Grand Magistrate: The Biography of Kiril Pordan

The reinstatement of the U.S. Constitution as the sanctioned law of the entire nation would affect the very social construct of the Republic. No Loyalist dares agree to such proposal, in the same way no former rebel can accept the *Magisterium Edict* as their law. This requires a compromise be found posthaste. And with Matthew Storm's Two State solution finding no traction from either side, another form of government must be agreed upon by both parties. Because of this, a special council is appointed to figure out a diagram in which both Democracy and Autocracy function as one.

The nine Vice Magistrates and six Resistance Generals waste weeks before even taking into consideration what their rivals have to say, and then months behind closed doors arguing a way forward. But after much deliberation, a fusion between the Constitution and the *Magisterium Edict* is composed. A form of government in which elections for political offices will be held by the people; likewise, the country's governance will again see the titles of Senators, Congressmen, Governors, and even Mayors taking into account the opinions of their constituents.

The seats of a Federal government will be the crowning jewel of this emerging governing movement. But the core of the United Republic is to remain the same, with a President, Vice President, Defense Secretary, and Secretary of State seeing their powers remain equivalent to that of Councilmen, Vice Magistrates, and a High Magistrate.

Undiminished stature. Utmost power. Unquestionable authority. The citizens of America would be electing their term-limited dictators from now on, and in turn, continue to benefit from the authoritarian trusted knowledge of their leaders.

This was going to be the new order of things. Citizens elected the person who'd be the ultimate ruler of the country, and that person would live up to the expectations for which they'd been elected. No longer would there be political parties vying for shared control, but one person who would choose an Administration deemed constructive and compliant towards the direction of their choosing. The citizens of the country would elect this person from amongst thousands, maybe even millions. And for six years, would just have to deal with what they'd chosen. Now, this person could be voted in as many times as the people wanted them, a lifetime even. Hey, it wasn't quite perfect, and it wouldn't be for years. But these early stages did allow Americans peace, as best as it could, at least.

Cecil Greenough

Grand Magistrate: The Biography of Kiril Pordan

The Interim Credit Encode will remain the entire country's means of survival. Depots will continue to furnish the everyday necessities of life. Factories will continue to span the nation, producing innovative items capable of perfecting ones existence. Arcological Bastions will continue to surpass design, giving man dominion over all things. And above all, with the threat of enemies desiring the destruction of the country never again to be considered an instrument of mere politics, the nation's Armed Forces will remain replenished by the mandatory service of capable citizens.

The first step toward a marrying of Democracy and Autocracy, a finalized draft of the Constitution of the United Republic serves its purpose in keeping calm. It is ratified on April 3, 2063, and the nation as a whole rumbles with heated debates of laws of government, bearing witness to the first ever fully functioning Anocracy.

It is a painful transition for some, but a promising sign that the United Republic and Democratic States, after twenty-seven years of war, can finally be unified as one. The United Republic States of America is what it shall be known as, and once again it will be a shining beacon of hope for all others to see. But for now, besides the already existing trials that await it, this emerging Anocracy has a daunting decision to make pertaining to the leadership of its country, as well as, the ultimate fate of Kiril Gustav Pordan.

Decisions that will determine the future behavior of the nation, it is the voices of those in power that take up the tasks in hopes of proving themselves worthy before the American people. The final act of the Magisterium Council, after months of deliberation, Kiril Gustav Pordan is tried in the Supreme Court on charges of treason, dissension, and human rights violations. Allegations all are aware should be faced by nearly all Americans, the former Grand Magistrate is made to suffer these accusations alone, and is eventually found guilty on all indictments.

In the end, the former High Magistrate's sentence is allocated by the very men and women he once appointed to power. Those who will no longer be Councilmen and Vice Magistrates but Politicians and Bureaucrats. It is them who pass the final judgment on Kiril Gustav Pordan, deeming his expatriation from the United Republic States of America an honorable verdict. And with the Islamic People's Republic being the only sovereign nation inclined to accept him, on June 19, 2063, Kiril Gustav Pordan boards a government flight bound for Baghdad, Iraq, where his arrival is much anticipated by those who still regard him as a great man.

Kiril Pordan was kicked out of the country. After sixty-eight years of his life, fifty-one of them as a soldier serving this country, Kiril Pordan was expatriated, and was sent to live the remaining years of his life in the Islamic People's Republic. It was a sad ending for a great man. And though many people still call him a tyrant and a killer, there's one thing everybody has to agree on; Kiril Pordan was the only man to have ever come so close to ruling the entire world, and lived to tell about it. That alone should classify him the greatest of us all. Grand Magistrate Kiril Gustav Pordan, may he be forever remembered.

Cecil Greenough
Grand Magistrate: The Biography of Kiril Pordan

Only one decision truly remains for the United Republic States of America now. One that will mend the broken trusts still lingering in the hearts of its citizens, solidifying the country as a whole. Who will lead America into its sanguine future? Who will be the first American President in thirty plus years?

The position no longer has the same meaning since its last inception. No longer the head of the nation's military, it now stands as its herald. Indeed, the President of the United Republic States of America is the most powerful man in the world.

On March 6, 2064, VEDETTE General Matthew Storm becomes the first of many to have his hat cast into the race for the USRA Presidency. A declaration not heard of in over thirty-one years, Arthur Havelock finds the proposition hopeful, and also decides to announce his bid for the United Republic States Presidency. A light of hope and freedom the citizens of the URSA find both symbolic and encouraging, the campaign trail for both nominees initiate into action with promises, ideals, and speeches of old bringing about a welcomed and peaceful frenzy across the land. And for now, America has found peace in place of war.

It's a bright future from then on for the United Republic States, at least for a while. You see the Bastions becoming the infrastructure of the entire country, and you see those same innovations spanning the globe. Just look around us, and you see the influence of the Bastions everywhere. Our Ecologies. Our Instruct Cores. Our lives. The United Republic States was the foundation for our modern society. The Interim Credit Encode was the first step toward the infinite procuring we now possess, and our self-autonomy owes its basis to Anocracy. I dare say the entire world owes its very evolution to the steps taken by these men and women of the past, and it all began because of the Great Divide.

Prof. Tamara Boggier

keeper, New York Republic Anthenaeum

The Great Divide. Europe does not lag after this war with the United Republic States. By no means. The first road toward self-autonomy was founded in Europe. Sure, one can make the case that the United Republic States enhanced the properties of all these things, but let us not forget the Great Demise also originated in the United Republic States. For all their advancements, did they spare us that dark time? No. So I commend Europe in its rise, and its ability to lead the world during such turbulent eras.

Prof. Jarvis Grimes

historian, *Superior and Biased: The History of the Royal European Alliance*

It was during these post-Great Divide years that the world began acknowledging the rise of An-Nur Islam. No longer were the Middle East and Africa regions of violence and instability. An-Nur dawned a new age on the Muslim and Mu'minūn factions of Islam, eliminating such classifications and giving birth to a unity never before seen. Logic. Compassion. Understanding. These are the things An-Nur embraced, and that is why you see it as the world's leading religion today.

Prof. Najiyah Abdullah Hassan

Crescent Moon and Pillars: The Rise of the Islamic Empire

Asia was and would remain the dominant influence throughout the globe for years, and then the Great Demise happened, and things went bad—for everybody. And yes, Europe committed itself in helping the nations to realize that self-autonomy was the way of the future. But it was Asia that once more broke the barriers of the world's darkness, giving birth to the Utopia we see being perfected even today. There is a reason why the Orient is the only Corporation right now in existence, while the rest of the world only now begins to Incorporate.

Tsun-chúng Hu

The Last Dynasty: The Chinese Republic's Ultimate Demise

What does the world fight for now? Knowledge? Dominance? Perfection? Without sounding like a Tellurian, maybe that's not what we need. You look at the days of Kiril Pordan, Matthew Storm, and you find something else being fought for back then. Hope. An understanding that we can never be absolutely right, and that things will always go wrong, but that there's always hope. You've heard the Determinists say that the more we forsake want, the more we'll find that we need it. I was just a child when the Great Divide came to an end, and a young man when the Great Demise ravaged our existence. And I see how far we've come. But I can't help but think where we Reverenese would be today if not for the hope of the past. Who we would've become if we'd still held on to hope? But I'm an old man, so what do I know?

Cecil Greenough

Grand Magistrate: The Biography of Kiril Pordan

Earth is a planet of over 7.1 billion people. It stands third in a solar system of eight planets, and five dwarf, yet stands alone. Many of its inhabitants are of different creeds, faiths, races, and ethnicities, but they all share one common trait—they are all human. And though they may have histories and myths as diverse from each other as the sands are from the seas, they are all the same. Herein lies the problem that has plagued them for so many millennia.

As fate would have it, the same trait that makes them human, is the same trait which begets their downfall—the want to survive. A need to endure, this driving force for survival often brings out the best in mankind: cultivation to philosophy, artistry to exploration—and his worst, in greed, tyranny, conquest, and war. A powerful, yet easily corruptible attribute, survival has raised human beings to the heights of godhood, while plunging them into the abyss of conflict and death.

This is Earth. This is where we live.

GLOSSARY

II American Revolution: United Republic conflict taking place 2059-2062.

II Civil War: period of conflict enacted between the United Republic and United States—2052-2059.

A

AEGIS: unification of the world's leading military during the Great Divide, resulting in a solitary functioning unit.

Affirmation Rectification: Executive order detailing the oath the United States Armed Forces take in serving their constituents, as well as, what is expected of those same nationals.

Afro Islamic Union (Afro Islamic Union): the designation of Arab and African nations extending from Arabia to the equatorial line of Africa unified by one form of government.

Al-Iithad al-Iislamia (Unity of Islam): Islamic conflict 2051-2058.

Al-Asas: a ruthless terrorist organization which existed in Iraq during the dawn of the 21ˢᵗ century.

***Almaseer-Ul-Adha* (Destiny of Sacrifice)**: name given to the allocations of Egypt, Sudan, and Eritrea to the Imperial Asiatic Alliance by the Afro Islamic Union.

An-Nur Islam: belief system formed out of the Islamic reformation of the 21st Century.

Anocracy: system of government combining Democracy with Dictatorship.

Ansar al-Islam: terrorist organization formed in opposition to Islamic partition.

AR2: anarchist offshoot of the ART movement based in the United States of America.

ART (American Revolution Two): American political group focusing on the Libertarian declaration adhering to the letter of the United States Constitution.

Article 412: proposition indoctrinating the principle of amalgamating all European banks and laws under one roof, as to strengthen the prowess of said region.

Autocracy: form of governance which adheres to the laws of one man.

<u>B</u>

Bastion: advanced arcology.

Boom Babies: term used to describe American children born after the nuclear attack on the United States.

<u>C</u>

Chief Lord: second most powerful office in the Royal European Alliance. A governor of a District (country) under the rules of the Monarch.

Children of Gaea, The: naturalistic belief system which preaches the love of Mother Earth, and the need to protect the planet from mankind's greed, wars, and religions.

Cleansing Hub: stadiums where Chinese Americans and immigrants are detained after the nuclear assault on China.

Confirm-Graf: platform used to track popularity of music shared on the Internet.

Councilman: an immediate official over Loyalists of the United Republic.

Custodians: third most powerful office in the Royal European Alliance. A governor of a Quarter (city) under the rules of a Chief Lord.

<u>D</u>

Deleted: to suffer an insulting death.

<u>F</u>

Feeb: 1) derogatory word to describe someone or something. 2) feeble.

Freelands: Democratic run countries during the Great Divide.

<u>G</u>

Gaea Makawee: 1) name for planet Earth. 2) Earth Mother deity of the Makaism ideology.

Global Magisterium: one world government recognized by those adhering to Autocracy during the Great Divide.

Grand Magistrate: sovereign leader of the Global Magisterium.

Great Divide, The: world-wide dystopian epoch spanning 2029-2062.

Grimaldi Defiance: militant organization operating in East Europe during the Great Divide.

Guardian: fourth most powerful office in the Royal European Alliance. A governor of a Sector (district) under the rules of a Custodian.

Guerreros: amalgamated military of all Latin and Central American countries.

H

High Magistrate: sovereign leader of an Autocratic Magisterium.

Hip-Fonika: 1) musical platform consisting of deep groves, heavy bass, and rantings. 2) genre of music used for religious, political, and anarchy propaganda.

I

ICE-chip: central processing unit allowing for all benefits pertaining to the Interim Credit Encode: financial, medical, and social.

Imperial Asiatic Alliance (IAA): Democratic empire of Asia.

Incessant Credit Encode: hypothetical genetic-based nanotechnology allowing a carrier all benefits pertaining to Credit Encode.

Interim Credit Encode: collective databank of all medical, social, and financial records.

International Guards: extended branch of the United States Armed Forces dedicated to the securing of the nation's Southern borders 2026-2029.

Islamic Peoples Republic (Islamic People's Republic): 1) Middle Eastern unified government, excluding the Arabian peninsula. 2) Designated land of the Mu'minūn.

J

Jihadi: a form of military consisting of all Arabian and North African militaries.

L

Latin Confederation: the designation of all Latin and Central American countries unified by one form of government

Latin Liberation Front (LLF): socialist movement focused on the unification of Latin America.

Level-Up: 1) respect given to someone. 2) allowing one more importance than others.

Loyalist: a cataloged citizen of the United Republic of America.

Loyalist Act, The: mandate put in place legalizing the detainments of all Chinese Americans and immigrants after the nuclear assault on China.

M

Magisterium: Autocratic government originating in the United Republic of America.

Magisterium Edict: redrafted US Constitution made law during the Great Divide.

Makaist: a devotee to the Makaism faith.

Makaism: naturalistic belief system which preaches the love of the Earth Mother, Gaea Makawee, and the need to abandon all man-made technologies, sciences and religions.

March of the AEGIS: military campaign conducted in the Midwest of North America 2052-2055.

Mod: 1) to become more than previously believed. 2) the goal of transferring ones consciousness.

Monarch: most powerful office in the Royal European Alliance. A governor of the collective Districts within the Royal European Alliance.

Mu'minūn: Qur'anic based rechristening of Shia Islam.

Mujahids: a form of military consisting of all Middle Eastern militaries.

N

Narnists: term used by members of the AR2 terrorist organization to describe their more violent associates.

National Offensive: military campaign conducted in the Midwest of North America 2043-2055.

Night of the Longhorns: uprising in the Southwestern States of North America.

O

Operation: Purification Schema: military campaign conducted throughout North America 2040-2054.

Operation: Red Star: international coalition military campaign conducted throughout the South Pacific 2025-2026.

Operation: Storm Front: AEGIS campaign conducted throughout the Midwest of North America 2055-2061.

<u>P</u>

Prometheus Flame: rogue internet sites dedicated to the world-wide distribution of rebel-run broadcasts.

Purification War: military campaign conducted throughout North America 2059-2062.

<u>R</u>

Republics: advanced cities raised out of the wrecks of war torn States.

Royal European Alliance (REA): the designation of all European countries unified by one form of government.

<u>S</u>

Sedition Repression Act (The Wall): mandate put in place legalizing the detainment and forced labor of all rebels.

SENSHI: military consisting of all Asiatic militaries under the Imperial Asiatic Alliance.

SENTRIES: military consisting of all European militaries under the Royal European Alliance.

Signal Runner: any person or thing gaining unparalleled fame on the internet.

SPINA: rebellion whose goal is to overthrow the United Socialist Russian Republic.

T

Treaty of Samad: peace agreement signed by both the Islamic Peoples' Republic and Afro-Islamic Union, ending the Islamic War of Ages.

U

UNDO (Union of Nations Defense Ordinance): a cohesive military unit consisting of soldiers contributed from all Union of Nations affiliates.

Union of Nations: a coalition of the world's superpowers.

United Republic of America (URA): designation of North American under the Autocracy.

United Republic States of America (URSA): designation of North America under Anocracy.

United States Resistance: insurgency against the Magisterium of North America 2040-2052

V

VEDETTE: all branches of military under the Magisterium.

Vice Magistrate: second most important position in the United Republic, and immediate official overseeing the Councilmen of the Magisterium.

<u>W</u>

Wall, The: 1) construction project utilizing the work of prisoners. 2) incarceration. 3) a death camp.

Western Alliance: Democratic government originating in the Southwestern United States of America.

World War III: Global conflict enacted between the Democratic Coalition of the United States of America, United Kingdom, and Germany against the Nexus Forces of China, North Korea, and Occupied-Russia—October 2, 2026 to December 29, 2028.

The Great Divide: a concise history of the future

CHRONOLOGY:

2025

May 9- Iraq declares freedom.

May 11- Asim Mustafa Abdullah, leader of the Al-Asas terrorist organization is executed in Iraq.

July 6- NATO Forces attack Iran.

September 14- NATO and Iraqi troops march into Iran's capital of Tehran.

November 2- Coalition Forces launch attack on Sumatra, Indonesia.

2026

February 23- SPINA defeats Russia's Silovik regime, hanging both the President and Prime Minister in front of the Kremlin.

April 3- China crosses through Mongolia, entering Russia.

May 4- Great Indo/Pak War begins.

August 18-China engages SPINA in St. Petersburg, Russia.

August 22- Jerusalem, Israel suffers nuclear attack.

September 16- China defeats SPINA.

October 6-China absolves its membership with the United Nations.

2028

May 10- Japan joins Democratic Coalition in World War III.

July 21- Chinese-Russian Forces seize control of Eastern Europe.

December 25- California is obliterated by a nuclear attack originating in China.

2029

February 14- Article 412 is agreed upon in Western Europe.

March 9- The nation of China is annihilated by American nuclear strikes.

2030

June 5- Imam Abu abd Allah Muhammad proposes his Islamic partition.

August 27- Islamic Diaspora begins.

November 10- End of Great Indo/Pak War.

2032

January 3- Creation of the Royal European Alliance.

April 9- Arnold Furlong bombs Union Station in Washington, D.C., killing 40 Army soldiers and 200 hostages.

June 10- Mahdi Abu announces the success of the Islamic Partition, giving birth to the Mu'minūn.

2034

September 4- United States Armed Forces engage the Executive office of the United States government in all out war.

November 28- White House is seized by United States Armed Forces, placing United States President under arrest.

December 23- Joint Chef of Staff Chairman George Hartsoe begins the detainment of all elected officials.

2036

October 25- Induction of the Magisterium Edict.

2038

August 25- 10,000 people turnout to hear Agnes Walsh in Charlotte, N.C.

September 17- Rebel forces attack the military base of Fort Bragg.

October 2- Fort Bragg falls to rebel forces.

2039

June 14- America's South is demolished by the Magisterium.

2040

March 7- First flight from the United Republic is taken to Europe. High Magistrate George Hartsoe is assassinated.

April 10- Kiril Gustav Pordan is elected II High Magistrate of the United Republic of America.

June 4-Launch of the Purification Schema.

2044

January 17- Kiril Pordan suggests the New World Order to the Union of Nations.

May 15- Launching of UNDO Forces.

September 11- UNDO Forces reach the United Republic of America.

2046

April 9- UNDO Forces conquer the Northeast Central Expanse of the United States.

July 22- Creation of the Sedition Repression Act

September 15- Enacting of the Sedition Repression Act.

December 10- Islamic War of Ages begins.

2047

March 4- Mahdi Abu calls for Jihad.

September 24- India is inducted into the Imperial Asiatic Alliance.

November 7- Birth of the Global Magisterium.

2049

February 10- AEGIS attack Eastern Europe.

August 21- Eastern Europe is conquered.

October 12- The RED WAR begins.

December 25- The Battle of Terrace Hill, Des, Moines, Iowa.

2050

February 3-The United States Resistance is victorious at the Battle of Terrace Hill.

February 6- Resistance leader, Jake Stockwell is captured in Rochester, Minnesota.

March 7- Jake Stockwell is executed by the Global Magisterium.

March 25- The Western Alliance attacks AEGIS in Baton Rogue, Louisiana.

2051

April 1- The commencement of Al-Iithad al-Iislamia (Unity of Islam) campaign.

August 2- Magisterium AEGIS Day.

2052

February 18- The March of the AEGIS begins.

February 23-the European Magisterium attacks the Northwest African regions of the Afro Islamic Union.

May 28- RED WAR cease-fire is broken by Imperial Asiatic Alliance.

2054

May 3- The Great Paranoia of the American Magisterium.

August 2- Nubian delegates meet with Imperial Asiatic Alliance.

2055

January 7- Alliance is formed between the Afro Islamic Union and Imperial Asiatic Alliance.

September 4- Operation: Storm Front commences.

November 7- The State of Iowa is conquered by the AEGIS.

2057

February 15- Eastern Europe declares freedom from Global Magisterium.

June 30- Kuzih calls on his Makaists to cease fighting.

October 25- The city of Port Arthur, TX is razed to the ground.

October 31- Both Texas and New Mexico are invaded by the AEGIS.

2058

February 10- Afro Islamic Union attacks Cadiz, Spain.

March 28- Islamic Peoples Republic withdraws troops from Afro Islamic Republic, ending the Islamic **April 12**- Treaty of Samad.

June 4- Mahdi Abu abd Allah Muhammad is assassinated.

September 15- Afro Islamic Union ceases attack on Royal European Alliance.

2059

August 19- The state of New Mexico falls to AEGIS.

November 2- Dia de los Muertos.

November 27- El Paso and San Antonio are seized by Guerreros.

December 31- Commencement of the Purification War.

2060

April 19- The Arabian AEGIS are ordered to surrender to the American Revolutionary Army.

September 12- Edward Davies proclaims himself Grand Magistrate.

2061

May 13- Latin Confederation Guerreros conquer the State of Texas.

May 21- Matthew Storm is made General of the American Revolutionary Army.

July 21- The Battle of Big Muddy.

April 28- The American Revolutionary Army attacks the State of Ohio.

October 17- The American Revolutionary Army conquers the State of Ohio.

2062

March 10- Battle of the Atlantic

October 2- Grand Magistrate Kiril Gustav Pordan is ousted from office.

October 19- The European AEGIS surrender to the American Revolutionary Army.

November 29- The North Carolina Incident ends and AEGIS Gen. Pamela Barnett is defeated.

2063

April 3- Anocracy is made law in the United Republic States of America.

June 19- Kiril Gustav Pordan is exiled to the Islamic Peoples Republic.

2064

March 6- The election of for the President of the United Republic States of America is initiated.

ABOUT THE AUTHOR

M.A. Martin was born in New York, and moved to Miami during his teenage years. A lover of Sci Fi and Military, his favorite writers are J.R.R. Tolkien, Edgar Rice Burroughs, and George Orwell. He currently resides in Brooklyn, NY, and dreams of the day when he can own his own transatlantic super yacht. When he's not writing, you can find him in the kitchen creating lavish dishes, or watching the latest movies.

Made in the USA
Columbia, SC
22 March 2020